MY
GOOD
MAN

MY GOOD MAN

Eric
Gansworth

LQ

LEVINE QUERIDO

MONTCLAIR · AMSTERDAM · HOBOKEN

This is an Arthur A. Levine book
Published by Levine Querido

www.levinequerido.com • info@levinequerido.com
Levine Querido is distributed by Chronicle Books LLC
Text and illustrations copyright © 2022 by Eric Gansworth
Library of Congress Control Number: 2022931727
ISBN 978-1-64614-183-8
Printed and bound in China

MIX
Paper from
responsible sources
FSC
www.fsc.org
FSC™ C144853

Published November 2022
First printing

for the Bumblebee,

walking our road together,
goals always the same,
hearts and minds uniting in that singular,
perfected sphere.

Contents

CONTENTS

Two Rows (I)

We discover each other side by side
in the water, traveling our own paths.

We emerge from different points of origin
and stay steady to our own unknown destinations.

We maintain our own customs, governing ways
of life and beliefs about the universe.

We each recognize that we move
according to our own desires and plans.

We respectfully do not cross streams
with each other, maintaining forward balance.

We see the open territory ahead of us and
acknowledge the mingled wakes we leave behind.

We share, between us, a peace we each maintain
by our dual presence in the expanse before us.

PART ONE

Distant Early Warning

(1992)

CHAPTER ONE

Assailant Unknown

G etting yelled at always makes me feel like a kid again, maybe because twenty-five is still semi-close to high school. Years seemed to take so long to pass before, but once you don't have a summer vacation to mark the year anymore, they fly right by. My job's as secure as a small city newspaper-reporter job can be. But my personality sometimes compels me to do things I should know better than to do. When I turned in the spec piece I'd worked up, 90 percent of me felt it was a good idea, and 10 percent of me felt like a cat intentionally knocking a water glass off the counter. My boss, Gary, the *Niagara Cascade*'s City Room Editor, called me into his office. You never get called in to hear you're doing a great job.

Shutting the door, I felt seventeen again, that state between Adulthood and Childhood. As a kid, you can make plenty of bad choices. Then one day, you blow out the candles, and suddenly you *own* it all. My sister and brother became legal for everything at eighteen, still in school. One morning, they could drive after midnight, buy cigs and beer, consent to surgery, get married, go in the military, all that . . . but they still had Trig homework and Cat Anatomy Lab. And as soon as Chester hit eighteen, he and Mona fled the Rez for a city apartment.

When it was my turn, the state bumped the rules to twenty-one. No longer a teen, not yet legal. Maybe college is mostly for those who could afford to not yet be adults. After graduation, people with vocational training got jobs, while some signed up for the military, and some got to take more years to decide who they were going to be. Right now, at twenty-five, my time was up.

But this trouble with Gary? I didn't even ask for it. You see, reporters were invited to pitch ideas for the Sunday Lifestyles Front Page. It had been fifteen years since the "Love Canal Toxic Waste" story broke, and if he said yes, well, though I wasn't from Love Canal, I had my own reasons for pitching the story.

"Look, kid," Gary said, before I even sat. "I'm shitcanning this Love Canal bit. It's not your beat. I know you put a lot of research in, but you should have known better." I wasn't surprised. "That's a rookie move not to know your beat." He was winding up.

"Well, what about this?" I countered. I had known better, and I wanted to stop that being-seventeen-again feeling. I'd try any amount of problem-solving to stop the yelling, even another pitch. "It's 1992."

"What of it?" He seemed genuinely puzzled, as if he'd forgotten why he hired me.

"Everyone's talking about how it's been five hundred years since Columbus arrived, all kinds of celebrations, and so on, but there *is* another side to that story, our side, and if you're really making people stick to beats, I'm the only choice." He thought for a minute, knowing I was the only Indian staff member, period. It was essentially why he'd hired me.

"Let's float a trial balloon," he said. "Something not so sticky in a city that's still got an active Christopher Columbus Society." Somehow he failed to see *that* was not my problem. "Work with me, kid. If you do well, we could *maybe* develop a series."

"I don't see folks reading a whole Columbus series. And I don't see me writing one."

"Are you dense, sometimes?" he growled. "Something current. Something interesting. How about on reservation people involved in medicine? People love that kind of story." I had two ideas immediately and headed to the volunteer fire hall off the Rez, where I'd likely find Hubie in the company lounge.

Inside the hall, Hubie grinned, hoping I'd notice his "Firemen Have Longer Hoses" T-shirt.

"Hey, Hube. Listen, I assume you know I'm working for the *Cascade*."

"Ain't you a little old for a newspaper route?" he asked, busting my balls and grinning wider, racking a pool game for us. He never liked to sit still much. Some of the other firefighters gave us side eyes and out of respect for Hubie, I ignored them. He seemed able to forget that when we were in high school, our mothers had been paid to clean the family homes of these guys, laundry included—and they'd taken perverse pleasure in making *special work* for them.

"So listen, I got another chance on a Rez story, a good one. Like that feature on Dusty earlier." He shook his head. "Anyway. I wanna write about people making a difference."

"Anyone I know?" he asked, suddenly eager. I explained I wanted to interview *him* for the feature. People knew him from his commitment to the volunteer firefighters. The Rez had no hydrants, and this company's water truck was often the first equipment on the scene. Happy to talk, he started giving me impassioned stories, until a siren blasted in. "Pick this up another time," he said, then shouted, "Come on! Hustle! Hustle! Hustle! We gotta go save some lives!" as they all jumped into their equipment. In seconds, they were transformed and gone.

We concluded the next week at his family place. When I gathered my materials to leave, he touched my arm. "None of my business," he started. "But, well . . . when you bring someone back, when the blue lips you been pressing yours against turn pink again, there's not another feeling like that on earth, Brian." Why hadn't he said anything like this during the interview? "This gig takes dedication. I love it. But your story? It's different. Take what Hillman give you. There's a story, right there."

I wouldn't put up with this comment from many, but Hubie had come so far from so far behind. I thanked him and told him I'd let him know about arranging for a photographer. I got it finished that night and left it in Gary's inbox.

"What is this BS, Waterson?" Gary said the next morning, waving my manila folder containing my piece. Getting yelled at twice in two weeks—a personal record.

"It's the story I pitched. I mean, the one you suggested. First in a *possible* series," I said. "I've even got a second one lined up already. I mean, you killed my Love Canal idea. Even after I'd read everything in the morgue and had a perfect follow-up interview."

"Told you before. Love Canal's not your beat." The *Cascade* editorial policy listed a preference that staff writers doing community human interest Lifestyles features should have an inside scoop vibe, if at all possible. He tossed my story down. "This neither."

"My pitch—may I?" I said, reaching for the proposal I'd developed from his prompt. "Was to profile reservation community members who'd committed themselves to serving others in medicine." Setting it back, I added, "How does this feature not fit that description?"

"Well, it's just—" Gary sputtered. "When I said 'medicine,' you knew I meant *medicine*. I thought you might do a piece on that game you guys play. Flaming Balls?"

"Fireball." He'd been trying to get me to cover this since I started. "I don't play."

"I didn't ask you if you play. I've heard you talk about attending. And you knew what I meant with this," he said, his eyes narrowing. "Kid, you're a decent writer and thorough researcher, but . . . a stunt like this will follow you." He assumed wrongly that I, like most of the other staff writers, was looking at this as a stepping-stone to a different job. My plan was to stay.

"You get this one, because I already reserved this week's slot for you. But this is *not* a series." I still didn't know what he was mad about. Maybe he already knew my family fell into that category people were curious about. "And cut it by two hundred words."

"Gary! That's almost a full rewrite. You know that!"

"You cut it or I do. Your choice. And maybe you'll remember this when you get another shot at Human Interest, but it ain't going to be soon. And when you do, they'll come out of *your* beat. You're not Love Canal. You're not Center City. You sure as hell ain't Lewiston. Your job is to open up the world of the reservation, as part of our local color."

"Hubie's story *is* local color. Local boy doing good."

"This story could be about almost *anyone*."

"Anyone who's an EMT," I said, trying to keep the smart-ass out. "Isn't that the point?"

"Your job is to explore the way you're different. Make it perky, inspirational. What are they saying these days? Celebrate difference. But in a good way. Not in a Running for the Rez Border kind of way." He saw my job as not building bridges, but ensuring everyone knew the distance between. One of our earliest treaties, the Two Row, insisted our relationship with Europeans was akin to our being two vessels, two groups, side by side. Some people read the treaty as a document affirming peace between the vessels. Others used it as a cautionary warning for anyone who tried to straddle—that having one foot in one vessel and the other foot in another was disaster in the making.

I got the photo shoot approved, so Hubie's image would be with the story of him rescuing people in need. "Wear your favorite shirt if you want," I added, when I confirmed with him. I'd initially discouraged him from wearing his "Longer Hoses" shirt if we got photo approval. "But if the photographer tries to pose you with a dreamcatcher, don't do it if you don't want." He didn't read the paper much, so I hoped he maybe wouldn't notice it had been gutted.

"No problem, Brian. I got the shirt on now. Truth in advertising," he said, laughing. "And my truck's dreamcatcher is fine. I caught my dreams." I wanted to explain that they were supposed to snare the bad dreams, but his good dreams had indeed found him. And it didn't matter to him that they came from a different Indian culture. "Give you mine if you need," he said, adding: "Not the T-shirt." We laughed. "Anything else? I'm your man." He asked me to save him a few copies of the Sunday *Cascade*. He hoped the piece might drum up new volunteers.

No sting from his past could take away Hubie's smile when some kid took in their own breath, coughing up water, crying new life he'd just jump-started mouth to mouth. He liked being the guy who coaxed back a spark. He was the guy who said "let's go save some lives!" when a call came in, and meant it. But most people he saved never knew their superhero. Hubie had steadied my balancing act, firming the foot in my home vessel, until the waves passed. I didn't have the heart to tell him he'd been my reward for doing a dreaded job.

Gary had insisted I document my cousin Roland's DWI, as he had years ago, shortly after I'd been hired. He ignored the fact that the *Cascade* got, on average, three reports a day from across the city and surrounding areas, but never missed publishing one from the Rez.

"You know how you got this job," he'd said both times I'd taken issue. "You think we don't get applicants with more experience and better grades from better places?" I knew what he meant. "How many times we gotta go over this?" He picked up the report. "Part of that job is that you write these stories, cousin or no cousin. Besides, you claim five thousand cousins at a place where a thousand people live."

"Like I told you last time. This is someone I grew up with. I mean, he's older, but . . ."

"Plenty of applicants in this folder, buddy. You gonna go work for the *Pennysaver*?"

So I wrote about my cousin's problem rather than punch my boss in the face, which would put *me* in the Police Blotter. Maybe he felt the heat of my protest and that's why he'd offered me this Feature Invitation. I had the feeling he was trying to make this job so irritating, I'd leave, and then he wouldn't be accused of firing one of the paper's only non-white employees.

"Remember, buddy," Gary said as I worked at my desk, chopping up Hubie's feature. "Salaried workers don't get overtime staying in the City Room." Whenever he asked for nearly impossible edits, he padded the request with lame comments like this.

"A roomful of noisy familiar people?" I said, "That's wired into my DNA. I *only* know life as a social person." Sometimes, I went home just to see familiar faces, to get the Rez wave as I passed someone on Dog Street, a quick wrist snap over the steering wheel, index and middle finger dangling. "I've been in my apartment for over five years, but the Rez is still home." This was my last chance to save my feature from being gutted. "The breadth of Hubie's story will speak to people, his years of dedication."

"And that's why we hired you!" He knocked on my desk, his signature exit move. I looked around: most coworkers I knew had already left. I could go to my apartment, but the place would be empty, a feeling I'd yet to get used to. This Rez Lonely Heart Syndrome was going to mess me up like it did my brother Chester. He paid rent on a city place he never stayed, sleeping on our ma's couch, more comfortable in the place he'd known his whole life.

It was Overlap, the funny time of night when people's shadow selves convinced them that a baseball cap and sunglasses were disguise enough to follow bad ideas. Half the Rez kept police scanners on, to hear these bad choice stories, so when the fax broke the news, I took a peek, and suddenly, any thought I had about features and the irritation of DWI reports was out the window.

Local, a police report. They always came in like badly written short stories; no names, only addresses, locations, descriptions of crimes. Probably Blotter material, but the details snagged me. To the degree I had a beat, this call was in it, in more ways than I'd have liked.

A Bite Mark Road man was found unconscious on the shoulder of Moon Road, the victim of a severe assault. Lying beside his car, driver's side door open, car idling. Ambulance to Our Lady of the Thorns. Critical. Assailant unknown. Every tiny detail was a face-punch.

"Unknown" seemed unlikely, but everything here disturbed me. I could write "Moon Road," but before it wound up in the next edition's Police Blotter, someone would have added, "on the Tuscarora Indian Reservation." Moon Road ran deep in the Rez's center. My family home was on Bite Mark Road, where the central artery met the eastern border. Tim Sampson, the brother of my mom's old boyfriend Gihh-rhaggs, lived at the sparsely populated southern end.

I hesitated to call the hospital, but the faded medicine bundle in my front pants pocket shot sparks along my nervous system, waking me. I could feel Hillman, my grandfather's brother, the man who gave me the bundle, waiting. Maybe he laughed, as I made a call to find out the beating victim's name, knowing, as he'd claimed years ago, that it would pull me home.

The hospital didn't kick out info, but I had alternatives. Even as I punched Hubie's number first, Hillman was probably adding another wampum bead to the two-man treaty we held. When I caved, as we knew I would, he'd look at me with indifference and say: *you knew you'd be back.* He would mean his house, but he'd also mean Our Lady of the Thorns

Hospital. I hadn't stepped through its automatic doors since I'd come close to dying there six years before.

I shut down my computer and headed to the one place I'd find a reliable source.

I went home.

CHAPTER TWO

Immediate Family

N ews travels fast, isn't it though?" Hubie said as I stepped into the volunteer fire hall's Members Lounge, banking a shot at the familiar billiards table.

"Does when you've got immediate access to crime reports," I said. "But I'm not here officially, not on the record. Probably Blotter anyway. Wire service details are fine, but—"

"It's him. Your buddy. ID'd him myself," Hubie said.

"So how bad . . . ?"

"Bad enough that I wasn't positive it *was* your buddy, at first. Someone took a tow chain to him. Even left it hanging out his open trunk, car idling and the trunk light on. I'm betting the blood on the tow hook will only match his, and that his are the only prints they find. Didn't ride in the ambulance, but what I saw? Definitely ICU. Immediate Family only."

"I remember," I said, fully versed in the Our Lady's Intensive Care Unit rules and regs.

"Oh yeah," he said, dragging it in a mock Rezzy accent. "I always forget about the time you . . ." Lots of people had no trouble discussing my ICU stint, as long as I wasn't there to hear. "But they don't check. They haven't found Meduse yet. If you claim you're family . . ."

"Thanks," I said. I didn't know where Tim's local daughter Christine, a.k.a. "Meduse," was living these days. I figured she still lived at home. "I owe you one."

"You're gonna owe me more than one in a minute," Hubie sighed, and paused.

"If you're not comf—"

"Skoutside."

We went out and leaned against his truck. He'd never violate confidentiality laws, but we were talking as friends, not reporter and source, so he gave me enough information to piece things together. As he talked, I flashed again on his current peers, those high school guys who, after gym or team practices, dangled sweat-soaked gym clothes in the locker rooms, middle fingers hooked on them. "Left something sweet for your mom," they'd cackle, stuffing them in gym bags.

They didn't do this stuff to the big Indian kids they were terrified of. Their resentment of that fear kept them aware which of us they could target. Our mothers had told us they needed those under-the-table cleaning jobs. They said if *they* could ignore gross behavior, so could we.

"So um," he said. "You totally can't know this. The 911 came from the pay phone outside the Shop-and-Dine, corner of Military, about 11:30. A woman under duress. Claimed she was driving by and saw him. She told dispatch they better hurry or they might find a body."

"Bold," I said, immediately wondering where Christine was, my stomach clenching.

"Those guys," he nodded toward the men in the lounge, "might buy that."

"But no one's on Moon Road late at night without a purpose," I replied. "And a *body*? Maybe she thought responders'd get there quicker."

"BINGO! Might make a good reporter someday," Hubie said, delighted in his own joke, like I hadn't heard it a thousand times before. He punched my shoulder, awkwardly, like he'd seen guys do on TV. "One look told me your buddy's seriously messed up." He shook his head.

"My buddy," I repeated. So inadequate to capture my relationship with Tim Sampson.

"There's surveillance cams at Shop N' Dine, but they haven't checked them yet, far as I know. Maybe you know someone who'd give you a peek. Bet'cha a dollar we know the caller."

"Sucker bet," I said. We both knew *anybody* who'd be on Moon Road at night. "Thanks, Hubie." We shook hands and he got to the building before I yelled back to him. I'd received a weird message at work. "Hey, DogLips wants me to call him. Something about the Summer Cottage. Any ideas?" DogLips was the father of Randy Night, a guy we'd grown up with: Mischief Personified. DogLips's real name was Douglas, but years ago, he'd taught his German shepherd to smile. It was a great trick until someone noticed that he and the dog had the same grin.

"Belongs to him, now," Hubie said. "Collected it to clear a deep hole in his dice game." This shack near my mom's house was called the Summer Cottage because it had been stripped of anything useful: heat, electricity, gas. If you scrounged wood, you could work its fireplace. It had become a gathering place for guys on the skids, drifting between homes and looking to party. "Let you know if I hear anything." Given the urgency of his message, DogLips was likely to track me down if I didn't get back to him quickly.

Hubie's confirmation of Tim Sampson's identity, combined with that "Assailant Unknown" 911 call, led my surgery scar to push itself more and more alive. If I looked, the giant midline incision would be as red and inflamed as it had been that whole first year. It had become a Bad News Barometer in my life. It felt alive and electric, a vertical line thrumming along my torso, almost unbearably sharp from below my heart to the area beneath the button of my Levi's.

I cut through the Rez to get to Our Lady, passing other haunted houses from my past. Maybe Christine's absence was just a coincidence, but if the 911 call led to her, it also led to Randy Night, and his father's call, and the ways all of our history was snarled and knotted together. As I passed by Hillman's house, his porch light flicked on, like a beacon.

The closer I got to the hospital, the sicker I felt. I hadn't seen Tim Sampson in over five years, an embarrassingly long time, all things considered. If I could do anything, I'd be compelled to. It was unlikely Hillman had orchestrated things from afar all these years, putting Gihh-rhaggs and then Tim Sampson and then their daughters in my path, sometimes years apart. But if he was behind this, I was sure that grin was becoming a full, hearty laugh, as all of his carefully chosen pieces fell into their determined place, waiting to be tightened.

In the hospital parking lot, I heard them, wildflowers, bushes, weeds, trees. The small nearby patch of woods was a secret place of healing, hiding in its own wildness. Scents blasted me as harsh as a shotgun from a homegrown joint, but the ER's automatic doors silenced them.

"Immediate Family?" a nurse asked inside, and when I nodded, she pressed the ICU electronic lock to buzz me in. For almost no one else in the world would I enter this ICU, but I had to act now. When Christine arrived, an ICU nurse would say "I didn't know you were related to that *Cascade* reporter." Christine would say "I'm not," and that would end my visits.

They'd outfitted Tim with a blood pressure cuff, duel IV stands, catheter/collection bag/measuring cup combo, an oxygen cannula below his nose, and an NG line from his nose down his throat to his stomach. Monitors counted his breaths, heartbeats, and blood oxygen level. All the apparatus made him seem smaller, a teddy bear with a big chunk of stuffing gone. He was almost unrecognizable. Massive gauze pads covered who knows what beneath his gown.

In the closet, Tim's shirt—sealed in a plastic biohazard bag, stained with blood—was the plaid flannel I'd given him, the last Christmas we'd exchanged gifts. The rest looked okay. His chest rose and fell as his vitals chased themselves on monitors. The rhythms were steady, rolling in and out like waves in the tide, or the first hints of a tidal wave. I closed my eyes for a minute.

"It's morning," a nurse said, awakening me, stiff in the visitor's chair. They'd let me sleep through the night. If he were out of the woods, they'd have booted me. "Cafeteria's open, if you want something."

I got up, and, reluctant, stepped out. Christine could show, and I didn't want to see her—or more rightly, I didn't want her to see me.

An EMT slouched at the station, looking at me intently. Hubie hadn't mentioned that Leonard Stoneham was on the crew. I didn't even know he'd completed his tours of duty.

"How is he, really?" I asked the nurse standing next to Leonard.

"Stable," she said. "Pretty good, considering."

"Tough," Leonard added. "Once a Marine, always a Marine." Leonard must have been the EMT who removed Tim's shirt. He'd seen the tattoo. His eyes bagged. He'd stayed all night too. "He'll come through. He's made it this long living out there." I left.

By the time I got back after a quick clean up at my ma's, my anonymity was blown. Leonard may have told the staff. From Tim's condition, I guessed at least five days before he might be transferred. That would be only a little less complicated. Ironically, I was going to finally have permission to write about this Love Canal survivor, but not in the way I'd hoped. Some days, I realized I hadn't thought this job through. You could never please everyone.

Lottie Darkwinter, the daughter of my old babysitter, Dusty, was a newly minted LPN on Med-Surg, the ward Tim would be transferred to. She claimed I'd made a fool of Dusty with a *Cascade* story I'd written about her beadwork. My first feature opportunity, years ago, after Roland had his first DWI. Lottie couldn't see the feature story was about her mother's dedication. She only saw the way Dusty had seen some things eccentrically, and the way I'd reported that eccentric view. On the plus side, Lottie was also afraid of my family—Hillman, mostly—but my ma's tea leaves and my own ICU adventure had only added to her wariness. It was going to take more than Lottie Darkwinter to keep me from reaching out to Tim, like I should have years ago.

CHAPTER THREE

Indecent Exposure

Trying to follow Tim's progress and stay in Gary's good graces at the *Cascade* the next few days, I fell short in both. My edited story was accepted, but I struggled to develop my next month's upbeat Rez column: "Dog Street Dispatches." They were shorter than the Hubie story I'd planned, but it was still a struggle. Only one vision came in my mind: Tim Sampson in that ICU bed in his threadbare hospital johnny, with the snaps undone, to allow emergency access if needed.

I had a ridiculous desire to put Tim's regular clothes back on him, like that would make this terrible situation go away. His jeans looked okay, but that bloody, torn shirt lingered. I picked him up a new flannel, a pair of jeans, and three packs of briefs and crew socks. Whenever he got transferred, I'd bring them for his discharge. The new clothes stacked on my dresser were like a medicine themselves, something I could do. Probably Christine had already brought things, but when your hands are tied, you ache to do anything, to coax a better future from the sky.

The little pyramid of folded garments every morning and night didn't let me forget I was avoiding reality. I drifted through evenings driving the Rez, pathetically hoping to stumble onto some clue to this violence, like an aging Hardy Boy, or Shaggy without a Scooby for assistance.

Catching the person wouldn't change anything, including those damaged places on Tim's body, but not being able to do anything was maddening. I just drove past familiar porch lights, wondering if people had bought new locks, like others would after news like this in the country beyond the Rez borders. Since Tim was white, though, it was possible they felt immune.

The Rez housed ten to fifteen families, depending on how you counted, but the same few ricocheted in and out of my life again and again. Hubie Buckman's, Randy Night's, the Darkwinter girls, and the Sampsons. The path of personal history was like playing pinball with four balls simultaneously in play. All you had were inadequate paddles, and you never knew who was going to trigger a release and need to be tended to, if you wanted to avoid Game Over.

"I went to see Tim," I said, stopping at my ma's. She was doing *Word Search* magazine puzzles and acknowledged my entrance by raising one eyebrow, like a cat turning its ears. "Maybe you could read for him," I suggested, after a long silence, "once he's transferred. I could sneak a tea bag in." She cut her eyes at me, to see if I were yanking her chain.

"You know I don't do that anymore," she said. "It's not me you need to talk to, anyway," she added. "I only see what's coming. Changing things, that's gonna need someone else."

"Not that desperate yet."

"Sometimes, if you wait, it's too late," she said. "We always think we have more time." I shrugged. "Our medicine's like that kind you tried at the college in at least one way. Only works on the living." Hillman, naturally, was the one she thought I should call. Any action I chose would rely on Tim, but I couldn't help him unless I completed what I'd started with Hillman, and then, only if Tim chose to accept. But he couldn't accept unless he knew it was a possibility.

As I passed Hillman's place in one last Rez Lap, the porch light blazed on again, one of his regular tricks. I headed to my apartment, instead, in the city where the world was less mysterious. If I mentioned my tea-leaf-reading mother or her medicine-man uncle at work, most people looked politely away. The ones who listened, would tail me, hoping to see their futures, wanting me to introduce them to the man who could give them a different hope—so I ran silent.

The drive to my place usually cleared my head after a rough story, or after interviewing a gunshot victim's relatives, hating myself for coaxing a hot quote to close the deal. The system-flush driving usually never failed to work, but not this time. Some part of me wouldn't let my ma's suggestion go, like she'd deflected my own medicine with a mirror, shining the idea back on me.

So I took a detour, back to Love Canal, which led me back to Tim even more. He'd come from this Niagara Falls subdivision, a ghost town these days. A suburban neighborhood, it had been the first proven toxic waste dump in the United States. A scattering of people who fled the place somehow wound up with us. Like us, they understood the idea of a homeland. But they weren't desperate enough to move back to their contaminated houses. Most former residents took the settlement, ditching their homes. Men in hazmat suits walking your street left an impression.

Occasional lighted homes still shone among boarded-up rows. Maybe the only residential neighborhood beyond the Rez you could take a nighttime leak off your porch without risking neighbor complaints. I sometimes drove the rows of mostly abandoned houses, but usually got noticed. Like the Rez population, people from Love Canal knew cars that didn't belong.

We had other overlap with Love Canal. A Rez road-maintenance job years ago, done to stop the buckling and heaving, included a "toxicity analysis" of the steel slag used in our road foundations. Love Canal residents were offered buyouts, but the Rez had finite borders. What were Bite Mark Road residents supposed to do? Wait to become Steel Slag Mutants.

As soon as I got into my apartment, I stood at the bay window and dropped my clothes to the floor. When you lived alone, no one cared where you left them. One nice thing about a third-floor apartment with a tree out front—you also didn't worry about accidentally flashing strangers. The decaying city rested beyond that tree, but its dense foliage still gave me glimpses I turned away from. After the surgery, this place, alone, was the only spot I felt comfortable unclothed. I generally avoided the mirror in such state, but even in the dark, shadowy reflection, I could see the large, mounded scar that divided my abdomen into neat left and right hemispheres.

The last person to see this scar was Hillman, when he insisted he could do something about it, then claimed I was the reason his fix didn't work.

All kinds of people had it way worse than me, even people I knew. Bug Jemison lost his leg before I was born. His prosthetic had become a defining part of his identity. He played the guitar with deep passion, could yodel like country singers with careers, but on the Rez, he was the one-legged guitar player. Some juvenile part of me thought if no one saw my scar, it wouldn't define me.

One major drawback had been my potential for an intimate life. It was embarrassing to be a virgin now, but I couldn't picture revealing my current body for the first time to anyone. In my head, all I could see was the rejection, the turning away, the repulsion. In the dark, I could enjoy the cool night air tingling on my bare skin through the slightly open window, like the perpetual breeze at our Rez house. Still thinking of Love Canal, I realized pissing outside was, strangely, one thing I really missed. My first weekend of *Cascade* Police Blotter duty, I'd logged six indecent-exposure arrests, almost identical: guys relieving themselves in the alley behind Third Street bars after last call. Patrol cars waited in the dark for this same bad urge over and over. My Rez habits weren't worth the risk, so I'd adjusted my behavior immediately.

My bare reflection here reminded me of what I knew I should do for Tim, no matter the complication. The giant scar from my sternum to pubic hair, my off-kilter navel, migrated an inch or so to the right, were strong hints of Tim's potential future, and a hint of what I could offer him, if I were willing to sacrifice. I crawled into bed, but sleep didn't come. I promised to give my ma's suggestion serious thought. I'd already learned to adapt to one new world as an adult. Maybe a second transition would be an easier one.

The next day, I wasn't as eager, but Hillman's door opened when I got to the porch. He hadn't changed much in the past five years. "So which part brings you back to me finally?" he asked. "The man down at Our Lady of the Thorns?" I started to speak, but he raised his hand and interrupted. "Or is it maybe the girl? I don't guess she's a girl anymore."

"Which girl?" How did this man who never left home know so much about my life?

"The one with the leather jacket," he said, laughing. "They're all connected, isn't it? And remember, if you want my help a second time, after you walked away once, no lies."

"No lies," I repeated.

"Do you still have the jacket?"

"Which one?" I asked. There were two tied up in this story.

"Which one you think I'm asking about?"

"Well what do you think, Mr. Know-It-All?" Hillman didn't seem to be an *Empire Strikes Back* kind of guy, but apparently even without exposure to Yoda, he'd seen his share of cagey mystical mentor movies.

"It's at my place, in the city," I said.

"You didn't leave it at your ma's. It still means something to you." He stood quickly and patted my abdomen. "I don't guess you fit it anymore, with that grown man belly." For the first time since the surgery, the scar didn't hurt. Most days, it throbbed in the background, but if I leaned into something—a railing, a table—it instantly awoke, sharp as ever.

"How'd you do that?"

"You still got a lot to learn," he said. "Should know better than to make me ask twice."

In the far end of my apartment closet, I retrieved the jacket he'd asked about. It still smelled new. The embroidery across the back was based on the primary album art from Rush's *2112*.

"And how did it feel after so much time?" he asked when I returned.

"Embarrassing," I said. The jacket was tight, but I could wear it, and zip it. It had been a long time since the little brown tag on my Levi's listed a twenty-eight-inch waist.

"You tried it on, anyway," he said, a statement. I nodded. "Well, if that betrayal is the worst you committed by the time we're done, I guess you been doing pretty good." I reluctantly agreed. I could tell that jacket was going to stay with me, more present than ever, since he'd forced me to see it again. The embroidered man across its back stood defiant against a blazing red star. Stripped of everything, he still dusted up with forces trying to control his life. Hillman agreed to tell me what I needed to know, how to fix Tim's injuries in ways mine hadn't been fixed.

"Hang onto this," he added. "It's part of your personal medicine. Will keep you humble. I see you only brung this one his daughter gave you, and it looks brand new. You never wore it. You still have the one Gihh-rhaggs's girl gave you first?"

"No," I said, "I deserved to lose that one. I gave it away."

"But did you give it away when you could still wear it, or after you got too fat?"

"I could have maybe squeezed another fall and spring out of it when I passed it on."

"Squeezed is the right word, I bet," Hillman said, laughing. "Okay, one New Yah's time of sacrifice is good enough."

"Before I tell you what you need, you gotta do one other thing, too," he continued, as I knew he would. I'd have to agree to practice what he'd given me. He looked good, but he'd slowed. He shuffled instead of walking when he saw me to the door.

"This life has responsibilities. You can't be willing to fix only those ones you think you owe," he said. I agreed, and met his gaze. "You said 'yeah' a little bit quick," he added. "This journey? Gonna be messy. You know, isn't it?" I nodded. "You know what I'm going to tell you to do." I knew it would somehow mean engaging Randy Night again, all these years later. "The man you want to help, the one who found some bad medicine on Moon Road? You think you owe that one's brother, Gihh-rhaggs," he said, finally. "What Gihh-rhaggs did? No one's fault but his own. But what about this one in the hospital? What makes you willing?" He sat down at the table again, knowing I wouldn't leave, that I understood we weren't quite through with our conversation. When I said nothing, he continued.

"You owe him something? You think I got secret knowledge. All I need is Eee-ogg and a careful ear. Every bit of news comes out in the end. But this one? You and him? No one has a good answer. Most say they didn't know you two were friendly. They say you're friendly with the daughter. And that ain't true either. Anymore, anyway. What you got between you and him? You tell me. And you tell me what this jacket has to do with it."

I began, thinking it started a bit before I turned eighteen. "Well, New Year's Eve—"

"No," he said, immediately. "You can't be dumb enough to think this story begins at the ending. I'm in this story now. Better try to remember where my strand enters the braid."

"You're kidding, right? When I was five? And you want me to tell you?"

"Earlier than that, but I'm not important. Could be good for me know what you understand . . . and what you don't. Anyways, it's not me you need to tell," he said. "Hope you got a rearview mirror on that truck. That's where you'll find the one who needs a talking to. I'm betting you already know who grabbed a tow chain, and once you know why, maybe you got a chance at helping him, too."

"What if I don't want to help him?" I was happy with Randy largely out of my life.

"Then you're not ready. You see? It's always gonna be this way."

"You help people who've done shitty things to you?" I said. The deeper I got into this path, the more I regretted it, but the path behind me had already closed.

"I helped *you*," he said simply. "And you did the worst thing of all. You walked away from the only gift I can offer. Made me think I chose the wrong one." He stood and put his hands on my shoulders, and then, leaning in, his mouth next to my right ear: "For a time."

"For a time," I repeated. Had he somehow compelled Randy Night to take a tow chain, and swing it over and over, into the father of the woman he shared a bed with?

"The world has a way of righting itself. That thing they call acid rain on the news? Even the acid rain leaves a rainbow behind. You had me worried. I'm getting old. But you still got that medicine bundle in the pocket of your dungarees." These days that medicine bundle was secured inside a little beaded and tanned leather bag. You'd think I might have lost it all that time ago, as a kid, but despite the calico print fading to a memory of itself, the bundle stayed. I'd misplaced it a couple of times, or it was displaced from me, but it always found its way home.

"I don't need to see it to know it's there. But here," he said, holding out a small container and another strip of what I now recognized was treaty allotment cloth. "You might need a little something extra this time. You think your job will be rough, helping that one with the Good Mind on his side. That one walking with the Bad Mind is gonna be even rougher. But you know one thing—the story always includes both of them."

Hillman wanted me to know I was still playing out the oldest story of our culture: the Good Mind battling the Bad Mind, the ways they roll the bones. I gathered the bundle and made a twist. For a few seconds, I felt that same sense of electricity I'd had with the first medicine bundle I'd gathered, intense arousal, like all my senses had been zapped with pleasure, a full body orgasm, and then, it dissipated, like that sharp odor in the air after a lightning strike.

Hillman and I had begun this journey six years ago. He'd forced me to look in his mirror, before I got dressed. I hadn't been that modest, so I didn't think it would be hard. But he added, "Remember, the Ganoñhéñ•nyoñ', the words before all others." The acknowledgment people called the Thanksgiving Address. "You remember, it's different every time. For each person. You start your Ganoñhéñ•nyoñ' here," he said, tapping the big purple welt at the top of my scar, at my sternum.

In the years since that emergency surgery, I'd replaced most of the pounds lost to the IV and the shaved hair had regrown, but the long, deep-purple trail never faded. It's not like I'd had a career as a fitness model. But acceptance was one thing; in the years since, I wasn't sure I'd ever really achieved the feeling of gratitude for anything the surgery scar brought me.

"So where do we begin?" I asked, now, though I already knew his maddening answer.

"Just like last time. Be thankful for all that the Creator has given you, and start here. Say thanks to this scar, first," he said. "That part of the story don't change. You gotta grow some. Gather your responsibility. You begin at the beginning. The words before all the other words. And you give thanks."

He wanted me to start where it made sense, giving thanks for all the people, animals, and environments that had shaped me. And even in absence, I understood the balance between desire and gratitude better. Before you could move forward, you had to acknowledge everything that had come before. And you acknowledged it clearly, so you didn't forget.

Two Rows (II)

We emerge from different points of origin
and stay steady to our own unknown destinations.

We maintain our own customs, governing ways
of life and beliefs about the universe.

We each recognize that we move
according to our own desires and plans.

We respectfully do not cross streams
with each other, maintaining forward balance.

We see the open territory ahead of us and
acknowledge the mingled wakes we leave behind.

We share, between us, a peace we each maintain
by our dual presence in the expanse before us.

We discover each other side by side
in the water, traveling our own paths.

PART TWO

Roll the Bones

(1970–1977)

CHAPTER FOUR

La Villa Strangiato

(1970–1971)

P robably this all begins with me, eavesdropping, step one of Eee-ogg, when I was maybe three or four years old. People paid attention to anything unusual happening at our house. You know that house in your town? The one everyone says is haunted? How the former residents moved under cover of the night and were never heard from again? How you looked away driving past, so no ghost lights would follow you home? Yup, that's ours.

Given the activities of Hillman and my ma, our label as Spook Central shouldn't have been a surprise. Some house has to carry it. Our Rez was small, so you didn't need more than one. In the movies, if weird shit happens—see *Poltergeist, The Amityville Horror,* etc.—white people just up and leave. If all it took were Amityville's buzzing flies and flickering lights to prove we lived with spirits, almost every Rez house would be labeled "cursed." But for us, it wasn't just the house. If none of us were in earshot, some folks claimed that we had a history of "Witchcraft." I pictured the Wicked Witch of the West, which I guess made me a Flying Monkey. You can take the Boy off the Rez . . . but the Rez pulls you, like the moon does the oceans.

Stories start somewhere. If it wasn't Hillman's practice, it was that, from the time she was six years old, my ma began seeing stories among the dregs of people's teacups. She grew up and got married, but people still sometimes braved her company to hear about their futures.

Like a bunch of Indian men, my dad caught Ironworker Fever, just after they got married and moved to Niagara Falls. He'd come home occasionally to plant another kid before heading back to ride the skies of Manhattan. I pictured him and all the other Rez guys suited up like Iron Man, red-and-gold metal costumes, flying across the New York City skyline in their jet boots. Always, I wondered after that atomic-yellow heart panel I believed was glowing in the center of his chest. My ma, Mona, Chester, and I eventually took the hint about where his heart lay, and headed back to the Rez to care for my grandparents, just in time to be there for my grandmother's last days. And since we needed cash, my ma opened back up for business.

Being my ma's customers required bravery. She told futures, not fortunes. She always pointed out what she'd seen to the person, but now that we needed cash, she sometimes made up nicer versions of the bad stories she saw in their clumps of leaves. In that way, we got by.

"How come you lied?" I asked one day when I was four. Her customer had left, and she was rinsing the cup, so she knew I wasn't reading it.

"Who says I lied?" She stopped putting away the cup and pan she kept separate.

"I could just hear it. You did lie, isn't it?" I didn't understand the implications of my ears.

"All I can say's that woman's house is on the right road," she said. Her customer lived on Dead Man's Road. A few weeks later the woman's husband fell from a skyscraper he was ironworking. My dad came home for the funeral, but he skipped conjugal explorations. Showing up in our lives after his full year away would have been messy. Gihh-rhaggs, a Love Canal refugee, used to shack with a woman down our road, but lately, every time I turned around, there he was, sitting in my favorite chair at our dining room table. When you saw two people who shouldn't be together more than three times, you could almost call that an official proclamation. Hot Eee-ogg burned fast like grease across the Rez. There was no way my dad hadn't already heard about this from at least a dozen people.

By this time, my ma had joined a group of Indian women cleaning the homes of white people in Lewiston. Sometimes, her job enraged her, and a certain mania with the Pledge lemon-scented furniture polish would overtake her. "Let's go," my grandfather Umps would say, grabbing me up as we flew out the door. "It's a Revenge on the Dirt Day."

"Why does she love Pledge so much?" I asked as we climbed into the Roadmaster one afternoon, hating the sharp lemon scent that coated the air, for days after. "It smudges soon as you touch it."

"Did you ever think maybe she doesn't want you to touch what she's polished? That she wants something in our house to look new?" He kept his eyes on the road as he talked, always extra careful when we drove. "I know. That's not the way you think. But you will, at some point. You'll want to get back to the way things were. You never can, but you can give yourself a gift for a little while." He paused again as we made our way off the Rez.

"What kind of gift?"

"Not a toy," he said, reading my mind. "She likes it," he said eventually, as we pulled into the lot of a little dairy store north of the Rez, "because when you Pledge something and buff it out right, it hides the scars of being battered around. Even for just a little while." He wasn't supposed to have ice cream, so I knew this was bribery for my silence about our second stop.

Umps was expected not to visit Hillman when I was with him, but these aging brothers had different plans. They reminded each other of the period when Hillman stayed hidden on the Rez while Umps had been shipped to Carlisle, where the boarding school tried to beat the Indian out of him. We had made numerous secret visits to Hillman, but the one that day seemed different.

"Wasn't expecting you today," Hillman said. "Not sure I have any ice cream."

"He's already had some," Umps said. "We're here for something else."

"That right?" Hillman said as I wandered around like usual. The two brothers usually talked while I drifted through the house unsupervised. Hillman would interrupt their conversation when I stopped among his drying plants, shout the plant's name, telling me what he used it for. "That's uhaHa-kyeha, good for bed-wetting if that's what ails you," he'd call and laugh, asking me to repeat it back.

"I'm beginning to think it's nearing time," Umps said. "Judy thinks I'm leaving bits of my mind around the house and forgetting where I put them. She ain't gonna trust me to watch over Little Man anymore, except when she gets that itch only Gihh-rhaggs knows how to scratch." Hillman didn't ask him if it were true. "Some girls down the road might need a few bucks for watching a little boy. Like those Darkwinter girls. Old Limp's granddaughters."

"Easy enough to take care of," Hillman said. The Darkwinters had some vaguely bad blood with us, but on a tiny Rez, even bad blood was negotiable. If you didn't trust someone on the Rez one hundred percent, you still trusted them more than someone from off.

"One other thing, too," Umps said. He suddenly had his brother's full attention. I heard difference in their voices too. "When Judy's been reading . . ." Hillman's eyebrows raised. "Don't give me that fake surprise. You pretend to live out here in the woods but you know everything. But you don't know this. Little Man can hear when she's not telling her customers the whole truth." Hillman's eyebrows shifted, but only a little, in real surprise. "If you think one of these kids is the one. This is him. I know it won't be for years, but this is the one to keep an eye on." I didn't like that, particularly. It was what people said when you were a mischief sort.

"Well, let's take care of that first thing, first. But I'll make sure we find just the right one. He's a little young to recognize the feeling, but that's okay. He'll remember." Hillman took me by the hand to his long shelf of cups filled with dried plants.

"Rhaw-nee-Hah Uh," he said, calling me Little Man in Tuscarora. "Move your hand slowly over this group here. Don't touch 'em, just over the whole group and tell me the one you like best." I leaned in, but he pulled me back. "Just the hand." I did as instructed and when my palm crossed over one cup, it tingled, sparked inside, excited, a surge of lightning thrumming from the center of my body to the fingertips. I was too young to articulate, but when I hit puberty, I recognized the feeling, like I was entirely aroused. I ran my thumb against my fingertips and felt them surge with an exceptionally pleasant, unfamiliar electrical throb.

"That the one?" he asked, and I nodded with enthusiasm. He lifted the cup. "Take one of them squares of treaty cloth beneath it." I lifted the first neatly cut square of identical treaty cloth from the stack underneath and held it out. "Take a couple dried leaves. Crush 'em up in the cloth. Pull those corners up and twist them," he said, and I followed his instructions. He tied the bundle with a small leather braid.

"Is it always going to feel like this?" I asked, wanting it to last, but also feeling the electrical surge was getting out of control, like the shock wave after an explosion.

"It'll pass, now that it's tied. You take this in your pocket if you go to Darkwinters, or anywheres you don't know the people so good." Again I nodded. "And if Kah-skwarih, Old Limp, kisses you, soon's you can without getting noticed, you rub this on that spot. That ought to fix you up."

When we got home, Umps had me hide my bundle with his tie tacks and cuff links, his "church wear," in his jewelry chest. On the occasions I was sent to the Darkwinters, he'd have me reach in and take it.

"You remember what Hillman told you?" he asked, the first time. "You put that bundle in your pants pocket. And if someone taking care of you makes you take them off, you just drop this in the front of what you got left on. Nobody should be asking you to take those guds off. You protect the bundle and it will protect you."

Umps had called things right, about what, out of courtesy, became known as the Day of the Car Aerial. We'd gone for ice cream again. He always chose some Old Man Ice Cream for himself that you wouldn't eat for money. Like Maple Walnut. "I guess we're going to Hillman's again," I said. Before he answered, a shadow covered us. Time got funny from there.

A huge farm truck came at us like a missile, crossing the first dip on Route 104. A cold wash ran through my blood. Ump's arm sprung out to brace me as we shot out my door toward the summer sky. Metal screamed around us. The Buick T-boned into a giant black boomerang, heaved into the ditch, headlights and fins pointing to the sun amid the smoke and settling dust.

That truck stuck deep into the Buick, steaming. The driver stared at us, frightened out of his own chest-rubbing. An ambulance man arrived a little while later where we sat on the dislodged bench seat, catapulted to the end of a swath we'd ripped through the cornfield.

I imagined our phone ringing at home, my ma Pledging the house, maybe even rubbing the phone table as its bells went to vibrating. She always wandered toward it, a minute or so before it rang.

Here in the field, the ambulance man asked me questions, encouraging Umps to sit still and sort of ignoring the things he said about the radio. Another ambulance attendant held gauze to the truck driver's mouth that grew a deeper and deeper red as the attendant held up various numbers of fingers and asked the man to count them.

This is where the story gets foggy for me, because it has grown in the years, twisting into the shapes people need it to. This is what people who weren't there claim, and what they believe.

One ambulance attendant turned to my ma when she arrived and said, "We think we should pull it out, but we want consent from a family member before we do," guiding her past the Buick and up to us. Umps stared intently into the vibrant cornstalks, the white dress shirt he wore for driving growing dark red, spreading from neck to chest and belly, a carnation in bloom.

"Dad?" my ma said, her voice light and strange, the voice she used when she didn't want to tell a customer what was in their tea leaves.

"Judy! What are you doing out here in the corn? You hate the crops!" He turned toward me and laughed. True enough, but he seemed to disregard what we all knew was wrong.

"Dad, how do you feel? Can you get up?"

"We better move him, ma'am, but first thing, we should . . ." the attendant said, moving closer, preparing to hold Umps down, should the need arise. My ma held him back, gently, just pressing on his white-uniformed chest with an outspread palm.

"It's Paul Harvey," Umps said. "I'm getting the rest of the story. He is one in a million, that Paul. A man you can always trust to get down to the facts." He listened intently, smiling and nodding, apparently in agreement with some point Paul Harvey was driving home in his cocky, confident way. Umps was the only one who could hear the broadcast.

"Dad," my ma said, walking behind us, holding his shoulder. "This might hurt." She stood over him, holding his jaw and tilting his head until he blinked in the bright midday sun.

"What are you doing?" he asked, and then she lay her right hand on the car's aerial protruding from the side of his head, an inch or so above his right eye. Her eyes opened wide for a few seconds, she smiled, waited a few seconds, then slid the aerial from where it had been lodged in my grandfather's brain. Blood geysered from the hole, spurting like a pump, beading on the aerial. The attendant stepped up and immediately held a heavy bandage over the wound.

"Dad, can you stand up?" my ma asked, reaching under his arm and helping the attendant lift him. "We need to get you looked at. You've been in an accident. Someone hit you."

"When?" he asked, standing and leaning on the bench seat.

"A little while ago."

"What happened to the radio?"

"I shut it off," she said, sliding the aerial in her apron pocket.

"You want to ride in the ambulance with him?" the attendant asked my ma as they strapped him to the gurney.

"You go," she told my Auntie Rolanda, who'd come with her, but stayed a good distance away. "We'll follow in your car, right behind."

"The little boy should be checked out too," the attendant said. My ma laid her hands on me for a second, the waxy smell of Pledge filling my nostrils.

"He's fine." She took my hand and walked us to Rolanda's car as if she were picking us up at someone's house. In the car, I asked her why she had waited so long to pull the aerial out. "I waited for Paul Harvey to finish," she said. "Dad always loved that man, but personally, I don't see what's so special."

This is what other people say about my ma and the car aerial. She refuses to speak one word about it, and my memory has likely reformed itself with others' embellishments.

At the hospital, they did what they had to, leaving a little dent and a star-shaped scar where the aerial had been embedded. That was the end of Umps' driving days and the end of our regular visits to Hillman.

Less than a year later, my ma spent most evenings with that Love Canal man, Gihh-rhaggs. Each time, Umps reminded her that she was still married. So, after a while, when she and her man were together, it was away from us. One evening, Gihh-rhaggs was supposed to pick her up, but she put the water on and poured water over a cup. The liquid darkened in swirling streams, and she told Umps to tear the tea bag. He drank it and handed her the cup. "Well?"

"Hard to say." She turned the cup this way and that.

"Is it time to pick out my favorite suit?"

"Dad, it just gives me what it does. I don't see much here." She was using her lying voice. He couldn't hear if she was lying, but he knew I could. I didn't know what she was lying about, but it wasn't good. She paused, trying to not see the truth.

From that night on, in bed, I'd wake to watch Umps' chest going up and down. Sometimes, I gently shook him awake, but I couldn't prevent the future any more than her lies could. The tea leaves themselves never lied. She had his best suit ready when we buried him a week later. I asked what she'd seen.

"His head growing like a balloon. It was gonna burst soon." That had not happened in any visible way, a depth-charge igniting somewhere deep inside his skull.

The person who had most raised me, day in and day out, was suddenly gone.

Hillman stopped over the first night and brought a pie that my ma set off to one side in the kitchen. When no one was looking, Hillman asked me if I knew where my bundle was. I told him it was in the bedroom. "Hold out your hand," he said, and tied a leather braid to my wrist. "This is so your Umps won't notice you before he heads to the Skyworld. Sometimes, when they leave their bodies, they want the littlest ones in the family to keep 'em company. You'll be invisible to him now, so you can go get your bundle. From now on, until it's your time to leave, you keep that with you. I was hoping we'd have more time, but it's always that way, isn't it, though?" I nodded. "Remember, if you see him, don't speak. Don't draw his attention. You can't stop what's happened and you don't want to drag out his journey, right?" I agreed. "I'll come back to take this braid off you when it's safe."

I wasn't supposed to go in the bedroom for at least ten days, until we had the Feast, leaving him a plate in the woods, to send him on his way. But I trusted Hillman and retrieved my bundle before my ma started cleaning out Umps's things, so he wouldn't linger.

No matter how much of my life I'd spent with Umps, I had to stay with the Darkwinters during his funeral. I took the bundle with me, and, sure enough, Old Limp, Kah-skwarih, did come near me, leaned over as if she were going to kiss my forehead. She stopped short, like I smelled funny. "Lena!" she yelled, standing abruptly, "come look after this boy, since you're the one getting paid." From then on, Old Limp kept her distance.

"Now listen," Hillman said, ten days later, when he came to relieve me of the wrist braid, "you're probably not gonna see me for a while. But that's okay. I'll be seeing you. It's the way things are going to be. I'll be back in your path when you need it." True to his word, he became scarce, hazy, like an unfamiliar landscape in your rearview mirror, distinctive feature still there, but going farther and farther away. When he eventually told me that all this time, I'd been training to take his place, he acted like I was supposed to be surprised, like I'd never seen *Star Wars* or *The Karate Kid*. The path is never as simple as it seems on those flickering movie screens. If Yoda or Mr. Miyagi had lived on a reservation, their paths might have looked like mine and Hillman's, but no hazy mist and music, just the spring of a pinball plunger, releasing and slamming me back into the Rez Mix, when I least expected it.

CHAPTER FIVE

Forbidden Fruit

(1971–72)

Gihh-rhaggs found a foothold at our house, as school started for me
a few months later. I met Randall Night there, noticing how he
refused to hold his right hand over his heart, standing out on the first day
of school. Because he was a member of a sovereign Native nation, he said
he couldn't pledge allegiance to another government. I had no idea what
he was talking about, but we were impressed with his denial of our teacher's authority.

By First Grade, Randall had a relationship with being sent to "The
Office" for breaking rules, which we quickly grasped was not a desirable state of affairs. We also knew by then that, come Friday, teachers
separated us into two groups, telling us this time was reserved for Bible
School. One group went to the parking lot below, but we lined up at
the front gate, where two women idled in large extended-passenger
jeeps with three rows of passenger bench seats. They could have been
kidnappers, but kids still stuffed themselves in and fought over window seats.

The taller, bigger woman threw her arms open in welcome. "Gather
round, children!" she yelled as cheerfully as she could. "I'm Miss Vestal,"
which I knew to be a lie, immediately. She was really a Mrs., the mother
of Christine Sampson in our class, and her older sister Hayley. Miss Vestal's short-sleeved flowered dress was cinched atop her belly, encasing her

like a sausage short of filling. She was Indian, but her pale skin was just this side of transparent.

"Hurry, now. Our time is short," she said, shooing all the kids who could fit into the large vehicles' bench seats, her routine. Despite her booming voice, Miss Vestal gave off a nervous air, like heat shimmers. "We'll be back for the rest of you in two shakes of The Lamb's tail, and in the meantime, Christine will tell you about Bible School." Then she jumped into our jeep's driver's seat. Christine, dressed formally, didn't seem up to the task. She'd been shy in kindergarten and wasn't much bolder now, a year later. Still, every day, she got on her knees, right on the lunchroom floor, to pray before eating. Braver than me, she made her own way in school.

"Where do those parking lot kids go?" Randall asked this year, making sure he sat next to Miss Vestal. He already knew, but he liked engaging with grown-ups. With any Indian adult of potential use, Randall would immediately start greasing his path. He'd already tried to impress the lunch ladies with his gap-toothed smile, and, instinctively, he asked Miss Vestal the kind of question she wanted to answer.

"Those are Catholics," she said, with a confidence that hinted at sinister meaning. These Bible School Fridays were the only times I'd been to a church. I'd been outside this one, the Tuscarora Protestant Church, when our pump broke, filling water jugs from its identical manual pump, but that was it.

"Now you children wait here in the entry, but Tami, you know how to lead for the Lord," Miss Vestal told Randall's older sister when we arrived. Tami snagged her brother's arm and they went in, setting up folding chairs before an easel, then sitting.

After Miss Vestal arrived with the last kids, she told those industrious young Christians that Jesus thanked them, but she eyed me up, in the vestibule. She hadn't singled me out to help like she had Tami, but I was in her mind. A new person had driven the other jeep this year, a younger, petite woman, dressed in a blouse and clamdiggers like my babysitters, Dusty and Lena. She wasn't from the Rez. Having never been told a bad future, she was a clean slate for me.

"So who are you?" Randall asked, sidling up to her, as she prepared the easel.

"I help Miss Vestal with these lessons," she started. "Now those of you who were—"

"Yeah, but who *are* you?" he repeated. "I'm Randy." Apparently he'd changed his name.

"Miss Betty," she said, as if he'd missed her name the first time. "You kids with Miss Vestal last year, go on ahead, and you new kids follow me."

Miss Betty revealed a large tablet with *A Children's Guide to Our Biblical Heroes* across its front, and set it on her easel. Its internal cloth pages had beautiful, color-rich landscapes, the first a wild, lush, unpopulated Garden of Eden. She called this the Lord's Flannel Board.

"Volunteers?" she asked, and hands shot up. On cue, otherwise reasonable kids gyrated like their chairs had been mildly electrified. She chose older volunteers who knew the drill.

"Okay," she said, opening a velvet folder, "now you each get one of these to put in the Garden, but remember, we don't get to name them because . . ."

"That's Adam's job!" her shills shrieked, selecting cardboard animals, jockeying for hot species like the monkey and toucan. After kids stuck their animals to the page, Miss Betty making the occasional correction, they sat down. She fixed two blond human figures in a pocket among the shrubs that we hadn't noticed. They were naked, but only visible from the waist up, the woman's soot-nehs discretely hidden by her long blond hair. At the end of her story, Miss Betty revealed an animal unavailable to us— the snake. She wrenched Adam and Eve from the shrubs and flipped the easel's page. Some loose animals fell to the church floor abyss.

She slapped Adam and Eve outside a large stone wall on Page Two, the dark sky an ominous gray like in late November. "How come they're wearing scaly underpants, like Robin?" I asked. "You know, from Batman?"

Miss Betty sighed, thinking I was intentionally challenging her authority, then clarified they were composed of fig leaves. She smoothed a partially eaten apple into Eve's hand and then peeled away a flannel patch in the upper right corner, revealing the giant hand of God, pointing at Adam and Eve. Indeed, they were being sent to "the Office," but Miss Betty was vague on their bad behavior. Their banishment concluded this year's first Friday Bible School lesson.

Randy asked if he could work the snake next time, and Miss Betty told him: "We'll see." She then smiled that polite smile like the women who told my ma she missed a spot, cleaning. "Usually, rewards come to those who don't question things. The ones who trust God knows what he's doing." He then asked on the ride back why Adam and Eve had been kicked out of the Garden. She said: "They were eating forbidden fruit, you know, questioning things they weren't supposed to."

They let us off at the school parking lot where we normally got the bus. "Forbidden fruit," Randy said to me. Christine joined us, maybe to offer an elaboration. Before she could say anything, he grinned and pushed me, saying, "That's what your ma's boyfriend eats on that hideaway couch in your living room." He'd never been to our house, but he knew where Gihh-rhaggs slept when he stayed over. Maybe Chester had said something to one of Randy's older sisters.

"They don't eat on the pull-out bed," I said. "The only thing they ever have is smokes."

"Didn't you see what Eve had in her hand?" he said, laughing the way he did when he knew things you didn't. "Gihh-rhaggs is eating the apple." I'd find out years later that "apple" was one name some Indians gave to other Indians who spent time with white people, and that Randy had a particular gift for vulgar turns of phrase.

LeKittia Night, Randy's mother, went by the name of Kitten, since it was easier for kids to remember. One May Saturday the next year, determined to make sure that Bible School wasn't our only outside education, she took a bunch of us on a hike near the spring and the quarry. One thing I'd noticed early on in school, the social lines were neatly drawn and rigidly enforced. Because the Rez was made up of about ten interlacing extended families, everyone mostly hung out with the cousins they'd known since birth, even in school.

I didn't have close cousins my age, and my ma and Hillman's unusual reputations kept me from being invited to the kid birthday parties of all but the most flexible Christian kids. Randy could be mean, and sharp, but also hilarious, and he had a talent for giving even the most boring day a hint of potential excitement. If I'd been stuck having just a couple friends my age, Randy was a good one to have.

That sense of chaos seemed to run in his family, since Kitten was dragging a bunch of us into the woods. She'd invited an equal number of boys and girls. "Now when we get out, you got to be respectful," she said. All the way there, she'd warned us that if she told us to jump, we had to do it. At seven, most of us took adult instruction as fact. We expected deep chasms and drop-offs that would require bravery and dedication. Randy sighed at this additional warning.

"Now listen," she said. "This spring is where Jigon`sae-seh lived. You kids know her?" Most of us shook our heads.

"Here, check this out," Randy said, digging into Kitten's bag. He'd heard this routine before. We passed around a piece of beadwork in progress that Kitten was making. Across the medallion, a woman talked with three men. One man had snakes for hair.

"Jigon`sae-seh was the woman who brought Hiawatha and the Peacemaker together with the Tadodaho. You kids know those names?" Most of us shook our heads no again.

"How come you just call that one the Peacemaker?" I asked. I could tell the other two names weren't in English.

"We don't say his name out of respect," she replied as we piled out. "But you kids learn these things. If you can learn that Adam and Eve oo(t)-gweh-rheh, you can learn about Jigon`sae-seh. If she didn't bring those arguing men together, there wouldn't be any confederacy. It was in her house." I'd heard the confederacy story before, but I couldn't recall a woman. "Without her, us Indians would just be wiped out and gone," Kitten said, sweeping her arms out like a lacrosse goalie. "Jigon`sae-seh could maybe see the future. She knew what white men were going to do to us, even before they got here, so she brought us together to survive." Christine and I exchanged glances. I knew her dad was white, and she knew my ma's boyfriend was, too.

"So when we walk around where her house used to be, we respect what we hear. Whatever I tell you? You do. No questions," she added, like we'd forgotten her earlier warnings. With that, we entered the woods through a path worn into the saplings. At the spring, the run of trees, boulders, brush, and mud looked like the woods behind our own houses.

We eventually wandered across the ruins of a building and asked if that was the house, excited. Kitten clarified that was an old sawmill, another alien word. Randy led a bunch of kids into a swampy patch where you could lose a shoe if you weren't careful. He'd already talked me into dubious scenarios in our few years together, but this was one of those periods where I was at the edge. A few of us had begun to take turns on his good and bad sides, someone else jumping in after you got burned, while you developed your personal timetable for forgiving Randy.

Gil Crews got stuck and was wiping mud off his jeans while Randy laughed his ass off. Christine crept next to me, a nobody too. She'd been eyeing up Randy the whole ride, knowing that Miss Vestal would probably not like her on this trip if she'd known the topic, but it seemed like she might also have a heart of compassion for my perceived deficiencies. With Gil suddenly in Loser Town, though, I guessed that space was freed up for me to spend the night at Randy's house. Kitten pretended not to notice as she gave us Five Thousand Facts About Jigon`sae-seh, but she was keeping track, as I thought she'd been.

Sure enough, when Kitten dumped all the other kids back at their houses, I stayed in the back seat and was suddenly on another adventure. Being a nobody sometimes paid off.

DogLips and Kitten hosted a regular dice game for adults on the weekends, and sort of had a built-in play area upstairs for people who couldn't get a sitter for their kids. Randy's cousins and some other Rez kids joined us while their parents rolled the bones. We told ghost stories upstairs, crowded around a stovepipe hole cut into the floor, eavesdropping. "I don't want to plant any bad ideas, if we let you watch this," we heard DogLips say to Kitten's nephew, Derek, still in high school. Derek's head bobbed, assuring them it was fine to let him watch *Bonnie and Clyde*. He was dying to harvest a bumper crop of bad ideas.

We grew bored and turned back to our own monster stories. A few minutes later, a werewolf's head suddenly flew up this empty stovepipe hole in the floor. Randy grabbed me, and we raced to report this breaking news. They feigned just enough disbelief to bewilder me.

While I described the werewolf's head with enough thoroughness for a police sketch artist, Randy snuck sips from his parents' beers. My ma and the Nights were not especially friends, but her boyfriend Gihh-rhaggs sat there, alone. He met my eyes, smiling a "keep your damn mouth shut" signal to me, blowing out the cigarette drag he'd just taken, like a gunslinger with the tip of his six-shooter. Miss Vestal's husband, Tim Sampson, hunched at the table too, towering over everyone. He frowned when Randy made his rounds of sips, but said nothing.

"What's wrong with your folks, man?" I said back upstairs. "We're in danger here."

"It's the mop," Randy said, laughing. "But keep it up. I snatch a sip every time we go."

"You're not supposed to do that," I said.

"You're not supposed to hog the heat, either, but we let you." The Nights had floor heat grates that blasted amazing rushes of warm air when the furnace kicked in. We had kerosene heaters that radiated a slow pulse of heat all the time. Nice, but nothing like that rush. Every time I heard it, I'd fly to the grate, loving the warmth rushing up my pant legs. It hadn't occurred to me that no one else was availing themselves of this pleasure. "We're pretending you don't stink too. My ma says, when she told me you could come over, that we have to make excuses for you."

"Exceptions," his sister Tiffany said, swatting him. "It's *exceptions*," she assured me.

During our next frantic werewolf-sighting report, Randy pointed with his lips to the mop. Its gray weave was easily mistakable for Evil Fur arriving through a stovepipe hole. Around the hole, we listened as those Texas sociopaths came to their own bad ending on the TV.

Someone knocked on the front door and a couple minutes later I heard the voice of Margaret, Gihh-rhaggs's daughter with the Rez woman he'd left, to be with my ma.

"Finally!" Tiffany said, standing up and dusting off the ass of her bell-bottoms. "Later for you losers," she added, heading to her room for a jacket. Margaret had her own car, and after a couple minutes of "don't get crazy out there" warnings, they were gone, two high school girls prowling for whatever high school girls chased.

When Kitten came upstairs later, we pretended to be asleep. After she left, Randy propped himself up on one elbow and looked at me in the dark. "I saved you from the werewolf."

"It wasn't a werewolf."

"You didn't know that, so, for real, I saved you. Now I want something. I'll tell you when the time is right. Just remember, you owe me." Drifting to sleep, I had no idea what that meant, but later I regretted being so eager to jockey for First Place in the good graces of Randy Night.

Before the sun rose, Kitten peeled my clothes from me and tossed them into a pillowcase with Randy's dirty clothes. I pleaded that I didn't need my clothes washed, but she begged to differ, and tossed me one of Randy's T-shirts and a pair of his briefs which I slid on and fell back asleep. Hours later, I awoke, convinced I'd had the weirdest nightmare until I looked under the covers. Randy was already up and wearing what he claimed was his only pair of clean pants.

"Come on, let's go down and get some breakfast," he said, tugging at the blankets I'd wrapped myself in. Delighted in my limitations, he brought cereal in for himself, and as the day went on, a sandwich, saying there was food downstairs if I ditched the covers. Down the hall, Tiffany and Derek discussed the pros and cons of a life robbing banks. Around sunset, Kitten returned. I got out of the bed and as soon as she left, I grabbed my clothes from the stack to change.

"Keep the drawers," Randy said, as I stood there, his shorts around my ankles. "I *really* don't want them back." He scrunched his face. I yanked them back up and pulled my pants and socks on, flinging his shirt off. Scrambling into my clothes, I headed downstairs, asking Kitten to take me home.

"Your ma's not home," she said, putting DogLips's clean clothes into their dresser. "I saw her out at the store. Gihh-rhaggs cleaned up at our dice table last night, and they were gonna go live large at the racetrack for a day."

"I don't care," I said. "Take me home."

Only two lights shone from our house when we pulled up: the outside light and a lamp near the chair nobody sat in since Umps had died. The Stones streamed out of the upstairs window, where Chester and Mona shared a tense truce across their linoleum floor. I made a sandwich when I got in and watched TV.

By a strange set of circumstances, at seven, I was the only one with a room by myself. Umps had never let Gihh-rhaggs stay the night, and my ma still obeyed her dead father's wishes, to a degree. So I'd inherited the large downstairs bedroom while my ma and Gihh-rhaggs frequently released the living room's hideaway.

While they were playing the ponies, and my siblings ruled their private kingdom, I drifted on the hideaway, awash in TV light. The next thing I knew, Gihh-rhaggs was lifting me off the mattress, a sharp alcohol scent streaming from his breath as he grunted. "Hey Ronnie Huh-uh," he said, butchering my Tuscarora nickname, carrying me to my bedroom. I couldn't guess how he knew Umps and Hillman used to call me Little Man. "Damn you're getting heavy."

"Wait, I want to watch the late monster movie," I said.

"No can do. I hit it big at the track tonight. You're going out to eat tomorrow and I don't want you spoiling it for your ma by being grumpy. Here, get these pants off. I'll hang them up." I had a sudden flash of my pants going through the wash at the Nights' and dug deep into the front pocket. "You won big, too, Little Man," he said, handing me the medicine bundle in a little plastic lunch bag. "Don't worry, no one touched it. Kitten Night told me she put it in the baggie when she checked to see if you had anything in the pockets. She gave it to me when I ran into her at the store. I don't know what it is, but you gotta be more careful with this. I know it's important to you."

The next day, Gihh-rhaggs had left my ma his car and some cash while he caroused somewhere on the Rez. Maybe without wheels, he'd found his way back to the DogLips Dice Game, rolling the bones, pulling in quarters by the stack. I pictured him raising his fingers to his lips, and I took that silent advice even now. I told myself that my ma had gotten up early and dropped him off somewhere out in the white world, where she'd later retrieve him from.

The four of us went to the Bradford House, a Colonial-themed restaurant where Indians who had enough money ate out. It was inside a Grants discount store, behind a stockade fence partition in a front corner, beyond the registers. The waiters and waitresses wore Pilgrim outfits, big buckles, white bonnets, short pants, and stockings. The counter was always lined with Indian men, smoking like the Buffalo Avenue factories, testing the "Free Coffee Refills" limits.

One spotted us and nudged the next, a slow wave of hungover dominoes, turning to look, curious how we had cash to come in. My ma glared back, daring them to ask. Some were my dad's drinking buddies, guys who'd helped him disappear for weeks at a time back when he still allegedly lived with us, sometimes lying to her face when she went hunting for him. Eventually, they turned their gaze away from her lava-hot stare, dropping their heads to their snotty eggs and corned beef hash and getting busy sweating out the previous night's beer. She dismissed them, spreading the menus before us, ordering us to pick whatever we wanted from the glossy surface.

We'd been to the Bradford House before, but this was the first time I'd been allowed to order. The Colonial waitress returned. Chester ordered an egg sandwich, Mona a fruit cup, and my ma a coffee.

"This," I said, pointing to the glistening Steak and Eggs special on the page. Gihh-rhaggs always got this. He came here so often he didn't even have to order. It just came.

"We're only supposed to order shit we can afford," Chester hissed after she left, punching me under the table. When our food came, everyone stared at the steak.

"Anybody want some?" I offered, but Chester just shoved each triangle of his egg sandwich into his mouth, whole. Mona ate the fruit chunks systematically, saving the one maraschino-cherry half for last. The steak cooled on the plate, soaking the eggs with blood. The bill was more than my ma had anticipated and she asked the Colonial waitress to wrap the steak.

It sat in the fridge for a couple of days. One morning, Gihh-rhaggs ate it with fresh eggs, offering me some from his fork. I shook my head, knowing the taste of that world had costs. He popped the wedge in his mouth and smiled, raising his pointer, reminding me we shared a secret. I didn't know what the big deal was. Maybe he didn't want to risk a table where he was king. She had a better poker face than he could dream of, but that didn't matter in dice. Like most of the Rez gamblers, he had his own superstitions, and perhaps he'd convinced himself that bringing my ma to a table where he was on a hot streak could change his luck.

My ma and Gihh-rhaggs would lie on the hideaway, those nights he stayed over, him talking his big dreams about the house he'd buy us in the suburbs until they started rustling the sheets. She'd never correct him, but we knew she'd sooner move us into the ditch on our property than leave the Rez again. She also never let him know that we ate lettuce-and-mayonnaise sandwiches more frequently than anything else when he wasn't there. She kept a lock on what our lives were like when he left our property and crossed the border to his other life. She was our Jigon`sae-seh, seeing the future and trying to find ways for us to stay together.

Gihh-rhaggs didn't know it, but some people would always see him as another white man we had to survive, one who could go back to his own world, any time he felt like it. Whenever we left the Rez, even for something as simple as breakfast, we had to be aware of our surroundings constantly, and avoid making even one wrong choice in selecting our nourishment. He could linger in our world without cost, consuming forbidden fruit on the busted springs of our hideaway couch, casting shadows across the room, ignoring the threat of God's hand emerging from a stormy sky.

CHAPTER SIX

My Good Man

(1973–74)

"My Good Man," that was what *she* called him. Good for what, was what most people asked, but all my ma would do was smile. He continued to hang around a lot as I made my way through elementary school. After a while, she had given the whole reservation a case of forced amnesia. Everyone forgot his real name, calling him MGM, which then evolved into Gihh-rhaggs, the Tuscarora word for "lion." He said it was because of his fierce growl and his thick beard and full mane of blond hair. He never knew the fluidity of our language, how we might say "lion," when we meant "lyin'." He could lift a full kerosene can to bring in, and enough time had gone by since Umps's passing that no one objected when she let him move in, during that winter.

My ma's house-cleaning gigs for those Lewiston white women bloomed into full time, five days out of seven, and most Saturday nights serving at cocktail parties for those same women. Sometimes she would get a party guest's wine-spill from a rug at the actual party, so it wouldn't have time to set before her regular day. Auntie Rolanda and Vera Blake would come at six o'clock every Saturday night, Rolanda carrying their little black dresses with the white collars on one hanger. That was their deal. My ma would drive Rolanda's car to wherever they were serving and my auntie and Vera took turns making sure their outfits were clean.

I'd stand on a dining room chair and zip them up after they'd gotten dressed, the backs of their white collars closing on my fingers like huge flower petals. The last thing my ma would do was take her teeth out and brush them in a dish of water and toothpaste. It looked like a much easier time than I had with my teeth and I wanted mine pulled, so I could also have those perfectly arranged removable teeth.

"When you going to find a man who's gonna at least help with the bills?" Rolanda would ask, in that voice she used before my hard-of-hearing Umps had died. Gihh-rhaggs generally stayed out of the way while my auntie and Vera were there.

"He does what he can. And besides, I don't see Phillipe making contributions at your house," my ma would say, as loudly back. Phillipe was Rolanda's boyfriend, a wild French Canadian who crossed the border whenever Rolanda's budget and wallet didn't agree. "And besides, My Good Man gets Brian up and off for school every day." True enough, but I wasn't sure my ma knew the whole story about him doing all he could manage. Not that I knew, either, for sure. Vera stayed out of things, quiet.

I don't remember when Gihh-rhaggs took over for my ma, in waking me. Chester and Mona feigned indifference to him, staying in their upstairs room most of the time. I imagined he felt clever at first, taking on the "job" of waking me up so I wouldn't notice he spent nearly every night at our home. The next spring, he was as much a part of our lives as the coffee cans we caught rain leaks with. He'd come into my room and do trampoline knee drops on the foot of the bed until I woke up. It was like waking to an earthquake five mornings a week. At night, I'd concentrate on willing myself awake the next morning, trying to train my ears to hear him enter the room or to sense him when he leapt. I wasn't picky. I just didn't want to wake up in the air for the rest of my school career. My ma was already scrubbing the shit from someone else's toilet long before I had to be up, so she figured since Gihh-rhaggs was there anyway, he could get me to the bus on time.

The first morning, he'd made coffee as I dressed and fought brushing my teeth. "You wanna keep those teeth as long as you can, junior. You never know when you're gonna need them." Then he offered me a sip from his cup and that was enough. "Good thing," he said. "There'll be plenty of bad habits to choose from once you get old enough. You'll like this, better," he said, pouring hot chocolate from the stove. He must have made it before jumping on the bed. "Your old man ever come around?" he asked. I shook my head. I'd been a later-life baby, a gift, a surprise, or more unkindly, a mistake baby. There were a fair number of us around the Rez. People got busy with each other, and if a pregnancy happened, well, that was the deal.

But my dad hadn't wanted more kids, said he had a hard enough time feeding those other mouths and still having money left over for his own pleasure, and he was sure my ma had gotten pregnant one last time just to spite him. He'd been looking for an excuse to fly for years, from what I hear, and I was just the one he needed. I hadn't seen him since before I'd started school, and even then, it had always been at a distance, from some far end of a crowd at different reservation events: community fair, National Picnic, Christmas bazaar.

I got to recognize his legs from afar because if he ever saw me coming, he'd make a quick disappearing act into the crowd. The year before at the National Picnic, I'd gotten within eight feet for several hours and he never caught on. I walked away as Fireball time rolled around. It wasn't like I could sneak up and capture him and suddenly, he'd want to be my dad again.

Gihh-rhaggs nodded and said it was time for the bus. He walked up the driveway with me and when the bus came up, Miss Betty opened the door, but she didn't look at me, staring out at Gihh-rhaggs instead. Lots of out-of-work reservation men waited with their kids in the morning to catch a glimpse of Miss Betty in her driving outfits, very different from her Friday afternoon Bible School styles. I didn't know then what impressed men about tight-fitting tank tops, but some older kids were kind enough to inform me. She had a smile for every one of those unemployed men too. Gihh-rhaggs looked back at her and nodded as she shut the door and got moving again. She watched him in the rearview mirror and he watched her and I watched the two of them until he disappeared around the bend.

He waited with me every morning as it grew warmer and there was less of a worry about me getting cold, or frostbit, or whatever he thought he was preventing by being there. He never waited in the afternoons, when Dave, the other driver, drove us home.

"How long you had that driver?" Gihh-rhaggs asked one morning.

"Dave?" I asked, knowing that was not who he meant. If anything, I got my dodginess from Gihh-rhaggs. He was the world's worst liar, but he'd convinced himself that if he didn't have to look someone in the eye, he could pull it off. When we drove around and hit his various stops, he'd offer me advice, what he called The Good Man Secret Handbook. He'd trained me to say we'd just gone for burgers on those Saturday nights we prowled his favorite places in the city. He liked my ma to think we just stayed home, but if she happened to call, we were telling the truth about the burgers, he said, "technically." He taught me his method was to stare at a point just beyond either ear of the person he was talking to. It's a decent technique and I use it often.

"The other one."

"Since I've been on the bus, pretty much," I said. There might have been others at first, but Miss Betty became the regular driver quickly, and any other faces rapidly faded to the point that Miss Betty had forever been our driver. Everyone liked her, not just the employment-challenged. Even the bad kids behaved for her, or at least in front of her. Across the Rez, Lewis Blake had an uncle who lived with his family. I don't know if his Uncle Albert was always a little off, but he sure was when he came back from Vietnam. Albert had struck up a waving relationship with Miss Betty, and after a while, they'd say hi back and forth, and she gave him cigs sometimes when the mood hit her right. Lewis told me his uncle sometimes suggested that he and Miss Betty were dating, and the neighbor kids found this way too funny. Lewis suspected kids from down the road would call his uncle if they knew he were home alone, and pretend to be Miss Betty. I was glad they lived too far away to want to consider me as a friend. This reservation can be a tough place on love.

I was beginning to think, as Miss Betty and Gihh-rhaggs became more friendly too, waving, saying hi, watching each other in the mirror, that there might be some real phone calls coming to our number. Did that bus stop at my house while we were all out for the day in our respective prisons? Miss Betty grew nicer and nicer to me the more she and Gihh-rhaggs became bolder, sometimes giving me a candy bar the way she passed cigarettes to Lewis's uncle.

I didn't know what Gihh-rhaggs did during the day, or if he had a job, but he seemed to never be without money. As soon as my ma and auntie left in their black dresses every Saturday night, he and I were out the door in his junker car. Mona and Chester had made it clear that they were not my caretakers and weren't wasting their Saturday nights on me. Gihh-rhaggs maintained to my ma that his car sometimes got stuck in second gear, so they usually rode with others whenever they went places together. But his car got the two of us wherever he wanted to be just fine when we headed out past dark.

Our first hit would be the Golden Pheasant, where all the women petted on me, buying me Cokes and potato chips and putting me up high on a bar stool to watch the pool or pinball games without getting in the way, while he went into the back room and rolled some dice. Sometimes, one of the guys would bring my barstool over and teach me how to shoot with the balls remaining, after someone had sunk the eight, and other times, I finished out the extra balls in Gihh-rhaggs's pinball once his opponents had used up theirs. I liked this the best, since the game, Fireball, featured art that looked vaguely like a superhero, and Fireball had a whole different meaning on the reservation.

We also regularly hit the neighborhood Gihh-rhaggs said he and his brother came from. They were Love Canal boys, growing up in a house filled with contaminants. He'd show it to me on those nights, but by then, Love Canal places had started being haphazardly boarded up. The neighborhood was beginning to look like *Night of the Living Dead.* Owners hammered up a few boards, enough to show they'd split on purpose, and called it a day. Even homeless crank-heads stayed away, and Love Canal had an almost 0 percent crime rate. The commonest criminals refused to flirt with cancer that epically.

Whenever he talked about it, I'd ask Gihh-rhaggs where his brother was now, and he'd just say "around." Even at seven, I knew a Mind Your Own Business comment when I heard it. How Gihh-rhaggs made his way out to the Rez in the first place was anyone's guess. The Rez and Love Canal weren't even neighbors. Maybe back then, all the Rez kids and Love Canal kids went to the same high school. It was hard to think of my ma in high school, adjusting her clothes in the Girls room when she got to school, to be a little more provocative for boys, dating, Eee-ogging about those dates, sneaking out late at night, whatever, but she did. I'd seen her diploma. Instead of Wheatfield, where I went, she'd gone to LaSalle, in the Love Canal district.

The official contamination news was still a couple years off when we cruised around, but Gihh-rhaggs, and probably most of his neighbors, had known something was wrong. He told my ma that he and his brother had slept in the basement of their home growing up, and during rainy seasons, the ground water leaking into their room often was iridescent, glowing in low corners, like *The Blob*. Sometimes, I overheard them at night. "You'll see, when I get up enough money for a lawyer, I'm gonna take the chemical companies to court, maybe the school board, too. I hear they had something to do with this." Sometimes, even later, he'd confess his greatest fears to her. "I swear, I'm gonna develop some wicked mutation or disease by the time I get old, and then you won't want me anymore."

"I'm not like that," my ma would say, and it was true. She didn't seem to think anything of our dad missing his big toe. It was just part of the way his body came.

"I swear, I took pictures of that glowing shit oozing down our basement bedroom walls. Those companies take one look at my pics? They'll settle out of court, and, baby, we will be set for life." As with so many of Gihh-rhaggs' plans, that one just disappeared.

His parents had decided to stay, even when he and his brother offered to help them. They said they were too old to move and asked to be left alone in the only home they'd known through their marriage. We'd sail silently by, before hitting the last few city stops of the night. At those, I mostly sat in the car. He'd detour and pick up fast-food burgers to leave with me, and whatever I didn't eat, he'd finish off as we made our way back to the Rez. Sometimes, he'd laugh a creepy little sound when talking about the people leaving Love Canal, saying, "Moving to much smaller accommodations," and only years later, when the contamination story broke, did I understand he meant caskets.

"Why you wanna live with us, anyway?" I asked one night as we entered the Rez.

"You don't want me to live with you?" I think it was the first time an adult had ever asked for my opinion, and meant it.

"I guess it's all right," I said. "You don't spill kerosene. But you're white," I added, as if this fact were not obvious. When my ma went for a white man, she went all out. He was about as blond and blue eyed as they make them; even his beard was blond and not that red-brown so many blond guys grow. As summer came on, his skin was burning or peeling, white or red; he never browned. "We have to live here. You don't. You could go anywhere, maybe live in those houses like the people on TV." I'd been to some houses my ma cleaned and they lived luxurious lives, with toilets and sinks, and their houses weren't wired with extension cords from the one set of outlets near the box. "Wouldn't that be great?"

"You could go anywhere, too. Your mom is the one who won't leave. I've been trying to get her to move for a while. Finally I gave up and came to live with her, since she wouldn't come live with me." I didn't buy this story. I might have been seven, but I'd already learned to add. I knew he'd been living with a woman down on Dog Street. I even knew Margaret, the daughter he had with her. If he wanted my ma to move off the Rez, it wasn't to give us a different life. It was because our house was a little too close to the last bed he'd been camping out in.

"Well, where would you live? Where'd you want her to move to?"

"Around," he said. "It doesn't matter. The point is, she wouldn't come because of you kids. She said she wanted you to grow up on the reservation, learn the language, all that shit. Are you learning it in school?" I nodded. "Does that name everyone calls me really mean lion?" I considered lying, myself, but then confessed that it did. "Hah, I knew it," he said, running his fingers through his beard. "They all wish they could have this proud mane."

"Maybe on their belts," I said. He probably didn't like that, but it was going to take more than a few hamburgers to win me over, even if I was learning to shoot pool and hit the pinball flippers long before I could ever reach the player position proper. He won major points with me, though, late in August, and I never made scalping jokes after that.

Gihh-rhaggs let me climb all over his car, treat it as if it were mine. He told me I could have it when I got old enough to drive, so I had better be nice to it in preparation. Kids from down the road would come over if his car was parked under the walnut tree. He was like my exotic pet. Some had never seen a white man that close before, not one as white as Gihh-rhaggs.

"Brian?" Randy Night asked one day we were hanging out, voice all wonder and innocence, which meant a bomb was dropping. "Is his pecker as white as the rest of him?" I told him I hadn't the foggiest. I'm sure they were intimately involved, I guess I knew it even then, but in our house, privacy was a premium. Without a bathroom and with a shortage of bedrooms, the only time you were ever naked was while bathing, and even then, it was either the upper or lower half. The first time I could remember being truly naked was when they started making us take showers after gym in second grade. I liked my privacy and never invaded anyone else's.

If Gihh-rhaggs came outside while we were playing, Randy would stare into his blue eyes, something he'd never do at his own house when the DogLips dice table was in session. He knew not to interfere with his parents' dealings. But here, Randy's chaos-loving side came out to see what kind of reaction he'd get. Gihh-rhaggs in response would smile and ask Randy what he was looking at, and Randy would abruptly retreat back to playing with me.

One day that summer, a group of us discovered we could reach a thick walnut branch by standing on the car's roof. Grabbing on, we could swing across the hood and down to the ground, just like using a Batrope on TV. We kept this up for a couple hours but then, abruptly, Randy said he didn't want to swing anymore. I just thought: more turns for me. He knew what I didn't, and about five trips across the hood later, the thick branch cracked, a loud and painful moan, like the noise a kid's body makes against the road after going over a bike's handlebars.

Randy and the others immediately called me "Tree-Killer" in as loud of voices as they could muster. They wanted anyone in hearing range to know I'd been the one to do the damage, before they went home to their own yards full of intact trees.

Our house was nearly in the woods, surrounded by trees, but my ma loved the black walnut growing outside the kitchen window. She collected the nuts every fall and though they stained her fingers black and the shells were tough as rocks, she cracked them and harvested every nut she could find. I tried lifting the branch and leaning it on the others, so she wouldn't know, but that night I lay in bed and thought about killing that tree.

The last swing had been a serious move that could get me a name for the rest of my life. Gihh-rhaggs was a dreadful enough one for my ma's old man. I participated in the ritual, and I most certainly did not want to go through life being named Tree-Killer. I'd hoped for a much better Rez name and had been getting to the age where one would come up on me unexpected, some unforeseeable life event changing my name forever. There was a woman named Buffalo Head just because she watched a movie that had buffaloes in it, with people who noticed her head was bigger than it should have been for her body. This move could be bad.

Worse than the name, though, was the idea that I had killed something, and the fact would not leave me no matter what I tried to think about. There were things I'd regretted by the age of seven, but up till then, those lapses in judgment had been retrievable, erased or held at bay by an apology and an expectation that there would be a payback at some point.

I already understood the vengeance of school children was not monumental, but still exact. For this action, though, no one was going to punch me in the nuts when adults weren't looking, or shove my head in the toilet at school until I couldn't breathe, then flush it at the last possible moment. No one would pinch my jaws open and spit down my throat and no one would stuff sulfur powder up my nostril over this singular death. None of the kids who'd watched me kill the tree cared about it. They just wanted to distance themselves from the blame.

I knew little of the ways of trees, but even as I lay in bed, leaves were falling, and I'd have to go out and face the corpse every day for the rest of my life, watching it grow gray, wither, eventually fall into decay, depriving my ma of her walnut harvest from that point on.

The next morning, I wasn't hungry. My ma was already hand-waxing someone's kitchen floor and Gihh-rhaggs was taking his responsibility of getting my breakfast seriously. He offered a number of things, cereal, eggs, pancakes, most of which we did not actually have in the house, but he was willing to go buy them. I refused even more stridently as he went along. I didn't want him to go outside and see the tree's corpse. He'd know my guilt for sure. Soon enough, though, I realized he'd inevitably need to use his car.

"I need to show you something," I said.

"I knew something was up. What is it? Are you sick? Something happen? Did you shit the bed or something? You can tell me. I promise to take it to the grave, if you want." I shook my head and took his hand, dragged him outside, and confessed to the murder. He frowned and pulled the branch down. He wasn't a tall man, but it was low enough for him to reach.

"I killed that tree. It was an accident, but I murdered it, by not thinking about it. Randy said so. He said everyone would remember what I did for the rest of my life."

"It's not dead. See? Look here." He lifted me up on his shoulders and showed me where the break was. I didn't want to see it, but he grabbed my hand and laid my fingers on the wet pulp. "It's still alive. This happens to everything. It'll heal over. You watch. You gotta quit worrying about this shit. This is like your craziness with the tornados this summer."

"Well, they said on the TV . . ." I started. I'd become aware of the Emergency Broadcast System a few months before, and anytime they did their tests on the television, I ran into the room and stared at the Civil Defense image on the screen while the warning tone filled my ears. Our house was over a hundred years old, had belonged to my grandparents before my ma, and it had no basement, not even a dirt cellar. Between the cracks in our floor planks, you could see the dark and wet earth beneath. I'd tried to negotiate with friends who had basements, like Randy, to see what I could give them in trade for room, in event of an emergency, among the commodity vegetables and their dads' porno mags hidden under the stairs. I'd secured reasonable assurances for my ma, Mona, Chester, and me, but no one wanted a white man in their cellars, and for sure not one as white as Gihh-rhaggs, though he'd been with us almost two years by then.

"I know what they said on TV, but I've lived here my whole life, and I haven't seen one tornado. It might happen, I suppose, but this tree will probably outlive you. Your kids'll be picking nuts off the ground. It's strong. Everything that's meant to survive does, and there's nothing you can do about it. Let's get rid of this branch and get some breakfast, okay?" We did.

Sometime months later in fall, when life was smooth, things changed forever, and the Emergency Broadcast System alarm never even sounded. Gihh-rhaggs had been right. The tree scarred over. My ma never noticed the stump, but I saw it every time I walked by and took to using the front door. In the mornings, Gihh-rhaggs would lay my clothes on the kerosene heater, so all I had to do was run into the big room, get into my warm clothes, and begin waking up fully.

The first thing I noticed that morning was that I awakened by myself. I'd finally trained myself to wake up before Gihh-rhaggs jumped on the bed. I waited and waited, and eventually peeked through the curtain that served as my door. There were no clothes on the kerosene heater. I tugged on a set, yanking back the curtain to see if the country had experienced a nuclear attack, and I'd slept through the Duck and Cover Drill the one time it had really counted.

My ma sat at the table, and as I got close, I thought she was laughing at something on the radio, rocking forward, her hand gripping her forehead. I touched her and asked her what it was. She looked up, not laughing, and, of course, crying. This was something I'd never seen. When she came home from work with her feet swollen like loaves of rising bread, she never complained. I'd asked her why, and she said complaining was a waste of the energy.

"My Good Man is gone," she said, and I immediately pictured Miss Betty pulling up early in her empty bus, so no one caught it, until she slowed to our driveway and Gihh-rhaggs grabbed his grocery bag of clothes from my ma's dresser, stepping onto the striped stairs behind the wheel well, allowing those folding doors to close on our life. She probably put the bus in motion even before he stepped beyond the white caution line. Those two were so sneaky.

"I bet I know where to find him," I said, picturing the large garage and fenced-in parking lot near the Rez border, where all the school buses rested when they weren't being used.

"He's dead," she clarified, straight out, like she had read me a headline from a newspaper. "That stupid car of his. Exhaust fumes, they think.

He was on his way home from the track, had this in his pocket. Hit a tree."
She pointed to the counter where we kept sugar, salt, anything she might
have used as seasoning, and the bucket of well water we drank from. "His
daughter left it on the porch this morning. The note said he was probably
intending it for us."

"How much is it?" I asked. I had never seen so much cash in my life.
We kept our few dollar bills orderly. I read off the names of the men, Jack-
son, Hamilton, Grant, Franklin, faces familiar only from the classroom
walls. It was easier to concentrate on these grim white faces than to admit
Gihh-rhaggs' goofy bearded face was gone. He looked a bit like Grant.

I walked out the door. His car wasn't underneath the tree. He'd been
wrong, I thought, looking at the walnut, or lying, after all, when he said
that this was the natural order, that things died, and things healed over.
All that shit. There wasn't a natural thing about that morning.

I wanted to tell my ma about what I thought was true of Gihh-rhaggs
and Miss Betty, then maybe she would stop crying. I knew it wouldn't be
right to say all the crying in the world wouldn't bring him back, but I
wanted her to stop. I got ready for school on my own. She sat, staring. I
bet she knew Miss Betty would be showing up, ready to get her morning
flirt in, and I was going to be just the person to set things straight. I waited
in the cold, trying not to think about the fact that Gihh-rhaggs was gone,
and trying to remember how I was going to tell Miss Betty off, even if it
got me kicked off the bus for good, and maybe even Bible School.

When the bus arrived and the door opened, Dave Three Hawks greeted
me instead. I asked him where Miss Betty was and he frowned, then
smiled, and said "Liz? Miss Betty, that's a new one on me." I nodded. It
had to be her. "She called in this morning."

I climbed up the few steps into the bus and stood at the caution line,
asking as casually as a seven-year-old can, if he knew why she had called in.

"Her dad died sometime during the night. They weren't close, but a
person's dad is a person's dad, right kiddo?" Dave looked up at me in front
of him and smiled.

"I guess," I said. I started to ask Miss Betty's last name, but then realized I had no idea what Gihh-rhaggs's last name was. I knew he'd had
another life, several, I guess, like any other cat, but I knew only a small

sliver. The rest was shadowy. For me, he'd only had the one with us, and no other life where he'd needed a different name than the ones we'd given him.

"Now get back behind that line and have a seat so we can get a move on, okay?" I crossed the caution stripe and he pressed in the clutch, shifted into gear, and pushed us on through the falling leaves.

CHAPTER SEVEN

True Crime

(1975)

After Gihh-rhaggs wrapped his car around someone else's walnut, my ma still needed to bring in whatever bucks she could, cleaning houses, so I once again got farmed out to almost anyone since Mona and Chester still insisted on their freedom. The wad Gihh-rhaggs left us seemed like it should have lasted us forever by my reckoning, but what did I know about bills? We were back to inventing food in no time. Ketchup soup thickened with half-off day-old bread tasted good after a while, in its familiarity.

The most consistent place I wound up was still with Dusty and Lena Darkwinter, each hoping to latch onto my cousin Roland the lacrosse star. I assumed my own charming self had brought them to fawning on me, but I soon figured things out. If their attention was on the wane, I'd casually drop that he'd asked about them the last time he visited.

Among the various houses I got dumped at, I'd developed a workable relationship with the Darkwinter girls, and so they were the ones I dropped the most information to: Roland's favorite foods, TV shows he liked, when he might spend time on Moon Road. I didn't know what went on there, but it was popular at night with no electricity poles chasing its ditches.

Their friend Margaret had a car, but she was never hip to my being along when they were snagging. Of the two daughters Gihh-rhaggs had left in his wake, Miss Betty disappeared, but Margaret was from the Rez.

That rift between her ma and mine was never going to heal now that Gihh-rhaggs was dead. When she'd show at Dusty and Lena's and stand around before peeling out, I'd know that they'd originally planned to go "snag-ging for mens."

"Well, kiddo, you blew it for us again," Dusty said, the last time. "We could have gotten us a nice time tonight. You gotta give us some info now." She was all smiles when she said it, handing me a Creamsicle, but she meant business.

"I don't have anything new."

"We could call her back and leave you here with my ma and dad and the dolls," Lena said. "And Grandmama," she added, as if an afterthought. Their parents were always around, usually working their trade in the back of the house, emitting clouds of blue smoke under the bare bulb and the amber strips thick with flies hanging over the kitchen table. You could hear three things continuously coming from that kitchen: their coughing, a drifting radio station, and the fading buzz of the most recent fly joining their suicide pact. Old Limp crept around upstairs somewhere. "And you know how funny things get with the dolls."

To drag her point home—like that was necessary—she lifted one of the cornhusk dolls from the high shelf above us and held it in front of me. It was wearing a traditional ribbon outfit, beadwork and velvet collar and cuffs, leggings. Their parents made an okay living doing the craft-show circuit and exercising their treaty rights of being members of a sovereign Native nation. As such, they were able to sell souvenirs to the tourists on the US side of Niagara Falls. My family was exercising our treaty rights by living in a house that would have been condemned and bulldozed any-where beyond the Rez borders.

The trinkets Dusty and Lena's parents made and sold were horn rat-tles, beadwork, jitterbugs, and yes, the cornhusk dolls that troubled me so. "I might just have to take this Magic Marker and draw a face onto this one here before we leave too. My mom says we're not supposed to, but we don't always do exactly as we're told." A lot of people said that if you put a face on a cornhusk doll, it would capture a soul and come alive and you were taking your chances with whose soul the doll was housing. Could be a nice old lady, could be a killer.

"He wears colored underpants," I said.

"Huh-uh."

"Yeah, dark blue, mostly. Some black ones and red too, like the white ones I wear, only colored." It was a piece of information I'd saved for a long time, discovering it once when Auntie Rolanda and my ma went to the laundry together. These girls had really wanted to go with Margaret, and they'd be surly the rest of the night if I didn't hack up something good.

"Blue underpants," Dusty said, her eyes drifting. "Like this blue? Or this one?" She pointed to various objects: a jar, a pillow, a beaded pincushion in the shape of a fancy ladies boot. I hadn't memorized Roland's underpants, so I conceded it was *probably* like the pincushion color. This detail would be something these girls would like. They were the kind who timed their ladies room visits during Clan League basketball games to maybe catch a glimpse of players changing in the locker room while others ran out onto the court. The girls sometimes hypnotized themselves while being paid to watch me. They'd forget I was with them as they talked their secret girl talk. This usually happened in their upstairs room, when they got out the scissors.

Dusty and Lena seemed to spend the money they got for watching me on magazines. They allowed me to flip through the ones they'd picked over as they explored new ones, deciding what warranted the scissors and what didn't. The cut-up magazines weren't that interesting since the sisters had relieved the pages of their best pictures to paste above their beds. Their bedroom walls were slats covering corncob insulation, smelling like a spent field at the end of harvest.

"Which one do you like best?" Dusty asked. She was never satisfied to just make and love this work herself, and always wanted comment on it, but who was I? A little kid was hardly an expert on art. I still favored super-heroes and had followed their lead, cutting pictures from comics and playing with them like toys. Spider-Man's legs, though, curled under and tore within a half hour of my releasing him from the page, like the legs of a fly when you held onto them. The flies hated so much to be held down that they ripped their own legs off to escape, but they never figured out that I'd tied them with sewing thread before I held them by one leg.

"Well?" Dusty demanded. I studied all the pictures and headlines she

and Lena had Elmer's Glued to the walls. They wanted me to give a different answer, but that seemed like a cheat. If they were really asking my
opinion, I felt an obligation to give it.

"This one," I said, pointing to the same one I had every time they'd
asked before.

"You always say that!" they both said, snapping their eyes and getting
up from the beds.

"What about this one?" Dusty asked, tapping one with a long red lac-
quered nail. A vague film covered this new piece. I think they'd been
attempting more advanced collage with glue sticks or shellac, maybe hoping to impress me. This was a picture of a woman running a vacuum
cleaner over a carpet, but the woman, in a dress, heels, and pearls, also
had a pair of antlers. She wasn't wearing them in the way a chief of the
Nation wears them, ceremonially, mounted on a Gustoweh, but the way
a deer wears them, erupting fiercely from her head, ready to rip out an
enemy's guts. A Sears-catalog man was glued on part of the page, so it
looked like the woman's vacuum was pulling the front of his underpants
right up its hose. One of them had written my cousin's name below the
picture of the Sears man, with an arrow pointing to him. The sisters had
cut out letters from a variety of magazines to caption this one, so its one-
word title, SNAGGING, looked like those kidnapping ransom notes you
see on TV.

"No, this one, still," I said.

"These new ones are so much better," Lena said, pointing to several
others. "That one you like, it was nothing. All it took was four cuts for the
picture and four more for the words."

"Then don't ask me," I said.

"We might have to get the dolls."

"You go ahead. It ain't changing my mind. I'm not saying this one is
the best. Just the one I like the best. Those others are like the museums,"
I said, hoping to make them understand in ways they already knew the
world.

Among the ways Dusty and Lena tried to snag Roland was to go to
every lacrosse game he played on the Canadian side of Niagara Falls, like
most of the Rez population. They weren't interested in the game, just

enjoying him running around the arena in the tiny uniform satin shorts. This limited view only held attraction briefly, and they'd wander out by halftime to hit the tourist area called Clifton Hill. They were convinced that Roland could sense they were showing me a good time while he dedicated his time to the Creator's Game, chased a hard rubber ball, bodychecking other men who got in his way. So they brought me along to check out all the bright lights and exotic happenings.

Most places to spend money on the Hill were flashy museums, offering lurid sights within on vivid outside posters surrounded by flashing lights. The girls generally liked to take me to the Hollywood Wax Museum, believing I'd be impressed by the likenesses of the Beatles and Batman, the only figures I recognized. They always claimed the Indian warrior was Fred Howkowski, but I'd seen pictures of him at his ma's house, and these girls were stretching their imaginations. I could see the Batman costume was passable at best. The blue parts weren't satin, the belt was wrong, and the blue shorts it rested on looked suspiciously like the kind Roland wore, fly flap and all. Even the poor lighting, glamorous *Pow!* and *Bam!* spraypainted on the wall behind the dummy, could not convince me that Adam West had ever worn the outfit.

We'd go in, nod, and back out, where the Hill was more interesting anyway. People wandered the street, crossed against traffic, and stared into the air at the tightrope-walker statue suspended over a crosswalk. Some watched the short films and other free exhibits outside those museums vying for our attention and dollars.

I generally tried coaxing the girls away from the Frankenstein museum, hunched like blight, with its balcony where the Wolf Man and the Mummy and the Devil would randomly burst forth from rickety-looking doors and leer at us from the second story, daring us to enter. The girls had tried to get me inside a year before, had paid the admission and we'd gotten to the steps leading into the basement entrance, before I had a meltdown and bailed.

It was knowing that monsters ran free on the second floor that bothered me the most. I didn't mind the immobile monsters behind velvet ropes, where you could admire their workmanship, but the idea of some prowling around the same hallways as me had been too much for my younger brain. By now, I knew that the monsters were men, probably college students working summers in sweaty masks and costumes, sneaking beers and snagging a grope occasionally from attractive museum-goers all in the name of fright. I was no longer alarmed by the second-story monsters, but was still deeply afraid the girls would resurrect my cowardice for their own amusement, reenacting my flight from the Chamber of Horrors.

"We saw something new at the museums the last time," Lena said, and when I asked her what it was, she acted purposefully obtuse, suggesting that if I got them invited to a family picnic, they might consider showing me their secret during the next lacrosse game. I made no promises. My ma tolerated others only as long as they contributed something to our general well-being. These girls were already being paid.

"So I heard a different reason the cornhusk dolls don't have faces," I said, trying to deflect the conversation's direction.

"Oh, yeah?" Dusty said, raising her drawn-on eyebrows. Mrs. Crews, our Indian language class teacher, occasionally wandered from her lesson plans and told us subversive traditional stories, ditching her number, animal, and food vocabulary lists. She told us she wasn't supposed to stray, so we'd pay closer attention. Being bad seemed more exciting than learning the four ways to say someone was eating. I liked her alternate version of the doll's history.

"I hear Corn Spirit made the original doll so kids could be happy, but that the doll was just always sneaking off to check out her reflection in a pond. Creator warned her to wise up and so the next time she snuck out, Creator snatched her face away with one quick pull. After that, she didn't have any more distractions."

"So where'd you hear that crock of shit?" Lena asked, cutting something new from a fresh magazine, planning her next wall panel.

"School," I said.

"School!" Dusty shrieked, and laughed like I'd just told her the dirtiest joke ever. "That old bitch don't know what she's talking about. Probably read that in some *Indians of America* book. Don't believe everything you hear, kiddo. You know what she was before she got all black-dress-and-string-of-pearls on us? A housecleaner!" She realized what she'd said just a couple of seconds after it was out of her mouth. She looked to Lena, who immediately began glue-sticking her new cutout on the wall, letting Dusty know she was alone in this mess.

"You know what?" Dusty said suddenly. "I'm gonna call Margaret this instant and see if she'll drive us across the border so we can take you to see the new secret."

I wasn't above bribery, but her housecleaner comment hadn't eluded me. Dusty knew she'd potentially thrown her income in jeopardy. Neither of us knew it was an empty fear, that my ma would send me with anyone reasonable so she could put food on our table and kerosene in our stove. Looking back, she didn't put me with derelicts, mind you, but she wasn't exactly scouring babysitting résumés with the intensity she used on the bathrooms of Lewiston's finest citizens.

"You know, she didn't mean anything by it," Lena said when Dusty went downstairs to use the phone. We could hear her negotiating with Margaret, making promises if Margaret would change plans and drive over the border to see this new thing. She reluctantly confirmed that I was still there, too. She came back up, smiling, saying Margaret would be there shortly.

I had my doubts. At lacrosse games Margaret and I didn't speak about her dad, pretending he'd never existed. One night, Dusty, Lena, Margaret, and I hid up in the arena's top rows, so they could smoke. I'd come with my ma and Auntie Rolanda, but gravitated to those girls, hoping they'd drag me along into their more fabulous lives.

I wanted to acknowledge to Margaret what we'd both lost when Gihh-rhaggs left us, but I was nervous, particularly after the strange funeral fronted by at least three different women and their children who had loved Gihh-rhaggs enough to see him out of this world together. I wasn't allowed to go, but Mona told me all about it in a more generous moment.

At the lacrosse game, I casually moved from the end where Dusty and Lena always kept a buffer between us, and sat down next to Margaret. I opened my mouth, wondering what would come out. I wanted to tell her how much he had meant to me, how much I missed our rides through the Rez and the city, just the two of us, when he would tell me his secret wishes and desires for our lives. The way he'd let me fall asleep in front of the

heater's blower and carry me to bed later when he was getting ready himself, the hot chocolate he made, the way he warmed my clothes on top of
the kerosene heater in the winter. But then I feared these were things he
either had or had not done for her. Really, I just missed him, and his lumi-
nous presence in my life.

I should have stayed put in my own seat, but I heard the words trail
out of my mouth and into the arena, where sweaty men whacked each
other with sticks and chased the bouncing, hard rubber ball. "Your dad's
dead," was what came out. It was technically an accurate statement, but
not at all what I had intended. I smiled, trying to soften its bluntness.

"That's not funny," she said. "You think that's funny? You want me to
say that when your dad drops dead? Shouldn't be too long." I snapped my
mouth shut and shook my head. It was as if she'd slapped me for loving
her dad as much as she had, and for being inarticulate about it. Dusty and
Lena pretended to watch the game, like they'd heard nothing.

"Well, bye," I said. No one responded, so I wandered away. I'd see the
girls, since they watched me. But after that, Margaret only spoke to me
indirectly, through Lena and Dusty.

True to their word, though, after Dusty's call, she showed and we piled
into her car, where we encountered another surprise. "Hi, Brian," Christine Sampson said, as I slid in. "So you're the one Margaret don't like."
Apparently Margaret kept her gas tank filled doing the same job as Dusty
and Lena.

At the Canadian Customs and Immigration Booth, Margaret and
Lena rolled down their windows and turned their heads in a studied, casual
way, refusing to remove their sunglasses, though it was nearing dusk. The
guard in the booth leaned over and asked our citizenship.

"North American Native," Margaret said, which the sisters and Christine repeated. Normally, I crossed the border with my ma, but I knew it
had become popular on the Rez to say this to Customs, Indians attempting to assert treaties. They were enforcing the Jay Treaty's acknowledgment
that Indians lived on both sides of the border.

"United States," I said when the guard turned his eye to me. My ma
always felt that letting authorities know you were Indian was a dangerous
proposition, and so I'd spoken the phrase she taught me to use whenever

we crossed the Canadian border. Lena smacked me and said, "He's a North American Native too. Just too young to know it." As if I didn't have eyes or live in our condemned-anywhere-else house. "Is that true, son?" the guard asked, and I nodded, which stung of betraying my ma a second time that night. He told us to move along.

A few minutes later, we were on the Hill, chasing down the girls' secret.

"Do you know where we're going?" Christine asked, as they prodded us to keep up. I shrugged. We passed the Houdini museum, featuring clips of his greatest escapes and actual props he used to constrain himself, chains, trunks, a cage, a glass water tank. Its sidewalk lure was a crystal ball on a table, somehow flickering the face of an actor playing Houdini inside the ball, dramatically inviting us to unlock his secrets.

"It's just a movie, and they project it behind the ball. Easy Peasy," Dusty hissed, a trick so primitive it was not worth even a sliver of her awe. The girls didn't stop to chat with Houdini's movie head as they usually did, making lewd suggestions as he begged us to cough up the admission price. We apparently had other secrets to unlock.

Turning the corner, we ran into a huge crowd, congesting the Believe it or Not! Museum's entrance. We'd already checked out the glass skull from some ancient past, the real skull from the man who lived with a railroad spike embedded in his brain, and assorted novelty skulls from around the globe. This museum hadn't warranted a second look before. It wasn't an issue of whether I believed or not, more one of whether I cared or not.

Given my age and height, I wasn't likely to see the big secret, but the girls had a way of working crowds, easing us in as if the others had been keeping our places in line until we got through Immigration. We burst out near the front and though I still couldn't see the exhibit yet, Margaret could. "This is what you dragged me out across the border for?" she said, glaring at Dusty. "That's disgusting. How can she go in public like that? I could be home watching *All in the Family* right now."

"Shut up," Dusty mumbled. "I told you I'd make it worth your while. I'm working on getting us invited to some party where Roland's going to be." Lying, she knew she'd already ensured that was never going to happen.

"We'll catch up to you," Margaret said. "At least Christine's not too chicken to go to the Frankenstein," she added, dragging her charge off down the hill. Christine's face suggested she didn't agree with that assessment.

"Ready?" Dusty asked me, lifting me by my armpits to her height. I could not believe my eyes, searching for the trick mirrors, listening for the motors, studying movements to discover where the extensions began. "Wanna meet her?" she asked, moving us up in the line, crossing the museum's open entry with the same confidence that had gotten us here in the first place.

The Giantess sat before me in a specially designed chair made of concrete blocks and accent pillows. A recorded introduction said it was made to accommodate her nearly eight-foot dimensions. Set at normal height, the seat forced the Giantess to sit with her knees jutting farther up than they should have. She looked like a humongous bird on a flimsy branch. This courteous Giantess tried to sit in a ladylike position, given her limitations. The chair was clearly a marketing ploy. Further inside the museum's foyer, her enormous wheelchair sat, which, aside from its scale, seemed made of average wheelchair materials. However, her size could not be a fabrication of anything other than her own assertive DNA.

"Hello young man. Would you like an autograph?" she asked, in an alien voice, strangely almost as deep as Gihh-rhaggs's had been, but soft, welcoming. She held out her gigantic hand to shake mine. I initially resisted, seeing the potential for pulverization should the conversation not go well. She was unlike the giants on TV. Ultraman, Godzilla, the Amazing Colossal Man, the *Lost in Space* cyclops, all were twenty stories tall but proportioned like average human beings. I had no doubt the Believe It or Not! Giantess was almost eight feet tall as her announcer claimed, but gravity and physics had done things to her bodily structure that Hollywood hadn't taken into account, curving her bones and weighing her down, her mass pulling her body away from her collar bones. Her clothes were designed to minimize these marks of her history, but anyone with a careful eye would know the world was never going to be kind to this woman.

A small sign next to a stack of glossy photographs of her in her concrete chair said autographed photos could be purchased for five dollars. I told her I didn't have any money, but Dusty offered to buy one, mostly because the crowd behind us was growing more annoyed with Dusty's pushing and cutting strategies, the longer we hogged the Giantess's time.

"Do you get any money for doing this? Sitting here and meeting people? The autographs?" I asked the Giantess.

"You know, you're the first person to ask that question," she said, smiling. "I live here, honey, and in return, this is how I help keep the place open. You understand?"

I nodded, picturing her being wheeled back to some secret room in the museum after closing time, watching all the lights of Clifton Hill blinking off, maybe even seeing Houdini's movie head wind down as they switched off the projector, making him disappear.

"Now, do you want that picture?" she asked, taking one from the stack and fastening it to a clipboard that had been resting on her lap. She took a ridiculously huge pen, like the pencils they gave us to use in kindergarten, and asked my name. I told her, and she signed it to me, turned it over, made a tiny X mark in one corner, handed me the picture, and told Dusty to show the checkout person the X.

"Can you believe that freak?" Dusty whispered as we walked away, but not necessarily out of hearing range. "How creepy. If you don't want that picture, I'll put it on the wall next to the deer-head woman," she continued. When we got to the counter, the attendant told us the photo was ours, compliments of the Giantess.

"I want to keep it," I said, knowing it was mine free and clear, a gift from the Giantess. I wanted to go back and thank her, but she was busy greeting new people with that same smile and offer of a big handshake and an autographed photo.

"Suit yourself, but I don't know why you wanna keep that, when you reject all my new wall pictures. They're a lot freakier than her pictures. All you can tell is that this bulky woman is sitting in a chair that doesn't fit her. I could take my own picture that way in a little kid's chair. Keep it. I don't care." I didn't budge, and we all met back up at the car and headed home.

"I wonder what the Giantess does with her free time," I said to Christine, while the older girls discussed their older-girl priorities.

"Probably watches TV like everyone else," Christine said. "What else is there to do?"

"I mean, you know, she lives right here, on Clifton Hill, but she can't ever go out into the middle without causing a ruckus. What do you think her bed looks like? Or her bathroom?"

"Like a regular one, only bigger," she said. "My dad doesn't fit in our bathtub too good, so his knees always stick way out, and the water only comes up to his belly. He says we're getting a hot-water tank soon, so he can stop taking baths." I could see that. Her dad was massive, towering over almost everyone else I knew. I was pretty sure the Giantess didn't have an outhouse like we did, but it sounded like Christine had real running water.

"I mean her life," I said, trying to work it out. "It just seems to be shaking hands and signing pictures, over and over, with that big dumb pen." She could never not be the Believe It or Not! Giantess.

"I wish I could have seen her," Christine said.

"How was the Frankenstein?" I asked. I was curious, but not curious enough to go.

"You know, the regular monsters. How scary can monsters be once you've seen them on TV?" I nodded, but was not necessarily convinced. "You think maybe Tallman would be a good boyfriend for the Giantess?" One of the other class stories Mrs. Crews told us about was Tallman, who came out of the woods late at night to peek into upstairs bedroom windows around the Rez. He minimized his loneliness by stealing kids who were still awake, offering them their dreams come true if they would just step out the window and join him. I slept on the first floor, but even if he came to the window on the rare nights I was allowed upstairs with my siblings, my dreams wouldn't be worth it. I was not a big thinker in that way.

"Well, they live on opposite sides of the border," I said. Tallman and the Giantess might have been a good pair if they could ever get together, but the world was against them. "She'd have to come to the Rez, 'cause I don't think the Jay Treaty would cover Tallman. Pretty sure he doesn't

have a red card." The older girls had done a reversal by now, eavesdropping on us, and began to laugh.

Margaret let us off at the road. She and Christine headed on while my
mom played the ponies on her own, Tim and Vestal Sampson chased their
own mysteries, and we walked up the driveway to the Darkwinters' house.
It was right about the end of news time on a Friday night, and we watched
the Mummy chase nosey archeologists on the late-night movie shows.
Later, in bed, when Lena started her dainty snoring, Dusty whispered in
my ear, "'K den, what piece up here do you *really* like best?"

"Same one as always," I said, pointing to a grainy black-and-white picture of a headless man's body lying in a ditch among the slugs and bugs, a
dark pool of blood saturating the fallen leaves while his head looked on
from a few feet away. Aside from being headless, he looked perfectly normal in his suit, like he'd fallen asleep in the ditch. I'd seen guys do that
around home, heads still attached, of course. Dusty had read me the story
from the magazine, even as she cut the picture from it and stuck it on the
wall. Investigators speculated the man might have had car trouble and
flagged down the wrong car or had picked up the wrong hitchhiker,
but they were only guessing. The dead man remained anonymous, and
the killer at large, living a life with secrets only he knew. Maybe the
man's throat, gurgling as it was slit, played a song of regret in the killer's
nightmares.

Dusty never understood why I preferred that picture over the ones
where she placed animal heads on human bodies, or why I could never
introduce her to Roland, or why, that night, I no longer cared if she drew
a face on any of her cornhusk dolls. I could take my chances. There were
monsters and heroes everywhere and nowhere, all at the same time, and
you never knew who was who until after you'd met them. I fell asleep eventually, listening to the flies buzzing on the glue strip in the kitchen, growing softer and softer. As lights went out on both sides of the border, I kept
my eyes closed in case anyone came peeking in that upstairs window. Most
nights the offer to step out through the pane and into a new life is less
attractive, but some nights you wait for the voices to invite you, if you just
keep still long enough.

CHAPTER EIGHT

Fall from Grace

(1976)

T he September we entered Fourth Grade, our worlds shifted seismi-
cally again, and mine would have bigger aftershocks later. The first
thing we noticed was our new bus driver, a guy with a scraggly beard and
boots so old, they'd split in dry rot, the pinky toe in his sock peeking out
the side as he goosed the gas pedal. No Miss Betty anymore. That first Friday, we were in for another surprise. We all knew Miss Vestal wasn't
going to be there. The previous Easter, she dropped dead at the kitchen
table, preparing for the big Church Easter Egg Hunt. She'd just sat down,
crayons and bowls of dye, a little wire halo to cradle the eggs, and vinegar
set neatly before her. I don't know who found her, Christine, Hayley, or
their dad, but I guess they thought she was catching a snooze with her chin
resting on the front of her blouse.

We assumed someone else would join Miss Betty for Bible School, but
instead, a new white woman showed up alone in the jeep and took us on
a number of trips. She ran us, as one large class, through epic renditions
of Christian kid songs, like "Happiness Is," using Miss Vestal's old dog-
eared cue cards. We all knew Miss Vestal's fate, but the new woman sub-
liminally deflected our questions about Miss Betty by telling us the story
of Jezebel, the Mother of Harlots. The cardboard Jezebel she slapped onto
the Lord's Flannel Board looked like Jeannie from *I Dream of Jeannie*. By
then, I was juggling plenty, so I hardly noticed the critique. Miss Betty had

been ignoring me outright since Gihh-rhaggs died anyway. I didn't dare ask anyone if something had happened to her, since it seemed like death was following me like that bathrobe skeleton who lugged around farm implements.

Even at school, where we expected stability, just as we got used to our new teacher, she up and left in mid-September, refusing to come back on Monday. The Friday before, she'd brought in her violin and attempted to teach us the Jig. She had no way of knowing that on the Rez, "jigging" was a word used exclusively to describe sex. That we knew this word at the age of nine proved we were the barbarians she'd suspected, and she declared she didn't go to school for four years to work under such conditions. That was The Word around the Rez, anyway.

All we knew for sure was that the following Monday, Mrs. Mistrovich, our First Grade teacher, came out of retirement. "Children, I missed you so much, I just had to spend another year with you," she claimed cheerfully, entering the room. I'd been back on Randy's out list for months, so long I couldn't even remember why, but his smirk when I looked his way told me my ball was back in play. "Randall Night!" Mrs. Mistrovich called sharply. "I see you haven't changed your ways any in the last three years." Instantly, he and I were friends again.

Randy's place as reigning king of our peers had been sealed during our time in Mrs. Mistrovich's first class. He'd developed a routine of being sent down to the principal's office for "unbecoming conduct." By November, she'd introduced a Christmas garland halo for Randy to wear as a halo during his office visits, and she watched him every time, to make sure he wouldn't remove it before he arrived. He secretly loved the halo and his solo treks down the hall, and he looked for ways to provoke its release from her locked supply cabinet.

Randy occasionally invited collaborators for his antics, but really, he didn't want to share. Before October of First Grade was up, Mrs. Mistrovich had hassled Christine Sampson to hysteria, insisting that Christine say letters were "lowercase letters" and not "baby letters." When Mrs. Mistrovich turned to demonstrate in chalk for us all, Randy had whipped a wooden "Upper Case" alphabet block at her head, leaving a small chip in the blackboard. Liberated for a brief moment from her mother's prim ideas,

Christine kissed her hero Randy at playtime on the monkey bars. After that, all the girls wanted to kiss Randy, and all the boys tried to mimic him. I was interested in the social benefits, but my cards had to be played right.

Back then, I thought I had only nine months to walk through the shadows, hoping Randy would never figure out my ma cleaned for Mrs. Mistrovich. To her credit, she spoke to me in class as if she'd never seen me at her kitchen counter, never sewn me a book bag with Batman on it, never left me cookies she'd baked. All had happened in the course of my ma's employment. In return, I tried not to remember the closet of toys and games her daughter, Wendy, would show me and then lock away after I'd mistakenly called her Cindy, which was her dog's name.

Throughout the previous school year, I'd experienced Third Grade in another one of my out periods. But I hardly noticed Randy's freezing me out for some unknown slight, or paid any attention to his antics. Lost in my own heartache, I searched our house daily for any trace Gihh-rhaggs might have left behind of himself. As Third Grade came to a close, Friday Bible School was consumed with slide show presentations of summer Bible Camp.

We had minimal funds for room and board in our actual house, so camp was laughable. Christine Sampson had appeared regularly in the slideshows, making Old and New Testament Arts and Crafts, running races, playing Bible Flash Card Games for prizes like Velveteen prayer bookmarks, or small New Testaments with the words of Our Lord printed in Stigmata Red.

After an appropriate amount of time had passed, I quizzed Christine about the camp. She said their days were spent learning to witness, so they could "spread the word" coherently, role-playing, learning fallback phrases if someone said "no thanks" to their invitations to be saved. She said it was okay, but at the nightly campfires, stories were strictly limited to ones with Biblical origin. Rez ghost stories were banned. Some kids claimed they were allowed to use the Lord's Flannel Board to aid their storytelling, which I didn't believe.

I also hung with a small group of kids like Gil Crews, who hadn't been told explicitly to stay away from me. This group occasionally was infused by whoever had currently fallen onto Randy's evolving shit list.

But now, at the beginning of Fourth, with Mrs. Mistrovich back, Randy waited on the monkey bars for me during recess. He hung from the top and whispered as I tried to see how high I could reach, "Remember that time I saved you from the werewolf and you owed me? I'm calling in that favor. And if you don't want to pay up, I'm gonna tell the whole class your mom scrubs the shit from Mrs. Mistrovich's toilet." He then told me what he wanted, and the idea so terrified me, my first instinct was to stall.

"I probably can't get what you want until Christmas," I said, a little shaken that he'd known my secret all along. "Maybe not at all. I don't always go with her now that we're in school."

"Christmas is soon enough," he said. "I trust you'll be good for it, 'cause you know what'll happen if you're not." He gave the nod, and suddenly I was popular again, other kids sharing their potato chips at lunch, stuff like that. My apparent faults dissipated in his radiance. I'd been spending so much time alone, this connection was like seeing sunshine for the first time after winter. I was used to my ma being off somewhere. Since Gihh-rhaggs had died, I never questioned when or where she went. If it came to where I couldn't stand it, I could always go down the road to Dusty and Lena's, but I'd have to bring my own food if I did. "You know," Mona had said one time, watching me study our minimally full cupboards, then pausing. "You could make things a lot easier around here."

"How's that?" I asked. It didn't really matter if I'd asked for clarification.

"You could run away. Then ma wouldn't have to pay someone else, or even me, to watch you and there'd be more food for us. Don't forget that whole Bradford House incident." The one time Chester had raised this forbidden topic at the supper table, my ma flung the water-pail dipper, dousing him. Right now, Mona and I were the only ones in the house. I ate cereal for supper and she made concentric rings in the table's oil cloth with her hot coffee cup.

Gihh-rhaggs was three years dead, but I still usually ate alone in the house, remaining silent if Chester tipped my plate onto his at our dining room table, and never eating in restaurants with my siblings. Sometimes, my ma and I got a burger, but threw out the wrappers at the fast-food place and rode home with the windows down. The Bradford House was strictly off limits. At Grants, even the smell of steak drifting over the stockade fence filled me with dread.

Suddenly, now, all the food in our house was spoken for, and not just the fancy items, like the Chef's Canned Ravioli we ate on special occasions. It was like being given secret-code labels for the first time and discovering my name on none of them. I didn't think I could live like that. Mona walked upstairs to play records, the Beatles. Chester wasn't home, so there'd be no requisite Stones tune to follow. I went to my dresser in my ma's room with a grocery bag, filling it with some clothes, including my three favorite T-shirts.

I headed north using the paths cut through the Rez woods. An hour later, I emerged into a field, and, above the corn, could see the only other Rez house I knew the insides of. Where else? Kitten opened the door before I finished climbing the steps. "Haven't seen you in a while," she said, looking into the bag. "Were you supposed to stay overnight, too?"

"Don't you remember?" Randy said, from the stairway, as if expecting me. "Come on." Once we reached his room, he pawed through my paper sack to see what I'd brought. "What are you doing here?" he asked, his tone suddenly sharp. I hadn't brought what he wanted. I told him I didn't have it yet and that I was running away.

"Running away?" Gil Crews asked. I hadn't even seen him when we'd entered. Since when were they friends again?

"Bass Head," Randy said, flopping sullenly to his bed. Randy called him "Bass Head" because fish had gills, and Gil had kind of thick, fish-looking lips. "If you were looking for a place to stay, and I was your friend, wouldn't you come through?" Bass Head said he'd do whatever it took. Kitten called us down to supper a half hour later, abundant rows of fish sticks and french fries lined up on tin sheets. I wanted more than the four that I took, but Randy would have kept track. "Hey, Bass," Randy said, twirling a fish stick. "Can you eat these? Isn't that like being a cannibal?" Bass dutifully laughed like that was the funniest thing he'd ever heard.

Most of the night, as soon as I'd fallen asleep, Randy poked me awake to list the things his good friends would do for him. When my ma showed up the next morning, I was exhausted and ready to go, though my bag of clothes was nowhere to be seen. Kitten had left early that morning for the wash and had taken my bag with her. By Fourth Grade, it was probably crossing a line to strip a kid out of his clothes for required washing if he wasn't your own, but it hadn't stopped her from hijacking my clean clothes. I accepted my loss and got in my auntie's waiting car. We did not discuss how my ma had come to know my location.

The next week, we had Columbus Day off. That turned out to be Mrs. Mistrovich's day, so I had to go with my ma. My teacher saw me in tow, smiled, and said she wouldn't be back until after we'd left. My ma's envelope was on the counter. Wendy walked by, looked at me, and said "Happy Columbus Day" before entering her room and shutting the door behind her. I could hear her playing Don't Break the Ice by herself, chipping away at the plastic ice blocks, trying to prevent the man from falling in. Did she play against herself, pretending she was someone else with alternating hammer swings? If she lost when she was Wendy, did she suddenly switch to the other identity before the man crashed to her floor? Cindy scratched at the door and was let in.

When my ma crawled inside the tub to work the glass doors, I found what I thought Randy wanted. I went to the basement to figure out how to keep them hidden until we got home.

On Tuesday morning, I showed him both options in the parking lot. "What the hell is this?" he asked, grabbing both. "This is the one I want." He threw the other back at me, which I stuffed into the Batman book bag I still used while everyone else had moved on to cooler heroes.

We started the day saying the Pledge of Allegiance and a quick rendition of "This Land is Your Land," while Randy sat at his desk, looking around as if he were a lone human among animals. The principal had long ago given all teachers instructions to ignore this behavior.

As we sang, Randy gulped air, swallowing hard, and when we concluded, he let the long, rumbling belch rip out into the morning announcements coming across the intercom. When the second one came, Mrs. Mistrovich retrieved Randy's strip of garland from her locked cabinet, and he stood up to receive it. We'd grown bored with this routine and opened our readers.

"Oh, it's breezy out here," Randy announced, after he'd been escorted to the door. "I better put my hat on, so my halo doesn't fall off." He pulled a pair of women's panties from his shirt, tugging them over his head, the leg holes providing sightlines. The class laughed and didn't see how Mrs. Mistrovich recognized the embroidered rose pattern, or the way she watched me instead of Randy, asking us to open to page thirty-three. As always, Jack's dog Zip chased Janet's cat Mitten, and Jack blamed his sister for putting her pet in the line of fire. I took home the other item I'd brought in the book bag, sliding the bag deep inside the closet. Mrs. Mistrovich went on through the fall, but Randy's halo never left the cabinet again, no matter his many provocations.

When Christmas break came, my ma told Mona that she had to stay home with me on Monday. Mona argued she had plans, noting that I always went with my ma to the houses. "Things are different now," my ma said, as she went out to wait by the road for her ride.

"What'd you do, order a steak at Mistrovich's?" Mona asked, sprawling on the hideaway that had become my bed. My ma carried out her loneliness in the downstairs bedroom now, while I got the late news, and a little *Tonight Show*, before I fell asleep. When I confessed, Mona didn't believe me, so I pulled the book bag from its shallow grave in the closet and brought it to her.

"No shit," she said, when I pulled men's boxers from the bag. "So Mr. Mistrovich swings free, like Rolanda's man." Auntie Rolanda's boyfriend, Phillipe, often lolled about her apartment in nothing but boxers, letting his equipment peek out a leg hole. Rolanda unsuccessfully tried to shag him into pants. Until Phillipe, I didn't even believe real guys wore them. Boxers were "TV white guy undershorts," what we saw whenever a sitcom required a locker room scene.

"Chester!" Mona yelled. "Get down here!" He promptly showed. "Try these on and listen to what this little shit has to say." He yanked the boxers on over his jeans, and after I'd repeated the events, with a few embellishments from Mona, Chester danced in front of our Christmas tree the way Phillipe twirled Auntie Rolanda about the room when they'd been drinking.

Then the impossible happened. They invited me to their room.

If I gave them the stolen goods. They thumbtacked them to a clear spot on the slanted half wall. Chester gave me the El Marko he used for

drawing rock-band logos on the wall. I drew the legs beneath the shorts
and then the paunchy belly as far up as I could. He and Mona continued.

Mona drew a big word balloon and wrote "Relax, honey! I need room
to swing free! Now hand me my beer!" and they shellacked a beer can picture cut from a magazine into his hand. Mona cracked the window, where
she'd slit the storm plastic, and set a pink cone in a tin ashtray. She put
Gihh-rhaggs's old lighter to the cone. The lighter had been buried in my
ma's bureau, so I didn't know how Mona got it. Small curls of fake-
strawberry smoke rolled toward us.

"You can lay there, if you want." She pointed to the furry, giant green
footprint rug that divided their room as she sat in the lopsided kitchen
chair. Mona lit a cigarette and slid Gihh-rhaggs's lighter under a fake bottom in her nightstand drawer, blowing smoke out the window slit. Chester took a couple drags. "You like that kid you been hanging around with?
The one you did the favor for?" she asked. "Tami and Tiffany's kid brother?"

"Maybe," I said, the most accurate answer I could give. Bass Head was
most likely at the Night house that night, enjoying the fish sticks that
should have rightfully been mine. I didn't know if the other poor kids were
as desperate for the Night Lifestyle and the reliable satellite group of
friends, but I suspected, like me, they only wanted to visit friends who
might dependably have food in their houses, maybe even the occasional
trip to McDonald's as part of the deal.

"Forget going over there again," Chester said. "This was pretty hilarious," he added, tapping the wall Phillipe, "but I been thrown out of high
school four times, and even I don't mess with the groceries. Coulda maybe
gotten away with it for any other kid. But those Night kids play for keeps."
He then punched my shoulder several times, emphasizing the next five
words: "Never. Mess. With. The groceries." He walked over to Mona, turning one last time to me. "Do well to remember that." He took another
drag from Mona's smoke and as he handed it back, said: "What do you
think? Is it time to maybe move him up here?"

I'd always believed Chester made decisions and Mona was the nego-
tiator, the wheedler. "Why'd you do it?" she asked, as we lay in the low
purple-bulbed black-light they'd stolen from some white kid's party. When
you turned it on, their posters glowed in the dark. It also made Chester's

dandruff glow on his shoulders, but anything I said could upset the balance again.

"Wendy," I said. "She locks herself in her room and plays her games alone, all noisy, when I'm there. What fun is playing a game alone? She just wants me to know she plays alone so no dirty Indian kid touches her stuff. And she told me, 'Happy Columbus Day.'" Mona was easy to play. "Bitch," I dared, and they laughed.

I didn't want to admit that I liked the attention, whenever Randy chose to shine it my way, and that I didn't want Bass Head to steal what I had, no matter how ridiculous or small. I wanted to live in a house where fake werewolves were all you had to worry about. Looking at the boxer shorts on the wall and thinking about the Night house, I suddenly suspected there was a life-size wall drawing of me, with my left-behind clothes, thumbtacked on some wall there, perhaps hidden in the basement, with a word balloon saying something like, "I ALWAYS SMELL LIKE AN UNEMPTIED POT AND LYSOL."

I heard my ma wandering around downstairs, beginning supper for us after cleaning up behind Wendy and her parents. "Changed my mind," I said, taking the shorts off the wall, "Gonna keep these, since I've already paid for them."

"You just bought your ass a ticket back to the hideaway," Mona said.

"Enjoy *The Tomorrow Show*, and late news," Chester added.

As time went on, occasionally I could smell the strawberry incense laced with cigarette smoke, and was sure my mom could smell it too. Sometimes downstairs, we heard "Satisfaction" from the second floor, and sometimes we heard "Revolution."

Who did they think they were they kidding?

CHAPTER NINE

Secret Identity

(1977)

O ur household rule about health: if no blood was involved, you were not going to see a medical professional. We only ever went to the Rez clinic if we were super desperate, and by the time you'd put it off, you definitely had a full-blown infection or broken toe that needed rebreaking to set, or whatever. After two years of my low-level complaining, I finally turned up the volume about my eyesight enough for my ma to hear. I was going to head from Elementary School to the big central Junior High in the fall, where I'd have to compete with three hundred white kids I'd never met, so I figured I really needed to be able to see.

After a few volleys, my ma finally considered my claims were not a desperate desire to look like Clark Kent. She didn't get that Clark *removed* his glasses to hit the skies above Metropolis. Marvel Comics knew that glasses were a superhero dead end, so Stan Lee wrote them right out of Spider-Man's life in his first few issues, like Peter Parker had never worn them. Stan and Steve Ditko flushed this lame accessory down the Marvel Memory Toilet. So, at noon, on the last elementary school day, I left the building with an early dismissal pass.

"Hey!" stage-whispered Marlena, one of the lunch ladies, leaning out of the cafeteria door. "Party's gonna start in a few." I'd miss the cupcakes and Hawaiian Punch cut with 7-Up in Dixie cups I'd been promised for six years. I explained I was on my way to my first optometry appointment.

"Well, I want to see your name on the honor roll and the merit roll," she said, slipping me a pre-party cupcake. I thanked her and nodded, having no idea what those were. "We need to show them what Indians can do. And it's up to you!"

Me? I'd struggled to maintain my math B this past year and things were only going to get harder. Its abstractions and unknown variables were of little consequence in my life, when "Solving for X" in real life was a serious daily challenge.

"You know, once you go with glasses, you don't go back," was my ma's greeting, once I located the car she'd borrowed. She was still convinced I was shooting for superhero trappings.

In the optometrist waiting room, I eyed the frames covering all walls, leaning toward the round gold frames, gradient-tinted lenses. Once inside the test, I looked into the headset like something Lex Luthor might torture Lois Lane with, trying to discover Superman's alias. The optometrist flipped switches, and only asked about comparative clarity.

"Okay," the optician said next, holding up rulers to my eyes, nose, and ears. "So let's pick out a frame." I stood, ready to march into the showroom and point out Plan A. "Where are you going, honey? I have the kinds you can choose from here," she continued, revealing a case, about the size of a portable record player. Inside were maybe thirty frames, strewn on top of each other, arms linked from the jostling they'd received. "How about these?" She pulled out a pair of sky-blue cat eyes with rhinestone butterflies in the points. "These are cute."

"If I was a girl on *Happy Days*, they might be," I said, sure this was some obscure optometry joke. "I know the pair I want. They're in the front room." My mom was out of sight, somewhere in the showroom, so I couldn't get her attention.

"What about these, then?" The optician held a pair like Buddy Holly's, waiting for me to slide forward. "They're at the high end of what you're allowed, but we could swing it."

"No," I said. "Out there, really. I saw them when I came in."

"Hon. These are the ones available to you. Those out there are for other people," she said.

"Adults?" I asked. "I've seen kids my age wearing wire frames. And

I'm super careful. I hate sports. The only time I got a third-place ribbon was because there were only three runners." I was pleading now, assuming it was a matter of persuasion. "And that was this year."

"Well wire frames are more fragile, that's true, but if you promise to be careful . . . Well, what about these? Is this closer?" She held out yet another pair of cat eyes from her seemingly endless supply. True to her word, these frames were metal. I tried them on and looked in the mirror, instantly transformed into a Batman villain . . . a female one.

"No, I'm sorry. I can't do that," I said. "Why can't we go into the other room and look at those? Do you not understand that these are girl glasses?"

"Don't *you* understand you're on Welfare?" she said, finally. Of course I understood we were on Welfare. I didn't know *exactly* what that meant, other than the fact that we weren't supposed to talk about it, and that once a month, we came to the city to be grilled by an unsmiling woman who asked if my ma was working anywhere, if there were other people living with us, and if I could give detailed accounts of what we were eating.

We'd practiced my answers. *No, she did not work.* Cleaning houses was "off the books," and Welfare didn't need to know about that anyhow. And no, *nobody lived with us.* Even when Gihh-rhaggs had been around, he didn't officially live with us, still getting his mail somewhere else, so that wasn't a stretch. Evidently our menu of hamburger gravy, lettuce-and-mayonnaise sandwiches, and the occasional SOS kept us safely in the Welfare nutritional expectations. (I later learned that SOS was polite for Shit on a Shingle, creamed corned beef and peas on burnt toast—close enough.) *No, we didn't get any pizza, no chicken wings, no fast food. Yes, I am sure. Yes, I understand that to lie to a government official is a felony offense.* But what did any of this have to do with my glasses?

"I know it, yeah," I said, my voice much quieter than hers. "But . . ."

"Your exam and lenses are covered, and you'll be eligible again two years from today, but as far as frames go, these are the only ones we're authorized to offer you. See?" she said, closing the case and showing me the neat Dymo Label sticker: "Welfare Medicaid/Medicare Frames."

"Well, what about if we pay for the frames?" I asked, immediately transforming into a new hero with limited powers: The Bargainer.

"Hon, if you can afford showroom frames, maybe you shouldn't be entitled to a Welfare check. We only sell the best, but they're for—no offense—paying customers. Look, hon, I know what it's like to be, what are you, twelve?" I nodded, though I wasn't quite twelve yet. "Maybe encourage your mom to find a job. There are plenty to be had, if you have some gumption. They're not the greatest, but they might be better than your current situation."

Even with my fifth-grade-math education, I knew: If your job pays federal minimum wage of $3.15 an hour, for five days at seven hours a day, and you take out Social Security and New York State Income Tax and United States Federal Income Tax and compound it with an undependable ride that costs five dollars each way, every day, and divide it by three dependent children, what do you have? Please use only a Number 2 pencil; show your work.

When my gigantic glasses were ready, looking like brown bedroom window frames, glee filled Chester's face. "Nice specs, Clark! Good luck finding a phone booth on the Rez. Don't forget your groovy shoes and your utility belt." Seeing Chester better wasn't a decent trade-off for the brown plastic rectangles that adorned my face.

Thus began my campaign to find work around the house, to afford frames on my own. I did trash, dishes, folded clothes at the Laundromat, and filled the drinking water bucket at the pump. That weekend, I wound up at the mall. While Randy pumped quarters into arcade games, I went to the new fancy optician, a sleek beacon of glass and chrome. Surely *they* didn't carry Welfare Clark Kent frames. I spotted a sweet pair and asked the new optician how much.

"Uh, let's see," she said, eyeing me up. She glanced at the small price tag affixed to the glasses. "Okay, here's the retail, and, will you be needing an exam?"

"No," I said. "I just don't want these . . . I prefer to have some choice in which glasses I'm going to wear," I decided.

"Many do," she said. "And that's good, because, you know, we would have to add new lenses, right?" Having not yet encountered advanced Geometry, I'd assumed they could swap my lenses out. She tallied the frames, new lenses, cutting the lenses, and a fitting. I thanked her for the total. Given the hours I'd already worked at home, I needed to find a whole lot more to do. Maybe I could climb the roof and patch the leaks. I amped up my campaign, reporting all completed work and asking my ma for my allowance, this thing I'd heard about so often on TV.

"What's that?" she asked, puzzled. Clearly, we did not watch the same shows.

"You know, weekly money for all those things I did around here this week." I listed all the work I'd completed again, sure she'd be impressed.

"You mean the work I do all the time?" she said. "You don't see anyone giving me an allowance. *Now* you see what I do around here, plus cooking plus cleaning plus paying the bills plus lugging in kerosene and a bunch of other plusses I'm too tired to think about." She set down the *True Romance* she was reading and looked straight at me. "Should I go on?"

"Seems to me you get an allowance from the Welfare office, or I wouldn't have to go uptown and lie for you once a month," I said. With my new glasses, the four-dollar price tag on the *True Romance* was crystal clear, and this was one of a dozen magazines she read regularly.

"Now what's this all about? What, you want some model or toy? Maybe we can swing it. Tell me what. Come on," she said, inviting me to sit with her in the swivel rocker. I stayed in the chair nearest the kerosene stove, switched off until fall now that it was June. I enjoyed the blowing heat when it was on, any chance I got. She seemed not to smell the pungent slop pail behind her swivel rocker, a swamp of table scraps and cooking by-products, hamburger fat, bacon grease, apple cores, and pig knuckles. I could never go near that chair without the odor swirling around me like a rancid tornado, and yet she was impervious.

"It's these glasses. I'm glad we were able to get them, and I'm really glad I can see again, but they're . . ."

"That damn Chester. Forget him. They don't look like Clark Kent glasses. They look . . ."

"I can see now, Ma. I don't need Chester to tell me they're awful. Look at Mona's glasses. Why'd she get to choose?" Glasses like this would be another visible sign of our secret, financially destitute life, just as I entered junior high. I'd had no idea when I was younger how we were just this side of a bad story, in part because my siblings had invented kind lies to tell me regularly. As much as they disdained the problems I caused them, they'd been down this road before me.

"I might as well be walking around in a new pair of Groovy Shoes!" I said, bringing out Chester's big ammunition. We'd faithfully watched *Rowan & Martin's Laugh-In* and reruns of *The Monkees* and *Batman* growing up, and desired all things Groovy. Mona used to decorate the upstairs bedroom with psychedelic drawings of swirls and daisies and bull's-eyes and paisley and bloodshot human eyes crying. Occasionally, she'd let me admire her avant-garde creations.

Grooviness sometimes entered our lives unexpectedly. Our ma would come home occasionally from the places she cleaned with bags of stuff, clothes mostly. Chester grabbed sports team logo T-shirts and left the rest for us. My ma would hold up a button shirt that was exactly his size and insist it was perfectly good. He'd hiss his disapproval.

"Look, man, for you!" Mona said to me once, revealing a pair of shoes. They were a deep-red shiny leather and had a buckle and strap, with designs tooled into them. They fit way better than my current shoes, but something seemed funny. "Man, those are the grooviest shoes I ever seen," Mona said. "Any in my size, Ma? Any other pairs?" she said, diving back into the bag.

"Only those ones, sorry. Seems like *your* lucky day," she said to me.

"Groovy Shoes?" Chester said, dragging the *oo*. He planned to say more, but my ma listed a bunch of unpleasant jobs if he didn't have anything better to do than consider my shoes.

I wore the Groovy Shoes, but when kindergarten rolled around, Mona encouraged me to give a younger cousin a shot at grooviness. My ma revealed a black lace-up pair, but I'd watched feet all year. Among the boys I knew, I absolutely had the grooviest shoes by far.

One morning, they were gone. When I protested, Chester clarified. "Those were from the free bags. We tricked you into wearing them before we had to get a new pair, and you can*not* wear them to school." He turned to my ma. "I told you! Bad enough we took him out in public in girl's shoes. Now he prefers them."

"You lie," I said, but Chester flipped open a Sears Catalog to the junior shoe spread of many Groovy Shoes, officially called the Mary Jane. And now here I was again in the land of Groovy Shoes, another signature of our poverty, courtesy of the optometrist.

"Well, Mona's been babysitting, doing other things for money," my ma said. "That's how she bought her glasses. I sure as shit I didn't buy them." Case closed. The summer went about as you might expect, people routinely asking if I was planning to step into the nearest phone booth.

One August night, my ma was four hours late, prepping for some party. Rolanda wasn't working it so that meant walking from Lewiston to the Rez on her own. She plodded in a little earlier than I'd expected, though. "Tim Sampson picked me up," she said.

"Why would he do that?" I asked. All kinds of people saw me walking the roads, and they rarely offered to pick me up, unless they thought there might be something in it for them. As far as I knew, Tim Sampson was occasionally a part of card-playing at our house, but after Gihh-rhaggs died, he stopped coming. I suspected maybe he was out shopping, and it seemed to me that Miss Vestal hadn't been gone all that long.

"Well, I guess he was being nice," she said, looking at me like I'd started dancing with no music on. I was about to suggest to my mother that she was being kind of naive, when she sharpened the image for me. "My Good Man was his brother. I imagine that counts for something in manners."

"He was what?"

Somehow I'd missed that Tim and Gihh-rhaggs were brothers. It was common to refer to older men and women in your orbit as uncles and aunties, but it finally clicked that when Christine referred to Gihh-rhaggs, she was describing a real family member. She was puzzled about my ache for him. We'd each learned not to ask people much about extended families; you never knew when things were going to get muddy. But she and I had found each other in shared grief, even if I hadn't understood how shared it was. I felt like an idiot, but in my defense, Tim and Gihh-rhaggs didn't look much alike, other than both being super pasty and blond. A number of white guys who wound up with Indian families fell in that same complexion category.

"Like real brothers? Like me and Chester?" I was trying to picture Tim Sampson, but because I normally tried to keep my distance, he was a little hazy beyond his size.

"Is there another kind of brothers?" Of course there was. There were half brothers and stepbrothers and foster brothers and adopted brothers, and secret, silent versions of all of the above, but she wasn't saying that.

"But they don't look anything alike," I said. Gihh-rhaggs had been average height and weight, at best. He seemed strong enough to do the things guys were expected to, but probably the only person he towered over was me. Tim Sampson was massive, broad-shouldered, and he always had trouble finding a place for his gigantic feet under a table where he wasn't accidently resting them on someone else's toes. Instantly, I had the insight that brothers could be quite different. No one comparing me and Chester would pick us out as brothers. But he was so much older, and a natural athlete.

It seemed funny that Tim had given my ma this ride home, but I couldn't say why. "What did you have for supper?" she asked, sitting in the swivel chair and closing her eyes. "I hope you didn't wander down the road till you got invited to someone's house."

"Can of ravioli from The Chef. Small one." I confirmed I hadn't opened the Family Size.

"Didn't turn the stove on, did you?" Our stove always smelled like gas, and since none of the pilots worked, we had to stick a lit match around the ring and take our chances. Chester's arms had become hairy, but his hands were bare as a young girl's from his stove use. If I'd had the heat vision my Clark glasses insinuated, warming the can would have been no problem, but that night, my utensils had been just a fork and can opener.

"You leave the newspaper off the pail when you threw out the can?" The newspaper sat on top of the five-gallon slop bucket, but in August, ten layers of newsprint only took your deodorizing power so far. "How much is in it?"

"Less than half," I said.

"Half full or half empty?"

"What's the difference?" I asked, and she laughed.

"Never mind. Maybe I'm coming down with something. Summer colds are the worst, and Mrs. D's boys leave snot-stiff Kleenex on the nightstands for me to pick up. Those boys, I swear must be sick constantly," she said, swiveling lazily. "Take it out? Way out to the second pile. Not where we burn garbage, but the one farther from the well." This was the one job I'd never done and definitely hadn't offered in my allowance lobbying effort. I knew how much I spilled from the two-gallon bucket when I pumped water. Water was one thing. Slops? Something else.

I grabbed work gloves. Inside the pail, Boyardee's face floated in the murky sludge, with a banana peel, a couple of pork-chop bones from Sunday dinner, and some mystery items.

Chester and Mona, were upstairs, listening to Black Sabbath, playing "Iron Man" over and over. For a heavy metal song, it made me sad, the way "San Francisco" and "Cat's in the Cradle" did. I grabbed the pail handle and held my breath. It wasn't as heavy as I'd feared.

Out the back porch, I looked at the path, several yards beyond the outhouse. We'd never been asked to do this one job. Really, we'd never been asked to do any. My ma accepted help with the same indifference that she accepted laziness. I'd tapered off on my helpfulness through the summer when it was clear the whole Allowance for Work concept did not penetrate the finite borders of our house, but I could do this.

Enriched by all our natural fertilizer, the bush line swelled in that patch, wild, green, and dense. The outhouse buzzed with wasps and flies. I grabbed the pail's handle and its bottom lip and heaved the contents on our mound of waste. Scurrying noises burst from the sludge pile. I hoped they were squirrels, but I knew better.

As I got closer to the house, Ozzy Osbourne bleated out his questions, wondering if Iron Man was alive or not, whether he had thoughts, and whether he was even a hero. Iron Man was more ambiguous than most heroes. He had resources we couldn't even dream of, and he could be anonymous if he wanted, behind that protective-armor suit. All he'd have to do was take off that outfit, and his powers disappeared. Of course, his atomic heart would still be there, pounding beneath his shirt, but conveniently, Tony Stark, like Bruce Wayne, was one rich bastard. No one would ask him to change his shirt or offer him a different one because his was embarrassingly threadbare. No one intruded on their lives in the name of doing them a favor.

Back inside, I poured water into the bottom of the pail, added half a measuring cup of Lysol, and set the newspaper back on top. My ma was in bed, covered up though it was still over eighty degrees. "You want anything?" I asked. "I could ask them to turn down the music."

"Nah, I can barely hear it. And I could put this radio on if I wanted. Glass of water? Did you wash your hands after you emptied the pot?" I went immediately back to the dining room and stuck my hands in the basin of milky soap water. I got my Batman glass from the cupboard and poured her water from the dipper.

"Here, reach into my purse, will you?" she said when I returned. Her purse was private. I didn't think Mona or Chester had ever lifted cash, but she never wanted to tap them into temptation. One quick movement could transform you into a thief, an action you could never undo, like being bitten by a radioactive spider, or pressing a button, launching your kid in a rocket to another planet, while you waited for your own to explode and take you with it. "See that little leather case? No, not my lighter, that other one, yes." I removed a slim case covered in a shiny black leather. "Open it," she said.

Inside was a pair of glasses with weird, octagon-shaped lenses. "We can get those lenses replaced with yours." The frames were almost nonexistent, a gold nose bridge and two gold arms that all mounted on little screws drilled into the glass. "They can cut them. Any shape you want. Not exactly what you were eyeing up, but the best I can do." I lifted them out and drew circles on the lenses with her eyebrow pencil, and looked in the mirror.

She was sick for a few days, but never missed work, and when she felt better, we borrowed a car and headed to the optometrist. "Let's not go to the one where I got these," I said. That optician didn't need to know we'd found a way around the limitations she felt we deserved. "I know where there's a different one." So, we entered the mall. My ma normally went to discount stores only, Kmart, Jupiter, Two Guys, so to her, these namebrand places and fountains and indoor goldfish ponds all had the same name: ENTER AT YOUR OWN RISK.

"Hey there, you back for those glasses you wanted?" the woman behind the counter asked. "How about it, Mom?" she asked, forwardly.

"Now which pair was it again?" my ma asked, pretending we'd been here together. The woman reached down for the exact pair I had eyed and handed them over to my ma. "I'm wondering," my ma said, "if we can take the lenses out of this pair," she removed the Clark Kents from my face, "and . . ."

"They won't fit, I'm afraid," the woman began.

"Now wait a minute, please. I wasn't done. I'm wondering if you could cut these lenses," she said, holding up my old glasses, then pointing at the new frames, "like the ones here." The woman was about to interrupt again, but my ma was having none of it. She pulled a little case from her purse. "And mount the cut lenses in these frames." Opening the case, she revealed the pair of gold rimless glasses with octagonally cut lenses.

"You know what? Let me get the optometrist," the woman said, replacing the fancy frames on the wall behind her and disappearing behind a partition. The same optometrist who'd tested my eyes downtown stepped out. Apparently, he worked at both places. No matter what, he already knew I had Welfare Eyes, despite my careful planning and attempts at hiding.

"Now what can I do for you?" he asked, and my ma explained what she'd wanted done again. He glanced at my glasses, the frames my ma handed over, and the ones on the wall. "Haven't seen a pair of these in a long time." He had a funny expression. "Sure you want to do this? These frames are, um . . . they're real gold. You could probably sell them to a jeweler who specializes in antiques, or just have them melted down and get cash for the gold weight."

"No, I just need to know if this can be done," my ma said, in a flat voice unlike any I'd ever heard from her. It was the secret voice of someone for whom cash value was irrelevant.

"I can try, but I'm not sure. We don't do a lot of these. I haven't seen a pair like this since my father was training me. Usually, we need to use these new kinds of lenses to—"

"Look, these glasses were made in the 1940s, and these lenses," my ma said, tapping on my left lens, "are made out of glass. You telling me glass is made different now?"

"I'll see what I can do, ma'am, but it's hard to recut lenses. If these break when I'm drilling, you'll have no glasses, and I won't be responsible." He paused. "I've warned you of the dangers. Do you understand that?"

My ma nodded. "Plus, a kid? Kids break their glasses. I've seen it a thousand times, and since I'm not selling you this frame, I can't guarantee it."

"Okay," she said. "I understand you're in business, and that this kind of sale doesn't do much for your monthly bills. If they break, and you need to replace them with new lenses, then go ahead. I'll find the money somehow. When will they be ready?"

"Normally, two weeks is standard, but I can have this done in an hour. I'll need the cutting and mounting fee upfront though. You understand." He took a box from under the counter and wrote on a small card. He seemed reluctant to take the two pairs of glasses and place them in the box. My ma removed a small envelope of cash from her purse. He rang it up, setting the receipt in the box, and took the frames in the back. "One hour," he said, disappearing.

"Let's stop in here," she said, further down the mall, in front of the York Steak House's fake medieval entrance. In line with our trays, she read the menu to me, omitting the prices. We sat and waited for our steaks, eating the pudding and french fries we'd picked up along the way. "Remember," she said, "when I worked that party, I got a bonus. Just don't expect much for Christmas this year. We'll call this Christmas in August. That's what they called that party I worked. They had presents, and a fake tree, decorations. They even turned the air conditioner on and made a fire in the fireplace. More money than brains," she said, laughing. "But without them, don't know where we'd be."

"Where'd those glasses come from?" I asked, cutting into the steak she'd ordered for me.

"They belonged to My Good Man," she said. "He'd like you having them." She'd been gone a lot that summer, and I'd spent many hours alone. I knew the contents of her drawers, even though I shouldn't have. I'd seen the photo album, an ancient Boy Scout compass, his driver's license, a men's ring, notes he'd written, though I never read those. But among the things she kept to reconstruct Gihh-rhaggs in her heart, I'd never seen this pair of glasses.

"Where'd you keep them?" I asked, forming the most neutral way of asking.

"Remember when I told you Tim Sampson gave me a ride? He wanted to know how we were doing, and I must have mentioned something about your glasses. The next morning, these were in our paper box with the *Cascade*. He said they were My Good Man's, and that he'd had them in his garage. Never had the heart to see if he could cash them in for their gold content. I guess that's what people do with them. Like what that eye doctor said." I couldn't picture them doing Rez Laps together, and that was a lot of information to cover in a two-minute ride.

"You friends with Tim Sampson now?" I asked.

"He was just being nice, and we're on his way home, anyway. Getting a ride from someone doesn't make you friends." Even at my age, I knew that wasn't exactly right. When you were stuck walking the roads, all kinds of people let you know they had a lesser opinion of you. They could be going your way, maybe even be your neighbor, and they'd blow right by as if you were nothing but someone's trash can whipping around in the wind.

We finished our lunch and walked back down to the optometrist's, where my new glasses were waiting. I tried them on and they were better than the ones I had longed for. "Do you want me to dispose of these?" the optometrist asked, holding up my old frames.

"No thanks," my ma said, trying on her neutral voice again. "We'll take them. You never know how soon these wild Indians might break their glasses and need to go back to their old ones." The optometrist smiled strangely. Even being able to see, I couldn't read it. Walking out of the mall, we passed the Waldenbooks, which had the magazine rack near the storefront.

"You gonna get your new *True Romance*?" I asked. "You don't have that one." The cover was easy to recognize as one not sitting around our house.

"I don't buy those magazines," she said, with an exasperation as if I'd accused her of robbing banks. "Mrs. D.'s daughter buys them. And you *know* she's not supposed to. I found them cleaning. I get rid of them for her when she's done." She added a sly little laugh.

"You wouldn't like it if Mona did those things."

"I don't care what she does with her money. But she better not be lying to me. And, about lying . . . do you understand why we don't tell that damn case worker what I do?"

"Because you're supposed to report all income," I said.

"If they found out how much you're unsupervised? Foster home for you."

"The whole Rez is one giant foster home when any parent ain't around," I said.

"Well, there's the way we know we are, and then there's the way we look to the outside world. You understand now why I taught you to say things just one particular way, when they interview you?" I did. I was forced to make my ma look like she was lazy and not looking for a job, just so she could keep the jobs she had and keep us together.

"Where you been, Clark?" Chester asked when we walked in the door, and then stopped, looking closer. "Wait a minute! It's not Clark! Mona! Come quick! Ma brought John Lennon home from the mall! Or is it John Denver? Or Radar O'Reilly?" Chester was trying to find some secret vulnerability in my new armor. Some chink even Ozzy Osbourne couldn't dream up, but he found no co-conspirator in my sister. Mona glanced up from *Rolling Stone*, recognition behind her Janis Joplin frames, peeking around every corner, looking for someone to buy her a Mercedes Benz. Our mother must have worked a Christmas in August party before.

"Go empty the slop pail," my ma said to Chester. He headed out, down the road, in his camouflage armor of neutral sports T-shirts that might have come from a regular store.

As the summer went on, I asked and heard different things about the shifting allegiances between Tim and Gihh-rhaggs, but most Eee-ogg was, at best, forty-five percent true, and you never knew which parts were false. The stories existed at variant points on the same plane. Vestal, like Auntie Rolanda, had believed my ma's tea-leaf reading was the Devil's power, courtesy of their rockabilly pompadour-topped preacher, Pastor Clyde. And because we were related to Hillman, Vestal had also believed my ma might try to steal Tim away with a snip of hair, a tea leaf he'd spit out, a paper towel he'd wiped his mouth on.

If we *had* these great secret powers, why would we be living at the edge? For excitement? We could cast a spell and be set for life, or get others to hand over cash like Pastor Clyde did, passing his "Collection Tambourine" through the congregation every week.

Some kids on the bus that fall noticed I'd gotten glasses, but even the occasional uninspired "four-eyes" from eighth graders couldn't touch me. The only person there who might have recognized them, didn't seem to, as she asked to sit next to me. I slid over.

"Nice glasses," Christine Sampson said, touching the temple. "If you gotta wear them, those at least look good."

"Thanks," I said. Should I mention their origin or not? It was possible Gihh-rhaggs had almost been as much to her, but that relationship had not been among the Eee-ogg I'd been able to coax out of the Rez's different pockets.

"Anything else new over the summer?" Like her sister, she was beginning to look different since her ma died. Her clothes hadn't always been church clothes, but as close to it as you might wear if you weren't in church. Now they were more causal. She had on a dark collared shirt with a little animal embroidered on it, a turtle. I wondered if that was her clan, but I didn't ask. It was always a little tricky for the more religious Indians to navigate traditional status and their church commitments. She'd always worn dresses or skirts and this was the first time I'd seen her in a pair of jeans.

"I bought *All the World's a Stage*," I said, ignoring her solicitation. I liked the Beatles and the Stones well enough, but both Mona and Chester were growing in different directions, music I had no interest in, like the Grateful Dead. They had cool album art but that was about all I found to draw me in. Randy and his circle were gravitating to that lame disco music, watching a local show that included disco dance instructions.

One day, flipping through the channels, I was stopped cold by a Special Announcement. My heart raced as it used to for the Emergency Broadcast System warnings that Gihh-rhaggs tricked me into ignoring. But in this case, it was a Toronto station, which seemed a million miles away. And anyway, it just announcing a program that was not a part of the regular schedule, a concert by Rush.

I knew who they were, a Canadian group, and they had a new song I liked, "Closer to the Heart," that was getting a lot of airplay on the Toronto stations. So I watched the concert, blown away that just three guys could produce so much sound. The singer's voice was unusually high, but that wasn't shocking to me. A number of Indian Social Songs included high parts for men.

The show was everything I'd imagined a concert might be, sweeping, brightly colored lights, explosions, exotic outfits, solos. As soon as I had enough money saved, I looked in the record bins at Twin Fair. *A Farewell to Kings* was their new album, the one with "Closer to the Heart, but *All the World's a Stage* was a double album live set. Mysteriously, the cover was a picture of the stage, minus the band, and displayed only the backside of a naked man standing against a bright red star in a circle. I had no idea this would become their signature image, but its boldness drew me in. Inside, they paid off the strange cover choice with a trifold jacket, including a ton of photos of the band playing live. I could only imagine how awesome that was, and immediately played the album any chance I got, though no one else at home shared my enthusiasm.

"I don't think I like them that much," Christine said, confirming I was likely going solo even in my music interests. "I hear a cool movie's coming out soon about a disco in New York City. Can't wait." Once again, Randy announced what was cool, and almost anyone in his sphere of influence followed. "You got your schedule?" she asked, pulling hers out of her bag.

"Yeah, right here," I said, pulling it from my shirt pocket. It seemed like the safest place.

"Far's I can tell, it's just me in my class," she added, relief leaking into her voice. "No one else from the Rez. No one will know about Mrs. Mistrovich being mean to me . . . or my big old meltdown about it." I almost laughed, but couldn't tell if she was ready to do that yet or not. I bet she hoped, in our new school, it wouldn't matter that her dad was a blond, white giant. "Hate being the dead lady's kid. I wasn't that happy being the Church Lady's Daughter either, but . . . no more worries there." Even these hopes she whispered, to avoid offering weapons to others.

My dad was largely absent, but still very much alive, and enough years had passed that my grandfather's loss was hazier. The absence of Gihh-rhaggs, though, still felt like a deeper gash. In both cases, we'd shared memories that now only I carried. I'd always figured that anyone with both parents at home would have found it the most awesome situation. DogLips and Kitten, for all the ways they were sketchy with others, seemed to really love each other, and Randy appreciated them. I mean, as much as he appreciated anyone.

Christine frowned like she wanted to say something. I was a little mad about her admitting life with both parents hadn't been perfect. But being mad told me I still had fantasies that my dad might come home one day, even if I was fearful of it. Maybe that perfect household didn't exist. What if I'd had the best dad I'd ever have, in Gihh-rhaggs, and hadn't taken full advantage of it? Did I really want to know what daily life with my dad would be like?

"Wanna share?" Christine whispered, pulling out a little foil sleeve. It was a semifull pack of Winstons. I glanced up and could see occasional clouds float out from other seats. Apparently, our new driver didn't care. "My dad smokes Marlboros, so I don't know whose these were. I found them in the garage. Maybe he changed brands." Her dad hadn't changed brands. I knew this pack had belonged to Gihh-rhaggs. Winston had been *his* brand.

"Sure," I said. "Could I maybe take one for later?"

"Don't be a hoggy-doggy," she said. "I offered to share." My ma kept new cartons in the fridge to prolong their freshness, so I knew these were going to taste stale, whatever that meant. I'd never had a cigarette in my life. She slid a half-used book of matches from the cellophane and lit the smoke. Though it had been years, I immediately smelled the essence of Gihh-rhaggs. I felt tears well up, but claimed the smoke got in my eyes, as she passed it.

"You gotta inhale, dummy," she said, smacking my arm. "If you're gonna waste it, give it back." I'd drawn smoke into my mouth and watched it roll out, knowing it looked too pure to be right. I tried a second time, and felt the scorch go down my pipes, and then felt light-headed and kind of sick to my stomach, trying not to cough as it curled around inside my lungs.

"I was trying to French inhale," I lied, exhaling as thoroughly as I could. Gihh-rhaggs used to French, pulling in a mouthful of smoke, letting it leak and then drawing it up through his nostrils. He always claimed it was sophisticated, but it left light tan stains in his mustache.

"My dad does that," Christine said. "You gotta draw deep and sharp with your nose, but first keep it in your mouth, and only open your lips a crack. I'd show you, but it hurts."

"When you smoke these up, can I have the empty pack?" I asked. I understood her not wanting to share the cigarettes, but trash? "I like the little designs." How could she say no?

"No," she said, instantly, not even asking why I wanted her garbage. "At the end of every day, when I get home, I put them *exactly* where I found them, and when they're gone, I'm going to leave the empty pack." I couldn't argue with her logic, and it's not like I had nothing from Gihh-rhaggs. He was helping me see more clearly than I had in years. "I'll share, though."

In the new school building, every kid from our bus drifted off. Like Christine, I was the only one in my class from the Rez. No one here knew we were on Welfare, that my ma was one of the unofficial team of Indian women, cleaning away the messy stains of life from white families' homes and clothes and bed sheets. No one would know the only showers I'd ever taken were in the elementary school boys' changing room after gym. They'd just think I was pokey when, every day, the gym teacher yelled at me that I'd be late for my next class.

When our homeroom teacher stepped into the room that first day, I could read his blackboard writing, thanks to Gihh-rhaggs, even from the far corner seat I'd chosen for maximum invisibility. Until I got back on the bus to go home, all my secrets were protected, hidden from everyone around me, safe and sound.

Two Rows (III)

We maintain our own customs, governing ways
of life and beliefs about the universe.

We each recognize that we move
according to our own desires and plans.

We respectfully do not cross streams
with each other, maintaining forward balance.

We see the open territory ahead of us and
acknowledge the mingled wakes we leave behind.

We share, between us, a peace we each maintain
by our dual presence in the expanse before us.

We discover each other side by side
in the water, traveling our own paths.

We emerge from different points of origin
and stay steady to our own unknown destinations.

PART THREE

Subdivisions

(1978–1981)

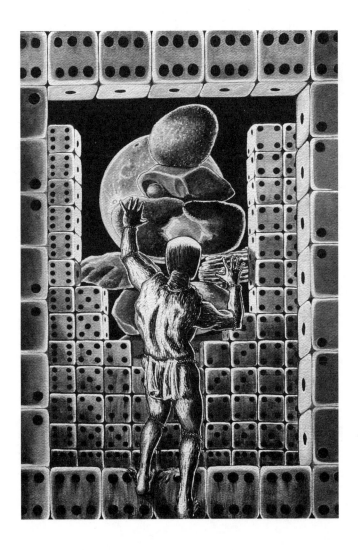

CHAPTER TEN

No Heart

(1978)

T he next summer, armed with new glasses, and music I'd discovered on my own, I grew accustomed to being alone. Everyone
from the reservation was on a search, and I was the only person who knew
it was a total bullshit effort. My cousin Benji, the new Dog Street Refugee, pretended to look after me, while Chester and Mona committed to
full-time surly teenage duties. Rolanda had dumped him off with us "just
for the summer," and my ma put him to the fake job of keeping an eye on
me. Benji thought his gig was easy, for indentured servitude. I could disappear into the woods at a moment's notice, later realizing he wasn't looking. He'd begun apprenticing for Chester and Mona: smoking upstairs,
burning incense, and listening to trippy music. The only times he came
along were when we hunted the Tin Man. He hoped that, if he solved the
Tin Man mystery, he'd gain a different fame than the kind his white leather
shoes had granted him.

Yup, someone claimed they'd seen a Tin Man, like the one in *The Wizard of Oz*, hanging around the Picnic Grove the week after National Picnic. As preposterous as it seems, the entire subsequent year delivered
sightings all around that area, so frequent and assured that the summer
daytime Bible Camp was moved from the Grove to the church, and even
attendance at Fireball was low at the following July's National Picnic. Our

whole community was nervous about what might lurk in our woods, growing brave enough to show itself several times. You ask anyone *now* about
The Year of the Tin Man, and they'll laugh, but if you pester, they might
tell you how they saw him, the circumstances, maybe even the date. Almost
everyone remembers that Tin Man Summer. No one has owned up to the
first sighting, no one remembers the first telling, but I do, because I was
the one who told it, and I plan on keeping my mouth shut.

Usually during summer days, we ran wild. "Like wild Indians," white
people would say if they didn't recognize you as one. A lot of reservation
parents worked, so we moved freely through the roads and fields and
orchards. We didn't have much guidance, but eyes were on us all the
damned time. The way I keep track of kids now is by the ghosts of their
parents' childhood faces. That was probably true for us, too, but we were
sure that, at the first sign of bad behavior, someone would speed-dial in a
Bad Kid Report to the appropriate mother's phone.

They'd know me by my new glasses and they'd know Benji by two
things, depending on who they were, or rather, who they hung out with.
His brother Roland's friends called him Labia. A few years before, some
Indian women had started nursing school, and kids passed around their
college books like they were sacred texts. Auntie Rolanda was particularly
fond of the *Taber's Cyclopedic Medical Dictionary*. She'd borrowed one to
interpret her boyfriend Phillipe's ailments, hoping to find magic words to
fix him, putting all her faith in the definitions and pronunciation key.

Benji pitched a wild fit when he couldn't find the words "cock" or "asshole" in the *Taber's*. Even when he found the word "pussy," the definition
said it meant "swollen tissue filled with green or yellow infected mucosal
discharge." "What kind of medical dictionary is this?" he said, then Roland,
in his post-Vietnam years, flipped to the word "vagina," showing him the
clinical illustrations with sharp lines pointing to labia, and other parts.
Benji looked up the word "labia," discovering it meant "lips or liplike struc-
tures." He looked in the mirror, claiming he was studying his labia. Benji
spread his labia in a secretive grin, entranced. Though it was only a line
drawing, that afternoon marked his first encounter with female genitalia.
On the Rez, your parents didn't have "The Facts of Life Talk" with you,

but *someone* did, usually an older cousin or someone else's dad. Benji apparently missed the boat, living the nomadic life.

Beyond Roland's friends, the rest of the Rez knew Benji by his white leather shoes with the big Pilgrim buckle straps. The shoes were all he had left from an encounter with a moving motor vehicle. Rolanda saw the zeroes on that drunk-driving-encounter settlement check and thought they were rich. For a while, they lived large in the city, heading to Arthur Treacher's, getting Chinese delivered whenever they felt like it, seeking out their futures in fortune cookies, learning chopsticks and everything else fancy they could think of. Suddenly, settlement spent out, they moved from their shabby duplex to an even shabbier apartment with one bedroom. Rolanda and her boyfriend Phillipe claimed that room.

Roland snagged the couch, but he spent that summer playing lacrosse like it was his job, trolling for women with their own place, largely successful in both endeavors. I figured he'd be out on his ass sometime before August and whoever he was sleeping with at the time would become the alleged "lucky lady." Fresh out of uptown sleeping arrangements, Rolanda moved Benji in with us to give her Breathing Room to Sort Things Out. As a parting gift, she presented him with a shiny white belt that matched his shoes and a bottle of that shine/touch-up stuff. He carried the bottle with him at all times in case of unexpected scuffs.

Mona and Chester hastily mounted a flea market Led Zeppelin tapestry to cover up the life-sized Phillipe drawing when he arrived. Benji had no idea his ma's boyfriend was still invading his space. He and Chester were the same age and shared a bed, without fighting.

I frequented burned out houses, which the reservation had in bountiful supply. Sovereignty laws left repossession-impervious land, but there weren't a lot of reservation houses idly waiting for new residents. I later learned that without mortgages, people's cash went into building materials, not insurance, so if a renegade spark happened to fly in your house, you were SOL. As a city Indian, Benji drew us attention on the occasions he decided to keep track of me. His nature was almost as exotic as when we were with Gihh-rhaggs. Whoever lived next door to the ruins might wander over to chase snakes with us. We were told to avoid some people, but still talked regularly with foundation neighbors and sometimes accepted their invitations to come in.

At one scorcher near the far northwest corner, the dislocated family had left for the city. Now, a month later, with the smoke cleared and the skeleton torn down, it was prime. Benji and I cut crosslots paths and, in under an hour, we jumped down the stone steps leading into the former basement. Those walls were littered with grit and burnt planks—bonfire ghosts.

"What you boys doing down there?" someone yelled from the foundation's edge. It was our great uncle Hillman. He was one of those men we were supposed to stay away from. Or, to be more specific, Rolanda told Benji to stay away from. If he was ever walking when we had a loaner car, we'd pick him up. My ma delighted in giving Hillman a ride in Auntie Rolanda's car.

"You come over here, rest up before you make your way home. You're Judy and Rolanda's boys, ain't you?" he asked as we scrambled. I hadn't changed that much. His question was more for Benji, who followed my lead to lawn chairs in Hillman's driveway. "There's a Vernors over in that there icebox," he said, pointing to an ancient Frigidaire deep inside his two-car garage that housed no cars. "Ice cream in the house, if you wanna make yourselves a Boston Cooler." I gave Benji the look that I was driving this particular trip. The last time we'd had both Vernors and ice cream in our house, at the same time, was *never*. "You just lift that screen, slides right up. It's on rollers," Hillman said, and Benji did, the wire grid enclosing the garage gliding up easily.

"Why you got a fridge outside?" I asked as Benji made sure the screen went all way up.

"Some things you don't need to keep in the house," Hillman said, smiling.

"Like medicines?" I asked, brave without my ma to walk all over inappropriate questions.

"You *do* remember, then. I didn't know what your ma has told you kids, or if you remembered our visits when you were a tiny person. That one's Rolanda's, right?" I nodded. "I bet he don't know about medicines at all. Rolanda was always the scaredy-sister. Dragged your ma into trouble when they was girls, but let her get one sight of a medicine bag or a false face, and she runs for the hills." He saw me smile when he said *medicine bag*, confirming I had mine.

"I coulda give you a few more years with your Umps," he said, "but he was old anyways, missing your Umma. Just as well he join her. Your ma thought that white man Gihh-rhaggs might move in, if your Umps wasn't always chasing his pasty ass off the property. Your Umps thought your dad would come back if Gihh-rhaggs left, but I knew better. Your dad and your ma each thinks they know what's right." I hadn't been here in years, and even though we were outside, I could smell the blended scents of his drying medicines hanging throughout the house. I remembered the plant that had made me tingle all over, a sensation I now recognized, and almost wanted to step inside to see if I could find it again. But with Benji here, there was no way.

"It's still in there, you never mind," Hillman said, cackling low, and I felt a hot rush come over me. "Time enough for that later. You been listening to me instead of thinking about things you're not supposed to?" I nodded and tried to focus more on him. "You better. This will happen to you, like it does to everyone out here. Your dad doing the ironwork and your ma cleaning the houses, ha! Those jobs make better lives for people who won't ever remember your name. Hard enough to come home from that job and face your family, but when two people gotta do that? Day after day? That's two people each carrying a world worth of struggle. Surprised they lasted long enough to produce three kids, but you're the last of that line."

"No arguing here," I said.

"That guy in there? He the one was hit by that drunk driver uptown? The one they call 'Lips?'" Close enough, I thought, and nodded again. "I offered to fix him up for his ma, too, when he come home from the hospital with that limp, but Rolanda said she didn't want nothing I had to offer. Even now, I could fix that little twist in his ankle, but she'd know right off you little guys had been over to visit me." He shook his head, disgusted, then looked up.

"You know, you almost came to live with me," he said casually, as if he were telling me my shoe was untied. "When your ma was struggling so much after the funeral? I told her you could come stay at my place. You got it, too, you know. Your heart knows or you wouldn't be carrying the little bundle with you now." I looked down, but you couldn't see that I had anything in my pants pocket. He just knew.

"Your heart. It's waiting for the rest of you to catch up before it opens the door and lets you see it again." He looked into the dark, to watch Benji, who had already drifted away from the fridge, eyeing up the neatly organized canisters all labeled in Hillman's handwriting. Benji sensed our pause and turned back to his task, opening the fridge.

"Anyways, your ma almost gave you to me, but then she said she'd miss you too much. You'd already dug too many roads into her heart." A lot of Rez kids were farmed out to relatives, but I never knew I'd almost been one of them. My life had come that close to an enormous fork in the road. Would I ever ask my ma if he was telling the truth? Was I prepared for all possible answers? Hillman faced the dark and yelled, "You find that Vernors?"

"What's this pie in here?" Benji asked, eyeing up the contents of Hillman's fridge. Just as he asked, the screen clattered, racing on its track and slamming the concrete. Benji dropped the pop cans as he ran over and they rolled under a skirted table, his face so stricken I knew he was not about to retrieve them. He grabbed me, lifting me straight out of the chair. "We gotta go."

"No pop?" Hillman asked, like he didn't have eyes.

"Getting late, and I gotta get this kid back home, or we're going to get an ass-whipping."

"You tell your ma where you been and you're sure to get one anyway," Hillman said to Benji, but to me he smiled and said, "What I got, your ma's got, and when you want it, it's yours, too. You'll know when you're ready, and you'll know where to find me."

As we got out of range, Benji pinched me in my armpit and twisted hard. He warned me that we were never going there again. "That pie in the fridge, when I went to touch it, it moved!" he hissed, scandalized. "Something under the crust, it jumped, like it wanted to touch me!" Benji, I already understood, was an expert at telling stories that he'd conjured out of nothing. He told anyone who'd listen that his ma was saving his settlement for his future, that she had big plans for him, despite the fact that he was currently sharing a bed with my brother in our house.

Hillman was pretty decent at predicting the future. Benji did get an ass-whipping that rivaled any other. Auntie Rolanda chased him straight through the bush line, not stopping as he entered the woods to escape her. He forgot she'd grown up in those woods, herself. I could've given him evasive maneuvers, but his attention was always diverted by his desire to join the half-baked hippy lifestyle my brother and sister were trying to pull off.

That encounter largely ended our Tour of Burnt-Out Rez Houses. The next week at National Picnic, Hillman bought me corn soup, and we ate under the tent, watching the hatchet throw. He even stuck around to catch Fireball that night with my ma and me. I was cheering for the Old Men running across the field chasing a flaming ball, scoring goals left and right on the Young Men. Chester was playing even though my mom thought it was too dangerous for a kid his age. I secretly hoped my dad was playing and that he'd feel me there, sending him my good vibes, and sending me back some of his own scarce good vibes, for my effort.

Hillman leaned to speak in my ear. "It don't matter who wins Fireball. It's a Medicine Game. The men out there, they play for the love of the game." The audience kept score, but the men played to be in touch with the Creator. I supposed that was why I wanted my dad to be out there, to feel the draw of home. You could only be on the Old Men's team if you had kids, so, maybe, kicking that flaming ball through the blazing goalposts would remind him he had some.

My hopes weren't as unfounded as you might think. My dad had seemed more present that year. He must have been squatting on the Rez—I think Roland had learned his "Summer of Shacking" philosophy from him—though given his habits, why any woman would have my dad was beyond me. Still, his recreational choices didn't stop *me* from believing he might come home someday, so I was just as delusional as anyone else who took him in.

The Sunday after National Picnic, Benji and I embarked on an early morning reconnaissance mission. Sometimes, in the insufficient strings of yellow carnival bulbs, people left things behind. A couple years before, Chester and I had discovered three whole six-packs of Pepsi, but he claimed two because I could only carry one home. I was hoping for a similar find, or nickels or dimes that had rolled off into the Coin Toss grass. Their place was always easy to spot because of the dead goldfish they left behind once everything was over, poured out on the ground to suffocate overnight. Benji scoured the Fireball sidelines, hoping fans had dropped change out of pockets or purses shouting for their team. He claimed he'd found three five-dollar bills the year before, but I believed that about as much as I believed in his settlement trust fund.

When I found dead goldfish scraps, I got on all fours and ran my fingers through the grass. By my second pass with nothing, I had counted thirty-three goldfish corpses. Looking up, I noticed the Cookhouse door slightly ajar. Jackpot. They'd forgotten to lock it up after the Picnic. I imagined more pop, maybe even leftover wrapped bags of cotton candy, potato chips, the works. Benji patrolled the far side, near the school, so I decided to take inventory first, alone.

I noticed only as I flicked the lights on that the padlock had been pried off. In a rumpled and stained sleeping bag near the deep fryer, lay my father. "The fuck are you doing? Trying to burn my eyes out? Shut that goddamned light off!" he yelled, and I obeyed. He'd already raided the chips and pop I realized were for the clean-up crews who'd come through later. "Jesus, what are *you* doing here? Your mother here making you scrounge for picnic left-behinds?"

"She's working," I said, not adding that weekends meant double pay.

"Working," he repeated, laughing, like it was something she couldn't possibly have mastered. "I'd like to see her scrub toilets a hundred floors up, like I have to manage. Working. I oughta just take you with me for a while, let her worry about where you are," he said, sitting up, oblivious to the fact that the Picnic Grove Cookhouse wasn't exactly appropriate living accommodations, even by my standards. "Gotch-ee! Let me see you." I stepped forward, but stopped. He smelled like shit, the literal kind. "Come on, I can't see you. It's dark in here. Is that glasses you're wearing? What are you doing with glasses? You been jacking off too much already? Nah, not a candy ass like you." I guess that was my Facts of Life Talk. He propped himself up on one elbow and the smell grew more intense. "All that reading bullshit. Don't ruin your eyes. I ain't getting you a new pair," he added, as if he'd had anything to do with the pair I had on. He stopped, realizing I'd made no progress toward him. "Would you come here!"

He reached out suddenly, faster than his damaged appearance would have suggested, grabbing my left ankle and dragging me to him. "Ain't you got a hug for your old man?" As he drew me in, the smell of vomit, an undercurrent below the shit at first, rose up. I pulled away and fell in the gravel, blowing the ass out of my pants. My ma was going to kill me. I crab-walked away as fast as I could. "God damn it!" he said, scrambling toward me, and I flew out the door, trying to slam it behind me, running, tripping, jumping the crick to skip the bridge.

Benji ran toward me, later claiming I was white as the skinned pig he'd seen at the farm across from our house. "We gotta go," I yelled, grabbing him by the arm, the way he'd wrenched me free from Hillman's lawn chair the week before.

"What? What is it?" he asked, my fear contagious, lighting him up with urgency as we disappeared into the woods, hunting the trail to our house.

"A Tin Man," I said, "in the john. Had his ax out and everything," I added, instantly regretting how stupid my claim was. How could I not have come up with something better than a character from *The Wizard of Oz*? I'd been writing stories secretly for a while, mostly trying to remember Gihh-rhaggs, my grandfather, the other people who'd disappeared. I definitely wasn't ready for the big leagues, if the best I could do in a pinch was a Tin Man.

It didn't matter, though. Benji, so used to inventing useful futures and pasts for himself, latched onto it the way he offered his white patent-leather shoes as proof of his wealth to anyone who'd listen. He grilled me thoroughly about my encounter with the Tin Man, inserting himself into the story with every new ridiculous detail I added, the dark, empty door in his chest where his heart was supposed to go, the fact that its lock was busted at the hinge, the stinky oil slick that ran down his oil-drum torso, smelling like old deep-fryer grease. By the end of the week, kids were spotting that Tin Man everywhere, and when fall came around, adults claimed him, too. I wondered if any of them had seen my real Tin Man when they looked, worried about what they might spot, or if they knew the ache of absent men themselves, lurking in the shadows with busted locks all their own.

CHAPTER ELEVEN

Checking Boxes

(1979)

P hilippe predictably pulled a vanishing act in the fall, so Benji went back to City Life and his belief in his settlement money. Mona and Chester, more experienced realists, developed new plans for themselves. They were tired of snagging rides now that they were both grown up, though they always had better luck than I did, or better knew how to be charming.

The previous winter, Rolanda's rockabilly preacher, Pastor Clyde, pulled over when I was walking home in a snowstorm. He drove the only Mercedes on the Rez, always clarifying it was a congregational gift. He handed me a snow brush through the window before unlocking the door. At the crossroads, he put it into park. I lived a mile to the right and the parsonage was a mile to the left. He said, "Be careful on the rest of your journey. You want people to notice you. I almost hit you." The car had been deliciously warm, but his message was clear.

I told my ma the story when I got in the door, because Rolanda was there. My auntie insisted he had urgent church business. Rolanda must have tattled, because the man she worshipped never picked me up again. I guess I showed him. Pastor Clyde had the nerve to come see my ma that December, a half hour after driving by me. He was trying to enlist her in his church, or at least snag some canned-good donation for the upcoming Church Christmas dinner.

Our house should have told him everything he needed about our lack of abundance, but even if we were wall-to-wall food, my ma'd have nothing to do with a church that had vocally criticized her tea-leaf reading. She also definitely wasn't in the business of allowing her sister to boss her around anymore, and she made these complaints to me right up to the second she answered the door. Still, she was all about being polite to white people in power.

That cootie plopped in the chair next to the heater and scarfed every cookie she offered. At the top of the stairs, I stuck my ear out between the curtain we used as a door. As Pastor Clyde expressed concerns for our souls, I thought he might need a primer on where my soul resided. If it wasn't good enough for his car, my heathen ass wasn't stepping foot in his church.

Mona had locked her Black Sabbath collection away, with her favorite records. Mostly by then I'd leapt to songs about oppression. Rush's *A Farewell to Kings* and *2112* were in heavy rotation, and I grooved to Rush's story of a man who found an ancient guitar and was then crushed by the government that had snatched all art from its people in the first place. I could see the parallels to the Dawes Act and the Carlisle Indian Boarding School's identity-stripping glory in this hard rocking concept album. Probably, a half hour long multipart song was too complicated for Pastor Clyde and all his "He Walks with Me and Talks with Me" hoopla. Did he think we didn't know that in Canada, Christian churches ran the residential schools trying to wipe us out?

In the box of abandoned singles, I found Mona's 45, "Indian Reservation" by Paul Revere and the Raiders, and at first put it back as too dumb. But the longer Pastor Clyde stayed, and the louder he hinted that those cookies sure had the Lord's love baked in, the less I cared. Most songs about Indians were pathetic. It was this, Cher singing "Half-Breed," or that stupid Billy Jack Tin Soldier song. I cranked the portable and gave Paul Revere a spin.

The Mercedes rolled out and I grinned right up until my mom opened the curtain door, armed with the big wooden spoon. "You will not embarrass me like that again," she said. I wasn't dumb enough to bend over, but the bruises she left on my thighs and ribs persuaded me to see her point.

I was young enough not to know how much Rez Influence Pastor Clyde and his Telecaster Church had. I couldn't grasp my ma's deep fears, wooden spoon in hand, that our weirdness was going to cause me trouble. On TV, if you confronted a problem, no one could touch you. And I was dumb enough to apply that philosophy at least one more time that month.

Our ma's strict rules about who could come into our house extended to romance, but Mona had kept her boyfriend, Harry, for over a year. My ma relented about Christmas dinner. Though Harry was a City Indian, I hadn't fully grasped how strangers would perceive our living arrangements. My siblings were ahead of me on that curve.

I'd saved enough for gifts: boxes of candy for Chester, Mona, and Harry, and a poker set for my ma, cards, chips, a carrying case, the works, thinking maybe they'd shake up her weekend games. I wrapped them in November, happy I'd be able to pass gifts out like anybody else.

Christmas morning, I opened my presents, some clothes—the rip-off gift you needed anyway—and a book called *The Monster at the End of This Book*, starring Grover from *Sesame Street*. I was too old for *Sesame Street*, but I loved monsters and still dug Grover and the Muppets. Remarkably, "Santa," my ma, also found plastic model kits of Robin and the Penguin, scarce Batman toys she never explained how she'd tracked down.

It seemed possible she had other things stored, anticipating a future when she couldn't afford gifts. The eight million cardboard boxes filling our house were packed with random items: baby clothes, a slightly used work boot without a mate, an enameled cooking pot, vases, speaker wire, razor rings for cutting twine, a belt buckle with no belt, a 45 rpm record adaptor, black electrician's tape, and a mostly used tube of Brylcreem. These Batman rarities felt like gifts from a Time Machine, and I was eager to share the gifts I'd planned ahead so carefully.

"Be right back," I said, when Harry arrived, as Mona helped brush snow from his coat. I pulled out the box I'd hidden behind Mona's dresser and discovered a problem. Downstairs, I joined the others around the dining room table immersing themselves in the aromas of dinner.

"I had gifts for everyone," I said, as people were joking. "But the rats ate them," I added, and every face at the table turned to my direction in unison. Mona and my ma laughed these odd sounds I'd never heard before, pretending they had no idea what I was talking about. Harry flicked his eyes to the others' faces, to see what the appropriate response to my weird joke was.

"Nice try, Cheapo," Chester said, adding a hissing noise through pursed lips, and a familiar Under the Table Kick. "You don't have to invent stories to cover up your selfishness."

"Really," I said. "It was Chocolate-Covered Cherries. Whitman, the good kind. I bought them at Towne Pharmacy, with babysitting money. I used wrapping paper from the sewing table. But the rats ate a hole in each one. Syrup's oozing out like blood." It was imperative that they know I wasn't making this story up. Gradually, Harry understood, exactly what my family was trying to prevent. "I can go get them and show you," I said finally, standing.

"Sit down, right now," my ma said in her I Am Going to Get the Wooden Spoon Voice. We largely ate in silence, but Harry scanned the places where our house offered considerable evidence that I'd been truthful. Mona watched Harry to see if he were going to bolt right from our table. Chester glared any time I met his gaze, and my ma only looked at her plate.

"We're gonna go downtown," Mona said after dessert. "Harry borrowed a car, so we can see the Festival of Lights." The city was trying this new experiment, to get tourists here in the winter. They'd built enormous holiday scenes, giant empty boxes wrapped like gifts, lights and trees, robot animals nodding their heads throughout the allegedly urban-renewed part of downtown. I'd only seen pictures in the Sunday paper. "Wanna come," she asked Chester, and he had his coat halfway on by the time she turned to me, reluctantly asking, "How 'bout you?"

"He's staying here," my ma said immediately. "Helping to clean up." Mona stalled a few minutes, but my ma handed her a coat and gloves. "You better get going, if you want to get there before they shut off the lights." This wouldn't happen for another six hours.

"You get those boxes right now," she said, before they were out of our driveway. When I brought the boxes down and tried to set them on the table, she slapped them to the floor, spilling half-eaten cherries and pink sugar syrup across the linoleum. "Here," she said, holding a bag.

"The cats ate the cherries. We have cats, and *they* ate the cherries," she said. They were both sleeping in front of the heater. Their diet consisted of our leftovers and free-range rodents. Though I still couldn't picture Skipperings or Rosencats chomping on candy, I knew it was time to be quiet. "Understand?" she finished. I nodded. "Wash your hands and put your coat on." We went to the garbage pile where she poured a small coffee can of kerosene on the bag, then lit it on fire. She'd discovered Gihhrhaggs's lighter and stolen it back from Mona. Mona's desire must have been in principle. She didn't notice it until the summer, the day she and Chester packed boxes.

"Where are you going?" I asked that June, as Mona suddenly began lining her bed with the things she wanted to take. Spread out that way, it wasn't much.

"City," she said. "I gotta be on the bus line if I expect to keep my job. If you ain't at the grocery store when you're supposed to punch in, it's adios to you. I can't rely on these vultures who want five dollars across their palms every time I need a ride. You'd think your own auntie might have sympathy." I knew what she meant. We went almost nowhere because we had to pay someone both ways. Rolanda, like her Pastor, was not a fan of inconvenience.

"Can I stay with you sometimes?"

"You ain't sleeping in my room," Chester confirmed, pulling boxes to his side.

"We'll see," Mona said, layering porcelain figurines in a flannel shirt and sliding it gently into an otherwise filled box. "Gonna be working a lot to pay rent."

"Could always just stay home," I suggested

"Not a chance," Chester said. "With the GM Employee plan, I'll have a car in no time."

"Is this everything you're taking?"

"Pretty much," Mona said, tossing in a couple of cornhusk dolls our grandmother had made. Their room was crowded with detergent shipping boxes, and it looked like an Andy Warhol art show I'd seen on PBS, when

I'd moved on from *Sesame Street*. "A few dishes if Ma lets us. Otherwise, paper plates. We'll be free. Maybe we'll eat at the Bradford House."

"Yeah, steak for me," Chester said. They only saw our mother in a light where every dollar had to be accounted for and given up begrudgingly. "Look, kid. The longer you're in the bigger school, the more things'll add up. I know Ma has you get in that Free Lunch line with the other Indians. Ditch that shit, soon as you can. Once those white kids know you long enough to remember your name, and they see you in that line, you'll be pegged as a welfare kid till the day you graduate." My ma had to give Chester lunch money through his entire high school career, despite this Impoverished Family Benefit's availability to us. "It ain't like at the Rez school, where Ardra knows your name, and you just don't get charged, lah dee dah."

"I gotta eat," I said. I'd heard other Rez kids get this same pressure from siblings.

"Find *any* other way. Listen to someone who knows better just once! In high school, they give out the pink Free Lunch tickets after the bell rings, so everyone can see you standing with the other poor kids. It's like the Uptown Commod-Bods line when we miss Rez distribution."

For my childhood, commodity cheese distribution happened twice a year, at the Old Gym. People catching up, telling jokes and swapping Eee-ogg. Everybody was in the same boat and the big orange bricks were passed out by people who'd take home their own cheese block, too.

But, if you missed Distribution Days, you had to head to the Human Services building. On the Rez, waiting was festive, but here, everyone in line kept their eyes down and didn't talk to anyone else as they shuffled through. A Human Services clipboard man asked my ma for proof of residence, passing us a large box from the stack behind him. It said, "USDA Commodity Foods," and contained the cheese, but also government peanut butter, dehydrated foods, canned vegetables, and a strange product we stared at in the parking lot.

"What do you suppose this is?" I asked. All the other cans were adorned with crude icons, in case you were illiterate: apples, corn, pears, peaches, squash. This can said, "Meat."

"Something we aren't going to eat," she said, separating Meat, oatmeal, and instant potatoes, and returning the box. The worker at the door said items couldn't be swapped, and asked why we didn't want them. "We just don't have any need," my ma said, and walked back out, leaving the box on a folding chair so someone who could use the contents might find it.

"I like instant potatoes," I said, trailing her, watching the box grow smaller as we left.

"Not as much as the rats do," she replied, as we got to the car. She never spoke of rats, so I knew she was making a serious point. After that time, we sometimes hit both Rez distribution and City pick-up, since the Rez didn't get all the extra items, just the Commodity Cheese.

Chester slapped his Commod-bod belly and got back to stuffing clothes into a box.

"Supper," my ma yelled from downstairs. Chester ran, as always.

"Can I have this?" I asked Mona, holding up the incense tray.

"I need that," she said, slipping it between the flaps of that closed box. "Look, whatever I leave, you can have. I won't ask for anything back that's still here when we walk out that door. Until then, leave my shit alone. C'mon, or we're gonna hear it some more." She expertly wrapped her arm around my shoulder and spun me around so I couldn't eye up my future.

A neat, small set of dishes was stacked on the table. Vapor from the serving bowl of spaghetti streamed up to the overhead lamp my ma insisted on calling a chandelier. "Those are yours," she said, passing Mona plates. "There's probably enough for leftovers, if you're careful."

"'Kay," Mona said, warning Chester with her eyes about seconds. "Ain't you eating?"

"Got stuff to do," my ma said, revealing a couple gallons of paint from beside her chair. "They were giving this away at Human Services, when I picked up commods last week. Housing Authority office is next door to Welfare. Didn't think I'd have a use this quick. Ro's taking me to Hector's for a couple brushes and rollers."

"How much she charging you for a ride?" Chester asked.

"Eat your supper," my ma replied. After years of city life, Auntie Rolanda was finally moving home, to a used trailer she had dragged next to our sagging house. The five bucks she charged for a grocery trip, payable up front, had become a regular revenue source for her.

"What are you painting?" Mona asked, observing the box of packed dishes on the table. We didn't have two dishes that were alike, but our ma was sending Mona and Chester's favorites with them.

"Room upstairs."

"What?" Chester and Mona said, turning to her, glaring at the paint cans, as if they were at fault merely for being in the house.

"It's your brother's now. I'm sure he doesn't want that nonsense you put up. We're gonna have a fresh start. Done packing?" The phone rang once, Auntie Rolanda signaling she was ready. Incomplete calls weren't charged to phones, so we had a Morse Code of rings.

"Fresh paint," Chester said, snorting. "Like putting a new glove on a mummy's hand. This ain't a Roadrunner cartoon, Ma. You can't paint a hole in the wall out of existence."

"If I'm not back by the time you're gone, leave your dishes on the counter. I'll get them."

"Did you ask her to buy paint?" Mona asked, as soon as the car door slammed.

"Didn't even know she had any," I said. I knew things about my ma that my brother and sister didn't, because they were gone so much. If she borrowed a car, we studied the random suburbs. A split level sat next to a massive Greek Revival, that sat next to a ranch. Almost the way trailers were sprinkled throughout the Rez. I asked once if she'd want to live there, if we won the lottery. "I should say not," she said, spitting the words. "I just want their blacktop driveways, not their neighbors!" I understood that. Our crushed-stone driveway was mostly murky mud and sludge six months out of the year.

But the paint was a mystery. "Guess she wants to do it now that we can have windows open," I offered. Chester's crude drawings and band logos would disappear along with Mona's outdated psychedelic floating eyeballs and peace signs. I'd have clean walls to do with as I pleased. When I realized Mona was leaving her clunky nightstand behind, I remembered Gihh-rhaggs's lighter, and wondered if she'd already discovered it gone.

Just then, their friends showed up. Randy Night's older cousin Derek had borrowed his father's truck to drag my siblings' minimal furniture into the city. Derek pulled a six-pack from the cab, what he called the first order of business.

I ran upstairs. Virtually all of Mona's boxes were sealed and the drawers emptied except for the old newspapers lining the drawer bottoms. She'd left behind a few albums and that box of singles, 45s of songs that weren't cool anymore, a couple decks of cards, and some nail polish in a lame color. The Pink Floyd pyramid stickers were dog-eared from where she'd tried to peel them from the vanity. Chester left nothing behind, not even the newspapers from the drawer.

"What are you doing?" Mona said, suddenly behind me.

"Just looking," I said.

"Well, it ain't yours, yet. Why'n't you help me, and then if there's time, I'll help you. Take those little boxes there," she said, pointing to a few that were manageable sizes. I loaded them in the truck while she carefully pulled tacks from her Dylan poster. When I got back, she stood, arms crossed, waiting for me. "Empty your pockets," she said. The Masonite she'd used to create the fake bottom of her nightstand drawer jutted out the top.

I did as I was ordered, confident in what I would find: my medicine bundle, my Batman wallet—empty save for an "If Found, Return To" card—a couple school pictures of classmates, and a lucky coin. It wasn't even a real one. Just an oversized fake Indian Head Nickel bar token Gihhrhaggs had given me. She patted me down, sure I had the lighter.

"Mona! Let's go! It's getting dark!" Chester yelled from outside the window.

"Come on," Mona said, escorting me downstairs. On the stoop, she lit a cig with matches and offered me a drag. I passed, not wanting to give her ammunition. She wasn't good with secrets, it seemed. "Tell you what," she said, blowing her first lungful into the still air. "Find that lighter? You can come up and stay the whole weekend, and into Columbus Day, in October."

"What lighter?" I said.

"Don't play dumb. You don't do it any good. I'm pretty sure you know where it is, or at least where it might be. If I had the time, I'd get it out of you, but we gotta go."

"Why do you want it, anyway? You didn't even like Gihh-rhaggs." Her eyes clouded and she stood as Chester and Derek brought the last thing out of the house, a small dresser my ma said they could have. Their other delinquent friends sat on the truck's hood, watching.

"That's my business," she said, dusting off the seat of her jeans and climbing in the cab. "Remember, that's *three* nights, in the city, with us." She climbed in, and they backed out of our driveway. I went into my ma's bedroom, to the dresser drawer where she kept her black scrapbook filled with pictures of Gihh-rhaggs, among girdles and bras and uneaten and unopened favors from every wedding she'd ever attended, like a strange, dissolving sugar cachet.

I looked through every drawer, but no sign of Gihh-rhaggs's lighter surfaced.

When my ma got home with a brush, a roller, and a pan, we began painting my new room. All the gallon really did was turn my siblings' marks into cave drawings in the dark. My ma noticed the nightstand drawer askew and gave a small, one syllable laugh as she adjusted the false bottom, pulling some papers that had been hidden under it, and sliding the drawer back in place. When I started moving my stuff upstairs, she simply said, "Don't get too comfortable."

"Why not?" I asked.

"The city and Rez Indians don't agree so much," she said. That was *her* experience with my old man bleeding through.

A month after my siblings moved, my ma and I lugged a box to the trunk of Rolanda's car, and we headed to Mona and Chester's. Their apartment was in a Sketchville Neighborhood a block from Rolanda's old duplex, in the small Indian section of town, walking distance to the Circle Club. Rolanda headed to the Slipko's Food King, a city grocery store. She preferred its shabby, uneven expanse over the brightly lit suburban ones where clerks hovered near whatever aisle Indians were shopping in. An Indian could still get end-of-the-month credit at Slipko's. Though she didn't need it as bad as us, Rolanda liked back-up plans.

At the apartment building, I pressed Mona's buzzer while my ma looked up and down the block, frowning, disapproving of the Skatey neighbors we could see and imagining the Skatier ones we couldn't.

Eventually, Mona unlocked the heavy door that opened to a small entry with another door, and then a hallway leading to her place. My ma made sure each of the locks fell into place behind all three doors, and nodded, noticing Chester's baseball bat inside, next to the door.

"Arlene still live in the back apartment?" my ma asked, testing the strength of the living room door's lock. She eyed up a Human Services envelope on the kitchen table that Mona quickly swept away. Was Chester drawing *that* logo on his bedroom walls these days?

The place had three large rooms with a small bathroom off the kitchen. Chester's "room" was a clothesline curtain dividing the bedroom in half. Their bathroom had three kinds of shampoos perched in a shower cradle, with two cups perching on the sink and toothbrushes leaning in them. I admired that they had a medicine cabinet and a real flush toilet, tile floor, hot- and cold-water control knobs, and a tub with a shower option and plug if you wanted a bath, just like the white people's houses where my ma worked.

The proof that this was their bathroom lay on the rack behind the toilet. There might have been chrome and stainless steel fixtures, but that rack held only classic Rez towels, threadbare and fringed on the ends, slowly disintegrating. One day, you'd try to dry off, and discover all you held were some strings loosely organized into a rectangle.

I used the john and flushed, watching the miracle as the water went from yellow to clear in a few seconds' time. Beyond the bathroom door, voices rumbled like a kerosene heater in the middle of the night, vaguely comforting but undependable, maybe going out on you as you slept.

"You want a pop?" Mona asked when I came back. They sat at the Formica kitchen table. "In the fridge." I looked at the few cans of store-brand pop next to the more abundant brand-name beer. My ma eyed up the empty grilled shelves.

"He don't need any. Just be needing to pee on the way home," my ma said. "Close that fridge. You're wasting your sister's electric."

"There's cable," Mona said, but I had no idea what that meant. She explained to me what it was and to my ma, she said it was free.

"Nothing's free," my ma replied. "You just pay in other ways." The TV came on and I could not believe the number of channels. A thousand

channels each for religion and sports, but I eventually found one with sixties reruns and hoped one of my shows might come on. They continued
their low rumble in the kitchen, just below my comprehension. Then it
got louder.

Suddenly, my ma was in the room with me, shutting the TV off and
telling me we were going to wait outside. The Skatey street seemed even
more ominous as we stood there, clearly not belonging. People stared at
us, not even pretending to look elsewhere.

My auntie eventually showed, but instead of getting in, my ma leaned
in and held her hand out for the keys. Rolanda did and said it was next to
the spare. My ma handed Rolanda's box to me and ordered me to take it to
the side, to the door beyond my sister's side entrance. A woman, Arlene,
immediately peeked her head out, nervously. She was Indian, one of
those city kinds who moved among us like familiar strangers at the
National Picnic. Her feet were bare and dirty, calloused and toughened,
like she often went without shoes and didn't care. "What do you want?"
she asked. "Who sent you here?"

I told her, and she eased, glad I wasn't somebody else. I gave her the
box after she agreed to deliver it to Mona, once an hour had gone by. I
handed over two dollars as part of the deal.

I tried to be stealthy on the walkway outside my sister's side door, but
there was no need. She sat at her table chain-smoking, staring at the wall
like there was a TV embedded within it. The table was bare, except for an
ashtray, a pack of smokes, and a book of matches.

At the trunk, my ma had the box we brought open, and she was ripping labels from various Commod-Bod cans: peaches, beets, applesauce,
pears, spinach, and few of the mysterious "Meat." She told me to walk
this box to Arlene's, with the same instructions.

On the ride home, we mostly listened to radio sermons Auntie Rolanda
favored. She wanted to remove the knobs and buttons so Benji and Roland
couldn't change the station on her. "Mind if we stop here for a few minutes?" my ma asked, as we approached the hardware store. I thought she
was going to pick up more paint. I'd hidden the holes gnawed through our
drywall behind small posters of my own, ripped from *Circus, Hit Parader,*

Creem, rock stars sweating amid fleshpots and spotlights, but they tended to buckle with nothing firm supporting them.

We passed Plumbing and entered Paneling. It was arranged according to price, and we started at the low end, working up. One at the end, called "rustic," was paneling made out of old gray wood with holes where knots had fallen out. It looked like our walls. People were willing to pay the most to have their houses look the shabbiest. She shook her head and we left.

"Too much," she mumbled.

"Why'd you tear off all the Commod-Bods labels? Weren't you saving those cans for the next time Pastor Clyde came a-begging?"

"He can get his own. Mona and Chester'll get hungry enough to open them at some point," she said, laughing a little. "I just added a little sense of excitement to their lives."

One day, the week after, when I got off the bus, my ma sat at the table, wearing the kerchief that meant she was going to the grocery store, waiting for her one-ring call.

"You going to Mona's store or that nasty one uptown Auntie Rolanda likes?" I asked.

"She don't work there, anymore."

"When did she tell you that?" I asked. I thought that had been the reason for the move.

"She didn't have to. I got you these applications for next spring. This will give you working papers, and this one will give you a job working at the school. You want a steady paycheck? It won't interfere with Medicaid or Food Stamps, or HEAP. Says so right here." She pointed one arthritic finger to a line on the application. I could hear her need to change things.

"Only thing? People will know why you're working there. Chester and Mona didn't want to clean up after their friends. It is better if you don't know the people you clean for, but you do end up knowing them, in ways you never wanted to. If you're quiet, they forget you're there. Now Mona don't know how to keep a job. Chester's fear of being spotted at Human

Services will keep him showing up to work on time. You gotta decide for yourself."

I didn't understand the application. She'd already checked most of the boxes, even the date, leaving me the signature line. A series of squares to check for yearly income was broken up into five-thousand-dollar increments. She had checked "Under Five Thousand Dollars."

"That should read '*Way* Under Five Thou,'" I said. She laughed, the first time in a while.

"Yeah, they don't have many checkboxes for people like us."

"Mona was checking her boxes, that's for sure. She went through every one twice, accusing me of stealing that," I said, pointing to the lighter sitting on the table.

"The one she stole from me?"

"That very one. Why does she want it?"

"I told her it was your grandfather's and that I gave it to Gihh-rhaggs, and Mona thought it should have stayed in the family—pretending like he wasn't family. To her credit, Margaret gave it back when she went through his stuff, and I put it away." Definitely more credit than I gave Margaret for. I didn't believe it, but I didn't have any more business in this discussion.

"But you know Mona," she continued. "Never respects people's things, but got all kinds of ideas about her own stuff. She thinks I don't know her. Ha! I know her better than she knows herself. She thinks I don't know someone already tried to break and enter her apartment. All it took was bagging groceries for one friend in college for her to quit her job. She thinks Welfare is invisible. Chester, though? He knows better, so he'll avoid any kind."

"Is this job Welfare?"

"You won't think so when you're doing it. You're gonna work for every penny you earn. And that's a good thing. You ought to know the kind of work I do to put food on our table. Six summers in a tough job should be enough for you to maybe think about something like college."

"College?"

"I got some applications right here," she said, revealing a folder. "Mona wouldn't fill them out when it got to the income section. She stuffed them in that secret drawer box. They'll be out of date by the time you're ready, but you should know what it takes to fill one out." The phone rang, and she left me with the envelope stamped, addressed, and ready, and the job application waiting for the last few boxes to be checked, Racial Background, Skills, Availability. The lighter, with its strange and complicated history of changing hands, she slid back into her purse, and then she stepped out and let the darkness envelop her.

CHAPTER TWELVE

Chess Champion

(1980)

When I reported to the school library for my first day of work, nine other kids from the Rez congregated in one corner, backs to the wall. Among the supervisors waiting to take us to our new jobs was Stewart Broad Moose. He sat with the other Indian guys, but didn't share their rhythm. When he for real got a joke, he laughed louder than anyone else. Among the kids, a few Rez faces surprised me, and their look said "You better not tell anyone about me," thunderheads behind frowning brows. It never occurred to them that no one went around crowing about our awesome Welfare and Food Stamps lives. I was just a better-known poor kid.

"Young ladies and gentlemen," a tight-ass man in plaid pants and a losing battle with a bald spot said, charging in at exactly 8:30. He abruptly opened his valise and read off a series of complicated instructions with coordinated numbers and placards, like at a wedding. "These are your bosses, your supervisors, and you will follow their orders. Keep your noses clean and you'll do fine. Obey them as you would me," he added, though we'd never met him before this morning. "I'll check in on you from time to time. You're to go with your new handlers and on lunch, complete the orientation forms in the folder with your name on it. Good day." With that, he rushed out. "This list of your names corresponds with the numbers your supervisors hold," he added over his shoulder.

As I stood, a hand from behind rested on my shoulder. "Waterson, right?" It was Stewart. "You're with me. Come on." As I grabbed my folder, he asked, "How come those Rez kids didn't want to hang out with you?" There was a whole list of possible answers, but Stewart, being either from another Rez, or the City Indian part of town, only knew public Rez stories.

"Some people . . ." I said, thinking. You almost never got to invent yourself without your family's story already tacked on your ass, like a birthday-party donkey tail, multiple cock-eyed versions sticking out. "Think they have privacy."

"They think if they get seen around *you*, other people talk?" he finished.

"That's what they think, anyway. Some of them will hang with me if I'm around certain other kids, but if it's just me? I guess my family has a little bit of a reputation."

"Don't you *have* to be poor to get these jobs?" He was doing the math in his head.

"Not that kind of reputation. Yeah, most of the Rez kids don't care if you're poor. But people tell themselves all kinds of lies for a little bit of breathing room, don't they?" White kids did not like other white kids to know if they were poor, but Rez kids might worry you could change their fate with a stolen hair clipping or snatched article of clothing. Not a lot surprised me anymore, but I was a bit by Stew's indifference to what my family's reputation might be. To him, I guess, a paycheck was a paycheck, and I could relate. I even suspected Randy Night would try to lure me back, once he'd heard I got a job. But he burned me bad the year before.

Shortly after we all admitted discovering the joys of Beating the Bishop, Randy talked a couple other guys and me into a contest to see who was the quickest. The winner would get the pooled twenty bucks. So we wouldn't be embarrassed, he gave us each a paper towel for proof, then shut off the lights.

Countless guys have fallen for this, of course, but they weren't being pranked by Randy. Once we got going, his older sister Tiffany, hiding in the closet, flipped the lights, revealing only me mid-stride. Randy and his accomplices had been rubbing wrists as a sound effect. I hadn't been able to live it down since. Still, I didn't exactly have a ton of friends waiting in the wings. If my having a job brought Randy back, as much as I hated to admit it, I'd follow along like everyone else. And besides, the Rez loved Eee-ogg, but an awkward kid prank probably wasn't juicy enough to jump to an adult like Stew.

"You grow up in the city?" I asked.

"Tenth Street. Right in the center of Skin City."

"Isn't there someone in Skin City that everyone else wants to hang out with?"

"There *was*," he answered, exaggerating.

"What happened?" I asked, knowing it would bring him pleasure to say.

"I moved out to the Rez," he burst out laughing, and I obliged him with a smile.

"So how come we didn't go through all the stuff everyone else did? No number, no assignment. I got my acceptance letter weeks ago. So I wasn't all last minute."

"Message in my box. The folks running this program tried to give me a last-minute girl. I wasn't about to be that guy working alone with an underage girl. People make shit up immediately. So they gave her whatever job was supposed to be yours. They only drop Indian kids at a couple places. Mostly bus garage, 'cause two Indian guys work regular there."

"Why do you think that is?" I knew about that trend and had figured I'd end up there.

"Never ask questions. Usually leads to more work. I'm a floater and working with me, you're gonna be a floater, too. Be good for your future."

"Why's that?" I asked. "What's a floater?"

"What's it sound like?"

"I'm guessing it doesn't have anything to do with the pool." The junior high had showers, but no pool, and we had five minutes to change out of sweaty gym clothes, maybe put on deodorant, and get to our next class. Showers so close, but impossible to use. A pool would mean I'd have regular access to a shower room and fewer days of bedroom wash-pan baths at home.

"Uh no," he laughed. "But there are perks to being a floater. Plus, every day's a surprise." Stewart was trying to spin the job. But the idea of cash in my pocket already had me committed.

"So, you got a license?"

"I'm thirteen."

"Oh okay. Know how to drive?" I shook my head. Cops only patrolled the Rez for urgent needs, so kids my age could and did drive, but I wasn't one of them. "You versatile?"

"Try my best to learn whatever you want me to," I said.

"Good enough. See, floaters are assigned wherever the district needs someone the most. Some weeks, you're a groundsman, sometimes a painter, sometimes mechanics helper, cleaner, custodial, whatever. Workman's comp deals are longer. Mostly the job's a week or two." It didn't seem practical to constantly not know what I was doing, but I didn't make the decisions. "You're only here for like two months anyway. We'll get you squared away." We climbed in an official school truck with a locked, embedded tool chest in the bed and headed out.

"If I give you a week assignment and leave you, can I trust you're not gonna fart around?" he asked, grabbing me by the jaw in one powerful hand. I assured him, removing his hand. "See, sometimes we're like the boy that's gotta stick his finger into the dike to fill a temporary need." He wanted me to laugh at his innuendo, or act clueless.

"I come from a long line of rule followers," I replied.

The first two weeks, we cut lawns, trimmed hedges, scrubbed rust off of playground equipment in prep for the paint crew, wiped down the vent grates for HVAC systems, changed out basketball hoop chains, trash-picked under bleachers, and detailed the superintendent's car.

He disappeared for hours on end, but I wasn't asking questions. If I did well enough, they might carry me through high school summers, and possibly short hours during the school year. Minimum wage—seven hours a day, thirty-five a week—delivered a double C note to scorch the pockets of my Levi's every two weeks. Anyone I knew who snagged one of these jobs, kept it, even if they didn't exactly talk about the requirements to qualify.

Like anyone who'd never had discretionary money, I had no discretion when my first paycheck arrived. At the mall where white kids hung out, I regularly prowled the Chess King, looking to jailbreak one of those black leather jackets lashed like a chain gang. Steel hoops linked these prisoners racked under track lighting. In theory, I could enter and say: "I'll take this one here." I talked about them so much, Stew eventually told me *No Jacket Fantasies Spoken While on the Clock.* The first payday, I torpedoed into Chess King, and demanded to try one on.

"Adult sizes, only," the commission worker said, folding shirts. I skulked down to Recordland, waiting for Randy to show up. I wondered what Rez parents told their kids about our family that made them keep their distance, but I didn't really want to ask anyone either. I just accepted that I had a pass only when Randy acted as a buffer. Also, being a solo Indian at the mall could be hazardous, so even after his exposure prank, I still hung with him in white-kid environments. The white kids were cautious around groups of Indian kids, but solo, you were easy pickings, if someone wanted to start shit.

I didn't come here that often anyway. I might snag a couple albums now and then, and after Christine had resurrected the ghost of Gihhrhaggs with his unfinished pack of smokes, I now purchased a periodic carton of Winston Lights, to remember him with, but that was about it. Mostly, I supported luxuries my ma and I couldn't have otherwise, like occasional McDonald's stops and her BINGO jaunts. We each got a little freedom. I eventually invested thirty-five bucks in a black leather vest from Chess King, a 40, like their smallest jackets, but you could wear them baggy if you wanted. Usually, it just held my smokes and a disposable lighter.

Those nights I was alone, I'd sit with the lights off, hoping my dad would sense a Disturbance in the Force and stay away. Over the last year, he'd taken to reading our newspapers and raiding our fridge for leftovers. He didn't usually start creeping around until the weather turned cold, but I didn't want to take chances. As insurance, I'd throw Bowie's *Station to Station* on repeat. The ten-minute opener, with the freak-out guitar imitating a train bearing down on you in stereo, would transport me to some ominous, fragmentary world I couldn't quite see.

Some nights, Christine would call, or I'd call her, and we'd talk about nothing for a couple hours, just sitting in the dark, looking at the glowing stereo dial and watching headlights travel down the road, all the cars going by on their way to more interesting places. Sometimes she'd talk about her goal to own a salon, but probably off the Rez. She didn't think she'd have a big enough Indian customer base and didn't believe other people would come out here to get their hair taken care of. Sometimes we talked about family, but often in roundabout ways.

I hated to admit that I was intimidated by her dad's size and impenetrable disposition, even if he was sort of a potential key to Gihh-rhaggs. I mean, it's not like learning new stories about him would bring him back, but it might have been nice to have some mortar to shore up the homes of my own memories. Mostly, I was glad she willingly blabbed her own future and didn't ask about any plans I might have, because in truth, I had none. I talked about my new job, but only in the most general terms, not even mentioning Stew. You speak an offhand comment, suddenly you're accused of dishing Eee-ogg about them, so I steered clear of that mess.

"Looks like me and you are gonna have some job stability," Stew said, on the third Monday morning. "Laborer at the garage is out on comp for at least two weeks." At the garage break room, I knew one half of the crew from my Rez life. Like Stew, Eddie Chidkin had moved home from Skin City a few years before, and I'd seen Lewis Blake's time card. Still, I was startled to also see Miss Betty when we walked in, now going by "Liz."

She'd gone full commitment with the tank tops and tight jeans from her bus-driving days, soft, pink flesh peeking out where they were torn. Like Margaret, she pretended that Gihh-rhaggs, her father, hadn't been with my family when he died, like he'd never existed. The man who'd loved my mom and me was not the same one who'd lived with her and died stupidly, because he refused to fix his shitty car-exhaust assembly.

"Now, Liz says you knew her dad in some messy shit," Stew said over lunch that first Friday. "You wanna keep your job? Keep your mouth shut for the two to three weeks we're here. She talks to you? Okay. But you don't talk to her. Got that?" She and I became two cats, stealthy and silent, with random hisses thrown in.

Cleaning johns was a daily duty. The ladies' was a maze of privacy booths. The men's had one sink, a urinal, a toilet, a bank of lockers, and a shower stall. Every single day, the floor beneath the urinal wound up shellacked with dried piss and corrosion, stray pubes preserved inside the midday steamy film like skinny insects in amber. The guys had such bad aim that Lewis and I secretly called them Stormtroopers, and we agreed to each do it once a day.

Our day started an hour after the real workers, and I quickly discovered the crew didn't leave the break room until we punched in. Wanting so bad to ditch my bedroom bath pans, that second Tuesday, I arrived an hour early, quietly locking my bike up and quickly showering before punching in. The best job perk. For about four days.

"The guys said to tell you to quit using the shower," Liz informed me Friday morning. Someone had caught on—I should have monitored the urinal puddle when I got dressed.

"Why can't I use it?" I asked.

"Just passing along orders. They don't want your Indian short and curlies in the drain hole to wash up between their toes." She turned her back, the matter closed.

"But none of them even use it," I said, knowing I was on shaky ground. "That's bullshit."

"So quit," she said.

I couldn't even go to Stew, since he'd suddenly started being a dick to me as soon as we landed in the garage. A couple days later, near punchout time, I found out why. Wandering upstairs for paper towel rolls, I discovered where he disappeared to when we floated. Though I hadn't been quiet, I sailed past the shelves, to find him grinding on Liz across a spare bus bench, his hand up her tank top and her jeans and his work blues bunched at their exposed thighs.

I felt like an idiot not catching on before literally catching them. Their frequent upstairs inventories. Their super long parts runs. Stew had taken Lewis and me a couple times to kill time cruising, so I imagined them doing the same. Were they so horny that they couldn't wait until night? Maybe the district had rules about workers not going out with each other.

Late the next morning, Stew stood over me while I kneeled on the floor, scrubbing the newest sticky yellow floor deposit.

"Be done in a minute," I said, "and *then* you can piss on the floor." I stuck the scrub brush in the urinal and flushed to rinse it.

"I need to know if you can be trusted," he said, towering over me, close enough to be awkward. Apparently, I hadn't gone unnoticed. I shrugged. "I'm not above kicking your ass."

"Got it," I said. "Good thing you have a shower available to you, for convenient cleanup when Liz decides to have Moose Knuckle stew for lunch." I wanted him to know I'd already heard his Rez Nickname. Guys made fun of how he wore his work pants at least one size too tight, giving him a moose knuckle. If he'd been raised the Rez, he would have laughed.

"What you saw is nobody's business," he said. Maybe Skin City didn't have the same sense of humor. "Talk and I'll beat your ass right now, have you fired, or both." Maybe he broke his funny bone when I caught him, literally, with his pants down. I saved that one.

"On the other hand," he said, his tone changing. "I could recommend you get afternoons with me, or here if that's easier, once school starts." He locked his narrowed eyes onto mine, so I'd know this was a huge favor. "You need cash and I want to help you out." I nodded. "Good!" He punched my shoulder hard enough to bruise. Man, I couldn't wait for this stupid trend to disappear. He added, "Let's get cleaned up for lunch. I'll be in the van." He pounded my locker and finished, "Something in here for you," leaving me in the men's room, alone with my silence.

Inside, a Chess King leather jacket hung on top of the flannel shirt I kept there for chilly mornings. I took it off the wooden hanger. It was a Men's 42. I slid it on and looked in the mirror. The sleeves hung so low, only my fingertips showed. But I'd grow into it.

Stew came back a minute later. "Knew you'd try it on. Put it back. When fall comes? You'll be like Bob Seger." He straightened my collar, then left, singing "Night Moves" with a surprisingly decent voice, mimicking Seger's sweet, aching delivery. I hung the jacket up, wishing I had one of those giant stainless-steel Chess King anti-theft hoops to keep it secure.

In the utility van, Liz was waiting. I tried not to think about what I'd seen. The electric buzz between them aroused me, even though I didn't want it to. I sat forward, hoping no one would notice. People joked about this problem all the time, but until it started happening to you, you didn't believe it. Even the idea of being turned on gave me anxiety these days.

"Guess we're stuck with each other," Liz said in the rearview mirror, while Stew ran into a convenience store down the road for subs. It took all my discipline not to ask her if she was sick of having Stew for lunch. I knew I wasn't supposed to ask about her dad, and I suspected that if I offered her any stories of my own, they might feel like betrayal to her. Before we reached the garage, Stew hooked into a school service road looping at a remote, wooded part of the property. A weathered picnic table sat in a clearing.

"One advantage of floating? You know *all* the good hiding places," he grinned, unbuttoning the top buttons of his work blues and yanking the lever that opened the passenger entrance. "Okay, kiddo, remember, I bought that for you in trade. Because you're a smart kid. You're a smart kid, right?" I agreed that I was smart. "Good. Now get out, and have a ball." He pulled four glistening Molson bottles and two subs from the bag, then handed me the rest. "There's napkins in the bag, and probably a little container of oil if you need it," he added, laughing.

"One more thing?" He handed me his portable radio/tape player. "Take this too." I wished he'd given me notice to grab a tape. I sat at the picnic table and faced the woods, washing my sub down with the two remaining beers, spinning the dial for tunes that would drown out their sounds.

Summer rolled into fall, and I kept my job. It became a pretty good life, for a while, but things change, even if you can't see them. Sometimes you glimpsed changes the first day of school, because you hadn't seen people in a while. Christine Sampson and I kept up our calls through the summer, but I rarely saw her in person. On the first day of high school, she debuted a new look, flirting with the Bad Girl New Wave image: Half-Pat Benatar and Half-Blondie. But as with most Fresh Looks, she needed someone to notice, and I guess that was me.

She slid next to me on the bus and lit a smoke, offering it. I showed her I had my own pack, in the inside pocket of my vest. "So what?" she said. "Just share mine. Then you can save yours. I'm skimming them from my dad." I saw the little Marlboro emblem as I took a drag. When you're passing a smoke back and forth, sharing an intimacy, you kind of get to know each other better, and take more liberties. Our morning shared smoke started to become a regular thing.

One morning in October, passing me the smoke, she asked how far I was in my half of our project. In Niagara County Geography, we were supposed to pick a partner from our neighborhood and map it out, with flour, salt water, adding knock-off Monopoly Houses and Hotels for residences and institutions. I gave an evasive shrug.

"I got the map drawn," I said. "That's something." I walked to so many places, I was pretty aware of my neighborhood. But Rez property was divided by tribal government rules. Family plots had multiple houses, some even deep in the woods. Most white kids' houses lined up neatly on equal-size properties, all the same distance from the road. This was called Zoning.

"I can see your face getting grumpy," she said. "No excuses! We gotta get it done. I'm not getting held back a year like my idiot sister." Teachers assumed you had a bunch of spare supplies just sitting around your house.

"My ma already freaked out at that stupid thirty-dollar calculator they made us buy for Algebra," I said. "I don't see a trip to the Craft Store in my future."

"I got stuff. We can just use mine," she said, her voice somewhere between hopeful and irritated. "My mom was Queen of the Bible School Crafts," she added, more quietly. The Bible School props had always been so polished, I'd assumed they were commercial, not homemade jobbies. "Don't get *too* happy. I'm *not* doing all the work if I'm providing all the supplies."

"Fair enough, but I don't want to be the first Rez guy facing down your dad inside your house." Hayley was older, so Tim Sampson had already gone through this once, but I had the feeling Christine was *Daddy's Little Girl*. Sometimes, she pretended to talk tough, saying the property and house were hers because he was white, but it all kind of sounded like a performance. She'd slip sometimes, and I'd hear a fondness in her voice I never felt, thinking of my old man.

"I could bring the stuff to your house," she said. "Most of it's in a big plastic bin."

"Also not happening," I said.

"Look," she said. "It's October, I'm not sitting outside and freezing my buns off cause you're a chicken shit." The thing about people with even a little bit of privilege is that they could not conceptualize other people's lives, except maybe for the lifestyles they aspired to. "How about we go to my cousin's. I'm babysitting her little kid, and she don't care. We can both smoke. My dad never stops in." She knew this was just another moron project, like I did, but she also knew that if she wanted to spend half her day in Beauty School, she had to pass required basics.

"Don't think I have much choice here," I said.

"You don't," she replied immediately. "I'll bring my kit, too. I can clean this mop up for you and it'll count as practice for me." She flicked her fingers through my hair, which badly needed cutting.

Naturally, the unnamed cousin was Margaret. Like Gihh-rhaggs's white daughter, Margaret had not said one word to me in years, and now they were both back in my life at once. It was like being dealt a bad hand with the same deck of trick cards every couple of years. We had a lot not to talk about, mostly her dad, but other mines were littered through this field, too. I didn't know if those half sisters talked, but when you had more than two people's version of the truth, you were asking for trouble. Still, I had zero other options. Harboring minor fantasies about college, I also needed this class. "Tonight! Six!" she clarified.

Christine waited for me outside Margaret's house, so we could walk in together. Inside, a Yahtzee game with a stack of quarters sat next to her box of craft stuff. "Hear you like contests with a little wager," Margaret said, and they both laughed a low, dirty laugh that meant Randy had successfully spread his story. Her phone rang before I could reply, and recognizing the voice on the other end, she instantly began flirting with *me*, like people did on TV.

"Christine, have Ronnie bring me a pop, okay? I'm in my bedroom." She used the nickname Gihh-Rhaggs had given me, butchering the Tuscarora pronunciation, rolling her tongue around it in a sexy way. She wanted her caller to think I was a big guy, construction worker type, regular paycheck, good benefits, long, thick hair swinging free—the works. Though I'd gotten hairier, I couldn't be further from the imaginary man she was inventing for the benefit of some invisible guy on the line.

"Thanks," she said, in a breathy TV Catwoman voice, when I got the pop as instructed. She winked, a weirdly adult gesture. Margaret was older than us, but not by many years.

Margaret took the pop and moaned like people do when stretching. "And could you light me a cig, too? On the nightstand?" she continued, pointing to the table in front of us. I lit two in my mouth at once, handing one off to her. I wondered when she was planning to leave, if Christine was supposed to be her babysitter for the evening.

"Well, what do you care?" she said into the phone, suddenly razor voiced. "Haven't seen your wandering ass in over two weeks. You have *no say* in who can and can't be at my house." Her mother owned the place, but I hadn't seen her since I crossed the threshold. I was kind of surprised she hadn't just kicked my ass out the door, herself.

"You wanna go out and play darts?" Christine asked.

"Darts more efficient at winning my money than dice?" I asked, offering my smokes.

"Just as easy out there," she said, lighting a cig off my hot ember, and we went outside.

"Who's she talking to?" I asked, barely hitting the dartboard mounted on the garage.

"Her man. Been gone more than a week. He's showing up to work so she figures he's off with someone in the city. You're the bait to lure him back to the reservation."

I didn't like the idea of some man flying back here to kick my semi-anonymous ass, but our only other option meant the presence of Christine's giant dad, who almost filled a doorframe like a massive cartoon Minotaur. It was time to rethink our bus ride cigarettes and my free haircuts, and Exit . . . Stage Left from this game. Some part of me had to ask, though: "And her old man would be?"

"Stew Broad Moose," Christine said, throwing her dart without aiming, landing an inch away from the bull's-eye. Now I was really ready to pay her off and walk home, never coming back. I sure didn't need to witness this bridge on fire between two half sisters.

"She thinks he's at the Circle Club, but he ain't," Christine said.

"How do you know?"

"If he wanted to chase Indian tail," she said, "he'd do just as well to stay home, where his woman will actually cook for him." This new version of Christine was like a Body Swap movie. The change was so dramatic, it couldn't be new. She was way more complex than the Goody Two Shoes disguise she'd worn in Vestal's presence. Maybe she was being provocative so I'd feel less embarrassed about being the scandalous subject of Eee-ogg. "He must like the round buns and tiny waists on those white girls. He'll crawl back in a couple days. Margaret will pretend he's not there, and then one morning, she'll wake up and kiss him, and that'll be that. He knows it, too. That's why he does it."

"No one snags someone else just to get their woman agitated." I didn't add that I had personally witnessed Stew's pleasure in his other snag.

"A lot you know, Mr. Lonely Hand," she said, laughing. I cringed inside a bit. I mean, it's not like I was the only one. Just the only one dumb enough to fall for that scam. "He thinks she'll feel lucky when he comes home, and she thinks he'll feel lucky that she lets his ass back in. Every few months, they drop these bombs on each other, to shake things up. Meantime she's gonna want to keep us out late, in case he comes home. She wants him to know *she* might be with someone. If you're not up for it, you might hit the road." I stood up, getting ready to peel. I hoped she'd find someone else to trim so she could get her credit. My ass was out of there. "I put a package of materials together you can take home, in case something like this happened. Just bring back what you don't use," she added, when my decision was clear.

True to Christine's estimate, Moose-Knuckle Stew kept perfect work attendance and resurfaced the next weekend at Margaret's. A couple weeks later, I punched in after school as Stew pulled up in the school superintendent's car, telling me to get in. He wasn't working at the garage then, but apparently had some assignment with the fancy Cadillac. "We still got an understanding, you and me, right?" I nodded as I got in the passenger seat. "I know you didn't spill nothing, or you'd be dead now. Why didn't it never occur to me you and Margaret would know each other? Fuck a duck! Your reservation's so small, I can't even take a leak without splashing someone else's shoes!"

"Try getting better aim," I said, and he leaned so awkwardly close, I leaned back.

"See no evil, you little shit," he said, yanking my cap over my eyes. "Get back to work."

At the day's end, I punched out as usual and started walking home. A couple minutes later, I heard a car pull into the cinders behind me and honk. Margaret had just picked Stew up. They should have been heading the other way, to the Rez entrance that led to their house. "Wanna ride?" she yelled, sticking her head out the window. My kryptonite. I even unwisely accepted rides from strangers on occasion, so I surely agreed to this offer. And the next day . . . and the next. Stuck with a convoluted and undesirable inroads into each other's life, we all decided to get to know each other.

One day, the following week, Christine was with Margaret and Stew, holding our project. I hadn't bothered retrieving it, because Mr. Turner had given us a B-, saying the layout couldn't be correct, the houses weren't lined up neatly, like everyone else's in class. I'd tried explaining that Zoning as he understood it didn't exist on the Rez.

"Thought you might want this," Christine said, handing me my half of our interlocking model. As I was about to disparage it, I saw the grade had been changed to an A, and pointed to it. Turner had never struck me as a generous man. "I showed him these," she said, revealing a couple of aerial shots of the Rez, proving our choices.

"You can thank me later," Stew said.

"And why would I do that?"

"I got 'em for her," Stew said. "Seen them up in the school office. Just dittos, but good enough." They were photocopies, not dittos, but I thought the finer points of office technology were probably not Stew's specialty. I could tell Christine had liked being the one to save the day, but Stew snatched it away in his need to be The Man.

"Anyway, I'm babysitting, but Margaret thought we could get some burgers at the drive-thru, and I can give you that long-promised haircut."

"You need it, Shaggy," Stew said, snatching at my hair with surprising quickness, tugging at it just a little too hard to be just a joke. He clearly did not like us all together. "But Christine here just wants a chance to stroke your head," he added, grinning.

"Leave 'em alone," Margaret said, as we plodded in the drive-thru line. "Don't you remember high school?"

"Pssshh, when I was in high school, if you were looking for action, you didn't ask for a haircut. Chickies were lining up for a serving of Moose-Knuckle Stew." I was surprised he'd adopted the nickname, but there was no denying his pants had to be uncomfortably tight.

"In your dreams," Margaret said. "I've seen high school pics. You looked like a heron in gym shorts, white knee socks, and a tank top." We all laughed so hard, I was shocked their little boy didn't wake up. He was strapped in, snoozing in the way back. He'd be wide awake and hyper in an hour or so, throwing himself around the way little kids tantrum. Stew was a filled-out man now but I could see how he'd once been kind of scrawny, like me. His arms were defined, but wiry and stringy, not thick, like the other guys who worked at the garage.

"It's a work night," I noted. "You guys going bowling?" He didn't seem to hang much with the other guys from work, but what did I know?

"Nah!" he laughed. "Why would I pay to get a shot at a trophy I'm just gonna put in the closet anyway?" He thought for a minute and then grinned. "Besides, they don't give trophies for the kinds of athlete I am."

"'Specially with that average bat and balls you're working with," Margaret added, reaching over and pretending to grab him, but he lifted his left leg to block.

"You sure you two don't want to just stay home?" Christine teased. "Or maybe just get a room or something? I don't care why I'm babysitting."

"Okay, we'll cut it out," Margaret said. "It's just almost always rutting time in Moose Country. I can have that anytime I want. Gotta win my jackpot. Can feel it in my bones."

"Can feel it in my bone," Stew added. Margaret side-eyed him and he shut up. So, it was BINGO, maybe the high-stakes kind in Canada, which made me think Stew was maybe originally from a Rez on the other side. I realized the way he likely operated now. When he vanished, Margaret would assume he'd hopped the border and headed to the Bush, but really, he was holed up with Liz, wherever she lived. Right as I put together my own aerial view of The Horny Life of Moose-Knuckle Stew, I looked up from my burger to notice him studying me in the rearview.

Stew didn't say anything at the time, but when we got back to Margaret's, he grabbed Christine's travel kit. "You should just start now," he suggested, clearing the table. "I'll even sweep up for you, so Brian here can have a shower before we leave. Like that, right, buddy? Better come with us to BINGO, 'cause we can't have a naked boy here with our babysitter if we're not home. Not with her dad, anyway."

"I don't know why you like keeping it so short," Christine said, running her fingers and brush through my hair to remind herself of its natural patterns, ignoring Stew. I knew the routine. I'd mostly had home haircuts from Beauty School Dropouts who owed my mom something. She put the poncho on me, then stuck my head in the kitchen sink, dunking me with the attachment.

"You know, like I do, that it grows out, not down," I said. Everyone pictured all Indians with super straight hair, cause of all those stupid wigs in cowboy movies, but easily half the Rez, including Margaret, had thick, curly, bushy hair like mine. "If I leave it, I just look like a shrub that grew a body." They laughed, but knew it was true as much as I did.

"See, look at these beautiful curls," Christine said, as she methodically cut them off and shaped the new layers. "You know how many perms I'm gonna be giving to get this look?"

"I don't want to look like a Chia Pet," I said. "No offense to the people who do."

"All right, you're done," she said after a few more minutes, with fake sadness, as she carefully lifted the poncho from me so no more hair fell on my shirt. "Look at all those abandoned ringlets all over the place. I can rinse you out in the kitchen."

"Nah, nah, he wants to shower before BINGO, don't you, buddy?" Stew said. "Can't concentrate on winning if you got all those little hairs pricking you everywhere, isn't it though? Got a towel and everything all set up just for you. Need a fresh shirt? Could borrow one of mine." Though being invited to shower at someone's house felt weird, it wasn't unheard of on the Rez, where running water was hit or miss. Saying yes once wasn't going to do any harm.

I made sure the door was locked and set the toilet cleaner in front of it, so that if anyone opened it to prank me, I'd at least know. I wiped down the tub and put everything back, and before I dressed, I held up the shirt Stew had left out, but it was a no go.

"Thanks for the shirt," I said, "but it's too big. I'll just shake mine out and put it back on." They all did the requisite fake sexy whistles as I walked through without my shirt.

"Put your shirt on, man," Stew added. "Now I'm hungry for chicken wings." A standard Rez joke said to anyone who was skinny and shirtless. The front stoop was chilly, so I gave the shirt a few quick shakes, and yanked it back on.

"Nyah-wheh," I said to Christine. "Looks great. I can't stand trying to wrestle a comb through it when it's long, and I'm not bringing a gigantic old hairbrush to school."

"Sit back down," she said. "I missed a few. Just take me a minute or so." I'd never really gotten used to having someone so close, semi-leaning up against you, so after a couple snips, I said I was sure the cut was fine.

I hoped they weren't trying to set us up, but felt relieved and then the sting of guilt when Christine acknowledged she was indeed staying behind to watch their kid. She wished us luck and gave me a dollar to play a card for her. While we played, I imagined her practicing darts at home, waiting for the next guy like me, believing the game would be an easy win. I could have passed on going, and stayed back with her, but both Stew and Margaret had been insistent that I could either go with them or they'd drop me at home. "I'm not paying my cousin here a dollar an hour so you two can go mess up my clean sheets as soon as Lionel's asleep," Margaret had said, and I couldn't tell if it was an awkward joke, or a serious concern. "So what's it gonna be?"

I'd promised Christine I'd play her a card, so I went.

Margaret and Stew were easier company than Randy Night. Not exactly nicer, but as adults, they weren't likely to pull the same kinds of pranks. At BINGO, they were friendly with a couple of Margaret's relatives, but it didn't seem like they had adult friends. Maybe I should have thought that was odd, but I was enjoying being treated like an adult for the first time too much to question things. That first night, Christine didn't say anything when we got home, except to ask if anyone had won. "All losers," Stew said.

Margaret, Stew, and I grew to know the ins and outs of every BINGO game in Niagara Falls. Our social life wasn't riveting, but they were each too interested in the other potentially cheating to tease me about my choices. I easily forgot they held secrets from one another. Margaret had maybe silently forgiven my young self by then. I didn't exactly trust Stew—always sure he was up to something—but I liked the fact that adults seemed to enjoy my company. I felt smarter, or funnier, or less like the kid who'd been dumb enough to get caught doing what most young guys do in private.

On nights they couldn't scrape up a decent BINGO layout, Christine came with us and we all headed to one of the two drive-ins, right up until the last weekend before they tore down the Star-Lite. I'd been stoked before the first night, but it was hard watching movies between their heads in the front seat, knowing Stew was copping a feel, ignoring their kid, and me and Christine in the back seat. He seemed proud of acting on his desires while others were around, like he wanted witnesses.

Some nights, I crashed on their couch. On those occasions, Stew would get up while we slept and set a towel and soap out for me on the toilet tank, though we never spoke of this. Things were good. I even planned on celebrating Thanksgiving with them, as long as Christine's dad wasn't going to be there. She'd been coming around less and less herself, unless she was actually watching the little kid, so it wasn't a worry. She also started to be hit or miss on the morning bus rides, too.

The day of, I helped my ma lift our turkey from its all-night oven bed. My siblings would be over later, and I'd be the only one not there. Later, my ma would borrow Rolanda's car and take Hillman over a big plate. Hillman believed Thanksgiving was a daily ritual, but he happily accepted home-cooked meals. The phone rang and we imagined it was Rolanda.

"Hey," Margaret said. "Whatcha doing?" I guessed she was going to maybe ask me to bring something.

"Helping my ma, learning some basics," I said, a lie, really.

"Learn by watching and helping," she said.

"Something like that," I said, stepping on the first land mine.

"So you know how to stuff the bird, then, right? Since you been watching and helping Stew do that for a while now." Her voice slid like a

drop-in winter windchill, from earnest curiosity to deadly observation. I
didn't know what to say. She didn't need prompting, eager to tell me Stew's
drunken Amateur Hour confessions the night before. Always practical,
she'd asked for details. He'd told her my presence on Parts Runs was the
perfect cover. No one suspected him and Liz during lunch, if they had
dragged my scroungy ass along for the ride.

"Well, you always said you knew he'd been sleeping around," I said,
thankful we'd gotten a long extension cord for the phone so I could talk
low from the other room. I was guilty enough, and kind of relieved in a
way, so I willingly stepped on the second land mine.

"True enough," she said. "I knew you two were up to something when
he kept trying to convince me you were sniffing after Christine. I knew if
I watched the two of you together enough, I'd figure it out. Wanna know
how?" she added in her Walk-This-Way Voice. "I recognized that jacket.
The one Stew gave you for keeping your mouth shut." I couldn't believe
he'd confessed to buying me that jacket, so I stayed silent. "Does it fit?"

"I'm growing into it," I said, quietly.

"You're probably not getting much bigger either, I guess," she said.

"Probably not," I conceded. "He had a good eye." I thought I'd made
it through the field, even without a map. "It was a little big when he bought
it." That's when I stepped right when I should have stepped left. "He's got
faults, but he's usually a decent guy."

"He told you *he* bought that? Has that man of mine ever told a truth
in his life?" Her voice was suddenly electric. "Know what else he lied
about?" I expected her to tell me Stew's last name was not Broad Moose.
Like so many Indian men, Stew wanted to measure up to our public image,
so they gave themselves more glamorous "Indian names." Margaret had
probably daydreamed for years, writing her future name over and over:
Mrs. Margaret Broad Moose. I typed his time cards at work, learning to
type as part of my newer work duties. IRS documents required his mun-
dane legal name, the kind most Indians I'd ever met had.

Rez women were more practical, most giving their babies their own
last names, unless the father was willing to cough up a ring to go along
with the offspring. Margaret had her mother's last name, and so did their
kid. So did Liz for that matter, and her mother was white. The only Rez

kids named Sampson were Christine and her sister Hayley. Should I tell Margaret that I already knew their big Fancy Indian Name secret, cutting her legs out from under her?

"*I* bought that jacket," she said—Land Mine Number Three. "*For him,* last year." My own legs suddenly went missing. "I thought it would look good on him, and he's normally a 40, but it looked funny, stretched across his growing pot. It was an end-of-season closeout. Final Sale. So, it was in our closet. When I saw you with one like it, I looked, and his was gone."

"You never said anything?"

"I did. *To him.* I got him totally lubricated on Baby Duck and he spilled it all."

"I mean, you never said anything to me," I answered, picturing Stew Broad Moose chugging the super sweet, fake pink champagne that was mostly known as a Girl Drink on the Rez.

"What for? The jacket fits, and your sorry ass can't afford one. By the time I found out why you had it, you'd creased it in all the places that fit you. You know, leather's like skin. It always wrinkles and refolds in all the places it gets stretched. I figure your silence was bought for half off." My secrets once again splattered all over me, once someone flicked the lights on.

"One last thing," she said. This was sure to be about Stew's real name, and she'd say she hadn't cared one way or another. Just his vanity. "It was Stew that didn't want you showering at the garage. He thought it was a funny prank on you. 'Cause he knew you wanted it so bad."

"But what about the towels laid out at your place?"

"All me," she said, and left air on the line, but I had no response. "My dad told me how you live. When he stayed with you guys, he'd come home to shower. We had a code. I'd put my bedroom blind at the top, and he'd know my mom was gone. In my head, I said he was washing off all the memories he was making, over there at your place. I laid out towels for him too."

Stayed with you guys seemed way better than *shacking up with your ma*, which was what she'd always said in the past. She allowed me to own the fact that when he was with us, he *wasn't* with them, his family. "Well, bye." She hung up, turning me back into an inarticulate kid again, just like in the lacrosse game stands. She wanted me to be aware there were all kinds of things in the world that would lose their value if I hadn't come by them honestly.

When I hung up, I asked my mom what she needed help with. If she noticed that I stopped hanging at Margaret's that Thanksgiving, she kept it to herself. Stew and I continued to work together, though he set me up elsewhere whenever he got assigned to the garage. I tried to forget my summer lunches, pretending I hadn't willingly been somebody's cover in trade for a stupid leather jacket, once again thinking I was getting two steps ahead, while someone else with better armor and more strategy quietly moved in for checkmate.

CHAPTER THIRTEEN

The New You

(1980–1981)

I saw Christine Sampson swimming at the dike, the next summer, a member of a large cast that changed almost every day. It was still August, but once in a while, a breeze would sneak in and bite where you didn't want to be bitten. Fall was coming, and the next school year with it.

"You still watch Spider-Man cartoons on Channel 11?" she asked, as we dried on boulders, sunning ourselves. I nodded, guilty. Made in the sixties, they went from barely competent to completely bonkers. Spidey fought his normal villains at first, but later, everyone behind the scenes was clearly using hallucinogens. Aside from the voices, it seemed like two entirely different shows. Canadian broadcasters were required to air a daily percent of Canadian Content, which was how I got to hear Rush on the radio initially. For TV, Canadian voice actors counted. If psychedelic Spider-Man was the only hero option available, I'd take him.

"Next time, right after, don't change the channel," she said. "That's what I want to do."

The next morning was one of the deranged episodes with watercolor skies like vomit splashes. Hamilton, a short jump across Lake Ontario, always beamed clear TV signals. The show after Spider-Man was a "live with a studio audience" show, called *The New You*. It starred a panel of women in too much makeup and hair spray, sporting outfits no one would ever really wear, giant hats and scarves that trailed like airport wind socks. The audience appeared to be seventy-five unhappy women. It was like *The Price is Right*, but for fashion and makeup. They randomly called an audience member's name, and gave them an overhaul, right on camera. They took a giant scissors to one woman and just chopped a huge braid off that had taken years to grow. Her face drained in panic when it fell to the floor. At the end of the show, they rolled a disclaimer that all audience members agreed to whatever changes were offered, in exchange for being on the show. I bet a lot of women thought they'd dodged a bullet that morning.

On the first day bus come September, it was clear Christine had begun escalating her own "New You" on herself, and she said she was finally officially enrolled in Cosmetology vocational school for half of every day.

We still shared morning bus cigs when she showed, and she still offered to trim me for old times' sake, but after the jacket incident with Margaret, we now had nowhere to do that. With my limited availability, she committed to her more adventurous subject—herself. She delighted in the greater chromatic palette to align her skin tone with her mood. I wasn't sure I needed a New Me.

Her ever-evolving appearance got a boost of inspiration from the one girl in our school who informed us her look was "Goth." I guessed this was short for Gothic, not Gotham, since it bore no relationship to Batman. That vampire girl helped Christine embrace the Doom and Gloom lifestyle, and the body shop boys prowled around her, because they thought she might be daring in a variety of ways, but they drew the line at Christine. The Indian boys thought she was too white and the white boys thought she was too Indian. No matter her inspirations, Christine was destined to carve out a largely lonely path.

Miss Vestal's dedication to Pastor Clyde after he encouraged Speaking in Tongues had raised some eyebrows, but Tim Sampson had also permanently carved out his place in our nightmares. Some guys aspired to get big enough to kick his ass at a party, but their beer-muscles faded once they were in the same room with this fearsome, impervious idol, buzz-cutted and towering over them at six foot five. His cheeks were so visibly ruddy, even through the dense stubble perpetually shading the lower half

of his face, you'd swear someone had just slapped him around. But I didn't
know a single person ballsy enough to slap those cheeks.

Somehow, he'd made unlikely permanent Rez inroads. Men in particular seemed impressed by his ability to smoothly navigate being the only
white guy in a roomful of Indians, and to sometimes even forget that fact.
But Christine remained a perpetual outsider. Pastor Clyde's rockabilly
Rez trading post church had been the perfect place for her in-between
genetics when she was a kid, fitting in with fringy types who slouched
there. But while he might play a cherry-red Telecaster with a twang bar
and banish cancer by laying on of the hands, he couldn't cure her stigma.
No matter her series of new looks, she'd inherited her mother's lozenge
eyes and her father's cheeks.

On that first morning of sophomore year, Randy didn't see Christine's
newest look until we arrived at the "Indian Rail." He'd successfully named
her Pristine when we were younger, but now her face held a pallor not usually found in living human skin tones, dusted in glitter, and set off by
heavy mascara. Her clothes were all black: cords, boots, a jacket, and a
T-shirt with The Cure printed across the front. She'd tied the hem in a
knot, off to the side, so her midsection peeked out. This look was finished
with equally black nail polish and a new Bad-Girl Hairdo, heavily sprayed
into loose, gravity-defying spikes that swayed on her head. It looked somewhere between a tumbleweed and a spider plant. You could almost see
cartoon cogs turning above Randy's head.

"Guess you had a busy summer," he started. Christine smiled and
shrugged.

"I mean, Clashing with those Titans and all that." And there it was. I
grabbed her arm to get us out of there, before she asked for the inevitable
clarification. The old fantasy moviemaker, Ray Harryhausen, tried to cash
in on all the *Star Wars* and *The Empire Strikes Back* hype. But new special
effects made stop-motion movies kind of a joke. High school kids went to
Clash of the Titans to get baked and laugh at the effects. I still loved it, but
I was in the minority.

"Do me a favor and run into my English class and make Mr. Haskell
hard as a rock," Randy exaggerated, like he was on a sitcom. Most people
at the rail thought he was just being vulgar, but he took pride in his insults.

When Christine just called him a jerk, he pleaded, "Come on, Meduse. Just get him to look into your eyes for a few seconds. He's already boring enough to seem like a statue."

I was surprised he didn't call her Tadodaho, the Snake-Haired Man from our history, but his dad might have "corrected" him with the belt for being sassy with a sacred story. He cut off the last syllable, knowing instinctively that "Meduse" was somehow a sharper nickname.

Most white guys didn't ask Indian girls out because they avoided coming out to the Rez, and Christine seemed to want to make her life tougher, referring to herself thereafter as Meduse, teasing her hair in even more defined spikes. She eventually even adopted a studded leather belt with real handcuffs for a buckle. She never tried the Indian Rail again, though, and found her calling among the other vampires skulking our high school's hallways, hiding from the sun and deciding the Castle Cadaver look suited her mood fine.

"I found us a place," Christine said one morning on the bus, passing me a Tim Cig, touching my own wildly growing hair. "And you are in desperate need." I was, but no one was looking my way, so having fashionable haircuts was not urgent. "Meet me at the ceramics studio during lunch." I wasn't eager to miss my guaranteed meal that day, so I planned to forget, but she knew my moves. "So look, Underwood says it's okay if I cut your hair in the far studio corner, long's we clean up." She grabbed my arm before I could hit the Smoking Lav.

"What's the catch?" No teacher ever cut a deal, not even one as dumb as this.

"I told him I still needed to log hours. I tried offering free services at the Rez Senior Citizen dinners, but you know how funny they are about their hair."

"I do," I said, "I'm always careful." Hair could be used against you in Bad Medicine, a part of your body you didn't want to fall in wrong hands. "So what's the catch?"

"We have to save the hair for him. He uses human hair in his projects." Hadn't she heard me? She assured me this was more Creepy Art Dude than Bad Medicine. So suddenly I was back to being her living Cosmetology "practice head."

"Okay, to be clear. This is just a cut," I said. "No dye, no bleach, and no 'Product,'" referring to the endless line of chemical goops that were available to apply to your head. "And most important. Please be careful. *You* have to move around *me*. My head, despite your best efforts, doesn't spin on my spine like your practice head turntable."

Toward Christmas break, this routine of haircuts and phone calls and morning rides started feeling a little tougher to manage. But since Christine was nice enough to make the effort for my benefit, I'd gotten her a waist apron with extra slots I'd glued in, so she could carry multiple tools at one time, instead of juggling back and forth. I gave it to her the last day before break.

"Let's try it out," she said. "You're kind of shaggy. Don't you wanna look nice for Christmas-morning-presents pictures?"

"We haven't had a camera since I was a kid. And with all the other shit you need, film, flashbulbs, developing fees, I don't see one in our future." I laughed. "I'm like Bigfoot. Very little photographic evidence." I was certain high school guys universally did not want to pose with gifts anyway, but I think the last photos of me were taken sometime around seven years old.

"Santa bringing you anything good?" Probably I'd get an album, maybe two if I were lucky, and the inevitable undershorts and the plaid flannel shirt that almost confirmed your family was on Welfare or Unemployment, or fast-tracking your way to one of those services.

"Rush has that new live album. Came out near Halloween." Anyone into Rush from our school already had *Exit . . . Stage Left*, because of a novelty feature. The audience featured on the cover was taken from the wings at the last Memorial Aud show. I'd been at that show, and I liked being on the fringes of Buffalo Concert history, but I hadn't been able to swing the cost yet.

"Want the standard cut?" This was sort of a joke. The standard cut everyone wore was something called Feathered Hair, but mine was too dense and wavy. On me, it looked more like wings than feathers. Still, she did her best. "What would you recommend as a good first Rush album?" She ran her fingers through my hair, developing a plan of attack.

"They're not exactly for everyone," I said, thinking of the stuff she listened to. The Cure was decent, what little I'd heard, but for Gloom and Doom Tunes, I preferred Bauhaus. I'd only started knowing about them and other new music because of Rush. A song on *Permanent Waves* was a celebration of a Toronto station, CFNY, nicknamed "The Spirit of Radio." It played all bands I'd never heard of. Still, I didn't want to be responsible for Christine buying an album she might hate. "They got some airplay with 'Tom Sawyer,' but man—"

"Ooh, I know that song!" *You and a million others*, I thought. A ton of people at that last show knew just that one song, an ocean of puzzled faces mixed in with us. They played "Tom Sawyer" about mid-set, and then people started drifting out, giving me a decent spot to sneak up to.

"It doesn't really sound much like the rest of their work," I said. "Can I ask you something?" I asked, before she could jump into another topic. "Seriously?" I didn't know how to ask, but this arrangement felt unfair to her.

"You going New-Yahhing this year?" she asked, ignoring me. This Rez tradition required a family car, or a coveted spot in another family's car, or a dedication to a lot of cold walking.

"I'm probably just gonna give out cookies this year," I said, being short on all those New Yah necessities. "Give my mom a rest."

"You could ride with us. Just me and my dad. Plenty of room in the pickup." I frowned, looking up at her. One of the strangest parts of getting your haircut was how close you were to another person. My family weren't really huggers. Okay, we weren't huggers *at all*. The last real contact I remembered having with any member of my family was sitting on my grandfather's lap. I didn't even want to figure out the number of years. When Christine leaned into me, or touched my temples to keep my head straight, it felt weird. Her hands were warm, warmer than my face anyway.

"My mom used to stay at the house," she said, quiet. "Now, we leave a sign up in the entry, take one apiece and one for the driver, if you want. My dad gets twelve dozen doughnuts and labels them all." You'd think someone would steal them, but New Yah was a community activity that everyone respected. If Eee-ogg got out that you'd done someone raw during New Yah, your ass would be cooked. "My dad still wants to give me this as long as I want it. Come with us."

"You know why that's never going to happen, right?" I asked. I should have spoken before she mentioned her mom, but she was quick. "Your dad?"

"What's wrong with my dad?"

"Well, besides him being able to lift me and crush my windpipe like Darth Vader . . . *every* dad of a high school girl sees *one* thing when a high school guy's sitting inside his house."

"And that would be?"

I laughed. "For all your Vampirella outfits, you don't seem to know much about real life on 'The Wild Side.' What your dad sees? A throbbing, pleading, bargaining and relentless crafty pecker. Doesn't matter how untrue. When the dad's the size of yours, he's gonna shake my hand, clamp like a vice, and smile the whole time. That's how dads remind young guys who has the upper hand."

"My dad trusts me to keep my Sergio's on," she said.

"It's not *your* jeans he'd be thinking about. Besides, I'm not much in the mood. Pretty sure that come summer, I'm gonna be out of a job. There's rumors about the school going on a strict budget. Before they can change even *one* regular worker's hours, they have to wipe all us kids out of the equation."

"That's, like, six months away. Besides, how do you know all this?" she asked, doubting.

"You know what they say about my family. We sense things . . . and . . . I pay attention to Break Room Eee-ogg at work. The mechanics helpers are worried."

"Well, no matter what, you'll always have someone to cut your hair," she said.

True to her prediction, she and her dad showed up in our driveway on New Year's morning, and she yelled "New Yah! New Yah!" in my face, even though I was inches away, in our open door. We laughed at our goofing on the ritual. "Get anything cool for Christmas?" she asked. I showed her the T-shirt I had beneath my unbuttoned flannel.

My mom had pulled one of her Christmas magic tricks again. She'd located the rare picture disc of Rush's *Hemispheres*, and a shirt to match. The regular *Hemispheres* Tour shirt had two pictures of a globe, side by side, but this one was from England. The back had a UK map with tour stops noted, and the front featured three floating brains, like the album back cover. I'd only seen one like it before, on this guy Leonard Stoneham. He was a year older, and I didn't know him, so I never had the nerve to ask where he'd gotten his.

"Nice," she said, touching each brain lightly. "Could always use an extra." As we laughed again, she pointed to my big serving bowl of cookies and asked, "One for the driver?" gesturing to Tim, a hulking silhouette in their pickup. I felt oddly exposed when Tim raised his hand and flicked his wrist, in a curt Rez wave everyone used. It looked weird on a white guy.

The second half of the school year went routine. The upheaval I was worried about came along right on schedule. It broke the Friday before Finals Week in June, "Play Day," when Upperclassmen formally humiliated Underclassmen for the last time. Kids screamed and laughed and staff just silently screamed as the district quietly rolled out an Austerity budget.

This meant nothing to the Football monsters dragging Academic Bowl scarecrows through Three-Legged Races, jocks grinding bird-framed kids' faces in the grass during the Wheelbarrow Race. I watched the news spread across the lawn like weeds, from one teacher's mouth to another's ear, over and over. You didn't have to read lips to know the story sucked. Budget cuts were coming, and no one was going to escape. I remembered the rule. They had to let go any Poor Kid workers who might take work from a union member.

"Isn't it about time for a haircut?" Christine asked, arriving with her usual opening volley after losing a class Tug-of-War. Her own hair had now evolved from spider plant into a sturdy aloe, with thick tentacles waving above her head, but she flipped the hair hanging in my eyes.

"No way they're gonna let us into the ceramics lab, Margaret's is out, and . . ." Sometimes I found myself complaining about the stupidest shit.

"What? Why you frowning?" she asked, pushing softly on my chest.

"Lewis and Maggi might survive the kid-worker purge, but I am the toast I predicted." I'd heard rumors Maggi Bokoni was involved with one of the groundsmen, though it seemed unlikely. The guy was easily thirty, and unless she'd failed a couple grades living in Skin City, I was pretty sure he'd be risking a lot by hooking up with her. Just the same, I was not adding to the Eee-ogg about anyone else's loneliness. "Gonna be out of a job in two weeks."

"You could work with me," Christine said. I shut up about my problems immediately. "Then I could cut your hair all summer, if you want, and after that, my dad will know you as one of the guys from camp, so when summer's over—"

"That church camp? Wouldn't lightning strike if I walked through the gate?"

"It didn't last year when Carson Mastick came. You should be safe," she laughed. "Randy, too. A lot of Rez kids. It's where we spend our summers. Keeps us out of trouble."

"Randy and Carson work at a *church* camp?" To the best of my knowledge, they weren't among the Rez demographic hypnotized by that Heavenly Telecaster. I didn't believe either had ever set foot in any church, let alone that one.

"We're not counselors or anything," Christine said. "That needs special training. It's a witnessing camp. The kids who go are practicing to witness for the Lord, to become members of the church. Hubie Buckman got CPR certified, so he's on lifeguard and swimming-lesson duty." I vaguely remembered he was on the Swim team and had been volunteering at the fire hall.

"Making out with their Resusci-Annie's probably the only action Hubie's ever had."

"You should talk," she said, irritatingly keeping that spark alive. "I bet you haven't even had a hickey, chasing Randy's sister all this time like a little leg-humping Chihuahua."

"How would you know about me and Tiffany?"

"There *is* no you and Tiffany," she said, laughing again. "There's you, back when you used to hang there, trying to catch a peek in her bedroom, or *accidentally* wandering into the bathroom when she's showering. Everyone knows that." *Everyone* knew because Randy would tell anyone with ears. "You don't have a chance. She's hot and only goes out with guys grown up enough to know what they're doing."

"Never said I had a chance," I mumbled, hoping she'd drop it.

"So, interested?" Christine asked, ignoring my statement. "Better job than nothing."

"Randy's *really* working at this camp?" I wasn't exactly eager to rekindle that friendship yet again, but I also had zero interest in staying home, broke all summer.

"He's talking about trying to join Carson's band, figuring he can get his skills up with a low-stakes audience, before finally trying out," she conceded. I'd heard about them, but I didn't know who else was in it. "You know, they're cousins. His other sister, Tami, already plays with them." I hadn't seen her at the Indian Rail, but Christine evidently had been hanging out at Randy's. He'd been a dick to her, too, but I had no room to criticize her decisions. "He helped cabins come up with a talent show song for the last weekend. Music director or something like that."

"Lucky him."

"He's gonna try to get Carson's band to play Friday nights and for Talent Show, I think. Randy's paid the same as us. Maybe extra for playing," she added, holding up her hands like she was strumming an invisible guitar. "And twelve-year-olds? Worst band in the world still sounds like rock stars to them." She glanced around quickly, to see if anyone overheard her.

"Pretty sure Carson wouldn't be able to use his real band name."

"Yea, no *Devil* names need apply," she said, with a disapproving hiss. "Dunno." Carson's band name, the Dog Street Devils, came from a name he'd made up for the friends who came to weekend-long parties he threw, in the burned-out foundation next to their property.

"Anyway, I still have another application at home," Christine said. "Special skills?"

"General maintenance and cleaning? Pumping gas? Typing?"

"Oooo, who could turn you down?"

"Tiffany Night, for one. Wait, do *I* have to witness?"

"Only the world around you," she said. So, that afternoon, I resigned myself away from one life and into another, out with the old and in with the new.

Two Rows (IV)

We each recognize that we move
according to our own desires and plans.

We respectfully do not cross streams
with each other, maintaining forward balance.

We see the open territory ahead of us and
acknowledge the mingled wakes we leave behind.

We share, between us, a peace we each maintain
by our dual presence in the expanse before us.

We discover each other side by side
in the water, traveling our own paths.

We emerge from different points of origin
and stay steady to our own unknown destinations.

We maintain our own customs, governing ways
of life and beliefs about the universe.

PART FOUR

Closer to the Heart

(1981–1985)

CHAPTER FOURTEEN

Campfire Legends

(1981)

My eventual acceptance letter instructed me to be outside the Human Services building in Niagara Falls by 8:00 the Monday morning a week after school let out. I was to look for a blue pickup and a guy named Leonard, the other groundskeeper. My ma had gotten me a ride to my pick-up point, who drove off, leaving me in the lot, sitting on Chester's duffle stuffed with two weeks' of warm and cold weather clothes, sneakers, swim trunks, personal hygiene stuff. My arrival was a week before the first campers, but Hubie, Christine, and Randy had reported a week ahead of me. There's not a lot of orientation in cutting a lawn and sanitizing a communal shower.

A security guard arrived a few minutes later, telling me the Welfare Office didn't open until nine as a blue pick-up pulled into the lot. "I know you," Leonard Stoneham said, rolling down his window. I was hoping he wouldn't remember me. "Guess I didn't recognize your name. Got a smoke?" He lugged my gear into the pickup bed with his. I hadn't known my ride's last name, but I knew exactly who he was when he pulled up. I expected the worst and tried to figure out any way to keep my bag in front of my shirt until we got to the jobsite.

"My own." I knew a test when I heard one. He asked if he could light his off of mine.

"Don't worry about the 'no tobacco' rule," he said. Our Do Not Bring

List included weapons, drugs, alcohol, tobacco, and *inappropriate reading materials*. "They put it in to cut it down. We can smoke, but not in front of the kiddies. Even find you porn if you got a need."

"Porn?" I said, giving him side eyes. How had some white kid heard this story?

"Inappropriate reading materials," he mimicked from our letter.

"I thought that meant, like, Stephen King novels," I said. Pastor Clyde's favorite rant was the Devil's Entertainment Empire.

"Yeah, don't tell that story to anyone else. It's pretty dorky. Offer stands, though. Whole summer's a long time." Our school was uptight. Most guys didn't really joke about such things, so I could only conclude Randy had been hard at work with his scandal story about me.

"I can wait till our week off around the Fourth of July," I said. "A beer, now . . ."

"Not an issue. That's on orientation stuff, in case parents help with the application. My third year. Stick with me, man. We'll be fine. The other grounds guy last year was a total asshole, disappearing on me, taking shortcuts, liberating my stuff. The booze and smokes I never got back. The *Penthouse*, didn't really want that back." We drove a while in silence until he said the one thing I'd hoped he wouldn't.

"Nice shirt," he casually mumbled, confirming where my *Hemispheres* Tour shirt had originated, probably the picture disc, too. Leonard lived in a garage sale neighborhood my ma and I frequented. The mystery shirt *had been* his. We both knew it. A year older, he spent a lot of time in a weight room and it no longer fit him. My ma had found it at Leonard's garage sale. "Looks good on you," he added.

"Thanks," I said.

"This job might help you fill it out, broaden your shoulders, chest." He flexed his bicep, and we laughed at his ridiculous Charles Atlas pose. Leonard and I were assigned as roommates in the Maintenance Cabin, and were told to gather at "The Big House," by noon, for orientation.

Pastor Clyde welcomed us, blustery and sweaty, decked out in his Elvis Presley pompadour. He conducted daily services and those of us who weren't *yet* saved were welcome to "a laying on of the hands" to start our path to salvation any day we wanted. I wondered who, besides

Randy, Carson, and me, had not been touched by those hands. Maybe Leonard?

I spotted everyone I knew, sitting in groups they'd been assigned. Counselors appeared to be college kids and older adults, one per group, overseeing. The leader over Christine and Johnnie—another girl from school—was a woman dressed the way Christine's mother used to, high-waisted old-fashioned dresses with lace collars. All employees called each other by their first names with "Miss" or "Mister" before them, as things had been at Friday Bible School. Apparently, for the summer, I was going to be Mister Brian.

Our adult, the lead groundsman, wore the standard work blues with a name tag embroidered: Roy. Leonard looked like a man next to me, but near Roy, Leonard still had a ways to go. Despite straining buttons and a little pot, Roy'd take Leonard in a fight without sweating.

"All right, listen up, Grunts," Mister Roy said, once we were separated. "Groundsmen aren't required to be in Large Group Activities. Can if you want, long's your Day Chart's complete. Day Chart'll be posted outside my bedroom door every morning. You're free during off hours, too, once camp starts. Curfew's one A.M. After that, front gate's chained 'til sunrise. One of our jobs, on rotation, locking and unlocking the gate."

Six of us shared doubles and Roy had the largest and best bedroom, solo. Since I'd already seen smokes, booze, and mags on his nightstand, I assumed he had a weapon there.

Roy continued, "What you do on your own time's your own business, but being dis . . . Being secretive, with common sense, will do you well. Once the kiddies arrive, if they need one of us, they ring the cowbell on our porch deck and wait. But you got a footlocker, so use it."

The first day, we moved floats into the lake and Hubie tested diving board depth. He was a committed swimmer, and his life as Doobie the Kid Who Failed Kindergarten was nowhere in sight. After mowing lawns and clearing paths, we cut and stacked wood for burning after the sun went down. At the end of the day, I could shower, so my camp room was better than home.

The main firepit was near the pool but I preferred the smaller lakeside one. After supper, we'd head there for "General Swim." My fake ID,

Leonard's sheer size, and my sad mouth-parentheses mustache allowed us to head out to the townie bars. Roy made it clear which bar adult staff went to once Pastor Clyde went home, so we could all avoid one another.

Mostly, I stayed with Leonard or the Dog Street Devils: Summer Camp Chapter. Leonard had a knack for becoming invisible, so he could hang with whoever he wanted, but often, just the two of us kicked back. Buying Mister Roy a case of his own granted us space in the Maintenance Cabin fridge, which Mister Roy and his buddies raided whenever they felt like it.

I got to know Leonard decently. The last night before kids arrived, we all sat around the lake firepit, most throwing on jackets over drying bathing suits. Randy played radio hits on his guitar, so we could half-assed sing along. It was one thing to sing well, another to play the guitar well, but he did both with ease. Later in the evening, he chose "Closer to the Heart," not exactly radio fare outside of Toronto, and not easy. Rush specialized in complicated riffs, but he'd stripped it to a manageable arrangement. I'm sure he'd practiced. He'd seen my shirt, somehow connected it with Leonard, and jabbed me the way only he could.

People drifted to bed, usually alone, but some workers knew each other better than others. Randy asked me if I'd drop off his guitar because he and Johnnie, Christine's roommate, were going for a walk. I said I'd take it to my room and he could pick it up in the morning. The fire grew smaller, and more people wandered away, until it was just Leonard and me.

"Why you lugging that asshole's guitar around?" Leonard asked.

"I wondered if he was your partner last year," I said, and he nodded. "The reservation's a small place. You learn to live there, knowing who everyone is, and how your lives are going to be for the long haul."

"The long haul?"

"I'll probably be there forever and so will he," I said. "Hubie, too. Maybe not Christine. Her dad's white, so she's got a fifty-fifty shot in either world. It's not going to hurt me to do Randy a favor here, and it keeps our good will."

"And what's he ever done for you?"

"It's not so direct. Like anything else, there are intangibles." The little

I understood about white life, the more I understood I had no way of explaining the differences, how I was storing for a lifetime of exchanges with people. You make enemies at ten, you might still be at seventy.

"Gonna have to drag your language back from Snootsville if you wanna talk to me, man." Leonard looked out toward the water. "Give me something solid, like the ground under that diving platform. Deep, but not deep enough that I can't dive and touch bottom if I want. Your other buddy there chose just deep enough that it's possible, but not so shallow that many kids would try it. It's doable, but you gotta *want* to touch bottom."

"Sorry. Intangible," I repeated, but I stopped. Did I have other words to describe it? That's why we have some words. We use them when there aren't others. "It's something you can't grasp, but you know it's there."

"Like faith?"

"I guess." Was I really the only nonreligious person here, aside from Randy? And Carson's guest appearances. There had to be others who just needed a summer job. Maybe Mister Roy.

"Like the deal with that car, there?" he asked, pointing to an upside-down car on the beach, its roof caved in. It sat near the stairs we used to navigate the drop.

"Well, that car is tangible, it's here. Intangible, not here. Tangible, here." I held my hands up like I was trying to balance separate things on a scale. "We can see it, even touch it, though I wouldn't do that without an up-to-date tetanus shot." The car looked like it was from the forties, maybe fifties, pre–gigantic Batmobile fins, surprisingly intact.

"But how it got here, that's what's . . . untangible?" I corrected him gently. "We got a rule," he continued. "If you got a specialty, you're allowed to do it. Your asshole buddy there? He brought that guitar last year, sang a few songs—Bammo! He's music director. A lot easier. So if you got some special talent, you could change. The one I tried out was the story of that car. We were supposed to come up with something to keep kids away from it, away from sneaking to the lake on their own. I told them last year that it was Bigfoot that did it."

"Original," I said. A few years before, *The Legend of Boggy Creek* hit it big at drive-ins, and Bigfoot was everywhere, even on that stupid *Six Million Dollar Man* TV show, except they finally revealed Bigfoot there to be an android. Even though that show was fake, science always beat out myth. Science and six million dollars, anyway, easily enough to kill a myth.

"You got to go with what scares kids. Bigfoot, they know, and it fits this place. Kids gotta believe they can survive. That's number one. And the fear can't be terrible. They need a fighting chance. Not too terrible odds. So, Darth Vader at camp ain't gonna cut it. That Cropsey legend about the crazy camp counselor? That'll just give kids nightmares. The escaped mental patient with the hook for a left hand? That's to keep horny kids our age from going all the way in cars. And zombies, or those crazy cannibals from *The Hills Have Eyes*? No parents in their right minds take their kids to those movies. Bigfoot's safe, but scary enough to work."

"Apparently he doesn't work well enough to get you the story-teller job."

"They offered. This keeps me in better shape than sitting around, making stuff up all day. I'm graduating next June and then it's off to the Marines. Early acceptance." The only people I'd heard talking about early acceptances were applying for "super competitive colleges." For the military, I suspected almost any applicant with all limbs intact and a reasonably stable personality probably got early acceptance. But I chose not to say, trying to understand their world, where you didn't say such things. "You ready to head up? This fire's burning down, and if we put some more on, it'll be another hour. We got lock duty tomorrow morning."

"I guess," I said. I'd been waiting for Randy and Johnnie to show back up. "One thing, though?" He sat back down. "That shirt? I just want to thank you for not saying—"

"Look, man. You think you're the only kid in our school wearing secondhand clothes? You think bad news *only* wanders the reservation? Every single house has some kinds of secrets." He threw one small length of wood on the fire, sparks shooting up into the night sky like a constellation, as he took in a deep breath and let it back out. "My mom bought me that shirt in England. I'd always wanted to get my picture taken in the crosswalk at Abbey Road, and when we were there, she got us tickets to see Rush. She was trying to find a way to tell me what she'd been diagnosed with a couple months before.

"Seeing it startled me. I tossed it in the garage sale when my dad put half our stuff up, to make room for the junk his new wife and her kids were dragging in." He poked embers, and they bloomed swirling clouds of a thousand miniature suns, warming their own lonely solar systems. "Don't know if I hated our house more when it felt too empty, or now that a bunch of someone else's history fills in the gaps. You feel like their new laughs are gonna squeeze the ones you saved right out of that house, when it belonged to your real family. You know?"

I didn't know what it meant to be alone in that same way. In Rez life, good or bad, you were never alone if you didn't want to be. If you were mourning after a funeral, and you asked to be alone, you might get that wish respected for a day, but that would be the max. Someone would drop off a warm meal to see if you were okay, even for just a minute.

"Now we don't need to talk about that ever again, right?" he asked, leaning against an ancient tree. I shook my head. The Rez part of me wanted to ask him some sly sideways questions, to see what he *was* holding back, if he really was done talking. But the part trying to learn his world was also learning to withdraw, and to respect others' privacy. I had the feeling he hadn't shared that story with many people.

"Gimme that guitar," he said. "You might as well know how to use it. 'Closer to the Heart' ain't hard. It's a couple hard moves, but mostly just a few riffs, over and over, strung together, like our jobs." It hurt my fingers. At breakfast, I asked the other maintenance guys if any knew how long it took to build calluses, and discovered Randy had already shared the story of his infamous prank.

Leonard didn't join in busting my balls, but that next night, after lights out, he spoke: "Listen, I wanna be straight with you. I am kinda involved with Pastor Clyde's church. I don't follow the rules rigidly and all that blah blah. I ain't ever gonna tell you it's a sin, and I ain't gonna rub my wrists together like those other guys, when we see a hot counselor." Just as I was about to drift off, he added, "Every guy does it. Don't let these lying jerks fool you."

Through the first course of campers, we learned maintenance mostly worked places no campers were at any given time. We were largely invisible, but often had some emergency job. Some kids were so backwards, or something—I never asked—that they'd shit in the corner of the large communal shower room. Whenever Shit Patrol came over the walkie-talkie, Leonard and I immediately headed out, knowing Mr. Roy would never stoop so low. We switched duties exactly every time, one with a shovel and one with the pump canister of disinfectant. I offered to always be shovel man. Having an outhouse, I was as used to that job as anyone might be. He insisted we split bad tasks down the middle.

"So, what's up for this week?" Leonard asked, as we got ready for bed the last night before the weeklong Fourth of July break. "A whole week of no Shit Detail."

"Just hanging on the Rez. No car," I added. It never failed to sound so ridiculous. It was almost like saying you didn't have a phone, or running water. At least we had a phone. "There's a Rez event I go to the weekend after, then it's back here the next Monday. You?"

"Well, me . . ." he said, hanging his shirt and pants up. "Probably gonna sit around and try avoiding my new step-whatevers."

"Brothers and sisters?" I asked, exaggerating.

"If you insist," he grumbled. "I bet some of my stuff'll already be packed up as they make plans for my room. And I'm still a year away. Fucking sharks," he said. "Anything else?"

"No, just catching up on everything I didn't get to do here," I said, grinning.

"Busy social life or your busy solo life?" he laughed. "Need a ride home?" I nodded.

Randy took my acceptance of Leonard's offer, somehow, as a rejection, so he invited me for an all-expenses-paid weekend to the National Picnic, the Rez event I'd mentioned to Leonard. If Randy tried jerk moves, I only lived a mile away and could walk. What would be the harm?

"Why you wasting time with that white kid?" Randy demanded immediately, picking me up in his dad's car the Friday night the Picnic began.

"Just drive." I had my first big paycheck in nine months, so I had a little to burn.

"Those Indian-white friendships don't never work out," he said. "They got no pride in who they are, no loyalty to who they been with. They don't know what a treaty is. Always going for the easiest thing. No sense of history like us," he added, when I didn't respond. "Your buddy gets a bump in his paycheck if he gets you to Come to Jesus this summer. He tell you that? If he paid any attention to my stories, he'd know how fast you come, and he'd give up."

"Shut up," I said, punching him hard enough so he'd know it wasn't in friendship.

"Easy! Easy! I'm driving here," he yelled, faking a swerve, then actually pulling into the parking spot. "I gotta drop my dad's keys off and he's supposed to cash my check for me. And I got something for you." Listening to rants was a cost of hanging with Randy. As with many things, he'd planned our adventure to the minute. His entire family seemed to function by manipulating others. So he led me to Exhibit A, proof of his philosophy about why Indians and white people just didn't mix.

Outside the RV DogLips had won the use of in his dice game, burgers and dogs warmed on a Hibachi. You were supposed to buy food from the Nation vendors, but DogLips didn't care about rules. When Randy opened the RV's side door, a massive cloud of cackling laughter and cigar smoke hit us like a fog. "Take off your shirt," Randy said. "I got a cooler one for you."

I peeled off my sweaty T-shirt as he held up a new one, fresh from a stacked box. It had been printed, like a concert shirt. A cartoon Devil with long hair and a breechclout rode a mean-looking dog. Spread across the top, "The Dog Street Devils" was spelled in flaming letters.

"What's this?" I asked. "I'm not in his band, and I don't live on Dog Street."

"Carson made them to sell at shows, doofus." The name had started as a joke on Carson, and he'd somehow turned it around, as if it had been his idea in the first place. "Put it on. It's clean. More'n I can say for this pus rag," he said, tossing my shirt aside with his middle finger.

The RV was crowded with men who only gave us a glance. In the smoky dark, DogLips and other men rolled dice, drinking and shouting. Through the center strip, I had a clear shot at Christine Sampson's dad, Tim, at the back, in a position I could barely comprehend. I thought it had to be a trick of the haze and gloom, but eventually, there was no denying the sight before me.

Tim swayed in rhythm, his left arm above him, bracing himself against the back cupboard. His work pants and white briefs stretched taut low around his hips, as he spread his legs to keep them from dropping. He slowly grunted and thrust forward, then back, gradually speeding up. In between thrusts, I could see a small woman I didn't recognize, leaning forward in a chair before him. His breath caught and whistled as he sped up. As his knees buckled, the work pants dropped to his ankles. "He sure can fuck face," someone said in admiration. The others cracked all at once, shouting "Fuck Face," like a cheer, shoving each other in glee. So deeply engaged, Tim Sampson had no idea he'd finally gained a nickname among his Rez associates.

DogLips passed Randy a couple fifties, telling us to make sure we went to the store with whoever made our purchase. DogLips turned to me, his eyes narrowing slyly. "This here's what happens if you keep getting caught with your pants down," he said, laughing. "But I paid for the hour, if you want a turn . . ." The crowd blasted another explosive laugh as I bolted. The last thing I saw was the woman lean back and take a deep pull from a beer, as FF awkwardly squatted, trying not to moon everyone, yanking up his pants.

The Night family played by even higher stakes than I'd thought. I could blame Tim for being stupid, but the truth was, we'd both been set up by different versions of the same bit of blackmail that never expired. Once you'd been exposed, that was pretty much it.

"What was that all about?" I asked, as Randy caught up with me, still laughing a cackle like broken glass. "How can you even be laughing!"

"She's from the city," Randy said. "Calls herself Little Eva. Her specialty is round-robin poker parties and dice games like that. She's, um, very popular on the party circuit. She's something like forty, but claims she's barely legal."

"Why?" Of the five thousand questions I had, I couldn't prioritize.

"When you're paying someone to do that, you gotta come up with some story to make it seem okay. My dad set it up to look like a party gig, but Sampson was the only customer. My dad says lots of women out here he'd make a good man for, but that he needs to loosen up."

"Your dad thinks Eee-ogg about Tim Sampson and a hooker is gonna make someone interested in him? Your dad better lay off the juice, man," I said. "There isn't a world I know of where that story makes any sense."

"You're just a kid. You don't know oo(t)-gweh-rheh," Randy said, trying to sound casual. Then he randomly punched me. "And don't be talking shit about my dad. He knows what's what. He said Sampson's old woman, after Christine was born, that was it! She closed up shop like a Ziploc bag, so Sampson, he's forgot what it feels like."

"Yeah," I said, "Like he doesn't—"

"Not everyone's like you," he said. I punched him harder. "Ow! Easy with those fists," he grumbled. "Don't injure my talented hands," he added, laughing. "But for real, it's crazy. Seen it myself. He don't even touch his pecker when he's taking a leak. He undoes his belt, then the pants." Randy told this story with glee, pantomiming as we crossed the parking field. "Slides the shorts waistband up under his nuts, with his thumbs. He's mastered the touchless whiz!" He swiveled his hips, like it was December and he was spelling his name in the snow.

"You did not see that," I said.

"Truth I did. Just once. Putting empties in the shed out back. He was so shitfaced, he barely made it out our back door before he started whizzing. Anyway, my dad's getting him drunk and having Little Eva take care of him. I guess she's like the Tutoring Center for getting off, so he'll remember that people enjoy hooking up." I just kept shaking my head, trying to play the scenarios where someone could be talked into what I'd just seen, but none added up. I wasn't super experienced, or experienced at all, but it still seemed unlikely. "My dad figured if Sampson was drunk enough, and with the regular gang, he could get talked into anything."

"And your ma thinks this is good plan too?"

"Don't be a dildo. She's in Ottawa, selling at some powwow. Quill work doesn't move here, but she likes snipping barbs, so she goes to Canadian powwows." Very few beadworkers I knew bothered with preparing porcupine quills.

"So your dad told her that while she was away, he was buying Tim Sampson a blowjob from a middle-aged uptown prostitute?" The summer before, I'd learned what hangovers felt like on mornings at their smoky kitchen table. DogLips and Kitten sipped coffee, looking at each other like two people who wanted to be together until one stepped out for good. People who couldn't wait for the rest of us to leave so they could be alone.

People who loved the smell of each other, even waking up in the morning. How could a fifty-dollar encounter compare to those silent smiles? These ideas didn't exist in the same universe.

"Anyway, I knew you wouldn't believe me, so I figured you'd have to just see for yourself. That's a white guy for you. No fucking shame, no dignity. The same for your friend Leon." I corrected him, but I could tell he was trying out new nicknames for Leonard, hoping to find the right burn. "He wants something from you. Probably just the Savior Bonus, but that puts it on you." Randy's logic was its own unique thing, and though I'd like to dismiss it, he had this way of searing ideas into your brain.

We arrived at the Smoke Dance competition. I couldn't focus. Since I didn't really know Tim Sampson, he was a bad example of white betrayal. I had no investment in his allegiance. But later that night, Christine showed up at Randy's party, and while we partied in the deeper back yard, the adults all rolled dice at a table near the house. Tim Sampson was rolling like everyone else, not acting at all like he'd been the main attraction a few hours ago. The whole time, I felt like I was keeping a secret from Christine. Her dad's private life was no business of hers, and for sure no business of mine, but he didn't even seem interested in keeping his privacy private.

I couldn't wash my brain of that scene. And beyond those complications, I'd become keenly aware that whenever I saw anything close to intimacy, something was poisoned in it. I kept wanting to believe that love might be out there somewhere, but I didn't know how to find it. It was bad enough with the image of Moose-Knuckle Stew and Liz lodged into my head. Now I had this even weirder version of an encounter added.

When I wandered home Sunday morning, hungover, the rest of my weekend a blur, I discovered several hickeys on my neck and less money in my pocket than there should have been. I could already hear Randy crafting a story for anyone who'd listen, that I was dropping twenties left and right once we'd found a ride, trying to look like a big spender, couldn't even keep track—in short, a sloppy drunk. Money lost was money lost, but I had to know one thing.

"Randy home?" I asked, when Tiffany answered. The line went dead.

So, I called back, and it rang and rang, until finally Randy picked up. "Something wrong with your phone?"

"Tiffany just hung up on you after what you and Meduse pulled this weekend." As soon as he said it, a hazy picture came to me. He and Christine had gotten me to believe that if she gave me hickeys, I could approach Tiffany and convince her she'd done it, herself. That she'd been too drunk to remember. Christine leaned in, with surgical precision, and worked one spot, then another, each time Randy cackling with fierce glee, seeing the fresh hickey. It sounds so moronic, in retelling here, but Randy had his dad's way of making you believe in the stupidest ideas, and it was worse when you were impaired.

In this case, it only worked because he'd had an accomplice. I guess Christine was just trying to do me a favor in achieving my desires. But who would do that? She wasn't remotely interested in me. Maybe she needed to be in Randy's good graces more than I did. Tiffany had grabbed me and slammed me across the living room to the delight of everyone there. I'd apparently been the second bill on the DogLips Night Entertainment Line-Up for the Weekend. I didn't bother asking how I'd arrived at Picnic with a full paycheck and by Sunday morning, had less than forty bucks left, mostly in fives and ones.

A little girl picked up the phone when I called Leonard on Sunday. "Suppose you're looking for a ride," he said, his voice chilly. I agreed I was hoping. "Well, tell ya what, I'll pick you up the same place I did before."

"That doesn't make any sense," I said. The Rez was between Leonard's house and the campground. Human Services was in the city and would take him twenty miles of backtracking.

"My truck, my rules," he said. "See you there?" I agreed. I'd learned from my ma to accommodate conditional rides. They indicated lower patience. So, she found me a ride uptown.

The security guard once again told me the time the Welfare office opened. "I happen to be getting a ride," I said, "to my *job*. Where I'm paid minimum wage for manual labor, a lot less than you're getting paid for sitting on your ass." I don't know what I was thinking, maybe that I was on public property and untouchable, but I was wrong. He escorted me off the property and told me that, if I stepped foot on again, even one more time, he was having me arrested for disorderly conduct. When Leonard appeared, he noticed our proximity.

"There a problem, officer?" Leonard asked, getting out.

"This wiseass with you?"

"Yes, sir," Leonard said, fake respect in his voice. "We work with underprivileged children at a camp that helps them to learn better social skills," he added, which was a total lie.

"How's this wiseass going to help them with that? He don't have any skills himself," the guard said, pleased with his own cleverness.

"He's our poor example," Leonard said. "We show them the costs of engaging with authorities inappropriately." The guard looked pleased that he'd recognized my social deficits. "And people with billy clubs. I'm his guardian. You know how it is with these Indians."

"Working here, where the Welfare office is? Man, do I ever," the guard said, entirely unaware he was being had, for just the few seconds it took for him to dig his own free-association hole. "Only thing worse is—"

"Assholes who think that an ID card is a badge?" Leonard said, in his same cheery awe-soaked voice, turning his back on the guard, helping me throw my gear in again.

"Both of you little shits better get out of here before . . ." He drew his baton from his belt.

"We are." Leonard said. "We're going to find a phone booth, where I plan to call my uncle in the mayor's office, and tell him how helpful you've been, Mr. . . . ." He glanced down at the guard's name tag. "Mr. Searl. I'm sure they'll be pleased to know."

"Oh, your big bad uncle scares me," Searl said. "I'm a dues-paying union member and I got time served for military duty when you were still running around in messy diapers." He slid his baton back in its holster loop, looking like he'd discovered he was in messy diapers, himself. "I know my rights."

"But no one else's," Leonard said, starting the truck. "You tell your-self whatever story you need to keep on being fulfilled by your job."

We got into the truck and left, heading back toward the Rez and the campground beyond, passing several phone booths. "You don't have an uncle," I surmised.

"I got an uncle, and he works at the mayor's office, but he does the same job we do. Except maybe Shit Patrol. Probably, they don't have that problem at the mayor's office. But that jerk back there don't need to know the details," he added, grinning. "He ain't gonna change, but maybe he'll reach for that club less. Enough about him. I see you got lucky since I've last seen you." He quickly reached over with deadly accuracy and pressed a hickey so hard it hurt.

"Don't even ask," I said, but told him the whole sorry story. "Can I ask you something?" I said, when I finished.

"It better not be about that shirt."

"It's not really *about* that Rush shirt. This past week? I remembered why you looked familiar, when I first saw you wearing it at school." Leonard Stoneham had been a big story in the city the year before. As careless or naive hikers had done over the years, Leonard had slipped and fallen in the Devil's Hole Ravine, a dangerous area in the Lower Niagara River Gorge. The water there was known as Bloody Run, after Senecas effectively retaliated against British soldiers in the 1700s. They always called the whites killing Indians "settling," but called Indians killing whites in response "massacres." Devil's Hole was not called a Settlement. I wondered if Leonard was a history buff. Most who'd fallen in were either critically wounded or washed away into the lower river whirlpool. Leonard was an anomaly. "I saw you on TV, didn't I?"

"Yup, you did."

"How bad were you injured? TV never said. You were just the Devil's Hole Miracle."

"Miracles have a funny way of playing out," he said, pulling into camp. "Touch my head, right here," he said, tapping his head above his left ear. The strange puffiness was familiar to me, like my grandfather's head after the Day of the Car Aerial.

"Now follow it." I traced a personal topographical map down his head. His survival seemed more miraculous with each inch.

"How are you still alive after that fall?" I asked.

"That girl you know, the 'Style Girl'?" He meant Christine. Camp Stylist was a euphemism for Camp Hygiene Monitor. Her duties included teaching proper washing, toothbrushing, showering, and in some cases, the concept of wiping, frequency of underwear changing. She also allocated plastic sheets and sleeping attire for chronic bed-wetters, and checked each camper for lice on entry. I did not envy her job. I'd cut a hundred lawns before I was willing to sit down with kids and tell them, yes, you do need to wash your ass, that it was okay, a good, healthy thing, even, as long as you had soap on your hands while doing it.

"Christine? Yeah, what about her?"

"Would she lend you her buzz clippers?"

"I wouldn't know what to do with them if she did," I said. I wasn't that keen on handling them, after they'd been through some questionable kid heads at camp. She of course practiced sanitation with all her instruments, but Science didn't always conquer Gross.

"It's easy. Just slap on the guard and you're all set. The Marines don't like recruits showing up to Boot Camp with their hair already buzzed—makes you look too eager. But I got a year to grow it back. Will you borrow her clippers and buzz my hair, before the kids get here?"

"What?" I was trying to figure out the punch line here, but none came. It felt like I was getting ready to stumble into a darkened RV and see more intimacies I should not be seeing.

"Look, you didn't share your world with me. I let you know I was stuck with my dad's screwed-up new family this past week, and you had something interesting to do, but you just didn't think I was good enough to enter your space, or whatever. Didn't want to be seen hanging out with a white guy at the big Indian event?"

"No!" The idea of some white kid wanting to attend was totally baffling. "Look, I just couldn't imagine outsiders being interested. Some of the Rez doesn't even go." I couldn't remember the last time my ma went. "It's just people hanging out, being with friends."

"Exactly," he said, quietly. "I thought *we* were friends. Or, we are, as far as I'm concerned. But you just cut me off, left me with these people who invaded my house."

"I'm sorry." I didn't know what else to say. "I am. We are friends. Okay, I'll get the clippers, but you really want me using them?"

"Just get them and meet me at our cabin," he said, grabbing our duffels.

I found Christine with Johnnie, painting Christine's nails black to match her own. Christine was willing to do me the favor, offered to buzz him herself, and came along.

"I want Waterson to do this," Leonard said, when we showed up together. He had an extension cord out and a towel wrapped around his bare shoulders. Christine admired his exposed chest and six-pack, defined with just a sprinkling of adult hair. She started to protest, but he stopped her silent with one question. "Have you told him the truth yet?" She looked down.

"About what?" I asked. "You know, I'm getting tired of always being on the outside of everybody's story." With that, Leonard plugged in the clipper.

"Buzz the hair off my head," he said. "All of it, but leave the mustache. Start at that place." I did as I was told and decided not to mention that his mustache was so faint, I didn't think the clippers would catch the hairs. The clumps fell to the rough planks of our cabin's front deck. Beneath his dense head of hair was a long, crudely worn road map, from just behind where his hairline began and all way to the back. "I *am* too good a hiker to fall," he said, in almost a whisper. "I've been hiking the gorge with my dad since I was seven." I put the fragments of truth together with what he'd told me through the summer. His mother would have been three months in the grave when he took a leap off the top of the gorge, hoping to make his last hike, ever.

When I was done, he unplugged the clipper and gave it back to Christine, who told him she'd buzz it again for him if he wanted, before we all went back to school that fall.

"I'm gonna shower these hairs off, or they'll keep me up," he said, shaking off his towel.

"If you shit in the corner, you're cleaning it up yourself," I said. He smiled, but no laugh.

"You should tell him," he said to Christine. "He ain't nearly as smart as either of you think." He walked toward the shower and toilet building.

"You want to tell me what he's talking about?" I asked Christine, as we watched him go.

"He doesn't *know* what he's talking about. White guys think they know everything. My dad? Thinks that's his house. Now that my mom's gone, it's mine. I could throw him out if I wanted. Start a new life with someone else. Someone from the reservation." She stood. "If I desired." Then she walked away. A big part of me hoped this was just her, repeating the ideas we'd all grown up with. The reservation was a finite piece of land, and though no one could stop you from marrying a non-Indian, you were always reminded that the land had to remain in the hands of someone enrolled. Kids from those families sometimes talked big like that, to show they understood the complexities of their lives.

If it was more than that, I began to wonder if someone had told her about her dad's RV adventure. I didn't think Randy was that big a bastard, but it was a packed camper. Word would get around.

Leonard and I fell into our routine for the night. The new campers would arrive soon, and at the campfire, I suspected he'd tell safe stories about benevolent hairy monsters who wanted to be left alone. "Why did you want me to cut your hair?" I asked, when we went to bed.

"Gotta get used to it. When my dad looks, he laughs, but he knows I'm a great hiker too." He paused, then pulled two beers from under the bed. "You really stupid enough to believe that girl sucked on your neck and gave you hickeys so you could impress some other girl?"

"That's why you were prodding Christine? Rez women are crazy bossy. If one's interested? You know. You might be the only one, but you'll know. So yes, of course that's why she did it, man. She has no interest in me, whatsoever. Now go to sleep," I finished, laughing a small, forced laugh, finishing another Bigfoot story for myself, one about wandering alone in the dark.

CHAPTER FIFTEEN

For the Driver

(1982)

Tim Sampson might have bought a ton of doughnuts every New Years, but in most Rez houses, we watched the weather while our mothers baked cookies—Christmas cut outs, Mexican Wedding, Italian Funeral, Russian Tea, chocolate chip, molasses, applesauce. This year, for the first time, I'd hit the age where I'd know what a New Year's Eve hangover was all about.

My ma's family played nickel-ante poker Saturday nights, and on New Year's Eve, they cranked it to a quarter. Some cousins and I reenacted *The Poseidon Adventure*'s devastating tidal wave, hurling ourselves across our living room, free-falling to the couch, over and over, practicing for the real thing at midnight, to do it right, as neighbors fired shotguns into the night.

This year, almost seventeen, I left Stella Stevens and Ernest Borgnine behind, their on-screen marital problems in care of my younger second cousins. My ma dropped me off at Randy's. She pretended it wasn't a drinking party. "You New-Yahhing with them?" she asked.

"Maybe," I said, "why?"

"Well, do I need to borrow a car to take you around?"

"If I'm home," I said, "I'll go with Joanne and Orville's kids." Rez old-timers insisted the New Year began at Midwinter, one moon cycle later. So, on January first, we spread the word that the New Year had arrived, like homeowners hadn't heard the guns and M-80s. Households thanked us with cookies. From the good houses, we negotiated for an extra—allegedly "for the driver"—which may have been true, at best, fifty percent of the time.

People came to our door either as the sun rose or just before the New Year's Feast at noon. My ma's cookies were the envy of the Rez. But folks prone to Eee-ogg claimed they were too close to Feast for the Dead cookies, allegedly flirting with death. So her willingness to make up her own rules added to the "relatives only" vibes of our New Year's Eve shindig. I wanted to be like everyone else, but going to parties at the Night House was like courting a human bug zapper. You were inexplicably drawn back to the humming lights, even if your wings burned off some.

My mustache had thickened to Good Enough to Buy Gas Station Beer. When Randy popped facial hair in the fall, we started looking ahead to checking out a New Year's Eve bar party.

"Hmph" was all my ma could muster. She'd been through this conversation twice before. "Well, see you next year, den," she said, pulling in. Randy's driveway was packed with cars, glowing in a dull frost coat. "Don't let DogLips switch dice midgame, and don't let anyone use their own." She hit reverse as my door shut, casting light into the exhaust cloud behind us.

The maze of vehicles told me who was inside, Dusty and Lena, Margaret, Moose Knuckle, others. So many people shouldn't have fit in there. One vehicle sheathed in ice slicked my insides with dread. Tim Sampson's truck had been there awhile. Meduse was probably with him, and things weren't the same between her and me, after Leonard claimed I was too stupid to notice her feelings. I used her nickname in a teasing voice, but it kept our conversations light.

I had to squeeze in the door. Meduse whipped around the entryway, grabbed my scarf, drew my head down, and planted one on me, her cold tongue tingling my mouth with cinnamon schnapps. I pulled away, and she yelled, "Happy New Year!" at me, while everyone hooted.

I freed myself from the scarf, dodging further excavations. She slapped my arm and told me to lighten up and celebrate. Randy handed me a beer in the kitchen. "What the hell was that all about?" I asked him when we got near enough to the stereo that no one else would hear us.

"Meduse must like the taste of your sweaty Adam's Apple, from when she worked those suck marks all over you." I'd yet to live this down.

"Want some snobs?" Meduse displayed a shiny flask hanging off her handcuff belt.

"No thanks," I said, "This is fine." I debated whether it would be better to correct her pronunciation, so other people didn't give her shit, or just hope no one else noticed.

"Suit yourself, Briney." A pet name? A nickname meaning I tasted salty?

I wandered away. She seemed drunk, and it wasn't even nine o'clock. I wanted to encourage her to slow down, but Rez Party Protocol dictated you were on your own, and if you became the entertainment, it was on you. I'd planned out how I was going to avoid being the official Sloppy Drunk this year; she seemed to be campaigning for the nomination.

"Your ma know you're here?" Moose-Knuckle Stew asked, lumbering toward me.

"She dropped me off," I said, looking for any other disasters migrating my way.

"All right, you little shit. Well, tonight's your night, then. Don't be puking on that jacket I gave you." He grabbed my lapels and knocked his bottle against mine, then let a Doppler Effect belch rip through the room, like a train disappearing in the distance.

"Well?" I said to Randy when we were finally alone. "Let's get the—"

"Gotta wait till my dad's drunker. Enjoy the party." Kitten yelled for Randy to get more ice, so he headed out the back door. Tiffany poured chips into bowls, ignoring me.

Tim Sampson sat at the kitchen table with DogLips, Kitten, Moose Knuckle, Margaret, and some men who'd been in the RV. Most had wives here, rolling dice with a big pot of bills, and promises piled in the center. Little Eva was decidedly absent, but a woman from Dead Man's leaned against Tim Sampson, thigh to thigh. He'd hold his cupped hand to her mouth, and she'd blow into it, touching his forearm. "FF, you rolling or getting blown?" DogLips yelled. Did the women know what FF stood for? Maybe they just thought he had a Rez Alphabet Name, the way people still called Gihh-rhaggs "MGM," all this time later.

We were allowed one album side for every two the adults wanted, and they had veto power. We settled for *Through the Past, Darkly*, pretty much everyone agreeing on early Stones.

"I brought some of the Cure," Meduse said. Her specialty: New Wave bands no one had heard of. "In the truck!" She tugged my arm. "Come get it with me. You still got your jacket on."

"It's too damn cold," I said, bold in my new adulthood. "Go find your own Cure." People laughed, but when I added, "try penicillin," they shut up and let Mick Jagger look for someone to spend the night with. Adults would laugh, retelling it later, but FF was currently at the table.

"Fine." Meduse yanked a ridiculous black cape from the coat pile, flashed its red satin lining.

"I'll just stand here," I said, from the porch, sparking a cig and blowing the first puff up into the sharp night, breath vapor disappearing as hazier smoke pushed through. "You go on ahead." She skidded to the FF Truck in these weather-unsuitable spiky black boots, snatching something from the front seat. "They don't have an 8-track," I yelled.

"This is even better," she said, leaning in deep. "Will you come here?"

"No one else wants to hear that," I said, joining her. "They'll just make you take it off."

"This," she said, revealing a massive piece of hardware, "is a boom box." It held a radio, tape player, two speakers, and a tiny equalizer. That would have cost a summer month's wages.

"How can you afford that shit?" I asked.

"Insurance. I told you before. Everything had to be in my name, since my dad can't own any land on the reservation. When my mom died, everything became mine and Hayley's, and she's out of here. Why do you think I can drink at this party at my age?" She seemed not to realize that half the party was underage drinkers. "Could throw my dad on his ass if I wanted to, right now, so he keeps in line." I guessed she hadn't heard about Little Eva. She grinned in the far-off porch light, taking a flask hit. I could hear myself mumbling similar things to no one under my breath when my dad appeared at my place. "Such a ratty jacket! You need to snag a new one!"

"We don't all have insurance, Vampirella," I said, hearing myself, too.

"Sorry, I didn't mean that. I'm not wishing sadness and loss on anyone but . . ." Increasingly, I was feeling like I barely knew her at all.

"Don't worry," she said, reaching up to stroke my cheek. "I know you're not like that." I stepped out of reach. She never acted this way, though Leonard's comments from the summer had stayed with me. Was this a new weird prank she and Randy cooked up? I was gonna have to stay on guard till we peeled, waiting for the trick cigarette to explode in my face.

"Look," I said. "Unless you brought tapes, you're out of luck. Only records in there."

"Covered!" she weirdly sang, revealing a case of cassettes. "Here, put this in your pocket, then give me a hand." She went into the truck and started struggling with the box. I glanced at the cassette she handed me, then took the boom box. The bench, shoved back all the way to accommodate her giant dad, still barely fit this very expensive toy.

"You can't take this in there." I slid the cassette across the bench, harder to reach. Before she could protest, I clarified. "Look, I'll bring this in, help you. I don't want you falling on those spikes. But that crowd? They'll eat you alive." The cassette she'd handed me was called *Pornography*. I'd never heard it. I'd heard The Cure, but didn't know their music well. "There's just no way a sixteen-year-old Rez girl announces at a party that she loves *Pornography* without getting grief. Don't you have enough of that already?"

"It's just the name of an album," she said. "And we both know there's real pornography in there, magazines probably on an end table," she added, a hint of bitterness coloring that last.

"It don't matter that *DogLips* has a bunch of porn in his house." She looked at me, and I looked back, meeting her eyes, so she'd know I wasn't another person goofing on her. "Only some people get a pass. And neither of us belongs to that group."

"You ought to know," she said. "But the way you come back here, over and over, I don't get it. You could have your own life." I held her tape player up to her face, so she'd see her reflection in the shiny back panel and notice that she, too, was at this party with people who mostly gave her grief. What she said stung, but only because she was right.

"Look. Where we live?" I said. "You can be *kind of* weird, more than in the white world, but there are still lines drawn, and you gotta already know that, right?"

She leaned into me and nodded, at least not reaching for the cassette. "Aren't you chilly in this flimsy jacket?" she asked again, tugging at it a second time. I nodded and grabbed the boom box, passing her the cassette case. I hoped she understood what I was saying. You didn't listen to Rush unless you were willing to take some shit. I'd been given enough to develop armor and accept teasing, and she probably had, too, but there was no need to beg others to hassle you.

Inside, we lugged them upstairs, trailing everyone our ages, all eager to hear this thing. Christine put on a tape. Instantly I recognized the synth plunge and thrumming drums that set up "Tom Sawyer." Rush had recently shifted focus in their sound and themes, singing about the baggage we're stuck with, social connections and misfires, similarities and differences, and how we balance our drives, between emotional and rational. They were ideas I loved, as if this band from across Lake Ontario were mining the mistakes of my life so far, and setting them to music.

The songs of Rush meant so much to me, I'd been trying to write similar pieces myself. They rhymed like lyrics. I knew poems didn't rhyme much anymore, but I had no musical talent. It was enough to write ideas and memories. There were poems about my grandfather, my siblings leaving, meeting the Giantess, the Tin Man, and of course, Gihh-rhaggs. They were poems I knew I'd never show my ma. I didn't plan on showing anyone, but *she* didn't need to be reminded of the sadnesses that filled her life like overstuffed boxes. Some of them grew from poems into paragraphs, stories, life too complicated to be contained in a box as small as a poem.

To everyone at this party, these stories would be boring, too intimate. We didn't talk about those things. And the Rush lyrics were buried in complex music, constantly shifting rhythms, not inviting for people who loved dancing. As soon as the next song, "Red Barchetta," came on, people got bored. I raised my eyebrows and Meduse hit the eject, flipping in Cheap Trick's *Live at Budokan*. Eventually, "I Want You to Want Me" came on. The music wasn't danceable, but people started squeezing close, grinding on each other to the beat like they were catching some Saturday Night Fever in the drafty upstairs of an ancient reservation house.

DogLips bellowed for Randy to get more ice as we slipped downstairs. Closer to the door, I stepped into the snow-packed yard, not bothering with my jacket. The back door opened while I tried balancing four ice bags. Lucky break, I thought.

"Hey," I said, "did you—" I dropped the bags. FF stood, one arm braced above his head, like the last time I'd seen him, his other hand behind his back. Piss steamed a vapor trail cloud off the snow mound in front of him.

"Did I what?" he said, continuing on, like a fountain.

"Nothing, I thought you were somebody else."

"My daughter?"

"No, definitely not your daughter." He finished with a little shiver, straightened up, and bunched his fists at the front of his jeans. He jiggled the fabric, before bending way forward, thumbs in his waistband, popping everything back inside. The bizarre singular dance Randy had acted out for me that summer. FF zipped up and lumbered steadily toward me, shattering deep impressions into the skein of icy snow beneath his boots.

"Why'n't you set those down and come with me," he said, relieving me of the bags I'd struggled with a few minutes ago, effortlessly tossing them next to the door.

"It's a little—"

"Don't worry about the cold. Here." He took off his puffy orange down vest and slid it on me, his arm surrounding my shoulders. Guided so forcefully, I had no choice. He turned us to the side yard instead of the back door, steady the whole time, more a command than an invitation. He kept the pressure as we reached the front, filled with cars and trucks cocooned in dense frost.

"Here, use this door," he said when we reached his truck, the passenger's side totally blocked by tall wild bushes lining Randy's driveway. I slid over, tossing the Cure tape in the glove compartment as FF got in. "Keys," he said, holding a gigantic, calloused palm before me. The enormity of him this close made me reconsider my current position.

"I don't—"

"Vest pocket." I stuck my arms out the armholes and found the pockets. In one was a set of keys, and in another, two packs of smokes. I considered claiming they weren't there. "Let's you and me take a ride," he said, starting the truck.

"Tim, I don't think that's such a good . . ." I started.

"You know," he said, "what is it with you Indian kids? You call me by my first name. No respect. It's Mr. Sampson."

"No," I said. "Not out here." He hadn't given me an easy path. I might as well actually engage him. "You're in Indian territory, and I was taught to welcome people, be familiar, to only be really polite when I don't like someone."

"So you like me then."

"I don't *dislike* you." What was I going to say? "Tell you the truth, I haven't thought much about you one way or the other, ever." Admitting terror didn't seem like the best strategy. I also never knew how people responded to my family's history with Gihh-rhaggs. I decided to leave his brother out of the equation. "I know you sometimes gambled at my ma's house, with Christine's mom." The word Christine felt like a foreign object in my mouth, one of those clamp things they used at the dentist's, but calling her *Meduse* at the moment seemed like a singularly bad idea.

"Yeah, Vestal never did like the games, even though Night said dice was part of the traditional religion. She refused to hear that, or approve of playing, much else in public for that matter. And once my brother died coming home from the track, whew, that was it for her. Proof of the wages of sin." All the while he talked, he'd expertly backed us out of the jammed driveway, dodging the five thousand cars randomly parked behind him. We drove up and down Rez roads in silence for a while, and then I asked if I could bum a smoke, since my jacket was in the house. He asked me to light one for him first, so I performed that stupid trick I used to do at Margaret's, sticking two cigs in my mouth and lighting them both.

"Don't you think people are gonna wonder where we are?" I said, watching the snow pick up, as I knew it would from the weatherman. The weatherman had also said to be careful out there tonight, and I most certainly had not done that.

"Nah," he said, all blustery, "they'll think you puked on your shirt and that I took you home, or that we made a run, or maybe nobody's even paid any attention. A lot of people at that party. Easy to go unnoticed. Here, let me have my vest back. It's warm enough now."

"I gotta take a leak," I said, sliding out of the vest as we neared a cousin's house.

"You just did," he said, driving on without lifting his gigantic foot from the gas.

"No. You did. I was getting ice. Which people are going to wonder about. They were expecting me to bring it right in." He turned down Moon Road, where a bunch of people partied in cars despite the temperature. We drove past without slowing. I hoped to recognize any car, but they were all hulking snow-covered mounds, vague movement and cigarette light behind steamed windows. On to Dead Man's and then Bite Mark, where we both lived.

The closer we got to my place, he sped up, our momentum carrying us on top of the new snow, gliding past my ma and her group frightening themselves, calling and seeing cards with quarters they couldn't afford to lose. The ride had that weird black ice floating feeling, like Luke Skywalker's landspeeder, fine unless we needed to stop suddenly. We arced around the corner with Snakeline, toward the Picnic Grove parking field where he'd become FF. He touched the brake lightly and turned the wheel sharp as we slid into the entry.

"Good a place as any," he said, shutting the truck off. "Go around back. I don't want you tracking deposits into my truck." No cars came, and we were nowhere near houses I could reasonably escape to, so I got back in after. "Let's try for some different scenery," he said. We passed the border signs and headed north beyond the Rez. I asked him what time it was. I could see the Twist-O-Flex watchband on his furry wrist, but he claimed he didn't know.

"You could get a DWI out here," I said. "This isn't the Rez. Not so forgiving."

"I don't need forgiveness," he said. "Put that radio on. Pick what you want. I don't get to choose with my little girl. Always that doom-and-gloom shit with her, or the noise you like." I found an oldies station playing the Beatles. Snow whipped around us, gathering on roads and all the trees. I didn't see one house on this road I'd never been down before. "Ain't gonna hear your group on this station. Go ahead and change it if you want."

"What makes you think you know what I like?" I said, as he slowed down and did a three-pointer, almost sliding into a ditch. "What are you doing?"

"Hitchhiker back there. Bad night to be hitching. Thought we'd pick him up. All right?" Was I supposed to pretend I had a vote? The hitcher jumped in, forcing me into the center, where I noticed, for the first time, that FF had a resonant scent. It wasn't the sharp wild odor of someone sweating in a summer basketball game. It felt closer to the scent of people who wear clothes they like too frequently, or too long. Not bad, exactly; more familiar, worn in.

I recognized a version from my own body on winter days when it was too cold to pump extra water pails outside, and too drafty for the bedroom pan baths. Those days, I allowed myself to smell natural, and told myself no one noticed. FF's scent was different, but still, I knew it, and knew it from somewhere else too. Eventually it came. He smelled like Gihh-rhaggs, or my memory of him. FF rested his arm on the seat back to give me more room and the surging scent became like a physical presence, nearly shoving me into the new passenger, who didn't seem to notice at all. In a way that defied logic, I suddenly missed Gihh-rhaggs as if he'd just died.

"Dangerous night to be hitching," FF said to our passenger. "Where you headed?"

"Anywhere," the stranger said, slapping his arms, clapping his hands together, cupping them and blowing in. "City, anywhere near the city. Thanks a lot, man. Thought I was gonna lose some fingers tonight." He wore a hooded sweatshirt under a Carhartt jacket, no gloves. Jeans and sneakers. He was ill prepared, at best, for walking outside on New Year's Eve.

"We'll take you anywhere you want. We ain't doing nothing, right? Just riding around and listening to music. No hurry," FF said.

"Um, okay, that's cool. Man, thanks again, I been walking for an hour. Cars don't slow down, let alone consider picking you up," the stranger said, relaxing, thawing.

"I always pick up a hitchhiker. How I met my wife. She picked me up one night walking home. I warned her that I coulda been anyone, and she was just this bitty thing." I'd never considered Vestal Sampson *a bitty thing*, but I supposed she had been, sidled up next to him. "She said sometimes you just gotta take a chance." I couldn't picture Vestal Sampson picking anyone up either. Like Pastor Clyde, she drove past me on many wintry nights as I walked the roads, and she knew that she'd go right by my house on her way home.

"Can I get a smoke from one of you guys?" FF nodded to me, pointing slightly with his lips that I should get them from his vest pocket. He must have picked up this Rez gesture from all his years of living with us. I lit three at once and passed the other two over. "You guys got any beers? I can smell 'em."

"All out," FF said immediately. "So what kinda music you like?"

"Don't know. Easy to please. Usually driver's choice, right? This is cool, can't go wrong with the Beatles." There seemed to be a marathon, one of those "Beatles A to Z" things. They'd been playing straight through since I turned the radio on.

"What would you think of a girl who paid enough attention to what you liked that she knew without you ever telling her?"

"Bitches like that get on my nerves, man," the stranger said, shaking his head and laughing. "Always hounding you and shit? Ask you questions and act like there ain't wrong answers? Nah, that wouldn't be cool." FF was quiet for a while, pretending I wasn't supposed to know what he was saying. Close to the city, the stranger invited us to a party that had been his ultimate destination. He insisted we'd done him this huge favor, and all kinds of nonsense like that, bumming another cig until FF declared we didn't have any more, which I knew to be a lie.

"This party was so good you were walking from Lockport to the Falls for it?" FF eventually said, when we passed into city limits.

"Gonna be a good one. You guys come in. I'll hook you up. Only a few more blocks, over the line into BC. Wanna say thanks for bringing me along." I'd lost track of the twists and turns FF had taken and hadn't realized we'd crossed into a bad place for me. Indians stayed out of Belden Center, and the B.C. Boys didn't come to the Rez. We kept order that way. "Just left Nancy Jay tonight," the stranger said. "Nowhere else to go.

They turn you out, don't care that you don't got no ride. Ain't complaining. Anywhere's better. So I knew about this party, figured what the hell. Didn't count on no one picking me up. Sure glad for your niceness, kindness."

"Nancy Jay?" I asked. Was this someone I was supposed to know?

"All right, well, this'll probably get you far enough," FF said, pulling over. "Your party's only a couple blocks up. We've got a few more stops of our own. Didn't realize how late it was getting. Now you be good and stay out of trouble."

"You know it, man." The stranger climbed out. "Least the next six months, anyway," he added, slamming the door. He pounded on the hood before walking off in one direction, then stopped and turned around to cross the street.

"N.C.J." FF said, enunciating each letter clearly. "Niagara County Jail."

"Jail! Are you fucking crazy? Why did you pick up a hitchhiker anyway? That guy could have killed us!" I said, imagining horrible things that would have, in truth, put someone in prison, not county lock up. This guy was probably in for what FF was doing right now: DWI.

"Do you honestly think many people are going to start shit with me?" he asked, reaching his hand over, covering the entire top of my head.

"Suppose not, but it's not like you're big enough to stop bullets."

"Wouldn't need to. Lotta lowlifes are opportunists. They pick the easy target. Me? I'm not an easy target. And even if they tried, they'd be flat out before they could pull a gun on me. Let's go get a drink," he said, pulling over. "I assume you have some kind of fake ID." He got out of the truck, expecting me to follow. Loud music poured out of a couple bars, neon blazing in windows. I could get into one of them, maybe even find a ride home, but I'd never been to this part of the city before, and aside from those few explorations with Leonard, hadn't entered a bar since I prowled around them as a kid, with Tim's brother.

"I do, but I don't want to have a drink with you," I said, outside the truck. This was not the New Year's Eve I'd planned for myself. Randy had probably already lifted his dad's keys and was even now partying in some other bar, while I was stuck near some old white guy with issues and mildly questionable hygiene habits.

"Ruined your plans, did I?" FF said. "You and that little shit planning to steal his dad's car again and go out? He tried that last year, at my house, and when he failed and passed out on my couch, you know what he did? Got the spins, lifted my couch cushions, and puked under them before passing out again. Which is why *his* folks are hosting the party this year. We caught him before he could leave the reservation a year ago. Dragged him back." He paused and smiled.

"I guess you didn't know that. You weren't cool enough last year to be included? Not useful enough? Now that you got these little whiskers," he said, lightly pinching my cheek, tugging at the longest strands of my mustache, "you got the power. Better use it now. Your buddy gets more than peach fuzz, you won't be so handy anymore. We were chosen last year 'cause my house is close to the border. He figured: easy escape.

"And the funny thing? He pulled off me hosting a party I had no intention of throwing, by promising my little girl that *you* would be there. Total lie, I'm guessing. *Did* you know we had a party last year?" I hadn't. I'd even asked Randy if there was one, and he'd told me his mom was sick. There were probably other parties around the Rez, but a lot of people just stuck to hanging with their gigantic extended families. My desire to have friends I wasn't related to was maybe more unusual across the Rez than I'd realized, but I was born in between cousin groups. I was too young for some and already beginning to feel way too old to do kids stuff. I helped my ma make cookies and worked my last *Poseidon Adventure* tidal wave routine with the cousins, wondering all night if anyone I knew was doing something more exciting.

"You wanna know what they call you when you're not there?" he asked.

I shook my head. No matter what, reservation nicknames were never flattering, and most often they acted like that yellow blood in *Alien*—acid, burning you with your own failings.

"I bet you don't. That's the way, isn't it? History tells me my little girl has a nickname, and that you know what it is." I looked for any place to go. Convenience stores were closed up for the night, the diner shut down. Outside the closest bar, guys took hits off a joint in plain sight, and as we approached, they smiled. I thought they were going to offer it to me, but instead they reached out to FF. "Thought you'd see it my way," he said, throwing his monstrous arm back over my shoulder and shaking hands with these grizzled men in the doorway, familiar with them.

For a regular night, this place would have been dead. That is, according to what everyone had told me about bars. How much fun they were, how packed with people out for the best nights of their lives. This room was semifilled at most, old men and women huddled and mumbling over drinks, copping a quick feel here and there among the shadows and occasionally laughing loudly. FF and I stepped up to empty barstools.

He ordered a double Irish whiskey neat for himself and a Coke for me, downing his immediately and knocking the glass on the bar for another. "Here, pay with this." He handed me a hundred-dollar bill and wandered off toward the juke box.

"I can't take this," the tender said. "Need my change on a night like tonight." I pulled a ten from my pocket, asking for a beer to be added. He took the ten, asked for ID, laughed at mine, threw it back, and brought me another Coke with my change. When FF came back, I held the bill out, told him he owed me and that I couldn't get served.

"Course you can't get served," he said, ignoring the hundred in my hand. "You're a punk. A punk who likes to call my little girl names. Maybe even sometimes to her face, I bet." He ordered another double, beginning to slur his words. "Besides," he said, "I need a driver. No way can I get behind the wheel right now."

"Maybe your friend from Nancy Jay can," I said. "I don't have a license."

"Who said anything about that? No Rush on the jukebox. Pay the man. We're going."

"I already did," I said.

"Not for that double I just had," he said, waving the new glass he'd just drained. "Could order another, if you want."

"Fine," I said, and paid out of my pocket again, heading for the door before he could order a third. "And I could have told you there'd be no Rush on the juke," I added, as we reached the truck. A delicate layer of frost was already forming on it. "Look, I really don't know how to drive. I've never even driven the Rez before. I know a lot of kids do, but . . ."

He held his hands up and repeated: "You don't think *I* can drive." I eventually climbed in the driver's seat and started the truck, trying not to hit the car behind us. "You're over-steering," he said. "Minor adjustments. When you see a curve, then turn, just a bit, keep in line with everything in front of you. Don't anticipate anything. Just respond," he said.

Mostly I responded, "Well, *you* fucking drive," and he'd raise his hands again. I kept flooring the gas, and then the brake, unable to get it right until he coached me, one slight increment of pressure at a time, to the point we'd reached an appropriate speed.

"Now just keep it there and relax," he said. "You don't want to draw attention to yourself. That's the way you survive. You learn to drive in a winter storm, you can drive in any weather. This is the way to do it." Every car in my rearview was a cop. I was sure of it. It was New Year's Eve, after all. My neck started to ache, the muscles tensing, my balls trying to push up into my belly, which was itself crawling up to my rib cage. I'd heard some kids on the Rez learned this way. I felt like an idiot having fallen for it, even with warning, but Tim Sampson wasn't from the Rez officially. He just lived there now.

By the time we hit the border to home, the wheel seemed almost familiar, vibrating against my hands. We neared FF's house and he told me to pull in the driveway.

I'd let go of the idea that we'd get back to the party. I could imagine people commenting on our return as we pulled in, then shutting up when we entered. They'd say, "Hey, look, it's Fuck Face and _____." I still didn't know, and didn't want to know, what they called me when I wasn't there. It was nearing midnight and the only person at the party who might really want to see me was Meduse.

Randy was probably long gone, but I knew without being told that I'd only been a potential ticket to a bar for him, nothing more. "Come on in," FF said, pulling the keys from the ignition, still pretending I had a choice. "I'll get you a beer. We're okay now. No cops." I could see the entryway, already set up for the kids who'd come by in the morning, but there were no doughnuts yet. He noticed me looking and explained he'd get up super early and they'd be waiting for him when the bakery opened. I'd never been inside their house, but it was warm and dark. Evidently, Meduse had taken to decorating in her newfound powers. Thick red-velvet curtains covered the sliding-glass doors opening to the deck. The dining room table was covered with a black cloth and *Phantom of the Opera*–type candelabras.

No goat heads? Upside-down crosses? Dead bunnies pinned to the walls? Chickens in birdcages? All these things I'd normally whisper to Randy stayed in my throat like hot hangover pipes on a Sunday morning. FF handed me a beer and walked me down the hall. "Thought you might want to see this," he said, opening the door to Meduse's room.

I was glad my ma rarely let anyone in our house; it would never even occur to her to open my bedroom wide to someone without my permission. Still, curiosity got me and I leaned my head inside. Most of my expectations were met: fake skulls, more candles, lace and velvet shrouding the mirror, posters of people in long hooded robes holding lanterns. A portrait-size copy of my sophomore school photo sat wedged into the mirror frame. "I don't suppose you gave her that picture." I shook my head. My mom had thought the school photographers shortchanged the order, but I'd paid for them myself with my job money, so she didn't complain.

I'd learned a month ago that someone had stolen the couple missing. One had wound up on the Music Room bulletin board with word balloons that changed weekly. A Jazz Band kid I'd helped dodge a fight brought it to me, modified—eyes crossed and the faint real mustache colored in, like a barbershop quartet handlebar. He included a sampling of the word balloons: MY MOM CLEANS TOILETS, MY CLOTHS USED TO BELONG TO THE WHITE FAMILY'S MY MOM WORKS FOR, I SHOWER AT SCHOOL CUZ I DONT HAVE ONE AT HOME, EVEN MY UNDERPANTS ARE SECONDHAND.

While grammatically incorrect, all were more or less true, and not things I broadcast. I tossed the others without reading. I had an idea of their topics. Only one person knew those details who also had access to the Music Room: Randy had been singing in hero worship of his cousin Carson for years. They both had amazing singing voices, and when they started partying, their voices grew more distinctive harmonies together. And now here was the second missing photo.

FF took it out of the mirror frame and handed it to me. On the bed was a black leather jacket sitting inside a gift box. He tapped one of the corners. "Go ahead, try it on. I'm sure it fits." He stepped out of the room and pounded down the hall.

"I already have a jacket," I responded after him.

"Not like that one, you don't," he yelled. "Look at the back. Go on, pull it out." The jacket had that awesome new leather smell, the kind of scent that rolled over you when you walked into a fancy place like Chess King.

Embroidered across the back was the eternal Man in the Star, from Rush's *2112* album, the backside of a man, naked, exposed and defiant against a society that tried to block beauty from its people's lives. Beneath the jacket, lining the box, were a bunch of tapes—the entire Rush catalog, maybe close to eighty bucks worth. I had nothing to play them on, and I was really hoping there wasn't also a boom box somewhere in this room, with my name engraved on it. I didn't like the idea that the money Vestal Sampson had ensured to help her family's comfort was awkwardly filtering my way.

I slid the jacket back neatly into the box, the way it had been folded, and wedged my picture back where FF had taken it from. I wondered how much Randy had milked Meduse for it.

"I want to ask you something," FF said, looming behind, blocking the door. I raised my eyebrows waiting, with no chance to escape. "Guess you know my little girl now listens to what you do. Doesn't sound like the rest of her music, so I imagine she uses it to think of you."

"Sorry, not my fault," I said. "They're not for everyone. I never recommend them to anyone anymore." No one ever cared what bands anyone else liked, unless it was Rush, and then people had some pathological need to tell me how much they hated them.

"That's not what I'm saying," he corrected, holding a giant hand out in front of me. His imposing size made me feel like I was talking to Ben Grimm. "She's played it enough that some is familiar to me now, but how do you get interested in the first place? It just doesn't welcome you. I mean, I know I'm old, and young music is for young people, blah blah." This was definitely not a conversation I imagined ever having with anyone, let alone this bristly, ruddy giant barring me from any exit, stage left or otherwise.

"At first," I paused, thinking about the TV concert I'd stumbled on,

"I saw a live show on TV. It was exciting. I'd never been to a concert at the time. And I'd never seen or heard anything like it before, and well, I wanted something of my own. In our house, we had to share everything. Even my music was mostly hand-me-downs. Rush was mine, free and clear."

"It can't just be that," he said. "I mean, difference alone ain't reason enough. You have to want it, right?" Did he realize he was asking me about his own choices? His life would have been so much easier if he'd just fallen in love with someone who was white. But instead, his love for Vestal, I guess, made him willing to give up the entire world he'd known, to live by our rules.

"It was enough to get me interested," I said. "But when I bought my first Rush album, the ideas in all the songs drew me in."

"The ideas? What do you mean 'ideas'? How can you understand what they're saying?"

"You can if you listen," I said, but Geddy Lee's voice was the thing people complained about the most, and I never understood why. He didn't sound that different from Led Zeppelin. "They made me think." I wasn't about to tell this giant who'd casually taken me hostage how they'd inspired me to write, too.

"Anyway, there's one song that's different from the others. I guess it's about a park in Toronto. It's about not being able to keep the things you love, about how they always become memories. There's rides, fireworks, midway games. Always reminds me of the short period your brother was with us. He took us to the field days sometimes, the county fair. He promised State Fair, but it didn't happen. It was the only time I ever knew my ma to be happy."

"You get all that from one song?" he said, squinting. "By *that* band?"

"It made me see the world different. What more can you ask of art?"

"Kid? You sound like you're my age."

"I hear that a lot, too. Anyway, it's called Lakeside Park. I'd like to go there someday."

"Lakeside Park? Does the song mention a lighthouse?"

"Yeah, a lighthouse and a pier. Why?"

"That's in Port Dalhousie, St. Catharines, not Toronto." He smiled a distant smile.

"I don't think that's right," I said, but he persisted. "How do you know?" I countered.

"I've been there. Used to take Vestal, when we were first seeing each other." His stone face suddenly wavered, like a surge of water had washed over it. "Listen. Don't rush through life. Enjoy being young." He stood back and let me step out of the room, then followed me to the kitchen, opening the fridge with the door wide open. "Got a cousin who works for an embroidery firm, so she got Christine a deal on that work, but still . . . She was going to bring it tonight. I talked her out of that idea. Didn't figure we needed to make that kind of scene."

"If you wanna stop drawing attention to yourself, you might want to consider taking a leak like a normal guy," I said, figuring I owed him that much. Pissing outside was expected for guys at our bonfire parties, so he wasn't ever going to have a shortage of accidental audiences. "The Rez puts up with a lot of weirdness, but don't expect people to let it ride in silence. Not my business, but you give people ammo with this nonsense," I added, tugging at the crotch of my Levi's and jumping around like he had. "People already make fun of that. I'm surprised you haven't gotten a name for it."

"If that's the worst? I'm okay," he said, sitting at the kitchen counter and pulling out the other stool for me. "Guess I can tell you the truth. I've shown you this much. That, uh, method? It was a joke between me and Vestal. After I discovered you can pull over and whiz along the roadside out here, she always complained that I found excuses to do it too often, enjoyed it too much." He gave a little chuckle. "Probably, there was some truth to that." He shrugged.

"Guys don't do that off the Rez?" It had been a common part of my life thus far.

"Only if they wanna get arrested for indecent exposure. Better learn that one before you graduate. Whip it out beyond these borders, you're gonna get an appearance." I'd evidently been lucky, because I'd surely been incautious leaving bars some nights with Leonard. No wonder he gave me such funny looks when I did.

"Vestal didn't like that I wasn't washing my hands after. So, one time, she's in the tub and I go in, and I do that, you know, that thing, as a joke. I'd invented a way, practiced, then showed her I don't *need* to wash, since

I'm skilled enough to keep my hands clean. Stupid, I know, but it worked. She laughed and laughed," he said, smiling, and nodding to himself, his voice growing foggy. "I miss her laugh," he added, a shiver running through him. "The most."

"The most?" The least likely thing you could miss about someone you loved.

"Everyone thought she was all uptight, but she wasn't. She went to the church, regular, but she could . . ." He paused, then shrugged his shoulders and looked directly into my eyes, the way I had with his daughter, earlier, begging her not to bring her Cure music into the party. "She could make love like, well, like you probably have fantasies about. I've been around enough to know that's not always the case. Some people are lousy lays. But anyway, afterward, we'd cuddle up like house cats on a winter night."

I drained my beer and set it on the counter, but FF didn't seem to notice. His broad monolith of a body was right next to me, a couple feet away, but his mind was in some other place where he found pleasures I could only imagine. I know it sounded ridiculous, but I was still waiting. I wasn't waiting until marriage and a honeymoon or anything like that, but I did want my first time to be with someone I cared about, someone who cared about me. The idea of love was a distant dream, but after that embarrassing mess with Tiffany and Meduse, I wanted more than just satisfying horniness. I knew how to remedy that on my own.

"I miss her every day, in every place we were ever together," he continued after a pause. "So when I do that, that taking a whiz trick, it's like she's still here, laughing while I tease her. That probably sounds as dumb as can be, but when you know heartache, son—and you will—you'll understand that every heartache has its own sharp edges and you'll understand the strange things people'll do to dull them."

"You mind if I—?" I said, holding up my empty, hoping to end this conversation. I didn't need to know these deeply private things about any other person. I didn't want him to have regrets in the morning and I felt like maybe I'd been offered part of someone else's load.

"Help yourself." As I got one, and then grabbed him one too, explosions sounded in the distance. "So this is the New Year," he said, taking his bottle from my hand, clinking it against mine and draining it in one long chug. "Make any resolutions?"

"Don't believe in making promises I know I'm gonna break," I said, shaking my head. I'd been the recipient of enough of those to last a lifetime. "You?"

"For your sake, I did. When I saw you outside at Night's place, I resolved not to beat your ass tonight, even when I had the chance. The way my little girl listens to that noise you like and cries, I'd swear you must be some astronaut stranded on the moon, and she's awaiting your rescue mission." He lit two cigarettes and passed me one. "Course, resolutions are meant most often to be broken. To show us our own weaknesses."

"Look, man. I've never done *one thing* to your daughter. We've been friendly forever and even pretty close friends, but you, out of anyone, gotta know how complicated it is." I didn't even know when Meduse and I silently agreed to stop hanging out full time; maybe when things had gotten too awkward after those hickeys and Leonard's accusations. "I'm the first to admit I'm nothing to look at, but being homely isn't gonna make me go out with someone I don't like in that particular way. I don't know why she's latched onto me. Maybe she thinks I'm the only guy who's lonelier than her? Maybe 'cause she used to cut my hair, but whatever her feelings might be? They're just not mutual on my end."

"You were friends, before. You said so, yourself, and . . . she's lonely," FF said, taking a drag on his cigarette, his breath hitching in exhale. "She's a nice girl, but she's lonely," he repeated. "Done what I can, but I can't be her world. I'm just . . . her dad," he said, as if this were not a significant thing. "She'd make an awfully good wife. True for life. What more could you ask for? I just want her to be happy," he finished, his voice breaking like glass in a fire. Those gigantic shoulders started to shake. I patted his shoulder, not knowing what else to do.

He reached over and I braced for getting clocked, and trying to find my way to the door before the second punch came. Instead, he embraced me, wrapping both of his arms around my shoulders, pinning me to the chair, his weight crushing as he heaved and wept. His bristly cheek felt like a wire brush against my own cheek, his tears, warm. If he'd done this to anyone at Randy's house, everyone in the room, maybe even the house,

would have burst out laughing, and would have later reenacted his "crying jag," writing it off as the byproduct of too many beers.

I tried reaching around, patting his back, my hands whispering on the
shiny surface of that downy vest, holding him in whatever way I could. I
guessed that's what you were supposed to do. He was so broad my hands
didn't come anywhere near touching each other, which was how I saw
people holding each other on TV. I realized in that moment I'd never been
hugged before. Not even when Meduse had given me the hickeys, zeroing
in with clinical aim, one spot, working it, and moving on.

I don't know how long we held each other that way, lost in our own
lonely chasms. I embraced him the best I could in return, trapped in my
own wonder, not moving, afraid the slightest shift would break this world
apart and shatter his resolve. Were you supposed to say things in situations like this, or was physical contact enough? I didn't know. Did you lie
and tell the other person everything was going to be all right? That didn't
seem like a lie I could tell right then.

Why didn't they teach this stuff in Health, instead of telling us the benefits of washing thoroughly, using deodorant, and the ways to shave, how
to put a condom on a banana, shit most of us already knew? FF eventually
lightened the weight. I didn't know how long was too long in the hug
department, so I stayed, decreasing exactly as he did. He finally let go, and
I slowly lowered my arms to my sides. He sighed and wiped his nose on
the sleeve of his flannel shirt.

"Vestal would know what to do, but I sure don't. What would be so
hard about taking her on a date?" He pulled another hundred-dollar bill
from the wad in his pants pocket. "Look, I know you ain't got much. I
remember the insides of your house. That was where I got into the habit
of going outdoors first." He shook his head.

"My brother warned me not to ask where the john was, the first time
he invited me to your place, because you didn't have but a little two-gallon
plastic bucket. That's when he told me a lot of guys go outside anyway. He
was always giving me tips about living on the reservation. Even if I hadn't
seen those cardboard walls inside your house, everybody knows your mom
and those other gals from out here wouldn't do that job if they had a

different choice. Nobody scrubs someone else's toilet unless they're desperate." He stared at the floor tiles, then looked up, his eyes redder, his fuzzy brows pointing like an arrow to his widow's peak.

"Can't you just take my girl on one date? I'd even pay for the costs." He set the bill on the counter. I would not get beaten that night, or any other night, at least not by him.

"The world doesn't work that way," I said. I pulled his other hundred from my pocket. It was a night of firsts: I'd never seen one in my own hand before then. I only vaguely remembered Benjamin Franklin was on some of those bills Gihh-rhaggs had left us. Yet, here was Ben, looking all smug at his high denomination, doubly smug on these tandem bills. I assumed FF didn't remember giving me the first. I could walk out of here with two weeks' pay in my pocket, free and clear. I slid the one in my hand over to join the one FF had just set down.

"The world always works that way," he said, looking at both bills. "What's it gonna take?" His eyes suddenly narrowed and his cheeks got redder. He pulled the wad back out of his pocket and peeled another bill from it, sure that he was going to find my asking price.

"Look, man," I said. I didn't like the direction this was going, and I knew of one clear way to stop it. I might get my ass beaten after all, but I couldn't bear the strangeness of this conversation anymore. Maybe he just didn't have a good sense of where to draw the line—the way he just showed me Christine's room, like that was totally normal. "I was in that RV. Picnic Grove parking? Randy had to see his dad. So you can stop pretending . . ."

How did you tell someone you didn't share their opinion that paying for intimacy was okay? I braced for getting my face pounded, knowing the chances were good.

"Pretending what?" He looked genuinely puzzled, like he had no idea what was coming.

"You can tell me about missing your wife. I believe you. I know what it means to lose someone, but not in that way. I also saw what you were doing with that scrawny woman in the back of that RV. Your pecker didn't seem too lonely that day." I grimaced, not knowing any way to say it but for the blunt way that was going to sound bad. "Trying to buy your daughter a date? It's not too far from what Little Eva was offering in the RV. You get that, right?"

"You got a big mouth on you, son," he said, after a minute, eyes narrowed, cheeks flushing with even more blood. I'd successfully snapped him out of his sadness.

"That supposed to be funny?" I asked, and held my breath. Neither of us moved.

"Maybe," he eventually sighed. He paused and let out a strange little clipped laugh. "Little Eva. What do you know about that poor soul?"

"She's a junkie and apparently she has some talents. You'd know better than me."

"I don't guess that she does, really. Figure her to be probably terrible. Missing some teeth, and the ones she's got are chipped. Looked dangerous," he said, the hostility in his eyes gone, his expression more like someone remembering a bet he'd lost money on.

"You didn't seem to mind. All that energy you spent with her leaning forward into you. That's how you got your nickname by the way. All your fancy thrusting, Fuck Face." Even as I said it, I could hear it sounded like I was calling him that name, instead of identifying it.

"That's what you think my nickname is? It ain't. If you listen carefully enough, someone always uses the real one. You've probably never listened close enough to hear mine *or yours*." He thought for a minute, studying me. "Maybe you just don't want to know. But me? You see, I don't plan to *ever* get married again. Vestal was it for me. The beginning and the end. But I got a good job, reasonable looks. There's plenty with less. Your mom, I bet, if I asked her out on a date, invite her to play the ponies, she'd go."

I didn't want to think about that, probably because it was close to the truth. She was lonely, too, I'm sure. She and my dad had lived together at some point, but I barely knew any details. The only person I'd ever seen her truly love was Gihh-rhaggs, and he'd been gone nearly ten years.

"Night's been trying to set me up with every fly-by-night floozy cousin that walks through his door. He ain't much of a buddy, but when he's all you got in the way of steady, door-always-open friends, you tend to forgive. A man gets used to heartache. I guess we're programmed to know one partner's most likely gonna go first. But when I lost my brother, I also lost my best friend." Tim paused, and drew in a breath. "I can't just be a dad as my place in life. I need to spend time with someone who . . . who knows *me*. Someone who knows the stupid shit I can do and is still okay being friends. Sounds like something a kid would say, when I hear myself speak it out loud, but maybe you know what I mean. About wanting a real friend."

Over the years, Randy had stuck wads of gum in my hair, stolen even my broken toys, drank more than his share of the beers we bought evenly together, smoked cigs without ever buying a pack, disappeared when it was time to cut more logs for the fire, mocked me outright to his white friends, and even purposefully wiped us out on a motorcycle we were riding in a stone driveway, always claiming he'd just been joking.

Like Tim Sampson with DogLips, I kept coming back. If I'd had cousins closer to my own age, things might have been different, but somehow, even back in kindergarten, we'd played complementary roles in each other's lives. If I walked away, I'd be walking away from everyone who'd have anything to do with me. Even if I decided to try hanging around more with someone like Leonard, he was as good as gone in a year. At sixteen, in my spook family, I wasn't quite ready to sit home every weekend or start all over again with new white kids.

"I had a good guess about why they brought that poor girl in. I knew what she was getting paid for and that I was expected to be the entertainment. Figured if I made a good enough show of it, word would get around. The way gossip travels around here? Those cousins of Night wouldn't have any more interest if I, what did you call it? Fucked face? Someone who fucked face on Little Eva, particularly with an audience? No one wants that man in their bed. I talked with her alone when they first brought her in, told her it would be okay."

"Warning someone you're gonna cum in her mouth gently doesn't make it okay." I could picture his hairy ass dimpling, remembering how far he thrust forward, how a shiver ran through him at the end. How he seemed to forget he'd had an audience. "You think that's gonna be okay if some guy says that to . . . Christine?" I almost wished I could stop remembering what I'd witnessed, but there he was, humping and grunting, and all those others laughing, and that broken woman on that ridiculous folding chair, leaning forward before him, collecting enough money for another bump, so she could forget what she was doing to earn it. I was never so glad that plenty of white people in Lewiston wanted someone else to clean up their messes.

"Did you *really* see what you think you saw?" he asked. I had to admit that I didn't. I could picture his ass and his briefs and the work pants falling around his ankles, but technically, his meaty thigh and Little Eva's long hair obscured the connection. I couldn't picture faking it without anyone catching on, but everyone in the RV was drunk, and I only caught a glimpse for a few seconds until I recognized what I was witnessing.

"Why would you do that?"

"I told you. Vestal was my beginning and my end. I take care of my own business when the need's too distracting, I can admit, but I don't plan to connect with anyone else. Ever. You understand? Night won't try to set me up anymore. I got my money's worth in faking a show."

"I thought he paid. That's what he said, when he gave us money."

"You still haven't gotten it," he said, shaking his head like I was a dog wondering where the ball went, when you pretended to throw one. "Ever notice you come home from their house broker than you should?" Of course I had. I'd picture Randy slipping into my front pocket when I was passed out, pinching twenties and tens. Sometimes I told myself that I'd spent it on beer I couldn't remember drinking. "Ever notice your buddy has money though he's never had a single job until recently?"

"I figured his dad . . ."

"Night's been lifting from both of us. I made sure my little girl didn't have any cash with her when we went over there tonight. Speaking of, we best get back there. She'll be ready to come home." He stood up and tossed the empties into a garbage can under the sink.

"Maybe you'd just give me a ride home? It's sort of on the way. I'd walk, but I don't have my jacket. It's still at Randy's," I said, picturing people going through the pockets, taking my smokes. That was all I ever left in it, these days.

"There's that one in Christine's bedroom. It's yours. She got it for you. Won't fit anyone in this house, and no one else likes that music but you."

He plodded back to Meduse's bedroom and brought the box out. "One date, that's all I'm asking. You can even use the truck. I'll teach you. Just, you know, no drunk driving."

"Tim . . . Mr. Sampson," I said, somewhere between what I felt I should call him and what he wanted to hear.

"Tim's okay, I guess."

"I can't do it. Can't take that jacket, can't go on a date. I have bought my way into almost every half-assed minor friendship I have, and your daughter doesn't need to know that life any more than she already does." I'd been the Bubble Yum Kid in junior high, spending all my babysitting money buying gum to pass out among the kids I wanted to hang with, and then the Winston Kid, as we all got a little older. Even before working with Leonard, I always offered to do the shit job. Maybe that was who I'd become: The Shit Job Kid.

"Look, I know she owns all this, and that she's threatened to throw you out if you try to make her behave, but buying her a date with me ain't gonna change whatever's wrong between the two of you. I mean, that's what you're doing here. You get that, right? Offering me money to go on a date? And I'm not desperate enough yet to become that kind of whore."

"I could still kick your ass tonight, son. Don't you forget it."

"I couldn't possibly forget it. You are easily two and half times my size. I've got eyes."

"Couldn't prove it by me, the amount of shit you miss in the world right around you." He grabbed the keys and put his arm back around my shoulder. "Let's go, Squier," he said.

"Squire?" He clearly meant for me to know that was my nickname, but I didn't get it. Low-level royalty? What did that have to do with me? Was Randy accusing me of being uppity?

"You sure you want to know?" I nodded. "Some song by a guy named Squier." Randy was keeping it up. Billy Squier. Hard to believe "The Stroke" made it on the radio. The entire chorus was a repeated demand that someone stroke him. I was never going to live this down.

We got into Tim's truck and headed toward my home. "Christine tell you that? About our finances?" he asked as we crept toward my end of the road our houses shared.

"You just hear things. And I know how Rez land rules work." He didn't need reminders that his life would always be complicated, that he simply could not own land within our borders.

"Yup. And I hear your ma can change hearts with her tea leaves. That's why Vestal stopped us from going back. She thought your ma was a witch. Thought she might take me the way she took my brother when you were a squirt." He drove, smiling, confident he was a handsome and desirable man, despite the prostitution scam DogLips Night thought necessary to get him laid.

"You think we'd be living the way we do if she had some kind of super-power to do shit like that? You think she'd want *you* if she could?"

He shrugged. Then: "I can feel it. Whatever your family gives off. *That's* what scares your buddy. He's *always* worried what people think. I can feel that thing, essence? In you and I don't even know you. Not really. I went to the party this year, figuring you'd be there. I wanted to see what all the fuss was, with my little girl. I hadn't seen you since you were a squirt. I knew you by the glasses I passed on to your mom for you." He reached over and tapped the gold glasses I still wore.

"Then tonight, when you were nothing but a punk, I wanted to hate you. Beat you. Something. But then here . . . I have never cried in my entire adult life, save the week Vestal died. Do you believe me?" I nodded, agreeing. Whatever he'd been holding inside that had gotten unleashed, had been there for a long time. And now that connection between us lingered, like the smell of woodsmoke on your clothes the morning after the bonfire.

"Something about you. Maybe knowing the shithole you live in and the way you act like you don't. Or the way my brother thought you were something special. Just made it pour on out. I don't know what. Seems impossible even now, fading, like that . . . at the kitchen counter . . ."

"Hug, embrace," I said. "It's okay. You can call it what it was, with me."

"Okay, that hug," he said, reluctant. "Still sounds funny. It was like some kind of dream. No one needs to know about that, right? What happened in my kitchen?"

"The hug?" I repeated. I wanted him to know that it also meant something to me, without coming right out and admitting it. "No. No one needs to know. Just you and me. I promise."

"This is yours," he said, offering me the hundred again.

"I'm not changing my mind."

"No, I understood that. This is about what I owe you. Night and his boy, they have an even split deal about the money they roll from people. You've probably bought me easily a hundred bucks of beers since you started going there. Do yourself a favor. When you go back, don't bring more than twenty bucks. Maybe make it all in ones. Stay away from fives. They're the easiest to lose track of. Bring only what you can afford to lose."

I took the hundred and slid it into my pocket without looking at it. "When my little girl gives you that jacket, just take it and say thank you, okay? I think she's planning on bringing it with her tomorrow. I know. It don't mean nothing, I know that, and I'll try to get her to know it, too, but for now just take it, okay? Just be kind? Can you do that?"

"I can." I couldn't explain the peculiar nuances of my friendship with Christine. I didn't understand them, myself. But if I faked feelings I didn't have, she'd know. And if she settled for fake love, that would be worse than the truth. It would be just another show for others. Another Little Eva deal, not as bad, but bad just the same. There was a good chance Christine would be here as long as I was. We had our whole lives to figure it out, I thought, as we slowed near my mailbox. "Thanks for the driving lesson," I said, as we idled.

"Anytime you want another, I'd be happy," he said. "You just pick up the phone and call me. You know my number."

"That's not going to happen."

"Figured. I wanted you to know, anyway. It's a sincere offer. And maybe the next time you speak my daughter's name, you'll call her Christine?" It was a plea.

"Yeah," I said. "You taking her out New-Yahhing? Just her again?"

"Thought so. Your ma still make magic cookies? Maybe put a spell on me? Make me not so lonesome?" After midnight, the radio marathon had continued, but it was Beatles Life after the breakup. They played only solo work: "Isn't It a Pity," "Imagine," "Photograph," "Silly Love Songs." "Your mom's gonna be surprised you're coming home tonight. She's probably figured she's lost you to that other world, where Little Eva and the rest of us live."

"The New Year's good for surprises. Keeps you sharp." I got out, and Tim Sampson drove on, back to the crime scene disguised as a party.

At my house, I looked in the windows where my ma and members of our extended family welcomed the New Year. They laughed, smoked, traded jokes and quarters, waiting for their kids to come home safely, but not daring to speak that fear. The whole group only got together like this a few times a year, but New Year's was a standing date.

The cold air was sharp in my shirt sleeves, but I walked back out to the lawn and looked up at the stars anyway, watched the Big Dipper become the Giant Bear that the three hunters had chased into the heavens, listening to those people still firing distant shots into the dark.

In the morning, I'd stay home, instead of shouting welcome across the Rez. I'd greet people coming to our door, sharing possibilities, giving out my ma's dangerous death-wish cookies to the bold. If Tim and Christine came, I'd make sure there was one for the driver.

For now, though, I stepped back through the threshold, to see if my cousins had felt Poseidon's seaquake yet, the deep ocean tectonic shift that would turn their lives upside down. Tim was probably reentering that other party, trying to find his daughter, and love her the best way he could as a new year awakened. My own tidal wave had struck me head on, out of nowhere. He'd left me capsized, sinking in an emotional state I'd never even known I'd wanted, until the moment it happened. I couldn't decide which was worse, not knowing what it felt like to be held, or knowing, with no one there afterward, to open their arms and welcome you in when you needed it again. How could you learn to love feeling vulnerable, your hull shattered and taking on water?

CHAPTER SIXTEEN

A Different Sun

(1983)

O n New Year's morning, Christine Sampson hopped out of her father's truck and carried three things up the driveway. I opened the door before she could yell, but she did, anyway.

"Um, brought you this," she said, holding out my old jacket, with some mud stains. I thanked her. "Grabbed it when you disappeared. You go with Randy? That's what everyone thought." Apparently, Tim had decided not to cover our evening together with her.

"I got sick," I said. "And someone gave me a ride home. I was too embarrassed to go in."

"I get that. I've embarrassed myself. Every once in a while." We both nodded subtly. "Brought you this, too. I saw it shopping and thought, there's only one person in the world who should have this!" She handed over the box that now had an awkward lie tied to it.

"Feels heavy," I said, weighing it as if I'd never held it before. "Expensive. Is that right?"

"You don't get to ask those questions with a gift, Brian," she said. "Just say Nyah-wheh."

"I'm sorry, of course. Here, step in." My ma was monitoring the intrusion.

"Chilly in here." She could see her breath in this room of our house.

"Yeah, just the way it is in here," I said, trying to dismiss. "But I didn't know we were doing this. This isn't part of—"

"Yes it is. Don't you remember the apron you made me? I use it all the time." I loosened the tape and opened each flap. "Don't be such a gramma!" she said, tearing the rest off. "My dad's gonna wonder what's taking me so long."

No, he's not, I thought. *He knows exactly what's happening, and he's happy to be sitting in his warm and toasty truck cab.*

"Wow!" I said, as she helped lift the box top off. "It's great! But really, too fancy. Too expensive." I held off the inevitable as long as I could. "I mean, I have a jacket, here."

"This one's different," she said. You could wear this in the winter, without layers, because it was thick with an insulated lining. The leather was designed to protect your hide in a motorcycle accident.

"I can see."

"Take it out and you'll really see." On cue, Tim honked his horn, continuing to pretend we didn't know how this was going to unfold. "Oh shoot! Hurry up," she said, helping.

I had to fake total surprise at the Man in the Star embroidered all over the back. "Oh man! Christine!" I said. "This is—well, it's frigging amazing! But it's just too much." The cassettes fell out of the box with the jacket no longer on top. I hoped I was selling a shocked look. It wasn't too big a leap—I still was at a loss for words. My mouth hung open.

"Okay, call me later," she said, taking a cookie from the box I'd set down. "One for the driver?" she asked, smiling and reaching.

"Wait, here," I said, "give him one of these, instead." I reached for the large gingerbread men from a separate container on my ma's piano bench.

"For my dad. *He's* the driver," she said, like I didn't know. "He don't get Oo-wee-rheh."

"Well, he sort of does," I said. Oo-wee-rheh, the Tuscarora word for doll, was also the word used on this day. You prepared a special treat for members of your father's clan. It had started out as gingerbread men. Most people now just made pie. My mom stuck to tradition, even though my dad's relatives didn't come to our house for this celebration.

"You're not gonna do that shittay thing," she asked, hurt flashing across her face.

"No! No, of course not. It's just for him." Some old-timers who still made gingerbread men did it to send a harsh message. If a kid's biological parents weren't married, or worse, were the same clan, just before they gave the kid the cookie, they'd break off its head and drop it in their bag first. The kids never knew why they got a maimed cookie, but their parents did. "Secret payment for all his smokes I've stolen," I whispered, and she grinned. It was a good enough lie, and she put the cookie in her bag, for the driver. She told me a lie and I told her one back, but I couldn't kid myself. Both benefited me.

"Call me!" she shouted and ran to the truck. I hoped Tim knew what it meant. I'd spent a lot of the night thinking about how we'd welcomed in the new year, just he and I, alone, talking, making a real connection like almost never happened here, both knowing we had no way to sustain it. It already seemed unreal, less than twelve hours later. The pockets of my old jacket were empty, which killed me a little. The fake Indian Head Nickel Gihh-rhaggs had given me, my lucky coin, had been in the chest pocket. An outdated bar drink token, with no value to anyone else, but someone had snagged it just the same. Still, I had my jacket back.

Back in school a few days later, it was as if Randy and I had never been friends, *again*, had never fought off werewolves as boys, had never steadied each other, drunk, so we didn't puke on our own shoes, had never pieced together a previous night from our shared memory pieces. But this time, I didn't care, and wasn't even trying to convince myself. I was finally done.

I loved the jacket from Christine, but it wasn't fair to accept such a gift from someone you didn't feel the same about. Home alone over break, I'd tried it on in the vanity mirrors Mona had left behind. The shimmering embroidered Rush image almost glowed against the leather. I'd fold it back in the box, sliding it under my bed, wrapped in plastic and another box, to protect it.

At lunch, I still sat at the Indian table, though now at the opposite end from Randy. When you shared a tight community history with twenty to forty kids, you could always find someone to joke with. It didn't matter if you weren't close friends. You had the shared history of our little community, the fun times, the embarrassing times. We could even joke about the mean hygienist who used to come to the Rez once a year to give us these deep-pink dye tablets so we could look in the mirror and see how gross our oral hygiene habits were. There might be a couple people you didn't like so much, but it was easy to stay at different ends of the group, if you kept it light.

Leonard and I both had Smoking Lav passes, so we caught up there. "Why are you smoking anyway?" I asked. "Aren't you gonna have to do all kinds of endurance shit once you're in Boot Camp?"

"Toughening myself up," he said, hotboxing his cig. "Only a few more months. Then it's adios." His Marines enlistment date was weeks after his graduation, and he was coasting. I asked him if that was his goal, to be a big guy. "I guess that's part," he said, goof flexing his biceps. "But sometimes, I think I signed up to belong to something less fucked up than my family."

"I can understand that," I said, thinking of what he was going through, his house transforming into someone else's while he was still in it.

"What you doing, Thursday night?" he asked. I shook my head. "D and D night at the Brick Spithouse. Five bucks."

"Dungeons and Dragons?" I asked. It seemed unlikely, but I'd heard of stranger hobbies.

"Ha! No, you weirdo," he said, laughing and raising his arms, growling in a sad dragon impersonation. "Drink and Drown. Get your hand stamped, then drink all night. They have wings and tiny pizzas that come around every little while. All for five bucks," he stressed again.

"So, listen, when I get back from Boot, we'll get together," he said that first night at D and D, each of us with a stack of empty plastic cups. "Have a blast!"

"Yeah, sounds good." I was supposed to act like I didn't care, but I felt myself already looking forward to it. I really enjoyed Leonard's company, even with the ticking clock. It was a novelty knowing I wasn't going to get robbed if I passed out. As long as I bought my share, and didn't expect much real conversation, I was good. We'd taken to shooting the shit on the phone, too, before he discovered the D and D. On those phone nights, we both just rambled on, mostly about school and our imagined futures, about everything and nothing. We were easy company. I'd forgotten how much I liked talking on the phone when you weren't constantly disappointing the other person. "We gonna be able to talk once you're there?"

"Not really. But as soon as I get in, I'll send you a letter with my address. I need you to write, okay, buddy?" He looked into my face, not wanting to plead. "I can tell it's gonna be lonely. Any connection to home'll be super helpful. I mean, my dad's gonna be busy playing house with his new old lady." I wondered how many other people he'd asked this same request.

"Of course, man. I'll write you every week," I said. "I promise." I was writing for my own pleasure anyway, so how hard would it be to make another entry, just for Leonard, sort of recreating our phone conversations as best as I could? "Why can't you use a phone?"

"They want you to think of only the family you enter Parris Island with. Far's they're concerned, you don't have any other friends or family. But we *are* allowed letters from home."

Other than Thursdays, which became a regular thing with Leonard, my evenings stayed pretty barren. I knew what it was to dread someone's phone calls, and I had no intention of becoming that person for him. On nights my ma didn't go to BINGO, I walked Rez roads, to smoke in peace. I didn't even miss Randy's parties that much.

With allegedly longer days, February still felt the worst. Snakey, salt-bleached asphalt traced my walks for the impossibly long "shortest month." I'd stroll past Margaret and Moose Knuckle's. At the "Summer Cottage", where my dad and other drifters passed bottles, I quietly drifted to the other side of the road. I had a sawed-off lacrosse stick looped into my jacket sleeve, in case trouble found my path. On Valentine's Day, a truck slowed behind me, stretching my shadow. Most days, I ached for company. Any encounter could be better than the long, epic, and brittle silent roads.

"Wanna ride somewhere?" Tim Sampson shouted, straining to roll down his passenger window. I'd drifted beyond my usual limit of making a bearable return in deep cold.

"You're not exactly pointing my direction," I said.

"Get in, you goof. I'll turn around." He shivered. I was so cold my balls felt like a walnut trying to push deep inside for any warmth. I got in. "Too frigid to be out there." He could see my old jacket, but he didn't comment. "For sure for someone who loves heat like you." He tilted vents my way. "Want one?" he asked, pointing to a six-pack on the bench seat between us.

"Too cold," I said, blowing warm breath into one cupped hand, holding the other up to the vents pumping joyous heat, as he did a three-point and headed us deep into the reservation.

"Antifreeze," he said, laughing. "Suit yourself." Near my house, he took the right onto Dead Man's. At a dark stretch of fields with no houses, he pulled over, and I gripped the stick in my sleeve. He was possibly just a *patient* vengeful father. "You know, you shouldn't promise to call someone if you're not gonna do it," he said.

"Did I promise to call you?" I asked.

"You know who I mean. Christine stayed home most nights last month, waiting for you to call." Among the people I hadn't seen much of, Christine definitely was up near the top. She spent half her day down the road at vocational school now, and we didn't share any classes. Sometimes, we'd pass each other in the hall, but that was about it.

"Haven't seen her on the bus," I said. "And for the record, I never said I was gonna call."

"But I bet you didn't say you *weren't* going to call," he said, like he'd had a spy microphone on our conversation. "I've been dropping her off at school, or she's been dropping me at work and taking the truck. Thanks for the cookie, by the way. Damn but your mother makes some fine cookies." I nodded. I guess that explained some things. The couple times I'd seen her, I'd said the jacket was too nice to wear in the winter, that I didn't want road salt stains on it.

He climbed out and headed toward the tailgate, like a Bizarro reversal of New Year's Eve. In the rearview mirror, his massive shoulders glowed and shivered in the red taillights and vapor, and when he was done, I pretended not to notice him come up the passenger's side. I debated a whack to the solar plexus and tried to decide which barren field might offer me a close shot at disappearing in the woods. I was young and might outrun him, but his legs were long.

"Hey," he yelled, clinking the passenger window with his wedding band, making that circling gesture to roll the window down. "Since you ain't drinking, you mind driving?" I opened the door to jump out, but he just stood there. "Snow's too deep here for those sad things you're calling winter footwear," he said, looking down at my dress boots. "I know how to dress for winter, so mine are OK. Just slide your skinny ass over. Cold out here," he said, climbing in.

"I'm not any better a driver now," I said. "Not like I've had practice."

"Yeah, you're a stubborn little fuck," he said, as I picked up the six-pack and slid over to the driver's spot. "Anyone else your age? Give 'em a chance to drive? An *invitation* to drive, you can't get 'em out of the driver's seat."

"I told you that night—"

"I know what you told me," he said. "Just shut up and drive. Don't over-steer and don't goose it, or we're gonna be stuck. Just ease onto the road." I pulled the shift down and the red tongue landed on the D. The truck heaved a little, and I slowly pressed on the gas.

"You gotta put *some* energy into it," he said. "Push down. Just don't floor it."

I pushed and got onto Dead Man's. He readjusted the vent to face me again. "I haven't really seen Christine," I said, a weak excuse, but I felt like I had to say something.

"She's moved on," he said, matter of fact. "She's got someone over, so I got time to kill. Valentine's. Figure I'd give her the house for a while." I took a left as we reached The Torn Rock. If I'd gone right, we'd leave the Rez. Randy's recently acquired El Camino wasn't in his driveway, and I wondered if it was parked at Tim's.

I didn't care much, but it still felt as if I'd been yanked from my own life like those TV actors who demanded too many perks from the executives running the show, thinking they were the star. Suddenly, their character just dies—no chance of coming back. My insistence on not being fucked over was too much. I'd been written out of their story.

"Chicken," Tim said, laughing. "Gonna limit our choices."

"You've got an open beer and I don't have a license. I'd prefer to acquire one before I get slapped with some violation." We cruised the northern strip and began a standard Rez Lap.

"Haven't seen you around Night's place." He raised his eyebrows. "Saving money?"

"Something like that."

"Let's see who's on Moon Road tonight?" he said, directing us further from my house.

"It's too early," I replied, passing by the turn. "Nobody shows up there until at least ten o'clock, closer to eleven, I'd guess most nights."

"That's not true," he said, cracking another beer. "It's always Happy Hour somewhere. How about we go to Vera Blake's?"

"Do you even know Vera Blake?" I couldn't see Tim at Lewis's house.

"I hire Juniper to help with stuff if it's too much for one man. He's um, what you might say, eccentric . . . but a hard worker." Juniper was Lewis's uncle. I guess eccentric was a word for it. Of the adults I knew who couldn't drive, Juniper was the only one who simply didn't know how.

"How about I just get out at my house? Then you can go wherever you want." Tim was trying to find a house where Valentine's Day didn't exist. Lewis's was a good guess. He had as much luck going out with someone as I did, close to zero, but they were just poor. When the rumor about you is witchcraft, no one takes any chances. Still, my misery was doing fine without company.

Maybe because emptiness was so familiar and tailored, I couldn't help Tim with his particular brand of loneliness. I figured it must have been hard as hell for a widower to deal with this one day of the year. That was the one card Hallmark didn't make—the one to your dead wife or husband. You just had to muddle through alone. Maybe he wasn't giving Christine her space. Maybe he just couldn't bear to be in his house.

"Why do you think Christine was so dead set on giving up regular school to go the haircutting route?" he asked as we did Rez Laps, over and over. In each other's company, we had nowhere to go. Most places I might go to were relatives of mine, and it would be too weird to show up driving Tim Sampson's truck. I assumed hanging out with me made no sense in his world either. "Wasn't she smart enough? I always thought she was, but what do I know? I'm just her dad. Dads always think their kids are geniuses."

Not true of all dads—mine at least—but that observation wouldn't add anything to this conversation.

"I don't know. I'm not covering, if that's what you're asking. I *really* don't know. Seems she found something she's good at." The college-track kids thought vocational school was for those who couldn't hack the academic side. I expected that attitude from people who took their school social standing seriously. It was a bummer to hear a parent having those thoughts too. Maybe my mom had set me up as a maintenance guy because she thought that would be my life. For all of her reading the tea leaves, she never really saw a future where any of us went to college, beyond showing us what an application might look like. Maybe my ma was afraid she wouldn't know how to fill out the forms herself. She barely even encouraged us to apply after, or hoped for us, the way Tim hoped for his younger daughter.

"Isn't finding her thing good enough? You believed in her enough to pay for her tools." The Beauticians Trainers probably laughed at the toolbox Christine lugged around every day, but Tim had made sure hers held everything on the Required and Recommended Lists. Christine had told me, herself. He'd even tried to dress it up, spray-painting it pink and slapping Flower Power stickers on—I couldn't imagine where he got those—but there was no disguising her Beautician's Case was supposed to carry Craftsman Wrenches, instead of Flat-top combs and curling irons.

"I suppose. Just don't seem like much of a future," he said, draining his beer.

"People are always gonna want to look better than they do," I said. "If she gets good at making people believe a haircut will change their lives, and knowing how to do them, she'll always have a job."

"She still cut your hair?" he asked. I laughed. Either he was in desperate need of glasses or just prodding me. My hair, clear to even the casual observer, was a home jobby now. Long hair was a legit Rez political statement, so I could just pass my shit haircuts off as "Tradition."

"What would be the harm?' he asked. "She cuts mine, and you yourself said she's probably gonna be successful at this."

"I didn't say that at all," I said, pointing us toward my home. "But if you're gonna put words in my mouth, those are okay. I'm sure she wants someone saying she's going to be good."

"See? How hard would it be?"

"It wouldn't be hard on *me*," I said. I didn't mean that in a vain way—we owned mirrors. All kinds of Indian men, when women saw them, those chickies would be willing to go all Captivity Narrative for them, fleeing their wall-to-wall carpet and Vibro-Massage Showers. My cousin Roland, even missing a couple bar-fight teeth, was still one of those Major Snags. But the traits my parents filtered to shape me were more like those "flies-in-the-eyes" Third World kids Sally Struthers hung around on TV, asking for your cash, to fill their bloated bellies. Christine's haircuts put me closer to the First World, or maybe the Second, but cutting someone's hair was a close thing. It would be hard to cut the hair of someone you longed for, to touch their face, feel them breathing on you, and not walk away agitated. If Christine still had feelings for me, I didn't want to remind her of what wasn't going to be.

I'd been familiar enough with that ache myself. Those times I stayed at Randy's, I rarely slept with Tiffany just one wall away. In the mornings, exhausted, I'd sit at the kitchen table with Randy, eating cereal slowly, hoping she'd come down for a cup of coffee in a robe. Kitten sometimes had Tiffany dump me off before she ran errands. I snatched glances the whole time, trying to use Gihh-rhaggs's old trick of pretending to look somewhere else, but keeping your eye locked the whole time. Her sighing and pounding the gas told me I wasn't fooling anyone.

As soon as she'd drop me off, I'd head straight to the privacy of my room, crash, and sleep most of the afternoon away. When I woke up, I just felt guilty and lonely, lonelier than I did on regular days. And if I was being honest, a good percentage was just me being horny. I didn't harbor fantasies we'd go out for real or anything. Proximity to her mix of perfume, hair spray, and Tic Tacs just sent me over the edge every time. If cutting my hair, being that close, was putting Christine through even the smallest sliver of those feelings, I couldn't be a part of that.

"You're getting better," Tim said, as I pulled into my driveway. My ma peeked out the window, to see who might be bringing unexpected freedom, a visit or an invitation for coffee. Her glance stayed, watching us, as I climbed from the driver's seat. "Wait," Tim said, sliding over and keeping the door open, dangling one leg to the ground. "You been driving with someone else?"

"You really think someone else is gonna hand over their keys to me? I just have a good memory," I said, leaning on the open door, feeling the faint blow of vent heat trailing out of the dash. "Thanks for picking me up. It was wickedly cold, and I'd gotten farther from home than I'd paid attention to. It was gonna be a long walk back." I held my hand out. "I really appreciate it." He took the hand and didn't crush it in that suspicious dad way; an earnest grip and squeeze.

"Like I said, any time." He reached the other hand up and gripped my wrist, keeping me in place. "Any time. I mean it." He looked at me directly, something we tended not to do on the Rez, unless we were mad and wanted you to know. But I didn't get that feeling here, so I mimicked what he was doing, adding my left, into a strange four-grip handshake. He nodded, then let go and pulled his leg in, settling fully into the driver's seat.

"Can I ask you something?" I still leaned in the open door. He shrugged and nodded, shifting position to look directly at me better, again. "What did you mean about me loving heat? You said when I got in—"

"You think I didn't know who you were, perched on the furnace vents at Nights' house? Little kids ain't shy about what they love. You don't learn to be guarded till you had love knocked out of you a few times, right?"

"I guess, yeah, but doesn't everyone love warmth?" I was embarrassed all over again.

"Only people who really know the cold love heat the way you do," he said. "If you want, for any driving lesson? You can turn the heat on as high as you like. I like heat. You know the number." I gave him the smallest of Rez grimaces to say no, a minimal pursing of the lips, and he read it, nodding in response. "Well, maybe if I see you walking? How's about that?"

"Sure," I said, grinning. "If I'm walking and you're driving by, feel free. If it works out any day, I'll drive you anywhere you want, as long as it's on the Rez." I said this like I had a hundred friends and was trying to balance all my social obligations.

"Doesn't leave a lot of options," he said. "Gonna have to leave these roads at some point." He waited in silence for a minute and added, "Son,

I know what it's like to be cold." I nodded, so he'd know I heard him, and stuck out my hand to shake again, a regular one.

"Kind of late for a school night," my ma said, glancing up from her sewing when I walked in. The late-night news anchor hadn't even come on yet with their *It's eleven o'clock, do you know where your children are?* tagline, so I didn't know what she was talking about.

"If you're a kid." I stood at the kerosene stove, its warmth radiating through my Levi's.

"I didn't recognize those headlights."

"Tim Sampson picked me up and gave me a ride."

"From where?"

What to say to that. From my life? From this house? From being a kid?

"Nowhere. Just walking."

As time went on, I recognized those headlights, in the oncoming lane, and then, at our driveway's end. He got the message that if he wanted to talk about a romantic future for me and Christine, I was done. In that way, we found our own way forward, our own awkward handmade topographical map tracing all the quirks of Rez life. He taught me to parallel park, to rock a snowbound truck, and—key on the Rez—a three-point turn. In spring, we went over the skill in mud. A couple times, he showed in an unfamiliar truck to teach me a standard shift.

After a while, my ma stopped asking who I was with. She recognized the headlights. But one night, coming in, she caught me off guard as I walked over and poured myself a glass of iced tea from the fridge. "What do you two even talk about?" she asked, sitting in the dark. It was a little past midnight; I guess we'd lost track of time out driving. "If you're trying to get with the haircutting girl, you're taking kind of long, or is there something like that Moose Knuckle thing going on? Getting messed up in other people's affairs is a good way to get your ass beaten and left in the ditch on Moon Road," she said. This was maybe the most forward conversation she'd ever initiated, and it made me understand she'd still been silently monitoring my life, after all.

"Nothing, we just ride around," I said. "He's been teaching me to drive so he doesn't have to drink and drive." I sipped the tea and then immediately added, "And no, I'm not drinking. He's the only one with open bottle, and no, I never leave the Rez."

"Well if you gotta to go to summer school to make up a class, don't come crying to me."

"Don't worry about it," I said. "I'm fine." Probably, I was closer to skating at the edge of being mediocre, but as far as I was concerned, that was fine. I thought about her question when I went up and got out of the day's clothes for bed. It was kind of hard, really, to reconstruct what we talked about. We'd become easy in each other's company. With Randy, I'd always had to worry that anything I might say could eventually bite me in the ass, but I never felt that way out driving. The unlikelihood of my friendship with Tim even faded below my level of awareness, most days. We just resumed whatever we'd been last talking about. It was the kind of friendship I'd imagined you might have with someone, the kind of good friends people on TV seemed to always have, but I'd never fully encountered.

"People probably gonna Eee-ogg," she said. "You start acting different from everyone else, you're gonna get noticed."

"You mean, like reading tea leaves?" I said. She had no response to that. Even as I said it, I understood, she'd probably paid more of a cost for getting involved with Gihh-rhaggs than she had for tea leaves. And what was Tim Sampson to her but one level of removal from the true love of her life, even if she wouldn't admit the intensity of their white-hot love before Gihh-rhaggs burned out?

As Tim and I continued talking, some names showed up often. Though I never understood what he did for a living, I knew the coworkers he liked, the ones he hated, the ones he liked well enough but didn't trust, and he knew that I spent Thursday nights with Leonard and some guys from school. Tim and I never made plans ahead. Some nights, I sat around hoping, doing homework and listening to music, and, I imagine, some nights he pulled in, flicked the headlights, and nothing happened, because I'd crashed on the couch or had other unexpected plans.

One night, in late March, near the anniversary of Vestal's death, Tim asked me to drive to Lake Majijo. It was a No-Man's Land, technically a

public park, but the only entry was on a Rez road. We'd gotten me a driver's permit by then, so I didn't put up any argument. "Mind if we get out?"
he asked. It was a warm March night, foretelling April. We climbed on
the hood, warm beneath my Levi's because we'd been riding a while, and
we leaned back onto the windshield, staring up at the clear late-winter
stars, the half moon rising on the small lake. The breeze was just a little
sharp, and on top of the sappy trees and wet earth, I would occasionally
catch that note again. Only now, I didn't think of it as Gihh-rhaggs's smell.
It had become Tim's, but it wasn't like you could tell someone you found
an incomprehensible comfort in their scent.

I sometimes felt like I could tell him things I couldn't even tell Leonard, and certainly things I'd never tell Randy, but it always seemed too
risky. I understood our new map looked weird to anyone outside of it,
because it looked weird to me, too. But I did not want to lose it. I'd come
to feel that I was destined to screw up any relationship I ever had, by crossing some line that was invisible only to me. So there were all kinds of
things I wanted to ask him, or even say, that I just couldn't. The truth sometimes was too much to bear unless you kept it sealed inside.

"Don't think I ever told you," he said, like he'd been reading my mind.
"We had another kid that we lost right near the end, just a bit before he
was supposed to come out." *He*, a son. I shook my head, but of course he
knew that he'd never told me. Losing a kid wasn't exactly a story you tell
casually. "Aaaand," he dragged, "when they took the baby, the garden he
was growing in had to come out too. No more kids on Tim and Vestal's
horizons." He wasn't prone to using this kind of language. Maybe this was
the way he told the story to himself, alone.

"That's when she turned to her Pastor Clyde and his Heavenly Telecaster," he added, a sour look crossing his face. "Playing their prayers
straight to the ears of Jesus. She traded our boy for a Jesus in the Key of C
Major. A different son to fill the spaces left by ours."

"Did you have a name picked out?" I asked. I didn't know what they
did with babies who were technically born dead. Stillborn, according to
Auntie Rolanda's old medical dictionary.

"Getting late," he said, glancing at his fancy radium-dial watch. "Better get you home. It's a school night. But how about you take us the long

way, down by Bond's and back to the Rez from the south side?" I agreed. It made me nervous to leave the roads I knew, to go off the Rez, even though I was better. But how could I deny someone who'd just revealed so much?

When we passed their house on the way to mine, Tim ignored the evidence that Christine was not home. He seemed also not to notice that he'd lost something, too, when Vestal miscarried, or was maybe he was just not willing to notice.

That night, after he dropped me off, I sat on my bed with a clipboard under the spiral-bound I was currently writing memories into, and wrote him a letter. What was happening over the past three months didn't make any sense to me. It was nothing I could tell anyone about, and have it make sense, but I was trying to be honest with myself and that meant admitting, for all my earlier protest, I didn't want it to stop. I had to tell him what he'd come to mean to me.

I didn't understand how Christine could lose one parent and frequently disregard the only one she had left, even if she maybe didn't mean it. Maybe that was part of what blocked me from feeling anything romantic for her. Was I mad that she had a father right there, who loved her as deeply as any father could, even if it led him to some extremely dumb ideas? How could she have him there every day and casually threaten him whenever she didn't get her way?

I started the letter, *Dear Tim, Dear Mr. Sampson, I call you this because I want to show you the respect I have for you*, trying to cover both bases in the way he lived in our world and still reckoned with his own world's expectations. *I'm sorry I couldn't take that money from you to go on a date with Christine the night we met, under such terrible circumstances.* I wrote, explaining that I appreciated everything else he'd done for me. I wanted him to know I understood the complications, the way he could have just rightfully pounded my face on New Year's Eve, and instead, changed my life the way no one had, except his brother, all those years before. *Maybe you fill the empty spaces left by your brother and by my grandfather before, or maybe you've just shaped your own space, making those throbbing aches less painful to endure. I don't understand why you took this chance, all things considered, our overlapping complicated histories, but I recognize how rare it is. And I feel it, every time I climb in the truck and we follow those twisting and curving and straight-on roads.* I added a few more things, but I could tell I was stalling. I hesitated at the bottom. Finally, I did one of the scariest things I'd ever done. I signed it *Love, Brian,* and I meant it. In the truck the next night, I handed the letter to him, sealed in an envelope, and asked him not to read it until after he dropped me off at home.

"Christine's not home tonight," he said, sliding the envelope in his shirt pocket.

"Like a lot of nights lately, I'm guessing." I was kind of relieved, to be honest.

"True enough. But I understand her not wanting to be home, especially this time of year." Easter was coming up: I wondered when he missed Vestal the most, the calendar date or the holiday overlap.

"The reason I mentioned that Christine's not home," he said, "is 'cause I want to show you something at the house. That gonna be a problem if she comes home while you're there?"

"Not for me," I said. "I still see her at school." Did she know her dad and I hung out some? Really, pretty regularly. Though she accepted all of my weirdness so far, this friendship with Tim was probably too peculiar even for her generous nature. I was living it, and I knew it was odd. She might find it totally messed up, coming home to discover me grabbing a couple cold beers from the fridge to watch some TV in her living room with Tim.

We went to their house and he took my jacket, hanging it on a wall hook as I followed him down into their basement, which I hadn't seen before. Gihh-rhaggs had told me he and his brother shared a basement bedroom growing up in Love Canal, before I realized who he was talking about. The full basement here looked typical for the houses where my ma cleaned: industrial gray floor, washer, dryer, utility sink, sump pump, shelving for stuff you always needed. Off to the back, the furnace was built into its own little room, surrounded by tools like I'd seen at the bus garage. He'd probably painted and decorated Christine's tool chest in here.

The whole far end of the basement was cut off, separated by a finished, paneled wall and a door nicer than the one on our house. A dartboard and protective panel made up one section of this barrier wall, all the darts surrounding the bull's-eye tight like the ass end of a peacock. How many nights had Christine practiced here, alone, honing her own skills at locking away her desires to find someone to love? How long before we wandered into each other's paths? When she offered me a smoke on that Junior High bus ride, did she think I was it? That all her dedication had paid off?

"This room's locked," he said, jingling a key chain from his pants pocket. "There's a key on the kitchen pegs, so if they want to, the girls can get in, but they know I intended this as my place. The place I go for privacy. They always had free roam of the rest." We looked through the door into this large room when he flicked a wall switch, turning on a rectangular hanging lamp over a pool table. A couple neon beer signs buzzed alive on the wall, framing a wet bar with a little fridge, a couple of stools, and a gun rack with the guns locked in place. One corner was filled by a big floor-model TV, a love seat, and a couple recliners. I had a hard time picturing how that TV even fit in the narrow paths to get here.

At the room's far end, another door led to what my ma always called a "dream bath." It had a john, a sink, and a shower stall, but no tub. Most of the houses she cleaned had one of these in the basement and she said these were time-savers. The shower didn't take as long to clean, but since she said these were used mostly by the husbands, the floor around the john needed more thorough work. I was familiar from my time at the garage.

"You probably know this, since no one can get a mortgage out here," he said, unlacing his boots and removing them before he stepped onto the carpet. "We worked on the foundation the first year we were married, and lived down here for almost the first decade, so we could scrape up enough each year to add to the upstairs. We figured since we were gonna be here for so long, we'd make it nice." He pointed to my boots and I pulled them off, setting them next to his, and we stepped in.

"We decided to start trying for that third a couple years after Christine was born. Vestal wanted another baby now that Christine was less interested in little-girl stuff, and I was hoping for a son. And, well, I had no objection to trying as much as I could," he said, a small laugh trailing. "This was gonna be the boy's room." He put his arm around my shoulder and walked me over to the last large object in the room. The more I looked at it, the more familiar it became.

"Other than my girls," he said. "This is the most valuable thing in my life." Standing before me on four perfect stainless steel legs was a Bally *Fireball* pinball machine. The glass-back scoreboard was a generic super-being: like Superman crossed with the Devil. A big blazing fireball framed him against stars and comets, and moons. Maybe like Superman, he got powers because his world circled a different sun. If he'd stayed in his own place, he would have been an average person. But here, he was more power-ful than any human. Why did Superman choose to help people? A sucker move, if you thought about it, the kind of shit you could only believe if you were willing to waste your quarters believing in heroes.

This man in red threw neat flaming balls at the player. The playing sur-face had the usual flippers, bumpers and targets, spinners, and trapdoors. He looked more like the Devil here, his cape fastened with a small skull and crossbones. I'd never thought of the Devil and Superman as having such similar stories, but some wiseass graphic designer had his own secret fun. Did the Devil miss being Heaven's right-hand man, or did he love rul-ing over human temptation?

"This table was so popular, they made one for home use a couple years ago, but the home ones are never as good. This is a genuine professional 1972 model, the kind you find in a bar. Gotta use these if you wanna play," he said, pointing to a bowl of quarters nearby. "Since it's a real one, designed to make money, you can't kick in a game except pumping those in."

He leaned over the far side, pressing his giant hand on the top glass, for balance, and suddenly the machine came to life. "I don't have it plugged in unless I'm playing. Leaving the lights off keeps the colors from fading." He took my hand in his, then with his other, grabbed a couple quarters, placing them into my palm. "Give it a shot."

"I know this game," I said. This was the most popular machine at the Golden Pheasant, the bar Gihh-rhaggs used to take me to. The owner bid to be in the test market, claiming the whole rest of New York might not have one. Patrons had grumbled when Gihh-rhaggs let me play out his balls, once he'd kicked someone's ass. Complainers whined that kids shouldn't be there at all, but the owner wanted to keep Gihh-rhaggs happy. I hadn't thought about it in years.

"You don't know just this game," Tim said. "You know *this* machine." He handed me a flashlight. "Here, look on the side near the wall. *Fireball* was one of the first pinballs that had art on the side." It wasn't elaborate, fakey flames and stars, Heaven and Hell, just like on the glass-back. Once videogames arrived, pinball had seemed like an Old Man game. Because pinball machines reminded me of Gihh-rhaggs, I still played when I came across them.

"What am I looking for?" I started to ask, when the flashlight caught graffiti scratched in those painted flames. It was a crude, pocketknife scratch, but it was distinct: MGM—100000.

"No high score markers on machines back then," Tim said. "To prove he could do it, one slow night, he played until he got too far. *We* watched it go from ninety-nine thousand nine hundred and ninety-nine, resetting to zero, like a used-car odometer scam. He scored that last point straight from the center. No accidental extra points. He was *that* good. Player Three. The machine always defaulted to Player One, and since no one who tried could match his other high scores on One or Two, choosing his Highest Score on Player Three made it almost impossible. As long as he kept kicking challengers' asses at The Pheasant too, his slate of zeroes remained intact. He wanted to have the proof and have it invisible. That's just how he was. There and not there. People tried, but his line of zeroes stays."

One of this game's unique features was that, at the end of every game, the numbers reverted to the highest recorded score—a crude forerunner to the High Score recorders on video games. Player Three was a rack of zeroes. I couldn't believe that all these years later, no one had found their way to playing the positions to use it. I ran my fingers across those letters and numbers he'd scratched in, and I knew he'd carved it with that weird lighter Mona had wanted to steal so bad. The contraption was like a Swiss Army knife: it was a lighter, a knife, a nail file, a corkscrew, bottle opener, and two little screwdrivers, one of each kind. Something that fancy? It was going to get noticed. She would have had to keep it in secret, all for herself.

"Go ahead," Tim said. "Beer in the fridge if you want. Just don't rest it on the machine. Be right back." He stepped into the dream bath, and I hit the game's plunger, sending my first pinball in over a decade on this machine careening into space. I watched it hit bumpers and get thrown across the star field, flying over the Devil Man's face. I ignored the climbing numbers.

These white brothers had spent their adult lives mostly with us, but to the best of my knowledge, neither had played Fireball as it was played on the reservation, two nights a year to celebrate the Creator's gift of sport. Arcade games kept you pumping in quarters to prove your skills with a scoreboard. This machine was maybe how Gihh-rhaggs and Tim reminded themselves that they lived among us, but weren't exactly like us. No matter how ensnared they'd become in our customs, they would always be men raised under a different sun.

"Hey, not bad," Tim said, coming out of the john. I was lame at video-games, but I had a decent knack with these. Still, I always got snagged on the ball traps. If I couldn't figure out how to release the trapped ones, my game was over.

"I never pay attention to the score," I said.

"I know all about the Creator games, son. Vestal never missed a Fire-ball game. But scores mean something to me, and they did to my brother." I'd never taken Vestal Sampson for a Fireball fan, but it was always played in the dark, so you never knew who might be in the crowd.

"Lemme show you," Tim said, leaning into me to take over my game. "How to get the most from your quarters." He hit the flipper gently and it fell to a sweet spot on the other flipper, and he slammed it across the surface, freeing my balls caught behind the trapdoors.

"You know," he said, casually careening his balls the way Christine's tossed darts found their way to the bull's-eye. "Of course you do. Since banks can't seize reservation land, you can add no home improvement loans on top of no mortgages." I didn't know. I figured we'd never got a bank loan because we lived on the skids. I didn't know this was a Rez-wide problem.

"I'm a pretty good saver, but we still had to eat and pay bills, and building materials ain't cheap. You might say this is 'The House that Fireball Built,' or helped build, anyway. My brother and me," he finished, letting his balls drop. "We were pinball hustlers. Worked with the guy who owned the Pheasant, who shared the cut." I should have figured out that Gihh-rhaggs wasn't just hustling cards in the back rooms at those bars. But the idea of betting on a pinball game seemed absurd. There had to be more reliable ways of getting cash.

"My brother liked challenges," Tim said. "And he liked high stakes. I guess that's the way most gamblers are. They think they can beat house rules, but nobody beats house rules, ever. Gambling odds are never designed to favor the player. You're like him that way."

"I'm no gambler," I said. DogLips Night's dice never held any appeal, and my mom's card games left me at a loss, considering how close to the edge we always lived.

"Sure you are, or you would've quit hanging around Night's kid years ago, when I first saw you as a little squirt. You must have known he was screwing you over before I told you." Whenever these brothers had sat at the dice table, Gihh-rhaggs never acknowledged me, so I'd thought he wanted me to be invisible. And I respected his wishes. They never acknowledged each other, either. You never wanted to give anyone the impression you came in with a plan to cheat, even if it wasn't true, so family members generally didn't interact in a serious game. I had just assumed Tim had no idea who I was. "Right? You had to know."

"What about you?" I said. "I'm guessing you still go there on some nights." Tim's life was none of my business, and yet it irritated me that he hadn't made the same break I had. I couldn't even say why. Maybe I worried the Nights would find a new way to exploit him. "I don't guess they've gotten any nicer."

"Nope, they haven't. But you accept the costs," he said, casually. I could hear myself explaining the same nonsense to Leonard, over a year before.

"Seems like a bad deal. I bet you even laugh when he calls you Fuck Face. Part of accepting the costs, right?" I wanted to reach into his shirt pocket and snag my dumbass letter. Not because anything I'd said was wrong or untrue. It just felt, now, like I'd maybe said true things in there that no one besides me ever needed to know.

"DogLips Night's got a knack," he said. "Keeping people on the line. Vestal knew about this machine. When The Pheasant's owner sold the bar, she talked him into selling it to her before the rest of the games went to auction. I can tell you, they ain't cheap. She didn't have enough so . . . she went to Night, hoping he'd float a loan. Him and Harvey Mastick. Make a good team. Night bought it outright, so she could pay *him* on time."

"With interest, I bet," I said, having seen that sad story over and over.

"Sure, with interest. He's no fool." Over the years, I'd seen folks sell Randy's dad and Carson's dad all the things they loved, hoping they'd get stable and get their stuff back. They called these exchanges "loans," but the folks desperate enough to show up at DogLips or Harvey's door never got back on top. So, they lost their collateral to other people looking for a bargain. It was how Carson got at least two of his guitars. Probably Randy, too.

"But here's the thing," he said, tapping his blunt fingers on the glass table, and the Tilt Warning light flashed on. It was a goosey machine, designed not to be messed with. "Vestal hadn't finished paying on it when . . . when she left."

"Don't even try to tell me he forgave the balance."

"Nah, I won't lie to you. Ever. You do enough of that, yourself, son. DogLips and your buddy there brought it over, a couple weeks after the funeral. Christine let them in. He even left a card taped to it. A picture of Vestal with the machine inside The Pheasant. And the card . . . Vestal had written it, telling me all about this. She'd kept it at Night's, already taped there, so I wouldn't accidentally find it. Reading the card was like having her back for a few minutes. I touched the letters she'd carved into the cardboard with her ballpoint. It seared my heart to feel those curlicues calling me from the past." His voice hitched. "Guess she was waiting for a special occasion, or maybe she had to pay in full." His breath came hard. "I don't know."

"But there was a bill for the balance, I bet."

"DogLips Night doesn't like writing things down."

"Man from an oral culture," I said, laughing. I didn't think Tim got the joke. "Okay, so he told you what you owed him. What was it?"

"Not everything's your business, son." His voice cleared instantly, as he gave me one of those rare direct looks. "You're a little too nosey for your own good sometimes, you know? Maybe you should work for a newspaper. Get paid for getting the scoops." I felt my neck get hot. More often than not, the things I'd learned by probing bit me in the ass. But no matter the sting, I'd always felt that knowing was better than not.

"What do you think DogLips's knack is?" Was it the same as Randy's? People came back over and over because he made your failings forgivable. People who hated or at least dismissed you, even the day before, he could give you his seal of approval and your life was different. Crawling back, *knowing* you were crawling back, was part of his price.

"His knack? That's easy. DogLips Night knows what's in your secret heart and he steals it when you're not looking. I guess you put up with it, because that house is so full of life."

"That's just effective thievery. Distracting you while he slides his hand in your pocket."

"The knack is, *sometimes*, he gives your lost thing back to you." I could see the attraction. I thought of all the regrets I had for not saying or doing some things, even though I wasn't even twenty, and I knew I'd lost some of those opportunities forever. Tim drained the beer he'd been nursing and stood up. "I better get you home. It's another school night, and you can't afford to screw up your grades."

"Pointless. All I'm doing is my time."

"Just the same, I understand you're a pretty smart guy. I don't wanna be responsible for you wasting your chances." He flicked off the main switch, but the Fireball still burned bright.

"You wanna take care of that? Don't want your colors fading, right?"

"They can burn a little while longer. Still got a couple balls left. Maybe I'll play when I come home." He handed me my jacket, and we headed out. The night air felt more like winter than earlier, which I hadn't thought possible. All the plastic grass, chocolate eggs, and pastel marshmallow Peeps jamming store shelves might have fooled you into thinking spring had arrived, but the wind cutting through your Levi's told you it was a long way off. We didn't say much most of the way as we neared my house, but something he'd said bugged me.

"What makes you think I'm smart, anyway? My ma doesn't even think I am, especially. She often says I miss a lot around me, with my head all adrift."

"I don't believe that for even one second," he said. Neither of them, though, knew I'd been secretly recording my memories, good and bad, to try and learn from mistakes—but also, I guess, to keep the color from fading. Nobody knew. It was just for me. My ma saw my only future as doing a Guy Version of her job, cleaning up the messes others had left behind, because they could afford to hire some desperate person to do it. Maybe she had some dim abstract hope I might try college, but that still remained a mystery world to all of us.

"Well, my biggest clue was that you finally quit carrying that stupid little club up this ratty old jacket's sleeve." He turned and poked a thick finger into my solar plexus. "Never carry a weapon that can be used against you." I silently watched Auntie Rolanda's trailer and then our old house grow large on the horizon, until he pulled into the driveway. I refused to let him know I was disappointed in the answer. I opened the door, and he grabbed my shoulder.

When I turned, he reached into his chest pocket and pulled out the envelope I'd given him, its seal torn. The letter I'd hoped would help him get through his toughest season of Vestal's absence.

"This took balls. I could *never* say these things, or things like this, even though I feel the same way. I don't know what this is. You and me. Friendship doesn't seem to cut it, but I don't know what else. But something beyond. You've got it here. I've felt every one of these times we've gotten together in the last month and a half. But whenever I try to say it, everything in my head sounds wrong. It's so easy for people to misunderstand what you're trying to say, and I'm getting old to start feeling the sharp broken-glass feeling of losing someone." He nodded and his eyebrows rose in the center, always like an arrow. He was trying to smile, but his lips quivered, and he pressed them hard together again, so they'd stop.

"When we lost our boy, Vestal hunted up her Jesus to get through. She was always calling him the Lord's son, or the Baby Jesus, like somehow he was up close and personal with her. That's not me. I didn't ever try to stop her, but that's not me. And now, somehow, it's like, without even trying, I found my own different son." He nodded as he said this, just slightly. He must have read the letter in the dream bath, while I played his version of Fireball. "*You* know how to get a hook in someone's secret heart, in ways

DogLips Night will never understand. *You* do it for the sake of the hook, the tug of connection between two people, the way its sharpness makes you feel alive. This hook," he said, tapping the envelope, "is not to reel someone in."

"I just believe there's gotta be other ways of living," I responded, telling myself as much as I was telling him. "Everything's an exchange, but not everything has to be commerce." I tried to say so many things in that letter I never could in person, where I was often clumsy and inarticulate, prone to saying mildly horrifying things that had not been my intent. I understood in this moment that I had reached him, touched him in the way I'd wanted, and now I didn't want to screw it up by offering something disappointing, like most of the words that fell from my mouth.

"Yeah, I knew that, at one point." He put the truck in park, like he was going to say something more. "Somehow . . . you forget," he finished, looking me in the eye, and then dropping his gaze. "Thanks for reminding me."

As I walked up the driveway, I thought about Gihh-rhaggs playing his zero game. In his own way, he understood the ways we interact. Everyone around him at that machine was either betting for or against him, for their own gain, but Gihh-rhaggs and Tim both knew what DogLips and Randy Night never would. They'd learned to play for the joy of connecting with other people, the feeling of existing in the same space together in the moment, sharing the air, and the electricity around you, not wondering who was bringing more, or worried about who owed whom. They'd found the tingling buzz of people being together and not keeping score.

CHAPTER SEVENTEEN

Semper Fi

(1984)

C hester fell into the same pattern as most off-Rez Indians who didn't live in Skin City. The idea of mystery neighbors was too weird, so he paid city rent, but stayed on our couch. "Hey Kato, the White Hornet's here," he'd say whenever Tim pulled in. "Time for your Rez Patrol."

Tim and I gained a steady routine and advancing comfort, digging deeper grooves into each other's days without trying. If his friends gave him shit, he never let on. Tim was the only one with a beer, calling me his chauffer, making me practice. By cap-and-gown time, I could do a three-point turn without thinking. Like most Rez Lappers, we'd circle, pulling U-ees at the border, swapping stories with others on the road. Eventually, we visited his Rez friends, never stopping at Randy's. If the people acted strange about my being there, we didn't return.

"Getting to be the time of year when people find out what colleges are taking them, isn't it?" Tim asked one night. He kept track of other people's future as if they were his own.

"I guess I've heard something like that." Almost every morning, someone would burst into Homeroom, telling friends they'd gotten their letters. People with family businesses they'd be expected to work in didn't participate. And I guess others just had opportunities lined up, too.

"Expecting any letters like that?"

"No, none like that," I answered. "Letters from a buddy in the Marines, that's about it."

"Why's that?"

"Well, that's all they allow you to send in. I like being able to write a letter that means something." He nodded. "Though he was able to send a package."

"No, I mean . . ."

"I know what you meant," I said. "I didn't understand the outdated college applications my mom had, and I was too embarrassed to ask kids in class. They always knew they were going to college." I didn't have friends among those getting pre-nostalgic about Our Last Whatever.

"Don't they have counselors at school? People who tell you about colleges? I know they don't talk with kids like Christine 'cause of vocational training, but . . ."

"They took us to some factories. The airport. And some guy from a school in California called Standford came and talked to us—"

"Stanford," he corrected. "Fancy place. That interest you? They talk about scholarships?"

"California? Shit, he might as well have been talking about trips to Mars," I said. "Who's gonna leave the Rez and go across the country where you don't know anyone?" Randy and his gang laughed when I'd asked how close the school was to LA. He knew I had no business California dreaming. I spent my time with adults, already beaten down by the world.

"Those are the only places?" he asked, implying I was leaving out information. "One guy from Stanford? No local colleges? Or like Rochester or Syracuse if you don't want to stay?"

"That's all I got invited to attend. Maybe there were others. I don't present well," I said, adding a little laugh. Though I'd spent seventeen years of my life observing the world, and had discovered in my letter I could reach someone on paper, whenever I actually opened my mouth, my words fell out like Boggle tiles, flat, disorganized.

I'd quit caring what classmates thought of me that year, gave up on serious talk and became a wiseass. As long as you busted balls, you had friends. It didn't take much, so I otherwise checked out. I was a ghost in my own senior class, with not a single plan after the end of June.

Before Leonard had left, we'd communicated in elliptical sidelong stories from our lives, like the way he'd made me understand what had happened in the gorge. He'd tell me a story he seemed to think was important, and I had to ask the right questions to get the rest. The drunker we got, the clearer the stories became. He also didn't know this was a very typical way of telling stories on the Rez, so I knew how to ask the right questions, and I told him some of my own. I left Tim out. I still did not have words to describe this friendship that I thought would make sense to anyone else.

Once Leonard left and sent me his Boot Camp address, I started straightforward and factual, but then thought about how we told stories to each other and began writing him longer, more detailed letters, like the one I'd written Tim. This was the one thing I was good at. Leonard had sent gifts from the PX at first, Marines T-shirts, with a bulldog and "oo-rah" screened on them. This was apparently a thing recruits said to each other to keep their shit together.

When Leonard failed Marksmanship, he had to go to a tutorial, finishing out of sequence from the guys he'd entered with. He said recruits a few racks over whispered oo-rah after Lights Out, helping him hang in until he passed. "Remember those words," he finished in the letter accompanying the shirts. "Two magic phrases to live by. Oo-rah and Semper Fi." *Semper Fi* I knew meant something formal—always faithful. Moose-Knuckle Stew had it tattooed on his arm. I supposed he hadn't seen the irony. Leonard would undoubtedly follow suit.

Leonard said not to send gifts, just letters about what was happening here. They helped him with homesickness. I kept up my end, but took my letters further. I told him I really missed him, how much I appreciated the way we'd hung out before he left. I understood his bravery in having me buzz his hair and letting me understand the toughest parts of his life. Sometimes I drew the Corps Bulldog Mascot and gave him encouraging word balloons to speak, on the back.

His letters grew shorter, factual, less lonely. After I asked about his new Boot graduation day, he stopped writing. Maybe part of becoming a Marine, writing yourself a different story. I kept extending my hand, though, so he'd know I was here, in any way I could be.

One April Thursday heading to the Smoking Lav, I felt gut-punched.

At the lunchroom vendor tables, a Marine recruiter had set up applications and pamphlets, and, right next to him, Leonard Stoneham sat at attention in dress blues. His head was practically shaved, like the buzz cut I'd given him. His scalp looked even more like the project maps Christine and I had made.

"Welcome, young man!" The recruiter drew a bead on me as I rushed forward. I fit the profile he was looking for. I pictured neighborhoods beyond Rez borders, guys coming home, speaking to younger brothers, cousins, neighbors, signing them up to get a pay bump, a few days liberty, a better assignment, places where young men disappeared and came home only on leave. "Hi," I said. "Thanks, I'm actually here to . . ." I started, reaching my hand out to shake Leonard's.

"These brochures explain the benefits of enlisting in the United States Marine Corps," Leonard said, filling my hand with pamphlets, instead of his raw-looking hand knotted with veins. "We offer benefits through your time, opportunities for advanced training in interest areas, toward a career or college, a choice some recruits make after their tours." He smiled a small, professional gap, teeth barely visible, as if we'd never met one another before. "Sergeant Johnson here will be happy to take down your contact information," he added, gesturing to the older man, and then greeted people walking by, as if they'd made eye contact. Most rushed by.

I figured it was required official Marine Representative Behavior. He was in uniform. At the end of the day, they were gone, pamphlets presumably left with guidance counselors. It was as if they'd never been here. Maybe he'd be at the Spithouse that night. Even as I had that thought, I understood its desperation. And yet, once it entered, I couldn't stop it from scurrying around in my head. It was a bad idea, but it wriggled away every time I tried to boot it out.

That afternoon, when the phone buzzed as I walked in, the call was surprisingly for me. Disappointingly it wasn't Leonard. I fortunately didn't have to say much, just listen, answer a series of yes or no questions, and then look on the wall calendar. I confirmed I was free.

My broader school speaking skills had deteriorated in the past year, I realized. I didn't raise my hand in class, or yack in the Smoking Lav beyond jokes, and my new job, digging holes and running limestone trails to keep jocks on target for their scholarships, left me mostly solitary. I'd come to feel comfortable talking honestly with Tim and most other conversations didn't compare. I didn't feel like I could call Leonard. What if his new stepsiblings refused to put him on? What if they said he wasn't there, when in reality, I might hear him in the background?

Leonard pretending he didn't know me, and vanishing before we could speak, continued to agitate me. I tried lying down and listening to *Signals*, Rush's most recent album. But its songs were so much about the subdivisions in our lives, all the ways we were disconnected from each other, how even when we wanted to reach out and feel another person meaningfully, it just made things worse. I put my clothes back on and reverted to walking the Rez.

I eventually found myself in front of Tim Sampson's place, already sweaty and chafing. It was one of those April gift days that felt like mid-June. You knew they weren't going to stay, but they were a joy at the tail of brutal winters. Tim loomed in his yard, trimming hedges with a cooler sitting nearby, and Christine's abandoned boom box streaming Oldies into the air. He'd stripped off his sweaty T-shirt and tossed it over the back of a lawn chair.

"Where ya headed, son?" he asked, setting the clippers aside and walking toward me.

"Thinking about going to the city," I said, an incomplete answer if ever there were one. The longer I'd walked, the more I'd figured I could try hitching to the Spithouse. Maybe snag a city bus. Maybe Leonard was there and could explain the past few months to me. I accepted that I still did things wrong and suspected my letters maybe weren't as helpful as I'd hoped. If I could come up with the right words in person, maybe it would make the difference. Other Thursday regulars I'd known the year before would be there, so I wasn't worried about a ride home.

"Long ways away, by foot. This what you do on your Thursdays?" he asked, nodding. I hadn't been to the Spithouse so much since Leonard had left, but Tim didn't know, so he just never bothered to check on Thursdays. "Whatcha got going on in the city? Girlfriend?"

"Nah, just some friends," I said, realizing in the same way I'd never told Leonard about Tim, I'd mostly left Leonard out of the things Tim and

I discussed. Having two white friends who didn't know each other some-how felt like I was sneaking around. "One of them's home from the ser-vice. We were supposed to hang out when he got home from Boot Camp. But then he had some troubles completing the requirements, and they seri-ously put him further back. And—"

"Then you never heard more. But you saw him *somewhere* today. Recruitment table?"

"Yeah, that's right."

"Marines. And he's home. Was he supposed to pick you up tonight?" I was at a loss. My idea now seemed so pathetic if I spoke it. We'd become pretty honest with each other, me and Tim, but I couldn't tell him the dis-tilled truth. I was walking to the city, hoping to get with an old buddy who might be there or might not, to fix something I didn't even know was broken.

"You wanna have a seat here for a minute?" The porch felt good, a relief to my sore feet. He offered me a beer, but I followed him inside and grabbed a Pepsi instead, pacing myself for later. He stepped into the bathroom, and I could hear the water running.

"You ready to make your first big drive off the reservation?" he asked, heading to his bedroom, a towel around his waist, sweaty pants bunched in his hands. "First by your choice," he corrected, laughing, coming out with a new pair on, still undone, a new shirt and a pair of socks in his hand. We grinned at each other. "Anyway, you want to?"

"Not really?" I said.

"Come on! Tell you what, we get you a license, I promise, you and me, we'll cross the border and you can finally see Lakeside Park. I'll be your navigator, but you drive."

"Where to tonight?" I asked in response to this strange offer, as he sat at the counter, putting his new socks on. "Not that I think I'm ready for a drive to the Falls, let alone across the border." I wasn't sure I could handle the details of driving and looking for the landmarks off the Rez. But he finished dressing and we were on our way.

"Where was it you were going?" he asked, and I told him. "Scene of the crime," he said, which I didn't get. Then it seemed to sink in. "That's where you've been spending your nights when you're not home?" Tim let

out some exasperated sound, the kind my ma would make when the February heating bill came in. "Could get your ass kicked at that place. And
then have to worry about finding a ride home? Not your place."

"What makes you think you know where I belong?"

"I don't know that, but I do know something about where you might
not belong, and Spithouse is definitely on that list. If you're going *out* out,
like to bars, should probably go to the Circle. That's where Indians go. If
memory serves me right, Thursday nights are D and D at Spithouse," he
said, and I nodded. "Hardcore drinkers out in force. They don't care how
it tastes, just getting buzzed to last through the night, or maybe to find
someone likeminded to keep them company. Either way, not a good place
for a youngster."

"I've been there lots of times," I started.

"You sure have," he said, laughing again. I hated not being in on the
joke.

"Um, I've never driven there? Obviously? So, I don't truthfully know
where I'm going." I could get us to the commercial district before the city.
Beyond that, I would be guessing.

"You can say that again. Been there when pool cues meet foreheads?"
I shook my head. "Didn't think so, but you will, and trust me, with your
scrawny ass, it's gonna be *your* forehead, but it won't ever be your pool
cue. Hope you find someplace else to hang around soon."

"I plan to do just that. But, um, first? I'm serious," I said, pulling over.
"Mind driving, since you seem to know where we're going?" He got out
and walked around, once again expecting me to slide across the bench.

"So where you gonna be hanging instead?" he asked, adjusting the
bench.

"I talked with a Marine Recruiter today. That's how I knew my buddy
was home. They were at the table together at school." Tim made that irritated sound again.

"Let me guess. By the time you got home, the recruiter had already
called your house."

"That's about right," I said. A year before, I'd have laughed at the suggestion. But I'd seen Leonard leave us in average shape and come home
less than a year later a powerhouse who could stop any bar fight at the

Spithouse. I'd gone most of my life being scrawny, and assumed that a build like Tim's was by genetics and good nutrition as a kid. Leonard's change made me see that, even if I'd never be a giant, I wasn't stuck always in the vulnerable position.

"That recruiter know you're friends with the Boot graduate?" I nodded. "I bet he told you you'd maybe be eligible to be stationed together." Before I could respond, he jumped back in, color rising on his cheeks. "Bullshit, by the way. They can do that, *if* you sign up together, but your buddy's already on a different path. You got set up. *You* signing up? That's a worse idea than coming to Drink and Drown Nights here. When's your enlistment meeting?"

"Monday, after work."

"Shit, that's not much time. Listen, come over tomorrow, okay? Never mind, I'll pick you up. Can you be ready by noon?"

"Ready for what?" I asked, as he pulled over to the curb and turned the key, pulling it from the ignition. "I'd have to skip school."

"High school is just some shit you have to get through," he said, opening the driver's side door. I realized we were parked down the street from the Spithouse. I hadn't been paying attention, so I still didn't know how to get here. "Aren't we going in? I could catch a brew."

"Thought you didn't like that place," I said, getting out.

"Just said *you* shouldn't be here." We crossed the street, and walking in, he held out a five as I showed my ID.

"I can pay my own way," I said, reaching into my pocket. "Appreciate it, thanks."

"Sure thing," he said, and we sat at the bar. I looked in the mirror behind the bar. We probably looked funny together. He was a middle-aged guy, catching a nightcap, and I was a punk, looking stoked in my new world. I didn't mind, until I looked deeper into the reflection and saw Leonard with another buzzed-head guy at a far table, toasting their futures.

"That your friend?" Tim said, looking at my expression in the bar-back mirror.

"How'd you know?"

"Been on that receiving end myself. You had the need to come so urgently, hoping he was here and hoping he wasn't here." I nodded. "Gonna be a kick in the nuts, but be the bigger man and say hi. Don't worry. I'll be here."

Nearing their table, I could see that the other guy looked Indian, too. "This Chatty Cathy?" he said to Leonard, who'd been watching me the whole time I walked over, expressionless.

"Yup. Chatty?" Leonard said to me, as if I'd always gone by this name. "Meet Chief. He's from a reservation, too. Where was it, Chief?" I stuck out my hand, but Chief didn't take it.

"I'm in a different tribe now," Chief said, shouting "Oo-rah!" into Leonard's face.

"Oo-rah!" Leonard echoed, drinking. A few people glanced, but this could be a rowdy place in general. "So who's that you're with, Chatty? Your dad?" he asked, flicking his buzzed head in Tim's direction. "Finally something in common?" They'd noticed when we came in.

"Friend of mine," I said. "How long you been here?"

"Few minutes," Chief said, nodding at the tall stack of empty plastic cups in front of each. "Going to probably call it an early night." He turned to Leonard. "Why don't you do a Head Call before we split, so we don't have to stop every five minutes?"

Leonard looked at the floor, neck veins pulsing as he sipped from his cup. He got up, faking a yawn and a stretch, then headed to the john. Chief turned to me once he was gone.

"I told him from the beginning you were gonna be trouble, that he'd let the wrong Indian latch on," he said, once Leonard was out of earshot. "He thought he should take a chance. Said he wondered why someone from the Rez here wanted to hang with him. He figured you were too scrawny to be any danger. He don't know scrawny Indians are more dangerous than big ones. We ain't never met, but I know how my Rez works. There's only room for one bruised apple in a basket, buddy, and this basket's mine. You move your little ass along." His fist quietly slammed on the table, shockwaves thrumming down the pedestal to the foot ring. I started to get up. What was there left to say? But he spoke again.

"You sure gave Crater there some miserable time in Boot." He looked to the ceiling, maybe debating whether he had time to say what he wanted, then back at me. "He belongs to a new family now. And one of the deals in Boot? When you get a letter from home? You gotta read it out loud to everyone. DI had a fucking ball with your letters. Funny your voice ain't nearly as high and girly as DI made it out to be. Usually it's the come-home-and-satisfy-me letters everyone wants to hear the most, but yours were pretty hilarious." I could imagine every supportive word I'd written, how easily they could be turned to make Leonard seem weak. Then I remembered how, the more I wrote, the less he responded.

"Thought I was helping him," I said. "Why didn't he just ask me to stop writing?"

"Any Marine did that? All our good letters stop too. Crater tells me the recruiter here's trying to sign you up. You running from the Rez? To be in the Corps, you should only be running to, not away from. You won't survive."

Leonard drifted back and drained his beer. "Coming?" Chief asked, standing.

"Your turn for Head Call," Leonard said. Apparently, it was code for: *Give me a minute to humiliate someone.* Leonard waited until his voice wouldn't carry.

"Meeting with the recruiter? You're gonna be a Marine now, Brian? You ain't Marine material. Chief tells me guys try the Corps as a ticket off the reservation. Said they always wash out. Never make it. Those letters . . . you're never gonna be tough enough to be like me."

"I wrote those to help—"

"Shut up. Chief said Indians only make friends with white people when they get booted by their own." He believed this bullshit made up by a stranger, knowing from me that everyone on the Rez was in some way connected to each other. It was one of the things he seemed mildly jealous of, when I told him the various stories from different times in my life, back when we shared things.

"I guess in your case, it was that Night shithead. I took a chance on you, knowing my own crazy world at home, but you're exactly what Chief said." He punctuated this rant, slamming his fist down quietly, too. They weren't wide swings, but the shockwaves thrummed down the pedestal to the foot ring as Chief's had, like they'd each become echoes of the other.

"You're not one of us. You just try on other people's clothes," he continued. "You can't just try on the Corps uniform 'cause there's nothing better to do. You're just like the rest of them." Who were *the rest of them*? I thought to myself. Indians? Non-Marines? People who hadn't jumped into the gorge? People without cars? People without scars? Nope. Couldn't be that one. He stood up and leaned in, finishing: "Find your own damned clothes."

"Don't you worry about that," I said. "If Boot Camp turns people into the kind of asshole you've become, then I definitely don't need to go there. No shortage of assholes in my life these days." I got up and walked to the men's room, leaving Leonard. The last I saw of him, he passed by the bouncer, on his way out. Even as pumped as he was, the bouncer was bigger. Leonard was still a boy trying on a man's body for size, waiting to grow into it.

"Where'd your buddies go?" Tim asked, as I walked up behind him, meeting his eyes in the bar-back mirror where the first dollar and all kinds of other shit was taped.

"They . . . they had to leave. Tired," I said.

"Tired," he repeated. "Just as well. Let's go. You should have an early night tonight, anyway. You've got an appointment in the morning." We left our still-full plastic cups. Bruno, the human wall who served as bouncer, nodded as we headed out the door.

"For what?"

"Not, for what . . . with who?" Tim unlocked my truck door.

"Okay, with whom?"

"Friend of mine," he said. "I called him from the pay phone. He owes me for something a ways back, and he remembered, without my having to provide the due bill."

"What kind of friend?"

"Different kind of recruiter. You didn't sign on the dotted line yet, did you?" I shook my head. I'd done preliminary paperwork at the table, for more information, but hadn't committed a signature to any piece of paper. "Good. When he comes to pick you up on Monday—"

"How do you know he's picking me up?"

"They always pick you up. Harder to back out. Nothing personal. Bodies are a recruiter's job, and you're another body. When he comes, I'll be there with you. We're going to tell that recruiter you have other plans. You tell him you changed your mind, you're going to say thank you for your time, and that you're sorry you inconvenienced him. He'll turn around, but you'll hear from that Sergeant again. He's gonna call you back and ask to meet you when I'm not around. But tomorrow, you and me, we're getting you enrolled in classes over at the community college for fall. It's what they call open admission. No tests can keep you out. Clean slate."

"What makes you think I want to get out of signing up?"

"I don't know where you're headed, son, but it surely isn't the Marines. The Corps draws a lot of hardheads like your friends there, people who need to belong to something, and who know *how* to fit into that thing. Know how to follow rules. How to toe the line. That last guy you were talking to? That other Indian guy?"

"I didn't know him. He's not from around here. He came home with Leonard because he didn't want to go back to his own home."

"Sounds familiar. Well, he decided, like your buddy, years before you ever met him, that you're not one of them. Your buddy could afford to be friendly because he knew the Marines were his future and you were his past. Every once in a while, people like him need to remind themselves of that something they belong to. That it's important for them. The right decision. You were the evidence of the other side, this time. You became everything that doesn't fit his new life."

"What makes you an expert on the Marines all of a sudden?"

"There is nothing all of a sudden about my life," he said, rolling up his right sleeve at the next light. "I knew my buddy would do me that favor. I didn't have to show him this as a reminder." On his bicep, muddy and hazy, in fading ink like you see on butcher-shop meat, still legible, sat two words. Buried in the blond fur and blotchy skin was that Latin phrase Leonard was in love with. I'd seen Tim with his shirt off numerous times, even just a few hours before, and never noticed it. "The due bill."

Good on his word, the following morning, we drove to the college and Tim introduced me to his friend who worked there, someone involved with admissions. We flipped through the register, listing the hundreds of courses being offered. I remembered my ma saying, years before, that we were so poor I'd qualify for something called Financial Aid, but that felt like too much to process, seeing all these potential futures flying by in small print. "I don't really know what to pick," I said. For the first time, I wasn't being told what to do, and I froze. What if I made a mistake? "What do most people take?"

"A lot of people come here for nursing," the counselor said. "We've got a great placement record. Or there's related medical fields," he added. "All two-year degrees." That seemed more manageable. "The first semester courses are all the same, but even if you change, they still fit for science requirements." None of that made sense to me, but I guessed it would soon enough. I agreed to let him register me in medical technology classes for fall. I didn't see myself being a nurse, but the other options looked okay. Tim and I had never talked about Hillman, but maybe he knew enough about the deeper Rez cultures to grasp that I was connected to our side of medicine. Or maybe he just remembered all those Rez ladies who came here, signing up for nursing. "Some of these high school classes count as advanced placement," the counselor said, looking at the list I'd written down. "You can get some credit for introductory courses for those."

"I got your entrance fees waived," Tim added. Maybe that was a tough thing to do. I knew nothing about this world at all. "And I can help you fill out the financial aid forms. I did it for Hayley." He handed me some forms already partially completed, with pencil asterisks where he said my ma had to fill in the numbers. I already knew the numbers from the earlier forms she'd given me, but still put them away to finish at home.

"Those guys at the bar?" Tim said, as we walked out of the building. "They needed to be faithful to each other, to some idea that helps young men like them feel a part of something bigger. You're already part of some-thing bigger. You've got to be faithful to something inside here." He tapped the side of my head, and then, my chest, and we got in his truck, heading to the Rez. "I don't know what it is, and you're probably too young just yet to know, yourself, but one thing I do know. What you are looking for? You're surely not going to find it on Parris Island."

CHAPTER EIGHTEEN

Open Admissions

(1985)

I looked my fetal pig in the eye. "I'm sorry, Algie, no disrespect intended," I said. I'd named him after the floating pig Pink Floyd brought with them on tour. His tongue lolled out the side. The first major discovery I'd made about the difference between high school and college: If you didn't do the work here, in college, you just failed. In high school, some teachers just let you pass so they didn't have to see you again, but that was not happening here. I had to do something fundamentally different. "I'd make a face at me, too, if I'd given my life up for an idiot who's gonna get a C, maybe a C+, if Dr. Freeland's feeling generous. And what patient wants to be in the hands of someone who's an average student at best?" Also, some teachers, professors, went by *Doctor*. Like Freeland. Since it was the first time most of us had encountered this title in a classroom, we were always screwing it up.

"Folks, when you're done cleaning up your area," Freeland said, "wrap your pigs and any extraneous scraps in plastic and put them in the medical disposal bin. Don't toss them. It's bad enough some of this formaldehyde aerosolizes in air. If you splash it, your mucous membranes will be exposed to more and the room will inevitably only smell worse. Remember, wash your hands with the provided Irish Spring. It is, we've discovered, the only soap that diminishes the odor some. Study hard for your finals next week. If you've been keeping up, you should do fine. If you haven't, cramming isn't going to help."

"Thank you, Algie, for the key lesson," I said, returning to my pig. My lab partner raised an eyebrow, but if there's one thing about being Indian out in the broader world, it's that people around you will buy that *anything* might be a ceremony. I shrouded Algie in the plastic wrap, as requested, and sprayed down the rubber-coated lab table, systematically removing all traces of my presence from participating in this process. Soon enough, all my molecules would be gone.

From my first day in class, I'd felt like maybe I'd made a mistake in my choice of major. By midterm deficiency warnings, I was starting to feel like maybe I needed an even bigger switch. I wasn't excelling. Apparently, I needed more than just a chance. Apparently I wasn't as smart as I thought.

My strong resistance to cutting into Algie also told me I was not meant for working on humans, at least with scalpels. "Dr. Freeland?" I asked, raising the little pig. "If you didn't do much damage, can your pig be, um, recycled?" It felt wrong to heave him into the medical disposal bin, so much sacrifice wasted. A couple other low-mileage pigs seemed in similar shape.

"Every student deserves a fresh subject," Freeland said. "Rather than revisiting someone's earlier mistake. Into the bin." Understood—I wouldn't want someone else's used pig.

The next week, Intro to Bio was the last final of my first semester, and I finished the exam early. I'd spent fifteen weeks in my pretend goal of being a medical technologist, because I'd signed up in a panic for one of the few reasons people from the Rez went to college. I wondered what my great uncle Hillman would think of fetal pig classes. Leaving the exam, I stopped in Admissions, where Tim's friend, Ross-something, worked. I never did memorize his last name.

"Got a minute?" I asked, knocking on his open door. Ross invited me to sit, offering me a cup of coffee and asking how it was going. I launched right in, just to be done with it.

"I'm near the end of my first semester. To be truthful, I'm not sure this is for me, after all. If I can't cut up a pickled pig fetus, how can I be responsible for medical events in people's lives? I'm considering doing a Withdrawal and didn't want you coming across papers without notice, thinking it was a mistake. I wanted to say, thanks for trying." I stood, reaching for my bag.

"Dropping a class might jeopardize financial aid. Let me check before you do anything." He went over to a file cabinet to grab my admissions folder.

"I mean withdrawing from school. I don't feel like I should be here."

"I told Sampson he was throwing his money away," Ross answered, closing the cabinet door.

"Look, this is hard enough. You think I want to be a failure at eighteen? Besides, Tim told me he got the fees waived," I said, annoyed. "Not technically *his* money."

"Fees aren't waived for anyone," Ross said, not bothering to sound like a diplomatic school official. "Sampson paid them, and you had a lot of favors called in to get you into those classes too. There's a waiting list for that writing class you've got lined up for spring. The anatomy ones you've got as well, for that matter. You wouldn't have gotten in otherwise for another semester. Maybe two."

"Well, who would do that? He doesn't have any pull here, I'm sure." Apparently, it wasn't on the promise of my future. Was I irritated at this guy, or grateful? I had no idea what to feel about Tim. One part of me wanted to stay, another wanted to go to the pay phones by the snack bar. The Marine recruiter's card was still in my wallet, with "Call any time, son" written on the back.

"I did it," Ross the Counselor said. "For *him*, not for you. And now I owe somebody for force registering you. You have no idea what this creative writing course cost me. It's got prerequisites, and it isn't even in your major. Or even *close* to your major."

"You owe Tim something big then," I said. I remembered that, if Ross rolled up his sleeve, I'd see the same blurry tattoo Tim had, the kind likely scarring over on Leonard Stoneham's arm. What had happened between them? Something major, clearly.

"That's business between friends. You don't ask why a friend wants something. You make a decision on whether the friend is worth it, and you act accordingly. I'm sad to see that Sampson was maybe wrong investing in you. He always was soft for head cases, even in Boot Camp." He laughed to cushion what he'd said, but it still stung. "What else are you enrolled in for spring? In addition to Creative Writing and Anatomy?" I explained I hadn't done too well in my major courses, even beyond Algie, and wasn't really interested in hospital work after all.

"Well," Ross said, sighing and standing. "What are you interested in?" Outside, it was growing dark, snow starting to blow. This guy surely worked on the clock and was supposed to have left twenty minutes ago. "This creative writing stuff?"

"I don't know," I said, pausing, then figuring I had nothing to lose. "I guess, yeah. Writing. Journalism. I like working on the paper here, the journal. I wrote that article about the spring-semester film series." I embraced the intoxication of those words. I'd never really told anyone about falling in love with the weird midnight movies. I'd discovered them briefly on a Canadian station that played wacky stuff on *The All-Night Show*, and from there, I had fantasized about seeing them, but no one ever wanted to go to the movies at midnight. When I watched the bizarre movies I'd desired that the college occasionally showed, it was like accessing a world previously closed off.

"I read that article," he said, which I figured was a lie. "Looks like a good lineup. Couple freaky ones too. That *Basket Case* one, I don't know." That was the one I most eagerly awaited. It had been on the Midnight art-house circuit for at least a year. "Creative writing's not too practical, but practical's not a requirement for higher education. What's wrong with journalism? If you're serious about a change, Communication's a legit different major. And when you finish, you take that degree to one of the schools we have transfer agreements with, boom, you've got half a Bachelor degree, right as you start. Buffalo State, or the university. You have options, you know. It's not that hard."

"Not that hard, if you got a car and the income to keep it legal," I said. It always came back to the physics of my life. If I stayed in college, it was going to be years before I owned a car. I knew Journalism was a fool's dream in a one-newspaper town, too. I'd read pamphlets on internships, independent study, travel abroad—awesome opportunities, in theory, but you had to have basic shit together to pull any of them off. I couldn't picture my community college classmates swinging the Semester in Paris they were advertising. Maybe all of it was a lie, so we'd feel like we were students at a four-year college. So we could pretend we hadn't needed the junior college Open Admissions policies.

"You could take out more loans, I'm sure. Have you looked?" Ross said, with all the awareness of someone who had a steady decent income, with some left over when the next paycheck rolled in. "And if you stick around in a different major, these bio classes could still count as science electives."

"I think you might want to get home," I said, getting up to leave. "And I should, too."

"Look," Ross said. "Don't do anything yet. Your financial aid has your next semester covered, and it goes straight to the college. Even if you drop out, you won't get it. Just hang in there and maybe we'll figure something out. Will you do that, for a friend?"

"Are we friends?" It didn't seem likely.

"No, but we share a friend. And if I know him, and I do, he's invested a lot in you. For him?" Ross got me in the one place I couldn't say no. "You have a ride home?"

"It's not that far," I said. "I can walk." He made me shake hands, and then I made my way toward an exit in a different part of the building. I took one last trip through the snack bar, buying another coffee to warm my hands for the walk. I didn't want him skulking up to me with a pity ride. The college was quiet. The next round of finals had begun, and anybody not taking one had hit it, before the snow picked up.

Creative Writing was an Elective, a course to make you a more well-rounded person. I had liked that even if no one ever saw my private stories, they would still be decently developed, at least for me. The college didn't have a major in writing, and even if they did, what would you do with the degree once you had it? Communications might be a good foundation for a Journalism degree, if I wanted to entertain a fantasy future. The activities around those classes were the things I'd enjoyed most about the college, but it wasn't like people were begging for news and insights about Rez life, and they sure didn't want plain old stories about it.

I had decent financial aid because we were so broke, but still, school was beginning to feel like just another lie to tell myself, another way to drift until the next forceful wave crashed into me. That connection Leonard had with his friend Chief? It had stayed in my head. Should I be faithful to dreams or reality? I never did know, but it wasn't for lack of trying.

Among the required fees Tim evidently paid was one for Student Activities, and I'd figured from the start if I were going to try this, I should make the most of it. The English people had something called the student literary mag, but it only came out once a year. I had already told myself I likely wouldn't be there a second year, so that was out, but I'd fallen in with the college newspaper crowd. The stained furniture and burnt coffee were the closest this place came to seeming like home. Like I told Ross, I'd even reported on a few on-campus events, after the paper adviser made fun of me for *loitering*. I'd written about the end of the semester party, food drive, a poetry guest speaker, and that movie series. I liked seeing my name in print. It was as good a plan to consider as any, I guessed. I had a few weeks left to think.

Just beyond the back Student Center doors, Tim Sampson's truck idled in the driveway circle. Sometimes, the way he showed up made me feel like I was living in a low-rent remake of *Christine*, the killer-car movie, but starring a sturdy old Chevy pickup instead of a red vintage Plymouth Fury. He flicked the high beams. There was no way out of this where I wouldn't look like an asshole, so I opened the door and asked what he was doing there.

"Came to pick you up," he said, like we were in my ma's driveway, and were going out for an early evening. "Want your help with something. The least you can do, since I got you into here," he added. I climbed in. "Christine's got herself a job at the hairdo place that other girl from the reservation owns. You know, over by the BK?"

"Say that's cool," I said. "It's what she wanted." I'd heard around that she'd gotten her cosmetology license.

"Yeah, I guess it is," he said.

"You had other plans for her?"

"Nah," he said, but then revealed he still had doubts. "My only plan was for her to be happy, but . . . I don't know, maybe she'll get by on that. You know how it is. No house payment if she wants to stay where we are. And it's a good enough house. Kept us happy."

"Don't be surprised if she needs a change of pace," I said, aware that DogLips Night's endless parties had their own special form of gravity that sometimes still pulled me, even in college. If it was that powerful on me, I'm sure she felt it too. It wasn't strong enough that I attended, but I was mad at myself for still having the desire. I worried it might tip in the wrong direction, now that I had time off. The amnesia Randy produced was like a paralyzing venom, once you were in range. Their parties were so alive, you stopped for a few laughs, and suddenly the next morning your head was pounding and your pockets were filled with echoes. "But even if she goes, she'll probably come back. We always do."

"That's what I'm hoping," he said. "You planning on leaving?"

"My feet are a little tired to leave town, just yet," I said. Where would I go? Had the Marines even been a legit option for me, beyond the desire for a quick escape? I refused the sustained pain of a tattoo, so Boot Camp was probably out of the question, anyway. That Recruiter card was just another in an endless series of punctured life preservers I had dragged along with me. I was a contrarian—a life based on following orders without question was a recipe for doom. I didn't have a path of my own, but I also had no patience for someone else trying to shape one for me. Maybe that was the long-term gift Randy gave me. I was well versed in what it meant to follow someone down a stupid path, just because you were too afraid to come up with your own.

"So I wanna get Christine a car for Christmas," Tim said as we headed to town. "Something reliable, so she can get back and forth to her work-place safely." I agreed it was a logical plan. "But you know. I'm in my fif-ties. What do I know about what's groovy?"

"Well, not the word 'groovy,' for one," I said.

"I know. Just testing you," he said. "But you're her age. Used cars are always a compromise. Someone got rid of them for a reason. I know how to spot most trouble, and even the kinds I can't fix, I probably know some-one who can, but . . . I don't want her to be embarrassed to drive it. Know what I mean?" I didn't, really. The idea of being picky about a car was beyond my imagination.

"I'm maybe not your guy," I said. "I don't know much about cars, and these days, I don't know much about Christine, except what you, yourself, tell me. Do my best, but in this? Your guess really is as good as mine. Or better."

"So how'd your first half a year go?" he asked.

"Semester," I clarified. "They call them semesters in college. 'Cause you finish the class. A lot of senior-year classes were that way too." I remained lame at real conversations most of the time, but I could drone on about college classes to avoid meaningful topics. I suspected he was asking how I was truly doing, and I was embarrassed to report that, even now, after fifteen weeks, I was not that informed. Somehow, when I looked up from studying, all my old friends had drifted out of my old life, or I'd drifted out of theirs. I had very little knack of finding new ones.

When all the disruption had settled, and I'd tried to make this go of it, I was still mostly alone when it came down to it. In that revolving door of people, Tim had been the one constant. Apparently, he had become my best friend. I couldn't articulate that again, without sounding weird and awkward.

We pulled into one lot and wind blasted our faces, no matter what direction we turned across the macadam. After a quick look, he settled on a blue Nova, and arranged to pick it up on Christmas Eve. It seemed like he'd made up his mind before we'd even gotten there.

"Wanna get a burger or something?" he asked. Leftover cold spaghetti awaited me at home, but I'd spent the last of my cash on that coffee. "My treat," he added.

In a corner booth, we watched snow accumulate fast. I was glad all I had do for the next few days was shovel the driveway and fill our kerosene heaters and the water pail, make sure the pump didn't freeze, catch up on TV, and try to help my ma coordinate her work rides.

"For helping me." Tim slid a hundred-dollar bill my way. He had a thing for this idea.

"Get out of here," I said, and slid it back.

"You're passing me this hundred dollars?" he asked, revealing two slips of paper.

"Yup, I sure am," I said.

"Okay, you just bought yourself a truck, somewhat used, for one hundred dollars," he said, writing this down on the piece of paper that already had other details, including the VIN, in his blocky handwriting. He slid it back to me, with the title and the keys to his truck. "I think you know how it handles. You've already test-driven it. Hope you don't mind giving me a ride home, though. Would suck to be out hitching on a night like this, wouldn't it?"

"I can't take this, Tim." I set my burger down. "I don't know what you're doing. What *are* you doing?" I'd secretly entertained fantasies that he was picking out the Nova for me when we were at the dealership, that my life was suddenly going to be easier, but deeply embarrassing fantasies were all they were. The story was so lame that I could barely sustain it in the time it took him to fill out the paperwork on Christine's car, feeling a bright rush of heat across my scalp, embarrassment burning my secret desires like a distress flare in the sky. Nobody does this kind of shit for you. I slid the stuff back across the table.

"Listen," he said, covering my hand with his massive paw, resting just enough weight on top for me to know it was pointless to pull away. "My brother was not a Marine. He couldn't be faithful to a thing in his life . . . until he met your mom. Maybe it would have just taken time, and he'd have fallen as usual, but I want right now to believe he'd changed. He wanted to marry your ma. He'd never married those women who loved him, so there were no divorce complications at his end, but she wouldn't divorce your old man. I don't know why. He's a waste, if you don't mind my saying."

"Said it myself enough times." We rarely saw each other these days, but I hoped he'd found better winter lodging this year than the Summer Cottage.

"Anyway, he wanted to marry her, adopt you, the whole shebang. He knew your brother and sister wouldn't go for treating him like family, but he thought you might be young enough. I've looked out for Liz and Margaret the best I could, but their histories have soured them on me. Best I stay out of their lives, even if they *are* my brother's daughters . . . my nieces," he corrected. "I mostly stayed out of yours for the same reason. Cleaning up after my brother could be a full-time job. You understand?"

"I do," I said, unwillingly letting a sigh escape.

"I was with him the night he died," he said, like the casual kick to the nuts someone might give you for a laugh during a Moon Road drinking party. "Guess you didn't know that. He dropped me off not two minutes before he wrapped that car around a tree. We'd been drinking, but not that much." He paused and looked me directly in the eye. "I didn't smell any exhaust problem. Don't know what happened. His taillights faded, and then that was it. But in the month before he left, one thing we talked about? That car of his. Said he was gonna make good on his promise to give it to you. Thought it'd be funny. I guess you left a butt dent on the hood? Anyway, he wanted it to be yours, or whatever car he had when you were old enough. And this," he said, sliding the keys and the receipt he'd just written, "is my way of helping him do that. I want to see his last wishes out. For all his faults, I loved my brother. Okay?"

I left the keys sitting there initially. "Your buddy at the college call you?" I asked, finally.

"What do you think?"

"So much for student confidentiality."

"The history we got goes a lot deeper and a lot scarier than student confidentiality."

"The Latin arm tattoo."

"See that!" he said, backhanding me on the shoulder. Even as a joke gesture, I felt his distilled strength. "Investigative journalism! Putting old evidence with new for a story. Do what *you* want to instead of what *other people* think you should be doing," he said, and paused. "But after you take these keys." His forehead shifted to that curious pleading frown.

I cleaned up our mess and dropped him off, our last driving lesson completed.

"So, anytime you need anything, you know where I am," he said. Heat vapors shimmered around him in the open door. "Tank's full, but if your pockets and that tank get empty, you get the picture."

"Thanks," I said. "Probably time for me to learn to do things on my own."

"Son, this is what I've been trying to tell you. No one ever does anything on their own." He then dropped his voice, adding, "Except maybe a few things we don't usually speak about, right, Squier?" laughing a little. His bringing up "The Stroke," for old time's sake, didn't sting the way it did coming from Randy. It felt more like an inside joke. "All seriousness though? You don't need this," he said, tapping the spot on his arm where his jacket covered that tattoo, "to stay true to what it means. I don't imagine you're going to New Year's at DogLips's place."

"Not invited," I said. "But even if I were . . ." I shrugged. "I guess that means you are?"

"It's good to seem predictable in some ways," he said.

He shut the door and disappeared in my rearview horizon, standing in his driveway, watching his truck become mine. I cruised through the Rez, out past the college, and made my way back to the border. There wasn't a single hitchhiker out and I was glad. I crossed back to the north end and passed by Randy Night's, then Hillman's place. He was one more person with designs on my future. When I signed up for medical technology, my ma said Hillman thought I should be studying the traditional medicines with him. That was his dream, not mine. I'd visit him on New Year's Day. We'd talk then. Maybe he'd still give me a cookie, one for the driver.

Two Rows (V)

We respectfully do not cross streams
with each other, maintaining forward balance.

We see the open territory ahead of us and
acknowledge the mingled wakes we leave behind.

We share, between us, a peace we each maintain
by our dual presence in the expanse before us.

We discover each other side by side
in the water, traveling our own paths.

We emerge from different points of origin
and stay steady to our own unknown destinations.

We maintain our own customs, governing ways
of life and beliefs about the universe.

We each recognize that we move
according to our own desires and plans.

PART FIVE

Vital Signs

(1986–1989)

CHAPTER NINETEEN

Late Night Double Feature

(1986)

You never want a college official waiting outside your Deviant Behavior class for you. "I took the liberty of checking your schedule," Ross the Counselor said, right off. "I know you don't have any classes slotted next, but are you free?" I agreed and followed him to his office.

"So you never told me you were Native American," he said, closing his door.

"Where would someone like me encounter someone like Tim Sampson enough for all that effort?" I asked. To me, that connection would have been obvious. "And besides, I checked those boxes on the forms I filled out almost two years ago."

"Missed that. There are opportunities for underrepresented minority students."

"I got state Indian Aid, the treaty-funded kind. Cash for textbooks with a little left to eat, if I'm careful. The other organizations offering financial aid to Indian students passed me by."

"You filled the applications out, yourself?"

"Who else?" I might have had a more productive day just going to the snack bar.

"I can't get you retroactive support. But why do you think we're here?" He seemed agitated I didn't know his job. "We do a lot of two-year degrees. In and out. Nursing job at Our Lady of the Thorns, ground-level accounting, we're great for that. But we also help people worried about going away to college, you know, dorming it. We have transfer agreements across the state, I must have told you."

I hadn't gotten that far in my thinking, struggling to balance school with the distractions of home life, the occasional lure of Moon Road partying to maintain some connection, remembering to pack fresh clothes so I could shower in the men's locker rooms before my first class. Not worrying about rides was a massive load off, but I hadn't been a good student in a long time. I'd had to teach myself how to study at a college level.

"This came in today," he said, sliding a Xeroxed sheet. "Thought immediately of you. It's legit. Pays, and the credits and benefits transfer to the state schools in Buffalo, I'm assuming that's where you're thinking about. Even has health insurance. Kind of unheard of."

The sheet was an internship posting for the *Cascade*, the daily newspaper in Niagara Falls. It offered chances to write for the paper—and not just Obits and Police Blotter copy—and experience in a city room.

"Not gonna lie. Probably it's a lot of making break room coffee and keeping the fax machine and copiers in paper." He'd highlighted a line in small print at the bottom: *Underrepresented Minorities Encouraged to Apply.* A spot I kept buried deep inside grew excited, but I refused to let it show. If you learned one thing living in a place of scarcity, it was to never reveal the things that thrilled you, because you were just inviting someone else to recognize that value and snatch it away for themselves, or simply for the fun of tearing it from your hands.

I applied, was interviewed, and told to add Internship to the classes I was taking for my final community college semester. Ross had called it, I ended up doing the *Cascade*'s version of the shit jobs I'd had with Moose Knuckle, but some of it was real, too. And when I had the opportunities, I worked like crazy, rewriting and rewriting, pushing my work toward professional. Halfway through the semester, the city room editor, Gary Hughes, assured me my internship position would transfer and stay active at a four-year state school, told me the *Cascade* offered a scholarship with a stringer bonus if I went straight on. I could keep working, gain experience, and maybe be an attractive candidate for the next full-time opening.

I was required to take the summer off officially, because I wouldn't start my transfer enrollment until September. Gary gave me an open-door invitation to pitch story ideas though that period, if I wanted, since he couldn't pay me or give me grades. In a good faith effort, he left me on their health insurance. He also admitted it would be a pain for HR to unenroll and reenroll me for such a short window of one summer. How could I say no?

I stopped to see Tim in May, parking behind his new truck in case Christine came home. I was making some changes in my life and I wanted him to know from me. "Talk to your friend lately?" I asked, as he racked the balls and I chalked a cue. Eight Ball had become the way we talked to one another, now that I didn't need driving lessons. We still shot the shit regularly, over a game, or his sacred Fireball machine.

"But you don't, really, do you?" I said. "You know, the one who set me up with another lucky break." I sunk one of each and called stripes, lining up my next shot with the bridge.

"I knew you were gonna use that," he laughed. "Amateur." He claimed the bridge was a gimmick for bad players, and I pointed out that he bought it. I thought the shot was hard, but it would set me up for a better next one. His shit talk still spooked me and I screwed it up anyway. "Ross? Sure, we talked not that long ago. Been friends . . . thirty years, easy. Talked about ways Christine might still find good in a degree. If she maybe got a small business or an accounting one, she could go out on her own if she wanted. Why do you ask?"

"And uh, thanks for sinking my first ball," he added before I could speak, easily knocking two more in. "Not that I needed help," he smiled. I didn't talk a ton about school with him. Would either of us ever be fully comfortable, entering without at least a little armor?

"He tell about the incredible internship he helped me pin down?"

"We don't always talk about you. Like I said, known each other a long time, and no offense? You're not that interesting." He smiled again, sunk another ball, and did a goofy hip-check on me, so I'd know he was teasing. I didn't know if he'd gotten better, or if he just chose not to tease competitively among his Rez friends, since they all played for keeps. "But yeah, I guess he said something about that. Are congratulations in order?"

"Yeah, I graduated a couple weeks ago. They don't give grades for internships. They write a report and say whether you passed or not. Looks like I got a good report." I missed again and he quickly cleared the table of his balls.

"Would have been quicker if I wasn't working around all that junk you left in my way," he added, pretending to miss the eight. Typical shit talk.

"If you say so," I laughed. "So they're gonna keep me on once I file for a transfer to finish my Bachelors, same few hours a week. My ma didn't want to have a party. You know how she is about people coming to our house."

"I remember you didn't have a high school graduation party. Didn't she know guests usually bring the graduate an envelope? I think Christine cleared almost six hundred bucks. You were there. It wasn't even a big shindig."

"Well, it's a transfer," I clarified.

"It wasn't the last time," he said, true enough. She and Mona had come to my high school commencement, but then we went straight home. "Did you graduate this time or not?"

"I did. Diploma and cap and gown and everything, but no one came. Guess she didn't see it as real since I'm not done. She gave me three hundred bucks that she said she'd have spent on a party, for both high school and this one." He missed the eight ball again, and before I lined up my shot, I told him one of the things I'd wanted to say. "I used it to get a deposit on an apartment near the *Cascade*, halfway between the Rez and the new college. Twelve minutes in either direction."

"Need help moving? Two trucks are better than one." I knew he'd insist, even if I declined, but I couldn't just keep taking from him without being able to give back in some way.

"I did. Over the weekend. My family, couple cousins, I hired Juniper to help with heavy stuff." It was a third-floor walk-up, and Tim's strength would have definitely come in handy with the bed, couch, dresser, and desk. But it didn't seem fair to exploit your friends because they'd been born with better bodies than you. "I had to do it quick 'cause I'm going to be out of commission for lifting stuff for a bit. That's the other thing I came to tell you. I gotta have surgery next week. Scheduled it a while ago and this seemed like the best time, all things considered." His brows immediately raised in the middle and the corners of his mouth drew themselves down. His eyes flicked around the room, like they didn't know where to go.

"It's not bad," I assured him. "Not *that* bad, anyway. I mean, no one wants someone else poking them with sharp instruments. It's gallbladder. My bad Rez diet catching up with me." Our Rez diet had a lot of fried food in it, and by mid–high school, I'd gotten used to heartburn and Tums, heartburn and Tums, for a few years. But this new, different heartburn I'd been getting on my right side felt different, and didn't go away, so after almost a year of it growing stronger I finally caved and used my new health insurance.

"What can I do?" he asked, setting his cue in the rack.

"Really, it's nothing. It's the kind where they make three tiny cuts, one around your belly button, two off to the side, and slide tubes up inside, along with a knife, vacuum, and tiny camera. Needle and thread too, I suppose. They said it takes an hour, usually, and I might go home the same day, but if not, the next morning. I just wanted to make sure you knew, 'cause I can't afford a phone deposit for my apartment yet. If I'm feeling good enough, that's where I'm gonna go." I set an index card down on the Fireball machine with my new address on it, and a *Cascade* phone number where messages could be left securely, once September rolled around.

"Best get it taken care of," he said. "Wish you'd have let me help you move. I mean . . ." He flexed his biceps, as a joke. Though he was big all around, a bit of a paunch made you not see that he did something to keep in shape. A weight bench sat in the unfinished part of the basement, and it didn't have a bunch of clothes piled on it. "What are friends for?"

"They're for being friends," I said. "One other thing I came here for was, just in case, to say that those things I put in that letter? Those years ago? I still mean it. Maybe even more now."

"Come on, kiddo. We don't have to be serious all the time." He sat in one of the recliners and gestured for me to take the other. "No one out here ever has serious conversations, do they? I mean, on the surface? Usually, you gotta decode about ten layers of jokes or offhand comments to figure out someone's being serious with you. It took me forever to learn that." I didn't know the answer. It had taken me years to realize that when I was young, my ma only let me visit kids at houses similar to ours. I'd been invited to other birthday parties, but she always had some reason I couldn't go. The Rez might have had serious households, but you'd never know. If you were at a community gathering, all conversations were saturated with laughing and puns, and mildly embarrassing reminders of previous goofs someone had made. Even in my lifetime, joking and funny stories had crept into funerals, as a way to celebrate someone's life and send them off to the Skyworld or Heaven, whichever place they were going.

"Just cause we're comfortable being serious with each other now, that doesn't mean all our conversations have to be that way, does it?" he said. I guessed not, but it had been such a relief to finally have someone like that in my life, I didn't want to lose the door to lack of use. Even tougher life lessons on the Rez involved joking. How had Tim ever adapted to our life? As we sat here, he leaned forward, fidgeting his hands. I could see he'd fully made the transition. He'd become more Rez than I felt at that moment. There were times I *wanted* to be serious.

Gihh-rhaggs had understood that, and he'd treated my worries meaningfully. I could see now that it must have been a pain in the ass to do. He'd wanted to be involved with my ma, but somehow, he'd gotten us too.

I thought I heard a car pull into the driveway, so I got up to leave.

"Bailing on me 'cause I'm kicking your butt?" Tim asked, smiling. I shook my head. "I can leave it, and we can pick it up when you're feeling good enough to lean over the table. No problem."

"That's all right," I said, nudging a couple of my balls into their pockets, scratching the game. "You might have someone else you wanna play with before I see you again."

"No," he said. "Not likely." His expression looked like sadness and relief together, overlaying one another, like a TV receiving signals from two opposing stations.

"Never know. I'll catch you later."

"We can do something else if you want, play the Fireball? I got a VCR and some movies here." He pointed to the big box on top of the TV. "I got two. Christine's man bought a couple cables and showed me how to make copies when you rent them." We never mentioned him by name, but I was fairly certain it was Randy. To say it aloud was almost like inviting trouble.

I stepped into the unfinished part of the basement, tugging my boots on. Though I grabbed my jacket, he kept walking along with me. "Cheaper than buying them. Look just like the real one and a blank costs five bucks." I gave a nod conveying: *cool, but I gotta get going.*

A VCR would be beyond my means for a few years to come, by my reckoning. Ironically, now that I had a car and a few college acquaintances interested in bizarre movies, the Midnight Show circuit was dying because of VCRs. I'd been hoping to pitch a Midnight Movie Reviews for the *Cascade*, but there might not be any left by the time I had enough experience to suggest that. *The Rocky Horror Picture Show* would probably stick around at midnight, because that needed audience participation, but unless you had great attendance cleaning up the mess of rice, water, toilet paper, cards, and toast afterward, theaters might not want to play it.

"I even got that weird one you like. Was gonna surprise you. That is one crazy movie. I glanced at it with the sound off while it was copying." I frowned. He seemed to be giving me just enough information to be unclear. "What's that thing in the basket? It sure is hideous." *Basket Case*, the story of two brothers, bound to each other in ways no one else could understand. At first glance, it looked like a moron movie. How did he know I liked it? Low budget monster movies weren't his kind of thing, and we didn't talk about movies. *Basket Case* was almost worth sitting back down, but I hadn't heard Christine come in after she'd shut off her car.

"I guess you'll just have to find out," I said. "It's not for everyone, but you might like it. It's got more to say than you'd think. But it's um . . . like me. A lot to forgive."

"Son, I'm happy to put it on. I don't have any other plans. Really."

"You go ahead," I said, sliding my jacket on. "We'll talk about it some time."

"Door's always open, you know that."

Outside, the air was still sharp, late night chill settling in the woods. Dew in the fields gave a rich earthy note, accompanied by a distinct scent. Christine's perfume was amazingly close to real roses. She was leaning on her Nova's hood, looking at the stars. The engine ticked, cooling.

"Hey," she said, not breaking her gaze.

"Hey yourself. Hope I wasn't keeping you from coming in. I heard you drive up."

"That why you decided to leave?" she asked, finally looking my way. She hooded her eyes with her hand, to deflect the harsh light from their porch lamp.

"No, we were done, just shooting a game of Eight Ball." I felt the urge to downplay my visit, to make it seem unimportant. "What were you up to, tonight? You and Randy—"

"Working," she interrupted. "We stay open late tonight. We run a guy's night. Well, *I* do. Business is mostly women, but I thought it was a fresh idea I could bring. Carla said I could give it a try. It's just me." She seemed both proud of her forward thinking and mildly annoyed that none of the other stylists were willing to take a chance on a different way of business.

"I guess there was demand?"

"At first, guys'd sign up for a time then head to JetPort instead for a couple beers and some wings. You know, guys. They don't want to be a beauty shop, so I got to thinking." She grinned and nodded, like the old Christine I knew who got excited about experimenting. "I started putting on different music, like 97 Rock, turned the TV to the sports channel."

"Did it work?"

"Yeah, amazing. That little bit makes them comfortable. I set up a couple lamps at my station instead of overheads. Forget they're in a salon when they're arguing about whatever game's on. Only trouble's cleaning up by myself. Guys ain't messier, but every night we mop with disinfectant, health department protocols. Even one station open, gotta do the whole floor."

"That's great. I mean, not all the work, but finding your own thing? Actually doing it? Congrats!" A handshake seemed too wacky, and a hug didn't feel right either, so I did the dorkiest thing and gave her a quiet clap, like they did for golfers on TV. "Aren't you nervous being there by yourself? I mean, a single car in a parking lot late at night only says one thing to the criminal mind. A lot of the robbery calls that come through—"

"Randy keeps me company," she replied. I could picture him sitting there, not helping, just drinking a beer in one of the waiting chairs, watching cable. "Usually he waits till my last client leaves, but if they're taking too long, he pulls in. I guess you get a clear shot of our lot from the JetPort."

"Pretty good wings. Don't imagine they're great on a client, though." I'd been in JetPort. Ten-cent wing and Labatt's pitcher specials. If I went out these days, it was with staff reporters to the place they favored downtown, or occasionally I'd head to Skin City and hit the Circle Club. I wasn't looking to flirt with a DWI, now that I had stable transportation for the first time.

"See you got on a different jacket than that one Moose Knuckle gave you."

"College friend of mine gave this to me, when he got too fat, and I gave mine to Hubie when I got too fat for the one from Stew," I said. "Funny, I'd never guess that Hubie'd drop all that weight and I'd gain it. Don't know if that's just reaching adulthood or quitting smoking, or both. Food tastes a lot better after you quit. I guess that was a good thing when food was scarce."

"Good when you get emphysema. I hear you really don't want to eat much, then."

"Yeah, I know," I said. "Seems crazy now, wasting money I didn't have on cigs."

"Well, my dad *did* save us funds, even if he didn't know I was skimming them for our bus rides." *Funds* was a very Christine word. It had always struck her as fancy, somehow.

"True enough." I didn't ask if Randy helped at the salon or not, and she was silent on why I wasn't wearing the Rush jacket. Neither of us wanted to dig up old ghosts. "Guess I better head out."

"Brian?" she asked, then paused. We looked at each other in stark illumination and shadow. "Why do you come here? I mean, it's obviously not to see *me*," she said. "I know how *you* pay attention. You'd know when to catch me at home." Over the years, I'd slowly come to recognize when Christine's white and Indian sides wrestled. No matter how bad you might want to know something, you'd never ask a question this direct to anyone on the Rez. Her directness in calling me out was not the way we lived in the world.

Even as I had this thought, though, I understood I was at least partly

to blame for her response. We lived more by action than word. That difference was probably why many mixed relationships were doomed from
the beginning. On the Rez, if you liked someone, you visited, and if things
went bad, you stopped visiting. Because our lives stayed in proximity, we
knew that words left permanent scars, where actions could be subtler. Her
Indian side knew I'd been telling her I didn't feel we had that kind of future
together, but my continued connection with Tim must have been confus-
ing. Finally, I could see how it would hurt.

I didn't know how to describe the status of Tim and me. The kind of
fancy college label might have been *Mentor*, but that was a school thing:
professional activities, internships. I didn't have a word for our relationship. *Friend* felt deeply inadequate, too. What we had was its own thing,
a connection I'd been wanting my whole life for, without even knowing, until I was in the middle. I lifted my hands before me and gestured
vaguely, palms open and empty.

"Do what you want. Thought he might start thinking about . . . been
almost ten years. But instead of going anywheres social, he's playing pool
here alone, thinking you might show." He'd had a social life after Vestal
died and before me, and he surely still did. She was maybe so involved in
her new life, she didn't know how active he was. Probably he was still
exploited at DogLips Night's table. "If you really care about him, you'd let
him move on."

It was pushy of her to make such a suggestion—pushy and wrong, but
I couldn't violate Tim's confidence. The things he'd asked me to keep that
New Year's Eve had to remain between us. Even if I was the only person
he'd ever told. *Especially* if I was the only person. It was his business that
he didn't plan on getting romantically involved ever again. I kept Tim's
confidence the same way I didn't offer my opinion on anyone's future
with Randy.

"No offense, but," she said, which definitely meant *Offense Coming In*.
"You got your own dad, and you don't give him a second look." That was
more of a Rez slam, a little bit of a body check about my family to criticize
my intrusion into hers. I deserved that. I wanted to say you can't build a
brand new house on a foundation that keeps disappearing, but I didn't
have a white side. I knew not to pull out the razor sharp daggers that left

the permanent scars. "Why do you need mine? First, your mom took my uncle, then you got Margaret. What if I'm sick of sharing him?"

"I don't know what to tell you." Her flash of anger surprised me. "Can't a grown man make his own decisions? Anyway, I moved to the city, so you don't have to worry about me stealing any more of your dad's time." Weak, but I didn't feel I should say what I was thinking.

Where I stood, she didn't want her dad so much in the first place. She and Hayley would sort out their eventual arrangements, and one would live here on their own, but it had no bearing on their affection, their love for Tim. "Just stopped to tell him something. That's all. No worries." Even turning the truck's ignition, I felt like I'd somehow stolen her father's generosity. There was no getting around that I was sitting on a bench seat that had been broken in and shaped to the contours of his presence.

"For what it's worth," I added. "You won't be seeing me here for a while."

"In that case," she said, strolling to the passenger side. "Wait a sec."

As she walked around, I noted: "Changed your hair." The spikey tendrils had been smoothed to something like Wendy and Lisa's hair from Prince's *Purple Rain*, a big swoop up top, narrow at her neck.

When I unlocked the door, she rolled the window down, shut it, and leaned in against the now closed door, looking at me. "If you're in the hair business, rocking some bold style's part of the deal."

"Good thing *Purple Rain*'s still a top rental at Video Factory, isn't it, though?"

"Around here, two years old is still flashy and new," she laughed, and I nodded. "Stylists sell people the fantasy that a haircut can make them new people. Even if it's ten years old style."

"You ever talk someone out of a bad hair idea?"

"Nah," she said, running fingers through her bangs. "What's the worst? In a month or two, try something else, but most want the haircut they had when they were happiest in life."

"Sounds risky. I assumed we were all supposed to get a grown-up cut at some point."

"Clients bring high school pics to give me guidance, so it's still a ton of *Charlie's Angels* cuts." She laughed a little again. Ten years out of date seemed about right for our area. "Maybe someday down the road, I'll ask some stylist to give me a Meduse, from the good old days."

"Don't you mean a Robert Smith? Ask for the Cure?" I said, immediately cringing.

"Yeah . . . the cure," she dragged out, searing me. "We were friends, then," she went on, now that I'd gone there. "Why didn't you ask Randall to stop calling me Meduse?"

"I *was* being a friend," I said. "If I tried to get him to stop, he'd only make it worse." Still insisting I knew Rez dynamics better than her, but knowing it was a coward move.

"Fair enough," she mumbled, then looked at me directly. "But did you have to join in?"

"Suppose not," I responded, breaking eye contact. Guilty as charged. "But . . . what does he call you *now*? How are you staying with the person who made your life so miserable?"

"You oughta know. I could have asked you that same question for all those years."

"Got me there," I conceded. "But Christine? I'm leaving. I've moved on." Moving to the city was likely to change my whole life, even among the few people I was close with. I worried about my skills at finishing my responsibilities on time, but it was time to grow up.

"I see," she said, pushing off the door, leaving the window. "Maybe my dad can get on with his life, now that he's got your permission." Walking away without turning back, she shouted, "Think about the haircut you're gonna be asking for in about ten years!" I left the window open as my cheeks stung in embarrassment. What haircut would I want? Could I even identify a happiest time in my life so far? Was it right now? This moment?

"Guess I've got time to think about it before I see you again," I called back, pulling out. I hoped that when she stepped in, she and Tim were nice to each other, that they'd find a way to negotiate their ever-shifting roles under that roof, with a little bit of kindness.

As I headed to the city, I had no idea how accurate my last comment was going to be.

CHAPTER TWENTY

I See You

(1986)

B efore I went under, the anesthesiologist asked if I had any questions. "If I need a transfusion, make sure the blood's from another Indian," I joked. "I don't wanna mess up my enrollment status by throwing my blood quantum out of whack." The anesthesiologist had a Reservation Humor deficit, insisting the odds were ninety-nine point ninety-nine percent against it, but he added *never say never*. Never say never.

I'd heard that awakening from anesthesia was rude and startling, because it would seem like no time had passed between going under and coming back up, instead of the swirling and gradual waters of regular sleep. As I drifted off, I wondered what that feeling would be like.

"What time is it?" I asked a minute later, opening my eyes. The truth was rude.

"He's coming around!" someone shouted. "Mr. Waterson, we're trying to get you stabilized." Words you do *not* want to hear emerging from routine surgery. I kept hearing the *Dawn of the Dead* movie trailer: *Imagine, if you will, that something has gone horribly wrong.*

"Six o'clock, now please, be quiet! We're trying to track your pulse." Five hours later than it should have been. The ceiling fluorescents sliding by above, making me sick.

Resurfacing later in the ICU, I felt tubes up my nose and scratching my throat. Dual IVs, and wires; everywhere I looked, wires trailed from me. I reached down softly, feeling the massive gauze pad covering my abdomen, and a spiking hot line of pain directly down the middle, like lit cigarettes. A trail of forty incredibly painful staples ran from my sternum to my pubic hair, now mostly tiny razor stubble with a strip of hair, an eyebrow above my equipment.

My bladder felt like I was a half hour into a concert men's room line. One last tube trailed from my johnny's hem. I gently raised the tube and my own equipment came along for the ride. Eventually, my eyes crossed over a nurse and orderly studying me, as I surveyed myself.

"Forty staples?" I asked. The nurse gave a gesture like: *More or Less*. "Catheter?"

"Yes, we had to catheterize you," she said, suddenly all *One Flew over the Cuckoo's Nest*, like she was sick of retelling me I had a plastic tube rammed up my plumbing. "Don't pull on it or you'll go back in restraints! It goes up inside your urethra and—" *Back* into restraints?

"I know what a catheter is," I said. "What happened?"

"The doctor will be in to talk with you shortly," she said. "Can you answer a few questions?" I wasn't sure, truthfully. The world seemed kind of wrong.

"Wait," I said. "My eyes are all screwed up." I reached up, finding no glasses.

"Over here," the orderly said, holding up my little gold frames. "Where'd you get them?" He came over. "They're really cool."

"They're antiques. You can't find them now."

"Neat-o. I'd sure like a pair that cool."

"Please, don't take them." I hated the chicken shit sound leaking through my words like noxious gas. I still wore the mysterious gift from Gihh-rhaggs, passed to me by Tim, the lenses swapped over and over. If this guy decided to steal them, I couldn't do jack. My pounding heart kicked it up a couple more impossible notches. A look passed between the nurse and the orderly.

"It's cool, buddy," he said, patting my arm. "They're safe. Nothing to worry about."

"So what happened?" I asked again. The orderly opened his mouth, but the nurse grabbed the tiny sleeves of his scrubs and pointed him out the door.

"Do you know your name?" the nurse asked. *My name?* That was not a you're-going-home-tomorrow kind of question.

"Waterson. Brian Waterson. Birth date? Social Security?"

"Name is fine, for now. Thank you," she said. "Doctor will be in shortly." She left.

To be clear up front: I had *not* seen a blinding white light, no brilliant doorway with dead, waving relatives in strap-on wings. What I remember seeing? A bright round spaceship above me, with a ring of smaller round bright-white spaceships embedded in its underside. I was sure they were coming to take me home. I saw a spool with a rope ladder before I faded out again.

I don't know why but this UFO report was the first thing I'd told Mona when I woke up in the ICU. She and Chester walked in now with my ma. "Good thing you're too lazy to climb," Mona said. I asked why. Any conversation was a desired distraction. When you're held together by forty industrial surgical staples, from sternum down to the place you don't want sharp office supplies embedded, you love distraction. "Cause we don't want you to leave yet."

As I told Mona more details about the spaceship, my ma asked me how I was feeling. I tried responding, but words ran to the far corners of my brain like panicky mice.

"You bring your tea bags?" I asked my ma, finally, concentrating to pull those five words together from the cloud floating just beyond comprehension. I didn't count on any longer words.

"Don't even joke," she said. She'd stopped reading years before, but she didn't need teacup dregs to see my sketchy future, not that I could drink tea, being allowed nothing beyond the dual IV drips in my arms and the occasional ice cube to unglue my sticky, dehydrated tongue.

Chester couldn't take his eyes off the monitors above me, and bursts of laughter filtered in occasionally from somewhere. The scarier things were, the harder we Indians laughed. Next, Auntie Rolanda, Roland, and other cousins blew through quickly, like I was a grim tourist attraction. Even Nadine, my dad's sister. Most watched the monitors above me for my vitals. I hadn't even told most I was having surgery, so I concluded they'd all heard what happened and got here pronto, preparing to say adios, just in case the next twelve hours didn't go so well.

The surgeon entered, looking not his confident self. "You had a tough time."

"*I* had a tough time?"

"Everything was going smoothly. We were closing and taking one last look around, and suddenly, you were filling up with bright red blood. We had to go back in to find the bleeder. A torn artery. Needed to be clamped and closed." He removed his glasses and studied the floor.

"What would have caused that?" I asked, my family all watching.

"I don't know. Maybe an extra artery connecting your gallbladder to your liver, more than the usual number. Some kind of mutation? It's the *only* explanation," he insisted. He had to go back in *minus* the convenience of the fiber-optic camera. I understood then that the huge cotton pad I felt, spanning my entire abdomen, covered the length of his incision, twelve inches.

"Mutant?" He shrugged, ignoring the obvious explanation. "Did you almost lose me?"

"There was," he said, pausing, "substantial blood loss." He was already choosing his words, as if he were being deposed. Had he already called an attorney? Have one on retainer? "You were transfused during the procedure and you're being transfused again now," he said. One of the IVs held dark fluid, nearly black, and where it drained, the bag was stained red.

"Brain damage?" If I put those thoughts together, the chances had to be lower.

"Possible. Slight," he said, then corrected. "Very slight. You're sedated, so you're foggy. I shot more anesthetic inside. Should last a few days, give you time to start healing." Weirdly, he shook hands with my ma, then flew out of the ICU before anyone could ask additional questions. Big Nurse said I needed rest. True, but being alone with those machines scared me.

Outside, some wild storm blasted the building, adding to the strange noises enveloping me. Worrying about the hospital's generator system, I watched blood drain from the bag and into my arm. I was the anesthesiologist's zero-zero-point-zero-one percent chance. A mutant. Maybe

A Mutant. Was I like the X-Men now? Would huge adamantium blades protrude from my split gut at will? Or could I shoot lasers from my eyes? Johnny Storm, the Human Torch, could blaze himself up any time he wanted, and in a second's notice, shut it off, change back to a young, muscular, wealthy blond man, holding onto the world securely by the balls.

Mutant. An X-Man. I felt more like Ben Grimm: the Thing. Sure, he was a member of the Fantastic Four, and could smash a building's foundation with one swing. But he could never stop being that mass of orange rocks, "the Thing". Sometimes, he tried wearing normal clothes, a trench coat, a fedora, dress pants, wing tips, and an ascot, of all things, instead of those little blue satin briefs that were his Fantastic Four uniform. But who could look into that fractured stone face, see those blue eyes, and still not think "monster"?

Grimm even chose his girlfriend in part because she couldn't see. He was sure anyone who could see him would never be attracted to him. Still, no matter Alicia's insistence, and no matter how much they loved each other, it's not like they could make love. The weight of his passion would crush her. The limitations of superhero physics were rarely explored, but the other members of the FF had more implied intimate lives. Reed and Sue had kids, and Johnny found Crystal, an Inhuman partner. Only Ben was banished, his form destroying the fantasy.

After the nurse escorted everyone out, she stepped back in, her expression softer.

"Your family's a little . . ."

"Boisterous," I worked hard to suggest, hoping to prevent whatever insult might have come out. "It's the way we do things. When America tries to wipe you out for several generations, you get a sense of humor about survival." I felt this moment of clarity fade as words became shapes and colors again, floating out of range. She gave me the sour look of someone who didn't like to hear about their own history. Their first response was always: *not me! I didn't try to wipe you out. I'm a nurse,* etc. They liked their buckskin-clad Indians crying their way through polluted lakes on TV. No matter how many times we told them that guy in the commercial wasn't even Indian, they insisted that wasn't the point. And currently being held together by sterile office supplies, in this woman's hands, I decided not to argue.

I asked her about the blood, how many units. "Four," she said, and paused, silently debating. "How did you know? I mean, nobody needs a transfusion with this surgery."

"Know what?"

"You know . . . how your uncle came before surgery to donate blood? Said you had the same type. We told him we didn't think you'd need it, but we did the match. We asked if it could go to the bank. He said that wouldn't be necessary, but . . . we meet all kinds in this job."

"Don't have one," I said. If she meant Auntie Rolanda's boyfriend Phillipe, hooking me up to a pint of Canadian Club would be the same as tapping him. She started going through her chart. "Didn't even know my own blood type till last week."

"Hillman was the last name," she said. "No first name listed here, only an initial. *A.*"

"*Great* uncle," I said. It had been years since I'd last had a real conversation with Hillman, that time with my cousin Benji. I chickened out whenever he tried to bring up serious topics in his sideways Hillman fashion. I'd just talk Rez news if I ran into him, or if my ma and I picked him up, walking. But the serious things he'd told me that one summer, about how I'd almost come to live with him? We hadn't brought it up since. There wasn't a first name, as far as I knew, but I couldn't explain that here in the ICU. It was one of those untranslatable places between Rez culture and everything beyond.

Later in the night, whispers from the machines told me I shouldn't get confident about my chances. Nobody's perfect. People make mistakes all the time. Maybe I'd heard this before. Part of that night, I believed I was picking up the nursing staff conversations through the room's intercom system. I asked the nurse where those voices were coming from. She said there weren't any voices. She speculated that I just heard the IV, regulating the drip. "Sometimes," she said, adjusting it, "the medication confuses patients. They get a little shade of paranoia."

Maybe some others came to see me. Much later, Gihh-rhaggs wandered in. "Hey, Ronnie-Huh," he said, still butchering my old nickname. I told him he forgot the last syllable. "Well, you're not exactly little anymore," he said, and that's when I knew it had to be a hallucination. It felt so real, though. I held out my hand and he grasped it, his grip a joyous warmth. "So listen," he said. "No, not to the machines. Listen to me. You're not ready yet. You got people counting on you. You know who." After a while, he added his other hand, equally warm. This incredible wave of love sunk in, but as my eyes fought to close themselves, I felt him separate and loosen his grip. "Okay, they only gave me a little while. Now I gotta go back." I didn't tell anyone about this visit, but it turned out he was right.

For the next few ICU days, I'd briefly come to consciousness and try to reassemble my past and massage the new, jagged edges of my present, hoping it would make sense if I could stay awake long enough. The move to the Med-Surg ward five days later was a change of scenery, but gurney bumps reminded you how easy your entire life could be split right in half.

A week and a half after surgery, I finally ditched the butt-gapping hospital johnny and got dressed to leave the hospital. Some other people beyond family had come while my body worked its magic. More and more, I could only think of the Rez as that giant pinball machine with multiple balls in play. We might try dodging someone else's trouble, but it often meant slamming into yet another person, because we weren't watching where we were going. We careened into one another, rolling with hits, never knowing what bumper we might trigger next.

Hubie Buckman, of course, came. As an EMT, he had an investment in anyone from the Rez in the hospital. Margaret came, but without Moose Knuckle, offering Eee-ogg that Christine was serious with Randy Night, which I'd already known. There were maybe other visitors, too. My ma said sometimes, if you had too many visitors, they restricted others. She said it was dangerous to keep tabs, to pay attention to who didn't show instead of the people who did.

After watching the surgeon yank my staples with the same little metal and plastic jaws you got at an office-supply place, I'd worried about buttoning my Levi's too tight. "I guess I can just hold them up undone for the trip home. Well, to your place," I said to my ma. "I don't think climbing the three flights of stairs to my apartment is a good idea." She was about to say something, when I discovered another artifact of my time in the hospital, as I tried putting clothes on. My Levi's hung loose on my sides, and my flat Indian ass gave them nothing to hang on in the back.

"Well," she said, and took in a deep breath. "We been talking about that."

Some cosmic hand somewhere pulled back a plunger on some celestial pinball machine, and an unexpected new ball stood ready to send me to some new unpredictable place. Maybe Galactus was going to ignore the Fantastic Four for a while and throw my life into chaos. I understood from the look on my ma's face that whatever she was going to say next meant my life had been changed, and as it always is with family, I didn't have much say in the matter. I'd know more once she revealed who the *We* of that sentence was, but some decision had been made while I was out visiting alien spaceships. I already knew I wasn't necessarily going to like that decision— I'd seen this expression often when I was younger. It was the look she wore staring into the fridge and cupboard when we arrived at the end of the month's groceries about a week too soon.

And in that way, I knew the tough part of this ride wasn't quite over yet.

CHAPTER TWENTY-ONE

Reservation Candy Hearts

(1986)

I went directly to Hillman's. How was my grandfather's older brother still so spry? He might not be the only remaining medicine man, but he was the last one working in the open. Not like, hanging a shingle with a spiral handprint out front, and dreamcatchers dangling from beneath it, or other ridiculous New Age shit. The Rez didn't speak of it, but if you needed something? You knew where to go. As soon as you say "Medicine family" off the Rez, though, suddenly some woman drenched in patchouli and turquoise was reporting her psychic dreams and secret high Indian cheekbones. Or a middle-aged blond guy with a sad possum-tail braid was asking you to bless his drum group's digs in the old growth he bought day-trading.

During the first month, I slept maybe eighteen hours a day. "Come on! Time to rise," Hillman said the second day. "Wash up or you're gonna get stink all over my house. Hurry up." All I wanted was sleep, but I pulled on Levi's and got up. "Good you lost that weight," he added.

"Not exactly a plan I'd recommend," I said, washing my face and pits, and stepping back in the room for a little more privacy, dropping my shorts and finishing. The scar was going to take a long time. I didn't want to look, but there was no avoiding it. Every morning, you woke up, and for the first couple minutes, you felt normal, like you'd forgotten. And then you absently reached down to scratch, and along the way, your fingers hit the new lumps of flesh, and you remembered everything all over again. You know your body was never going to be the same. You saw people walking around shirtless, thinking nothing of it, and you knew your days of doing that were forever gone. Even if I could have avoided all of that, I still had a whole list of dos and don'ts, to avoid splitting open like an entrails-filled jelly doughnut.

"How'd you get fat, anyways? Always scrawny when you were a kid."

"Quit smoking," I said. "And, food tasted better? And I had regular access to food?"

"Yes, that's not how we use tobacco, but I hope you didn't throw them out." He revealed a pack of Marlboros from his shirt pocket. I didn't recall him ever being a smoker. "It can still be used in a pinch. Our medicine's a little different from what you get at Towne Pharmacy from the man in his little white coat. When I learnt, about your age, things weren't easy like you have it. Medicines? They understand this. They take your intention into account. Understand?"

Even sitting up zapped my energy at first, but I was supposed to move around. Eventually, I was able to awake more and for longer stretches. Our first endurance test was to stand at his big plant table as he told me the names of each, pointing out identifying features, and covering the basic treatment uses. "Now, don't just nod at me like that Bobblehead Batman you used to have. Repeat. Only way you're gonna learn. And this is just the first layer." When we started, I leaned on the table, then later stood on my own and then walked around with him.

In the sixth week, he put my ass to work on small, low-intensity jobs, since I wasn't to lift anything heavy. I mostly helped him keep house. Each night, we'd go through the treatments that were supposed to make my scar disappear. "Is this gonna be okay?" I asked, as he slathered on a mixture he'd heated with some water. "I'm not sure I'm all the way sealed up, yet."

"Don't matter, even if you ain't. Just a different entry. You saying you want me to stop?"

"No, I'm just asking. I mean, skin is sealed up for a reason, right?"

"I ain't been peeking, but it seems to me you got the right number of holes as everyone else," he said, laughing, gently pushing on me to recline.

"Now you remember the three medicines that are in here and the order I mixed them?"

"I'd have to be an idiot not to remember," I said. "You've been doing this every day."

"I don't make guesses about your smarts. I can see you're a smart-ass." As I lay there, motionless, he'd explain their interaction to me, remind me when and where they were harvested, and when I repeated everything with him, he added further information. "You sure you're paying attention?" he asked one night, acting casual.

"Of course," I said.

"Pretty quick answer," he said. "Better be sure if you're gonna be my replacement. Well, no one can replace me, but guess you'll have to do." Was I supposed to be surprised when he sprang my alleged new life on me? He acted like I'd never seen Ben Kenobi telling Luke Skywalker lies about fathers, to kick his ass in gear and get those droids out of his dusty shack on Tatooine.

Hillman was going to be deeply disappointed when the end of summer came along. But in the same way he'd begun training me without my giving any indication I wanted it, I'd send him the same message when I went back to school. I didn't object to learning what he was offering, but the idea of changing your entire life path because some old relative decides you need to? Well, that was Indian life from an era before I was born.

Throughout the summer, my ma would stop by with prepared meals. Every day, he poured tea in her presence, and ripped the bags, casting our futures. She refused to take the bait. I wondered how deep she was in on this. Was she just hoping for the best in my recovery, or did she know Hillman's entire plan? I was too weak, still, to be alone in any sustained way, so I went about doing what I was told, surprised at how easily I understood everything. My lack of skills in Western medical education didn't give me a disadvantage here.

In the mornings, I'd memorize harvested plants. Afternoons were outside, gathering plants, but only in the right way. He'd say something, and I'd repeat, adding all earlier parts before the newest addition. It was like that Simon game, the disc with blinking lights and noises. What he'd insisted—that the whole world was interconnected medicine—became clearer.

He said medicines would speak to me. Eventually, I heard them as clearly as I've ever understood anything. Evenings were filled with stories, about his work. By July, I was strong enough for National Picnic. But if I wanted to go, I had to find my own way.

"Before I go, I want to know something," I said. I figured if he'd decided he could just try to will my future to change, I had a right to some answers. "If you can do this, healing me—"

"You're not feeling healed?" he asked. His tone sounded like concern on its top layer, but beneath, I could hear that he could be snippy too, if he wanted. He was assuring me: I wasn't thinking about this path as thoroughly as I might. Most Rez families had some thread of this belief. There were qualities within your family you were just expected to follow, though most weren't insisting you change your life to suit their desires. As with so many aspects, you weren't told directly anyway. The paths were just put directly in front of you and you were expected to keep going. With most, you were free to seek out a different path if you were called to one, but you also knew that it was harder to find this path a second time on your own, because you'd already been invited and screwed it up. There were consequences to passing up on invitations, even subtle, unasked invitations like this one.

"Well, yeah," I said, but I'd had enough medical-type classes and lived long enough to know how the body functioned. "You're *supposed* to heal after surgery. That's why they only give you so much time off. But okay, let's say it's working. Let's say one day, I'm going to be able to look in the mirror, or run my hand down my belly and not feel like a monster. If you can do this, why didn't you do this for Benji, after he got hit by that car?" Usually, around Picnic time, I thought of him and the Tin Man, and every other suspect thing people believed in.

"Well, remember what I said when you were little?"

"About Benji? Sure, but you weren't exactly forthcoming."

"Weren't exactly ready, were you? I didn't work on that one 'cause

Rolanda got herself a bad case of the Jesus Eyes, from that fool with the guitar."

"Jazzercise? The ladies in spandex program? No way for Rolanda," I said, laughing.

"Jesus Eyes," he enunciated slowly, like we spoke a different language.

"If you're saying what I think," I said, "Most of this Rez has a bad case of the Jesus Eyes. Way more than the Jazzercise."

"Oh yeah, oh yeah," he said, laughing himself now. "You see lots of people lining up to visit me? They come when they don't see praying or the Towne Pharmacy medicine doing what they want. Bargaining chip for them." He changed his voice instantly to a mocking whine: "Oh Jesus, fix my kid and I'll stop going to the Race Track, I'll quit helping myself using the nasty magazines, I'll put more in the collection plate." He waved his hand, like flies buzzed around him, and went back to his voice. "Come to me only after you've used up all your other Belief Bargaining Chips? Nothing I can do to help. You believe in what I do, or you don't."

"That's it? So Benji's leg is screwed up and only going to get worse, because Rolanda goes to her hillbilly church? I mean, if you've got all this medicine, aren't you being stingy?"

"More tricky than that. We'll talk when you're back from Picnic. Your mind? Stuffed with clouds right now. You say you wanna catch up with people. Lie to yourself. But I know it's just one single person you're looking to see, even though you know your gut is gonna throb and flash like a K-Mart Blue Light Special from being up and around so much. If you can't admit to yourself that you're looking for him, what good are you gonna be if you find him?"

We hadn't discussed this feeling at all, but it had been six weeks since I almost climbed up into the Flying Saucer. Tim Sampson hadn't come, not even once, to the hospital or Hillman's. You can't ask someone why they didn't come when you were in seriously desperate shape in the hospital. Hillman, as he maddeningly was, understood everything. I wanted to give Tim the chance to tell me why he hadn't come, so I went to Picnic, with just one explicit desire.

I saw Christine and Randy together there, in the distance, but she snubbed me like we were in the middle school lunchroom and she didn't want me eating at her table. I *did* catch up with quite a few people I'd grown up with. Seemed like a lot knew what had happened to me, and they wanted to know why I was staying at Hillman's. Eee-ogg takes its own natural shapes, like a tree growing twisted in a crowded woods, shifting to the needs of others.

The Rez was small enough that if the person you wanted to see was at Picnic, you would run into them, often without even trying. I didn't ask anyone about Tim and no one volunteered information either. Either he had stayed home, or he made himself scarce when I showed up. Maybe he showed around the time for Fireball. It was the one time you could go and be invisible, since the only light was the moon, the flaming goal-posts, and the ball being chased across the field by forty or so men playing for keeps. Sometimes, a guy chose to take the hit in his chest and you'd see a momentary flare, but it was easy enough to stay in the dark.

I went back to Hillman's and dropped off to sleep with my clothes still on, smelling of kerosene and burnt grass, and didn't reply when Hillman asked if I'd found my answers. On Sunday, we went back to our routine. There was a conversation coming about my paths that we weren't going to enjoy. I decided to get to it sooner rather than later.

"So, listen," I said one night in August, over supper a few weeks on. It was a struggle, but when it came time to walk out the door with my bag, I just couldn't do it silently. I knew he was counting on me feeling guilty, but I'd already found who I was going to be as an adult. After wandering lost for so long, Tim had helped me discover my true desires. "Is there some rite of passage I have to go through when we're done?"

"Right of passage? What's 'at? Like a right of ways or something? Always the walker, not the car. Even if they're not at a crosswalk." I could never tell when his generation of Indians was joking. Their stealthiness was part of the joke, even if there was no audience to appreciate it.

"No, a trial—" I started then stopped. He liked watching those court TV shows, so I knew where he'd take this. "A challenge, a sacrifice I have to make."

"Almost getting killed wasn't challenge enough for you?" he said, digging back into the pan, for any last few spoonsful. As my elder, it was his right not to ask if I wanted some.

"It was, for me, but that wasn't related to this."

"Everything's related. Think you're done learning? If you ain't learned that basic step, we gotta start this oo(t)-gweh-rheh all over."

"No, I got that. I understand," I said. "But Hillman, I have to go back to *regular* school. I start back in September." I had another two years, maybe one semester shorter if I took overloads. My scholarship required that the degree be completed without interruption. If I screwed up, the college would just fill the spot with another journalism student, and I'd be another unfinished story, nothing to show but a series of student loan payments waiting for me.

"The place where we are," I continued. "It's an okay stopping point for now. I need school."

"What you think we been doing? This is school. A more useful kind, too."

"Yeah, well, I can't live on it," I said. "I don't know how *you* pay bills, but I need to plan for a steady income. I'm already well versed in Poor. I wanna try something different."

"Big mistake to walk away," he said. "Of all the possible people, I picked you."

"Well, aside from this being the first I'm hearing of it from you, practically, I *also* have plans that I made before you thought this up, plans you didn't make."

"Not true," he said, casually. "You told me to get ready for this plan when you were four. Hearing the secret voices of others? That's not one of my talents, but I know a person walking the Medicine path when I see them. Even if they don't know it. I waited all these years for the world to put something in front of you, so you'd have to look up. The world would tell me when you'd come. And finally, here you are. You think your sister and brother got a little bundle? You need to keep going over this till you got it, till it's right there in your mouth. You don't have to go digging in your head."

"I'm there." I didn't believe that the world had put me in the path of a shitty surgeon so I'd get back to Hillman's. But he also didn't understand that I had no need for refresher courses—that I remembered it all. I had no idea how it happened, other than his relentless repetition. This structure had gone on every day with no variation, gradually, until I'd learned. Like how you committed songs you don't even like to memory, with enough exposure.

I never had aspirations for Hillman's way of life, but our plans don't always align with others' maps, their passions and beliefs for you, on a collision course with yours.

"I remember everything." I walked over to his long table and named off every medicine there, what it was used for, who you couldn't use it on. "I'll come back, through the year, as I can. I appreciate what you're offering. I get the responsibility. I'll show you. I've kept it. I have a good memory." The pain was low-level abstract, but the midline scar, splitting me in two with a thick and purple line, showed no signs of going anywhere. My head was full of knowledge, though, from the reservation's only open medicine man.

"You're supposed to take over when I go," he said, bowing his head, then looking up.

"Hillman, don't give me the Sad-Dog-Who-Ate-the-Bacon Face. You're better than that."

"I am better than that, isn't it though?" he agreed, and changed back to a normal expression. We both laughed, breaking some of the tension that had been spinning around us like a dust devil. "I got serious plans for you, and time's running out."

"You're too ornery to go anywhere," I said, but I didn't know how old he was. Even the healthiest people didn't live forever. "Look, I scheduled that surgery for when I did, because I already had plans I didn't want it to interfere with."

"I guess you didn't have your ma read for you ahead of time."

"She refused," I said. "Look, I appreciate, so, so much, that you were willing to use your medicines to help me recover in ways that frigging surgeon blew off. But that was all this was supposed to be." I'd already packed my bags and they'd been neatly lined up under my bed. I stood up to clear and wash the dishes and put them away. "I can't just become someone else because my family said I should. I have to complete my education."

"Why do you think I'm doing this? You ain't becoming someone else. This here's your born-into path," he said. "Search your memory." He stopped there. I stepped into the room I'd been using and slid the few bags with my belongings along the floor, to the door. As I began situating them into my truck, he slowly walked over to lean on the truck bed. "Something's gonna bring you back, just you wait," he said, banging on the quarter panel, like a used car salesman.

"Listen, I know you want me to stay, but if I don't reactivate my classes, I lose my scholarship, my health insurance, the future from this internship, a potential career, everything."

"Not everything," he added, revealing the medicine bundle I'd carried most of my life. "Just from that path. Hard to get back here if you change your mind. You know already. Things have a way of getting lost." He opened his hand. "Leave this on the floor on purpose, did you?"

"Must have fallen out when I took my pants off last night." I reached for it. He'd quite possibly snuck it while I slept from the pants pocket where it lived, to reveal this very moment.

"Must have," he said, as I took it. "Guess you weren't ready, anyways. I been wrong before, but you understand this here. It's gonna be you needing me next time, not the other way around. Maybe not for you. Maybe for someone you love."

"Ha!" I laughed, unable to stop, even knowing it was rude. "My ma says there's no real Indian word for love. I even asked her. So maybe we don't believe in it." Every Valentine's Day, we joked that candy companies were missing an opportunity by not producing Reservation Candy Hearts, with terms of tolerant endearment like SHIT ASS or declarations of coupling like SKODEN? OR GWANDEN!, or K-DEN, or WILL YOU *EVEN* B MINE? Of course, Indians made up less than one percent of the population, so we didn't have much purchase power.

"Maybe she meant we got more words than you could handle, 'cause you don't know them in your own life. Is it maybe that?"

"Hillman, I'll be back when I can fit it in. I just have stuff to finish."

"Better hope I'm still here when the words for love finally speak to you." That was about as direct as he was likely to get, but I guess I'd already begun adapting to life off the Rez, where you made your own decisions and your family might make encouraging suggestions, but that was it. The more white people I knew, the more I saw they were charting their own lives, their families wanting them to grow into the adults they wanted to be. It was strange, and probably some people I grew up with would feel abandoned by such a hands-off approach. I didn't want to admit I'd begun liking the taste of that other world enough to add it to my own understanding.

That was how we left it as I stepped back into the world of textbooks and meal plans. Hillman couldn't see how preposterous such a résumé would look: Newspaper Man by Night, Medicine Man by Day. My internship had already begun to reveal ways my community navigated life every day. He made his offer, and, if I wanted it, I'd have to find a way.

CHAPTER TWENTY-TWO

Secret Origins

(1986)

When I pulled into my ma's, she already had things set up, apparently expecting my return. I told her a short version of my departure but she acted like she knew it already. "Anyway," I said. "I just wanted to let you know 'cause I'm going back in the fall, and I'm not ready just now to finish what Hillman started, much as you two might think."

"Do what you want. I brought you to Hillman 'cause I thought he could do something for you," she replied, picking up a magazine, never looking at me except as a reflection in her window. I could still read her lying voice, but if this was what she needed to tell herself, okay.

"He did do something," I said, thinking it had not been what I'd hoped.

"Open your shirt," she said back, in a second, no hesitation.

"You know what's there already." I was irritated that I'd let myself believe him.

"Open it."

I pulled the tails out, revealing exactly what she knew she'd see: the waistband of my Levi's yanked low, accommodating my new life, the thick purple scar. Every morning when I got dressed, my mirror reminded me of what I'd declined to do to Algie, my fetal pig.

Despite the surgeon's assurances after removing the surgical staples, the tissue still puckered and stayed amoeboid, like a thick line of violet-black candle wax drippings in a straight line. This was occasionally broken up by a thinner thread of white tissue, patches of how the scar should've looked. I'd become my own wampum, my own treaty belt negotiating the places between life and death. "Still there," my ma said, like I didn't have mirrors.

"That's not what he did for me. It was something else."

"That's why *I* did it. After all his pestering to take up what he does, finally, I gave in."

"You gave him *me*, not you," I corrected. "Even if it took you almost twenty years." I doubted she ever thought Hillman would tell me.

"You didn't have to say yes. You could have decided to never step across his threshold."

"How do you say no to a question you've never been asked?" Even saying it, of course, I knew that I did it all the time, in that subtle, action-level Rez language. She ignored my question, to illustrate. So, I dropped it. "Did you tell me everyone who came to see me?"

"I told you three months ago. I wasn't there every day. I can't keep track."

"Could you tell who, if you read for me?" She understood that it was important for me to know who'd come, but my desire didn't mean she'd cooperate.

"It doesn't work that way. If you don't know, how can I know?" I'd been there with her when her tea leaves told her things I was sure the drinker didn't know. But asking someone to explain something they'd done their entire lives, and barely understood themselves, was a challenge. "If you're staying here, bed's all made up. Fresh," she said, like we'd agreed this was the day I'd return.

"Did you ever read for Gihh-rhaggs?" I asked her directly, ignoring that last.

"No. You know that," she answered promptly. She wanted to remind me I was willfully chipping away at the wall of silence we'd constructed around him years before. She almost never talked of Gihh-rhaggs anymore, even in oblique terms.

"He gave lots of reasons that he should be checked on. He never pretended to be a saint."

"I told you before. I only see what I see. No control. Besides, I was mostly done reading when he came into our lives." I wondered how often she went through her scrapbook, if it glowed at night, calling from her dresser. "He knew what he had in me, and I knew what I had in him." Sometimes, growing up, I heard her sliding that drawer open, looking through pictures, wondering if in accumulation, they added up to something she was happy with. "Some things you don't need to know, while you're enjoying life. The end of the story should stay unknown until you're ready." She paused, then added, "And quit calling him that. You know his name."

I grabbed my things and headed to the staircase leading to my old room.

"Wait," she said. "That's my room, now. Your stuff's all down here. In there." She pointed with her lips to the downstairs bedroom I'd shared with my grandfather, and, for a while, all by myself. The same one she never moved into until Gihh-rhaggs was gone.

I opened the heavy curtain we used as a door and though I'd only been at Hillman's for a few months, the strong sense of home blasted me, a breeze blowing through. Even the hottest days felt ten degrees cooler here than anywhere else in the house. Now, the long lingering days of August heat felt sharper, like autumn moving in early, planning its stay.

I folded my pants on the chair near the foot of the bed. The room was wall-to-wall thrift shop and "curb sale" dressers white people left near the road with the rest of their trash.

Shadows grew across the ceiling above my bed, changing patterns. Were these fleeting images what my ma saw reading tea leaves? The world got smaller, an ember winking out.

Around midnight, I woke up and went out to take a leak. The cicadas hushed as my feet grew wet with dew. By the time I got back to the house, they were back at symphony volume, racing to the end they never got to, and my ma was sitting in her chair, though I'd sworn she'd already gone to bed. Next to a cardboard box on the table sat a teacup, with a new bag of Red Rose on the oilcloth. The kettle was on the stove, but the gas ring below hadn't been sparked.

"Do you know what the Jesus Eyes is?" I asked her, sitting at the table, in my usual chair.

"Ha!" she laughed. "Hillman's favorite insult. What do you think it is?"

"Well, I have probably a decent idea, I'm not stupid," I said, but she chose not to affirm or suggest otherwise. "But I felt like there's more he wasn't telling me. I know you don't think he fixed me the way you wanted, but we were talking about Benji and his messed-up leg. He said Rolanda had a bad case of the Jesus Eyes."

"All this time and you still don't know? Guess you're not as smart as you think."

"Ah, so good to be back in my loving home," I said, laughing. "Come on, you're the one who dropped my ass off over there."

"Okay, got me there," she said. "It's not officially fall, but most crops are well along enough for it to be okay. Now, this isn't my belief, but it's Hillman's. It's the old one. And you only get the highlights. You want more? Find it yourself." I suddenly glimpsed her life. She also hadn't been asked to become a tea-leaf reader. It'd just happened somewhere along the way. She'd discovered her own doorway into the shadow world one day, unaware she'd locked herself out of a million other doors by opening that one. I wondered if there were silent struggles on those rare occasions she cracked that door open again, once she'd gotten it closed.

"You know how Rolanda's always butting in with, 'oh you're going to Hell for this, Jesus ain't gonna let you into Heaven if you do that, he's got an eye on you,' blah blah blah, like Jesus and Santa Claus were the same thing. And when things go bad, she prays for Jesus to forgive her. When she says she wants to get into Heaven, she's really saying she don't want to go to Hell. Always thinking about Satan, how all his bad choices turned him from the chosen one into the fallen angel, and she's always thinking about how she don't wanna be the fallen angel, but she's pretty sure everyone else is gonna be?"

I nodded, thoroughly familiar with my auntie's views, and all the ways she mashed up a variety pack of selected beliefs to bend to the way she wanted to see the world. "That's not the way our world manages," my ma continued, her Rez accent growing stronger. She talked about the Good Mind and the Bad Mind, or the Clear Thinker and the Clouded Thinker, all the ways our story was about two sides, always shifting the balance, but both necessary. The Good Mind provided for us, but in return, we were just supposed to be thankful for what we had, not ask for additional favors.

"The Bad Mind reminds us of struggle. And you're supposed to be thankful for both. There's no sin to conquer, no Hell to be banished to," she concluded, then added: "There's the easy and the difficult! Like demanding the difficult be conquered? Like telling winter you're gonna conquer it! If you don't have the dormant season, you don't get the growing season."

"Okay," I said. "I guess I've got that. But what does that have to do with Benji and me? Or you and Rolanda? Or Umps and Hillman for that matter?"

"Well, some of that's Rolanda's business, but I'll say, she wasn't thankful Benji made it through okay. Some lawyer told her she'd have a better case if Benji had some pain and suffering. Then, when it was over, she asked her Pastor Clyde to lay his hands on Benji's leg, to straighten it out. And when it didn't work, she asked him about God answering all prayers."

"I already know the answer to that one," I said. "Benji told me himself that Pastor Clyde told him sometimes, 'God answers prayers with a no instead of a yes.'"

"There you go. You remember a few years ago, when that strange woman showed up, asking me to read her leaves?" She didn't have to say that strange *white* woman. No one on the Rez admitted they'd made the suggestion to the woman. My ma sympathized with her nonetheless. How did you not feel bad for someone whose child just vanished one day? "Remember what I did?"

Of course, I remembered that, too. "Why'd you refuse to read for her? What did you mean about how the answers you gave would only cause sadness?"

"Heartache. Not sadness. Not the same thing," she said, a fine distinction. "So your memory's that good? You've learned all you needed from Hillman in one summer's time—"

"I never said that. Not once. I said that what he'd taught me, I hung onto."

"Okay Memory Boy, think of everyone you ever knew me to read for. What they got in common?" I hated these questions with multiple true answers. So easy to be wrong.

"I remember," I said, after pausing. "You know—*really* know—every-one you read for. All from the Rez. Even if you don't hang with them, you know about their lives before you begin."

"And how come it's important?" I was going to have to take every step, myself.

"'Cause you know what they want, even before they walk in the door." Did she want me to suggest she was a huckster? I'd seen fake psychics work a room of a few hundred people, because all of them had unfinished busi-ness. I didn't understand what my ma did, but in this very moment, I grasped that it had something to do with memory. Collective memory.

"I had no connection to that Love Canal woman and her missing boy," she said. "Just what was on the news. She was tired the way new mothers are. I've been an exhausted mother. But after that? No bridge for us to meet in the middle."

"So when you read for someone, let's say you read for . . . Tim Sampson . . ."

"Tim Sampson. Just yanked that name out of the air, did you?" Con-versations with her were always games of chess but with magnetic pieces, and she had a much larger, secret magnet under the table, silently control-ling the next move.

"You mentioned Love Canal," I countered. "Wasn't a big leap."

"Did you notice your father didn't come see you?" she asked. My par-ents had never divorced, and I never dared ask Mona or Chester how long the periods were when he supposedly stayed with us. That was an answer I didn't want. But right now, I really wanted to hear about the details of my time in the shadow world. How did Tim just refuse to come when I was in serious trouble? He had to know.

"Nothing for Dad to mooch," I said. "So I never *expected* him to show." I felt my feet slide forward across her imaginary life-size chessboard.

"So this is all about what you expect from others, then? What you think you deserve?" she went on, making no move to light the ring of flame beneath the kettle. "You can't know what's going on in other people's lives," she said. "Just because you were in the hospital, all the demands in everyone else life just keep on coming. Think of people who expected something from you, maybe some still hoping," she said. "Don't you care about their needs, their worries? Are there people you've wanted to help, but you just needed to sit home and be by yourself?"

Of course there had been. One of the hardest parts of being a reporter was being in the position of telling someone's story, then moving on. They might feel attached to you, because you were attentive and listened carefully, but it was part of the job. In their desperation they believed you could do something more, be a hand for them to hold. Naively thinking you could or should maintain relationships with the subjects of your stories was one of the first warnings they gave you in Foundations of Journalism. You needed to stay detached for the good of everyone.

"Dusty was there, isn't it? Pretty sure," she added, prodding my silence.

"Don't believe so," I said. "Think I would've remembered."

"That box there is your old funny books. The ones you liked best still on top, so you know nobody else was digging in them. *What If?* and *Secret Origins*." Your family knew you in the strangest ways that others didn't, even down to your favorite forms of escape. I guess that's why most superheroes had little in the way of family. They couldn't have someone holding their secrets over their heads. Batman went back to Crime Alley every year on the anniversary of his parents' murder; Superman kept a miniaturized Kryptonian city in his secret Fortress of Solitude, while the rest had become Kryptonite, his shattered homeland turned to poison. Who would Bruce Wayne be if his parents got to grow old together? You assume Kal-El would likely trade his abilities for a life as a normal man on Krypton, but how could he not love being Superman?

Still, Dr. West hadn't suggested I'd become a hero after the ICU, and he didn't take the responsibility, either. It was an accident, he claimed, caused by my being "a mutant," more like the Marvel heroes. Peter Parker's uncle was killed because Peter was lazy as Spider-Man. And you knew every time Ben Grimm looked in the mirror, he didn't feel very super. How could you love the Gamma Rays that had, in addition to giving you tremendously impossible power, turned you into a rock-covered untouchable loner?

"If you want me to read for you, turn that burner on," my ma said in the dark cicada symphony. "But what I tell you, it can't be changed. I can only prepare you for the future, and since you know my tricks, I can't even tell you a nice version." She reminded me, in that moment, that *I'd* started this ball rolling before I ever started school, when I could sense she was trying to help someone accept their future by telling them a gentler version of it first.

"I guess I'm okay not knowing what's coming until it arrives," I said, and went to bed.

Gradually, I healed more. As fall came on the horizon, I moved back to my apartment. You could have a secret identity everywhere except your own home. I didn't need to revisit that operating room, to understand my life was changed, forever. All I needed was to stand naked in my bedroom mirror. Accepting my new life, I swore I'd never set foot in Our Lady of the Thorns again. Hillman, amid his plants, laughed and sat back, waiting, as he'd grown accustomed to.

CHAPTER TWENTY-THREE

Bleeding and Leading

(1988–1989)

B ecause of our long, complex history with education, the Rez set up systems to encourage people to commit. Things got risky at sixteen, when you could drop out. You'd think just being recognized for your accomplishment wouldn't have that much of an impact, but it did. We called the celebration Moving Up Day, its goal to acknowledge education milestones. Anyone hitting one was invited as a formal dinner guest at the elementary school, for a certificate and a gift made by women in beadwork class. I didn't receive an invitation when I finished community college, and it felt like a sharper absence than I'd thought it would.

Two years later, I'd completed my Bachelors, and one was extended. By then, I'd changed from intern to official *Cascade* staff reporter almost seamlessly, and I'd stopped attending classes, my City Room duties increasing in hours. This was going to be my last Moving Up Day.

Your invitation came with two guest tickets. I gave one to my ma, of course. Traditionally, the second one went to a close family member who'd helped you out, or if you were ready to go public with someone you'd become involved with, the ticket went to them. As my ma had always insisted, public affection declarations were just not the way we did things, unless you were getting to the pregnancy-showing stage or the sending-out-wedding-invitations stage.

I stopped first at Hillman's, and he was at his table, exactly where I'd left him two years earlier. I'd seen him in between at occasional events, where he'd act like I was one of those kids whose names he couldn't remember. "I'm going to my final Moving Up Day," I told him, sitting.

"That sounds about right. They still give these out at Mr. Nyah-whehs," he said, getting up and tapping a calendar hanging by a little bulletin board in his kitchen. A little convenience store just off the Rez named Mr. Thank You made special calendars for the year-end, customer gifts just for us, using our word for thank you. Everyone on the Rez had at least one, usually in the kitchen. "Doesn't seem like you're gonna finish your real education. I got no little beadwork gift for you, anyway, but if you do decide to finish, this here will all be yours. Everything."

By rights, his land and belongings would go to a family member when he passed. Often it went to someone of his children's clan, but he didn't have any children. We were the kids of his brother, so we belonged to our mother's clan, but family was still family and with no others in his clan, it would go to one of us. I wasn't sure my siblings had ever been inside here. I didn't know about Roland, and to the best of my knowledge, Benji had made only the one trip.

"I don't enter that building myself, except for the Senior Citizens meals," he said.

"Elders," I said. "They call them Elder Events now."

"I'm not a Senior Citizen anymore? Learn something new every day," he said, giving a fake surprise face. "So you supposed to mind your elders?" He was telling me not to offer him the ticket, so I respected his desire.

At home, I wrote: *In case you'd like to come* on a sheet of paper, added the ticket, and dropped it in the mail to Tim Sampson. He'd been at my high school one, for Christine, and presumably he'd gone to one for Hayley. I left my address off. No one else would be sending him one, and he could make his own decision. I still had incredibly mixed feelings, continuing to feel his absence from my time in the hospital and its lingering state. Some days, I was too exhausted to feel the absence, but in so many ways, I'd never have gotten anywhere of my own choosing without Tim having shown me the door of possibility in the first place. And yet, he had chosen not to cross a threshold when I'd most needed him to. In a few days, I'd have my answer. We didn't even have to speak, just be in the same room.

It seemed impossible that he'd skipped two years of community events, but I had no idea if he'd regularly gone or not before. The only time I'd ever seen him at National Picnic was during the Little Eva incident, and he wasn't exactly walking around the grounds visiting people, that time.

A lot of people ran on Indian Time, purposely late, but I arrived to the Moving Up early. Just inside the door, the lunch ladies' laughter echoed in the distance. A mural of a spearfishing Indian man still dominated the entrance. It had always seemed so breathtaking when I was a kid. We saw ourselves in media so rarely, that mural was strong personal magic, cultural medicine.

"Whatchu doing here?" Dusty Darkwinter said, stepping out of the gym.

"Graduated. Got my invitation," I said, reaching into my jacket pocket.

"Teasing," she said. "Made your beadwork, myself. Lots of ladies sign up for class when they got a kid moving up, to make the one for their kid." I'd heard she'd become the organizer. "I got rules. Nothing extra fancy for your family member. We want everyone to feel honored."

"Makes sense." Dusty had always been a prankster, so her customization of mine was either going to be serious or subtly ball-busting.

"Gimme a hand bringing them?" she asked.

"Hang on, I gotta stop here," I said, hitting the Boys' Room. The adult restrooms were locked, Staff Only. I was used to seeing tiny classroom chairs and desks, but there was something strange about standing at a urinal where the flush bar was below the fly of your pants.

"What's the matter?" Dusty yelled, opening the door a crack. "Can't find it?"

"Coming," I yelled back, leaning over to wash my hands with that pink-powder soap. She already had the boxes of beadwork loaded onto a cart. "You clearly didn't need my help."

"Maybe I wanted company," she said, stepping away from the storage room. "Shut the door, then tug on it to make sure it locks. This cart sometimes is a fierce pony. If it gets sassy, you can help." I grabbed the opposite handle and felt what she meant. It had one wild wheel. Peanut butter cookie aroma filled the hallway.

"Working for the *Cascade* for real now or what?" She motioned with her lips for me to open the lunchroom doors, revealing tables in the same tiny scale. "We got a few minutes." Rejecting the Indoor Voice we used when this doubled as our library, she yelled, "Marl! Them cookies ready?" Marlena came in and set a plate before us, asking if this were my last Moving Up Day.

"So you didn't answer my question," Dusty said, making a cookie vanish in two bites.

"I don't exactly know what you mean."

"You emptying the trash and brewing coffee, or writing articles?"

"Officially a reporter now," I said. A number of people worked in white-collar places. We just usually didn't get far before someone, somewhere, slammed the brakes on us.

"So these days you're emptying the coffee, writing the trash, and brewing stories," she said, laughing, but meaning it, just the same. "You know why you're there, right? For real?"

"Cause I committed, and made my grades, and worked my ass off?"

"Aww, honey," she said, like she was soothing a kid with a bee sting. "That's so cute. Like when you went to school here. Hey Marl?" she yelled, and Marlena peeked back around the corner. "This guy eat all the veggies on his tray?" Marlena laughed and shook a dishrag at us, like she'd been told a particularly good joke. "Think of all those starving kids who went away to the Boarding Schools, and how they'd kill for your salad and your green beans."

"What's your problem, Dusty?" I hadn't seen her in years, but I didn't recall crossing her.

"Just don't want you getting a big head is all."

"What's wrong with enjoying some success? I mean, I've only been doing it a couple weeks. Don't I get to hope I might enjoy it a little?"

"We don't get that luxury," she said. "You get cocky? You get lazy. And pretty soon, you're gonna have to write a shitty story about someone you know. Or they're gonna make you defend a story they put in the paper. *That's* what you're getting paid for. You try writing a nice story about, say, me? Me and beadwork, and Border Crossing? See how enthusiastic they are."

"I *could* do that," I said. People were doing spec stories all the time. I'd already had a plan for my first spec proposal, but I could shuffle and make one about Dusty a priority. "Let's set things up. I'll start tonight. I'll write about you teaching women how to beadwork—"

"And men, if they want," she said. "Whoever wants. The more people do this, the better it has a chance to survive." And right there, she was already giving me angles. I could do this.

The custom beadwork Dusty made for me was close to the standard feather and mandala she'd taught her class to do. But for mine, she'd added a glass-heart bead in the mandala center, with red glass veins tracing the leading edge, the blood running through a community keeping it alive. I was glad we'd run into each other, and not just to catch up. Tim didn't show. As the night went along, Dusty seemed to know who my no-show guest was, and asked if we minded her sitting with us. If my ma was puzzled my second guest was my old babysitter, she didn't let on. When I got home and shut off the light, the empty chair at our table glowed hot in my mind. I didn't know if I should feel more sad or mad. I'd tried writing several letters over the past two years, but each time, I couldn't finish them. I went through periods of driving past his house regularly, and other periods of avoiding it, depending on which choice felt less like an ache at the time. I couldn't get past the fact that he hadn't come.

When I proposed Dusty's story to Gary, the guy who'd hired me, he said I should wait my turn before proposing features. I accepted that answer, believing the *Cascade* editorial staff would be more supportive and inclusive once I'd established myself. But as Dusty had hinted, the Rez was most often in the paper for crime news. A couple months later, I pointed out that pattern, and thought surely they'd understand if I were clear. The story I'd just been assigned also had a direct personal connection to me. I had to say something.

"You really think people from the Rez go to the city, steal shit, and then drag the proof home?" I asked Gary, noting the fairly frequent Blotter report of stolen cars that got stripped and dumped on the Rez. "Would you?"

"Can't speak for the criminal mind," he said. "Our job is to report where stolen cars are found," he added slowly, as if I were not a natural

English speaker. The same old song, just a new singer. "The facts, not speculation. *Not*," he emphasized, so I knew he meant business, "to guess how
they got there. Foundational rules of journalism. News is one thing. Juicy
news, something else, then sports, and then Opinion, coming up the rear.
That's why we have a clearly identified Opinion Page."

"The *Cascade* identifies the exact location *only* if the stolen-and-
stripped car's on reservation land," I said, showing photocopies I'd pulled
from the morgue to prove my point.

"You're the ones who keep saying you're a *different nation*," he said,
shrugging.

Dusty had no meaningful relationship to my field of work, and yet,
she'd known. Even now, well into the real job, I was mostly assigned
Police Blotter and Fire and Ambulance Calls. Still paying the dues. She
also knew that when a complicated Rez crime story came in, I would be
tagged for the byline, as the reporter from the Rez.

To make matters worse, whenever someone from the Rez was
arrested, everyone in the city room gave me editorial eyebrows. You
know: *how come you let this shit go on?* The last time, I'd said to the whole
room: "If I stared at you every time a white person got caught commit-
ting a crime, I wouldn't have time to do anything else, now, would I?"
Most dropped their eyes and clucked like chickens.

"Look, Brian," Gary jumped in. "Come on in and shut the door." Once
inside his office, he offered me a seat. "Your colleagues, they're suburban
kids who've grown into suburban adults. Like me. When they took these
jobs, maybe they thought they'd break the next Watergate, the next assas-
sination. Most want to jump to a major market. No one—except you—
enters with small dreams. The big story they might really hit is going to
be another Love Canal, but we don't want to think about that. We live here.
No one wants to believe they live in a toxic wasteland."

"So why do they get to pick and choose?" I asked. "Is it going to be
like this until you hire a second Indian? 'Cause I don't really see you doing
that any time soon."

"Brian, *we* don't know all white people in the county, but *you* know
most of the Indians. It's why you get the big bucks." He laughed because
I *didn't* get big bucks. "When everyone else here signed their contracts,

they didn't know they'd mostly be getting quotes from grieving people whose kids got involved with a domestic abuser. I mean, you never pick this job because you want to hear: 'Yes, I knew he was going to kill my daughter. She chose to live with him.'"

I'd seen enough bad relationships to agree, mostly off-Rez. I wasn't pretending it didn't happen at home, but if you roughed up someone at on the Rez, they had family who might school you on your bad ideas. White guys in my high school forced girlfriends to walk with their heads down, so they didn't accidentally see another boy. Never understood how those girls got involved with shit heads like that in the first place, but I'd seen it often enough to know it was a thing.

"Those optimistic ones are the worst," he said. "But you're not optimistic. And you want to stay here." Even new to the formal job, I knew people didn't buy newspapers for happy stories, unless the happy story was about them. My job was: whatever they tell me. "There's bound to be other Indian news. If I want perspective pieces from local reservations, you're our guy. And you know, if you stick around and everything works out—"

"Why wouldn't it work out?" I asked.

"You see? There?" he said, tapping crumpled papers on his desk. "You interrupted your boss. These kids who grew up in Rose Courtyard and Misty Meadows? They know you don't do that. You have to learn to play nice. Didn't you ever play any team sports?"

"Not a one." I flashed on how disastrous my attempt at the Marines would have been.

"That figures. In the meantime, you know the policy about bleeding and leading. You should be happy I'm giving you front-page shots."

"Look," I said, deciding I should at least be up front about why I was resisting today's particular assignment. "I've done these for two years, never complaining. The last one that came in? It's my cousin. Isn't there some rule about avoiding conflicts of interest?" Roland's name had slithered through the fax the day before: DWI. Gary insisted that Blotter copy always identified a perp with "an illegal blood alcohol level at the reservation border," calling it a Public Service.

"We're too small for conflict of interest concerns," he said. "You're from the reservation. Your beat's going to be the reservation. You know almost anyone there. Correct?" I nodded, the scar pinching and spasming. "You're in an unusual position." I'd been hired *to* have a stake in the story. I'd have to keep the balance and, he assured me, I wouldn't always be successful. "I took a chance on you. Made an investment. You got two choices. Let me know." I could write stories about people I knew, or look for a different job.

"But Gary, this is my *cousin*," I said again. "Don't you have cousins?"

"Don't you say you're all cousins?" he asked. It was not entirely a shitty remark. "Okay, say it is your cousin, your *real* cousin. That means you have incentive to get the story right. Tell you what," he continued, perking up. "This new multicultural BS is picking up steam. If it takes off, we'll see about maybe upbeat features on reservation life. In the meantime, I promise, we'll work up a column to rotate upbeat Happy Snappy stories about communities around the region. You can write short perky reservation stories there. Maybe by the first of the year. Give us time to get things in place. Until then, you know our tough decisions in the Big City Newspaper Life."

I did what Gary said and got on with my life, with an annoyed cousin. But that exchange, and my willingness to write the story of Roland's DWI, paved the way for a rotating Niagara Communities Sunday Lifestyles column and allowed me to eventually develop my first *Cascade* feature byline, a Sunday piece on treaties, focusing on Dusty. Beadworkers like her kept treaties alive, the only private people to legally "engage in commerce" in the Niagara Falls park, for helping save colonial asses in the Revolutionary War.

The feature would help her, too. A laminated clipping on her table would give her an edge. "It's my right as an Indian to not pay two dollars to cross the border!" she shouted at my recorder during our interview. "My sovereign right! And it's gonna stay that way. As long as, what was it? Oh yeah, as long as the grass stays growing and river flowing. Something like that. You know what I mean. And you keep that in."

It was an honest account of Dusty's life. Beadworkers dedicated incredible hours into pieces, and, invariably, customers tried bargaining. *Cascade* fact-checking policy required me to note that the "crossing the border freely" wasn't about bridge toll. Within a week, Dusty had a new nickname. Now she was Two-Buck Dusty. Sometimes just Two-Buck. As with everything, she laughed and moved on, beading a hatband with a two-dollar bill upfront.

When Dusty set up at Culture Night the next year, she had the feature laminated and pinned to the Pendleton she always put under her items for sale. I went to chat, but her daughter Lottie snapped her eyes at me, telling Dusty she was going for food. "You know kids," Dusty said. "She thinks this article's making fun of me." I glanced at Lottie in line, and she whipped her head back the other way, so I'd know she was snubbing me.

"Guess you didn't teach her to snap eyes like a pro yet," I said, and we both laughed.

"White girl moves she's learning in school." I'd seen it happen once Rez kids hit middle school. "She don't know how this works," Dusty said, tapping the feature. "Customers don't read. They see my pic with the article? My prices get to go up, but they still buy from *me*, 'cause they think I must be the best if I was in the news, isn't it though?"

"You were in the news?" I asked, goofing like I hadn't written the story. "Oh yeah! It's right here."

"You know what I mean," Dusty said, flashing me her palm. "She'll be happy when I show her the bank book, so she can go become a nurse like she's already planning."

"*You* know I wasn't making fun of you, right?" She had to know that wasn't my intent. "I'd never do that. I finally got to write about community. And you gave me the idea." I felt like an idiot, even as I was trying to sound like a hero, but somehow, it didn't stop me. "I wanted your work to be a wake-up call for everyone, to embrace their identities as Indians."

"Look around," she said, gesturing to the room. "We already do that, Brian. Maybe you should read your own articles, isn't it though?" I was a chump to have thought that was my place to say. My community already embraced their lives, with the same, almost invisible strength they held on to every sliver of our history and shared culture.

I was beginning to understand this job's risks in ways Dusty already had, even from the outside. Maybe her love of *True Crime* mags had made her aware the news pie chart showed a gigantic wedge of Bad News dominating a little slice of Good. Because of Dusty, every now and then, I got to write positive community pieces, even if I was mostly the proof that the *Cascade* wasn't biased. If they'd hired me, how could they be accused of harboring anti-Indian sentiment?

"Hey there, Cousin," Roland said from behind me. I was surprised to see him here, but you never knew where he might pop up. "On duty or off right now?"

"Culture Night, just here to enjoy, check in with old friends, family, have a little corn soup and frybread, see what's happening."

"Oh yeah, just checking," he said, sipping our strawberry drink that always disappointed non-Indians. It had no added sweeteners or syrups beyond the strawberries mashed into it. "Most people don't even come unless they got kids or grandkids at the school." A few people were like me, but most either had kids here, were demonstrating a traditional art, or had a vendor table.

"Well, what are you doing here, then?" I asked.

"Oh, I help Dusty set up and break down her table," he said. Funny how, all these years later, one of the Darkwinter girls had finally snagged their snag, to the degree he could be snagged. "And our kid watches the health table. Probably be running it someday."

"You don't have any kids," I said, and just as I did, he pointed with his lips, at Lottie.

"Some kind of reporter you are," he said. "Good thing, though. Means it don't get around much. She don't know, herself." He pursed his lips and looked down at the demarcation lines on the gym floor. "Probably better that way. Then she don't know what trouble her dad is. She can just read about my messes in the paper and toss it away like everyone else."

"I'm sorry, Roland," I said. "I tried to get out of it any way I could. But Lot—?"

"Shhh," he interrupted. "Told you, *she don't know* either. My mistakes are my own. Lot of people make the same one. I just got caught. You *should* be taking those stories on. Make sure they're told right. If you can't get rid of them, make sure no extra oo(t)-gweh-rheh gets added." He went back to wandering, looking at the mini-longhouses the school kids made, beadwork vendors, snow snake and lacrosse stick examples, and the other displays celebrating our culture.

Lottie sat next to Hubie as he took blood pressure, offered advice, and she passed out specific pamphlets to give to their table visitors. Lottie would be surprised to discover she had one big blood connection with Hillman, as scared as I was guessing she was of this side of medicine. She couldn't see what I was trying to do, the ways I had to keep balancing the two sides of my own life.

I knew a group of Eee-ogg-loving people made comments like: *How come a big old Medicine person needs a regular job? Must not be any good. The Chosen One shouldn't need steady income or a college education, right?* Even Rez people who didn't know the Two Row Wampum themselves still formed their attitudes around it. The boarding school legacy had left many people suspicious of advanced education. Trying to balance a super traditional side and a side in the white world was viewed with suspicion, depending on what you were doing.

Even though she was still in high school, Lottie already knew it would be impossible to be a full-time medicine person now, so she planned to do it the American way. She talked big, but really, she maybe seethed that Hillman had shown me a glimpse of a life she'd never be offered, then left it for me to decide.

And instead of saving lives, I dedicated my life to talking about them.

Two Rows (VI)

We see the open territory ahead of us and
acknowledge the mingled wakes we leave behind.

We share, between us, a peace we each maintain
by our dual presence in the expanse before us.

We discover each other side by side
in the water, traveling our own paths.

We emerge from different points of origin
and stay steady to our own unknown destinations.

We maintain our own customs, governing ways
of life and beliefs about the universe.

We each recognize that we move
according to our own desires and plans.

We respectfully do not cross streams
with each other, maintaining forward balance.

Test for Echo

(1990–1992)

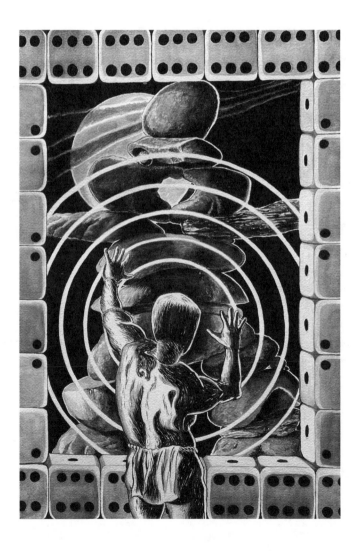

Ed. *The Niagara Cascade* recognizes our region's rich diversity and will regularly feature columns from *Cascade* contributors, on a rotating basis. We hope this column is the first in a long series of inviting our readers to get to know their hometown a bit better. Our first entry is by Brian Waterson, our Native American correspondent, from the local Tuscarora Reservation. Brian was nurtured by our college internship program, as part of our active engagement with the spectrum of communities in our readership population.

Dog Street Dispatches, January 1, 1990, "New-Yahh, the Feast" by Brian Waterson.

Happy New Year! Or as I was raised: New Yahh! New-Yahh! Once you know people outside your family, you notice you don't share all traditions. At Tuscarora, we have two long-standing January First rituals. Because our history has been orally shared, recorded by outsiders, you'll find multiple origin stories. Some say we borrowed them from our German neighbors. Our traditional calendar lists the New Year closer to February, so some say this holiday let Old Time Indians know the outside New Year had come.

Early on New Year's Day, children and some adults bundle up and go house to house, shouting, "New-Yahh!" As a reward for their news, they're given a baked good. Children belong to their mother's clan. But if you visit members of your father's clan, you add the word "oo-wee-rheh" (doll), and you'll get an extra special treat to remind you they're family too. Often, kids ask for two cookies, one for them and one "for the driver" taking them around the Nation, but I wonder if the drivers, often dads, really get the cookies that had been negotiated for them.

As traditions change over time, I wonder if we might someday have a new tradition, to thank adults who aren't your mom or your dad but who help raise you, shape you into a better person. Sometimes, they're the driver, and sometimes, they're the navigator. I hope we find ways to thank them for their support. In the meantime, Happy New Year! New-Yahh! And don't forget to show your love for your family, and always remember something special, for the driver.

Dog Street Dispatches, July 1, 1990, "The Two Rows, Border Crossing" by Brian Waterson.

Readers faithful to this column may recall my very first entry was about holidays and rituals, around the New Year. As with other traditions, I didn't become aware that an event I attended wasn't universal until later in life. For this column, I thought I'd explore a similar event, one that takes place in our city, every year, which most readers of this newspaper have likely never heard of.

The Annual Border Cross celebration commemorates the Jay Treaty of 1794, ensuring American Indians free travel between the US and Canada, in recognition of our original territory being on both sides of what is now an international border. The celebration involves a yearly parade that eventually crosses one of the two bridges in Niagara Falls and concludes in a gathering with games, food, speeches, and other programming. The event begins on one side of the border and ends on the other, taking turns every year.

For most of my younger life, I was entirely unaware the event was primarily a political event involving international treaty law. For many young people, it's like a big party where you get to see cousins who may travel great distances to participate. You check out what the vendors are selling, watch some dancing, and though you know speeches are occurring, you only become aware of their importance gradually, at your own rate.

Like many of our treaties, the Jay has some relationship to our first significant treaty with others: The Two Row. Negotiated first with the Dutch and then eventually with New York, the treaty is simple, featuring two lines, representing two vessels traveling side by side. The vehicles represented our two ways of life. We did not interfere with theirs and they didn't interfere with ours. The space in between was to represent peace, calm water. Some leaders have maintained that it is impossible to have a foot in each vessel, but many members of local Native communities work outside the nation. They also have relationships with people from each vessel.

You could say that a helping hand from each might help steady us in our journeys. It takes a commitment from everyone to maintain the peace between the vessels, an embrace, a clasping of hands. These days, I'm aware of the importance of maintaining treaties, but usually, when I attend the Border Crossing Celebration, it is to celebrate those friendships, those helping hands that were extended my way when I really needed it. Nyah-wheh (thank you), to those who have made my life better in our shared journey down the river, and for all the peace between, and all the borders we've crossed together.

Dog Street Dispatches, September 12, 1991, "Mystic Rhythms" by Brian Waterson.

This month's column is a little change of pace, but bear with me. One of my favorite bands has a new release. I've seen every one of their concert tours since 1980, even going to Toronto once. Yes, they're Canadian, Rush to be specific. Some people might stop reading right now. Rush is one of those "love them" or "hate them" bands, with little in between.

"What's an Indian doing liking Rush?" is maybe the weirdest and most common reaction I've gotten. Among non-Indian friends, music taste is often tied to their identity. But what does that leave Indian music lovers? Buffy Sainte-Marie and Redbone? Link Wray? Fine enough, but we need something more than "Rumble," "Starwalker," and "Come and Get Your Love." "Mystic Rhythms" sounds like it might be a Native song, but it's not. It's by Rush, off their *Power Windows* album. Traditional social songs are great, remembered for generations and learned when you're young, sitting in with adult singers and drummers, maybe learning rhythm on a horn rattle to begin, but they're not exactly my go-to music while driving or working.

I have Rez friends in a band. They've gone by different names, but mostly the Dog Street Devils (borrowing the same beloved nickname as my column). They play songs by The Stones, The Beatles, The Eagles, Prince, AC/DC, The Dead, Fleetwood Mac, Hendrix, Lynyrd Skynyrd, The Who, Led Zeppelin, Springsteen, and for our parents' generation, some Johnny Cash, Hank Williams and Jimmie Rodgers, and a little Patsy Cline and Loretta Lynn, depending on who made it to the gig. They don't make a living, but they have fun, playing parties and the occasional bar. I listen to the bands they cover, but they don't cover a lot of what I love. I need the real thing.

Which brings us back to Rush. Their music is complex, with multiple time signatures, and high upper-range vocals. In truth, multiple time signatures and tough range vocals *do* describe traditional social songs. Closer than most. But that's not the point. People can't really say why they love some music over others. It's personal, even if you're the only one being moved. I found Rush through the music, but stayed for the lyrics. I learned about French history, the Holocaust, left and right brain theories of brain science and psychology, classical mythology, exotic cars, Shakespeare, Hemingway, Tolkien, Coleridge, and the controversial writer, Ayn Rand. None of these influences had been a part of my life before Rush. Their words spoke honestly to me, before I found someone I could be honest with, in my real life. And even if we lose touch with those people we care for, when we most need them, we still have familiar music for comfort.

Their new CD is called *Roll the Bones*, a slang term for dice games of chance. You might wonder the origins of this slang. I know for sure there is a game of chance in the Haudenosaunee creation story. And the dice involved? The skulls of self-sacrificing chickadees. When Rush comes to town for this tour, you can be sure I'll be there, not as a reporter, but as a fan, someone touched when someone else rolled the bones and took a chance on them.

Dog Street Dispatches, November 21, 1991, "Thanksgiving" by Brian Waterson.

One of the first questions you get when someone understands that you're Native is whether you celebrate Thanksgiving or not. As with so many things, the answer to this question isn't nearly as easy as you might think.

On the one hand, we do, on the last Thursday in November, gather as extended families. The meal often involves turkey and dressing, some version of cranberries, a pumpkin pie among the desserts, and the TV playing a parade in the morning and then any number of football games throughout the day.

If you're lucky, you may have some traditional corn soup and cornbread and frybread too, as part of your meal. But even this is not as easy as it may seem. Some Native families say that frybread came about as a result of being cheated out of the food supplies promised in treaties, and that it was not traditional food. But in my experience, frybread is special-occasion food, and traditional food, and it's tied to meaningful days throughout my life. It may have started out of some people not holding up their end of a deal, but it hasn't stayed that way. Relationships change and grow. They become their own thing, and no one else can insist that your tradition is not your tradition. You may develop a tradition with someone special in your life accidentally, because of some magic spark in that moment, something you both wanted to honor and preserve. Keeping them as a tradition is a way to protect that relationship, because our connections to each other are more fragile than we might ever imagine. I am thankful.

Within the larger communities of Native peoples in this area, we also have a different belief about Thanksgiving. Without going into an elaborate explanation, I'll just say it is a traditional Haudenosaunee (Iroquois) custom to give thanks every day for the opportunity to live a good life and appreciate the people, places, animals, and plants that enrich your life. It is also spoken at the beginning of important gatherings, as a good place to start. Sometimes people mistake it for a prayer, but it is more an address, an acknowledgment. If you happen to be friends with a Native person, locally, and you ask them if they celebrate Thanksgiving, don't be surprised if they say "yes, every day." They are being serious, and this Thursday, like all days, I'll be thankful for every opportunity that has come my way. Some things, some people, I'll be more thankful for, and will always remain so, but don't we always hope that for the people we love? Wishing you and your loved ones a happy Thanksgiving, however you celebrate.

Dog Street Dispatches, February 13, 1992, "Words for Love" by Brian Waterson.

This year, my Communities column arrives close to Valentine's Day, so it seemed like a great opportunity to talk about different ways people express love. My grandparents and parents were fluent in the Tuscarora language, but even now, they are afraid to teach us. My grandparents had been sent to the Indian Boarding Schools, whose main goal was to "Kill the Indian and Save the Man" (a topic for a different column). They came home, but the fear of seeming too Indian stayed with them all their lives, and they passed it on to my parents' generation.

So I am not fluent, and most of what I've learned has been in Language Classes while in elementary school, and bits of slang still commonly used. Most of us have gotten used to asking our parents the Tuscarora words for this or that thing we want to know. English is a noun-based language, largely about things. Tuscarora is more about verbs, actions. Because they're so different, our parents feel it's safe to give us individual words. They go through some mental process and give us something close enough. When you ask for phrases, things get more complicated. Sentences don't move back and forth easily. The space between is approximate.

A while back, I asked my mother the Tuscarora word for Love. Her answer stunned me. She said, "there isn't one." Now for those of you buying cards, candy, plush white teddy bears holding little red hearts, or jewelry this week, that answer will seem maybe overly harsh. Her quickness stunned me, but it didn't seem too far from my understanding of affection in my community. I've seen the same romantic comedies the rest of you have, and I've seen my share of couples trying to pull off the Big Romantic Gesture. After all, Niagara Falls is supposedly the Honeymoon Capital of the World, so *Cascade* correspondents see such displays fairly often, covering community news.

I can't speak for everyone in my community, of course, though I always try for an accurate balance. For this delicate topic, I'll stick to my own observations and experiences. People in my community move in together, get married and have children, though not necessarily in that order. But we also socialize most often in larger groups. You may never know for sure a couple is actually serious until you see a wedding invitation or start hearing rumors of a shower. That's maybe a little exaggeration.

Fortunately for me, I have a family elder who was old enough to remember the boarding schools, but who luckily dodged the experience. He was willing to share some insights with me beyond my mother's terse answer. He said that in the boarding schools, when residents got too chummy and familiar with each other, school staff would separate them and move them into different housing, so they'd be forced to be alone again, forced to use only English, which made them easier to monitor. Expressing affection in front of others was dangerous.

After telling me this disheartening history, my elder smiled and said that love is like weeds. Even in the toughest environment, it finds ways to adapt and grow. He said that it always finds a way, and noted my grandparents as examples. Maybe that's why Valentine's Day relies on so many props. People hope that a teddy bear will say those words people find so terrifying. My elder never did tell me a Tuscarora word for love, either, but he did say love is an action, so maybe there are thousands of different ways of describing that action.

When tomorrow rolls around, instead of hunting that right card (you're probably too late, anyway), reach out and touch a person you love, connect with them, hold their hand, embrace them. If they love you, they'll probably embrace you back, and even if this is not the love of your life, won't it still be nice to know someone thinks enough of you to reject fear and commit to hope? To risk expressing that feeling of connection just for you? Won't it be nice to do that for someone you think might benefit from the embrace? Happy Valentine's Day.

Police Blotter, May 3, 1992, "Apparent Samaritan Becomes Violence Victim" Cascade Staff

An anonymous midnight tip lead to an apparent assault near the north end of Moon Road on the Tuscarora Indian Reservation. The victim, a longtime resident of Bite Mark Road, was discovered unconscious in a field next to his idling vehicle, severely beaten. Authorities speculate the weapon was the victim's own tow-chain, already secured to the vehicle for a presumed attempt to render assistance to the unknown assailant. This discovery was made in response to a 911 call reporting an unusual sight on the sparsely populated road. The victim was taken by ambulance to Our Lady of the Thorns Hospital, listed in serious condition. Anyone with potential information is encouraged to call the police tip hotline.

Two Rows (VII)

We share, between us, a peace we each maintain
by our dual presence in the expanse before us.

We discover each other side by side
in the water, traveling our own paths.

We emerge from different points of origin
and stay steady to our own unknown destinations.

We maintain our own customs, governing ways
of life and beliefs about the universe.

We each recognize that we move
according to our own desires and plans.

We respectfully do not cross streams
with each other, maintaining forward balance.

We see the open territory ahead of us and
acknowledge the mingled wakes we leave behind.

PART SIX

Entre Nous

(1992)

CHAPTER TWENTY-FOUR

Taking Inventory

It took six years, two Roland DWI stories, and facing mortality, but I'd finally re-entered the one place I swore I'd never step foot in again. Despite my ma's claims that there's no Tuscarora word for love, someone I loved needed me, after six silent years, to deliver on an investment that had been made in my future. As Tim slept on in the ICU, slowly reknitting himself back together, I needed to wake up, open my eyes, and, finally, risk it all.

Hubie kept an eye on him for me, after I could no longer pass for Immediate Family. Several days in, Tim had been transferred to Med-Surg, but Lottie Darkwinter worked that ward, the Sixth Floor of Our Lady of the Thorns. Even these years after I'd written about Dusty, Lottie maintained the grudge. She also knew I had medical coverage, so I wasn't beholden to her special off-the-record Rez treatment plan. We were like magnets flipped to repel one another. Lottie was afraid of Hillman, but my mom's tea leaves and my departure from the ICU added their own color. And that story had only grown in the Rez imagination in the past six years.

"What are *you* doing here?" was the first thing I heard, getting off the elevator. My luck she'd be at the nurses station during my initial attempt to visit. "You shouldn't be here."

"Not your decision," I replied, walking past. For Med-Surg, I was free to visit unless Tim himself objected. He looked better already without that drainage tube, spaceship halo lights, the closed-circuit TV channels of his body, and that hover mattress. He must awaken sometimes. Soon enough, he'd be fully conscious. Even when he did awaken, though, he might not remember my visit.

A large square dressing still covered the round arc of Tim's belly. Out of the ICU, he still wasn't remotely out of the woods. He'd probably had a splenectomy. *Major surgery, commonly resulting from a traumatic abdominal blow,* my anatomy professor noted inside my head.

While I was relieved he didn't have other visitors, Christine's absence felt wrong. If these events led to her, they also led to Randy Night. It's possible I just hadn't bumped into people with the right Eee-ogg, or people stayed quiet, knowing my level of involvement was personal.

Lottie followed me in a couple minutes later, staring into the crinkled pages on her clipboard. "Immediate family only," she lied, trying to use her notes as a prop to chase me away.

"Lottie-dah?" I used a Rez nickname she hated. "I know the drill. He's not in ICU anymore." I sat in Tim's visitor's chair. Some part of me was so tempted to tell her to be nicer to me, since we were cousins. But it wasn't my place to change the course of Dusty and Roland's lives. I'd done that enough already.

"Better not be bringing anything in here, either." I displayed my palms, holding nothing except a Visitors Pass and my keys, on a beadwork fob her mother had made for me. "Well, I don't think you should be here. Christine probably don't, either," she said, adjusting his sheets.

"Then it's good that's not up to you, and that she's scarce, and that his roommate doesn't mind," I said, gesturing at the empty far bed. She huffed and fled. Christine *could* make that call. Until that happened, I'd be here after Lottie's shift and before the announcement for visitors to leave. Tim's labored breathing was at least unassisted now.

In the dark distance, someone wondered how effective their beating skills had been. What would have triggered Randy and what did Christine have to do with it? Admittedly, I could miss a lot, seeing them only fleetingly at Rez events over several years' time. Five floors below, ICU nurses on break flanked the work entrance.

As if sensing my thoughts, Tim moved in sleep, coughing. He tried to cross his ankles, but the foam straps covering his calves restricted movement. His eyes were open, just a hair, but he didn't seem to see me. It was like he had access to a different dimension right now, other worlds blocked from the rest of us. His eyes drifted closed again.

A young nurse entered—shift change—perky with a uniform swarmed in pastel cartoon characters. She checked the machines monitoring Tim, expertly sliding by me, and smiling. "I'll be his nurse tonight," she whispered, putting a card with her name, Mo, next to the Nurse slot on his bulletin board. "Just be a minute." She recorded numbers and changed an IV bag. "Has he been awake since you've been here?" I shook my head. "He's in and out, happens with people in this condition. He might not even remember the first few days in the ICU."

"You get a lot of people here in this condition?"

"I'd *like* to say we don't get many people like this, but that would be a lie. Usually, it's women. Women from the men in their lives. This one's extreme, but your dad's a pretty big guy, and in decent shape." I didn't correct. "Probably what saved him. Lot of people might not have made it through what happened, but it doesn't seem like much short of a tow chain *would* bring this guy down." She absently patted his leg. "Wasn't that what they said?"

"Yeah, a tow chain," I confirmed, having typed in the news item detail myself.

"This world," she said, and left. I followed soon after and did Rez Laps instead of heading to the city. Catching the person wouldn't change anything, including those damaged places on Tim's body, but I felt like I was supposed to do something. In truth, I didn't know what I was looking for. That world I walked away from was always there, waiting. Last week, after I'd begun the rituals of Giving Thanks that Hillman insisted I do, evaluating my entire life, I began to hear them again.

The hospital's automatic doors silenced the natural world singing around me, but when the doors slid open again, they'd resume, like a chorus of cicadas, singing, and waiting. The air was still crisp, not the thick swelter we'd have by July. The scent of river water drifted out of the dike through my vents while peepers hummed in my ears.

By the second night, Lottie had switched to evening shift. I waved when I got off the elevator. If she thought she was stopping me, she was more clueless than I'd suspected. I looked forward to seeing Tim, even sleeping, coming together beneath those surgical staples. She whispered to the nurse next to her, then gestured for me to follow her to the visitor lounge before I could make my way to his room.

"Lottie, if you think you've come up with some other way to prevent—"

"Shhh, be quiet and listen," she said, as we entered the vacant room, suddenly serious. "I want to tell you something. I know you're not really his family."

"This is not news, Lottie," I said. "We've been over this."

"No, that's not what I mean." She kind of moonwalked to the door, to make sure no one else we might know was in the hall. *Subtle*, I thought, and laughed. "When Christine comes, there's always someone with her. From the Rez. He's more your age. Acts like her snag." She knew who she was talking about, and I did, but if she refused to name him, I'd do the same. Eee-ogg was like this. If you didn't speak someone's name, technically, you hadn't been talking about them. It was a ridiculous justification, but everyone operated by this same rule.

"Yeah, I got an idea who you're talking about. Tall? Kind of dark, but not super dark. Long hair? Lanky looking at first, but really, he's all wiry muscles?"

"Very funny." I'd just described half the Rez Male Population. "Anyways, he comes with her, but never goes in the room. That's not how we do things now, isn't it though? Always goes to the lounge, and starts flipping the TV channels, even if other people are there."

"I do have an idea," I said. "But, as you've noted, it's not really my business now, is it?"

"I figured you might know him," she said, seeming disappointed I wasn't going to name him, either, but I knew the rules of Eee-ogg as well as she did. I wasn't sharing my opinion based on her intentionally vague description. "But . . . I seen that hovering behavior before. Guys always with their woman, don't let them get mail, answer the phone. Know what I'm saying?"

"I do. Not usually at home. Be bad to a woman from the Rez, you're looking for trouble."

"If it ain't from her, it's from her family," she said, acknowledging the way we kept things in balance, even without police. It wasn't perfect, but it worked as well as most social services programs. Like Hubie, Lottie was trying to tell me something she thought important, but also trying to stay out. The next night, I didn't recognize the nurse at the station, on the phone and transcribing, but she looked up and smiled. She'd known what I'd see in a minute.

"Hey, son," Tim said, as I walked in, and then scrunched his face as I almost yelled, so relieved to see those eyes open. "Fuck! I keep forgetting I can't smile with these stitches in." He frowned a little. Even more important, he had his bed raised. He was practically sitting up. These were our first words in over six years. I was never so happy to hear someone's voice.

"Sorry!" he yelled, himself, inexplicably. "Didn't mean to swear." I suddenly noticed he had a roommate now, a guy in his sixties. The man and a visitor nodded and grinned, then continued their hushed conversation.

"Christine been by today?" After all this time, and with so much to say, I had no words, or none of the right words to accomplish the job.

"Couple hours ago," he said, not seeming to think our long silence was worth noting, acting like it was perfectly normal for me to stand before him lying prone, at his most vulnerable. I remembered that feeling, pretending to visitors you weren't wearing a threadbare shapeless cotton smock, some slippers and nothing else that wasn't medical equipment, but his denial felt deeper. "Christine's getting the place ready for when they let me out in a couple days. Soon as the gut engine gets revved up. They been giving me food I don't want and pushing to make me finish. The old if-it-goes-in, it's-gotta-come-out idea. I said give me a box of that chocolate ex-lax, but they said nature has to take its course." He spread his arms. "Like nature had anything to do with *this*."

"Police been by?"

"Nah. Told them I don't remember anything. Just barely remember heading down Moon Road, then suddenly I'm here. Told them I'd be sure to call them if anything came up."

"Really," I said.

"Really," he repeated, and grimaced. "Maybe you wanna stop over in a few days, when I'm all settled in back at home." He looked down and paused, seeming to formulate his next sentence carefully. "I mean, if you want to." His mouth moved again, and I couldn't tell if it was a grimace or a smile that time. "Same old place. I haven't moved." We both let out single note, grunt laughs. For all of my desire to see him awake, it was so hard to say what I wanted.

"Christine helped me do a quick washcloth bath. I didn't smell anything, but *she* did, and now that I got a neighbor, he's probably happy too," he said, raising his voice again. The neighbor, introducing himself as Alvin, laughed politely along with his visitor.

"I've smelt myself worse," Alvin volunteered. "During haying season." The visitor agreed, and stood to leave, telling me to take good care of my dad. Before I could correct him, both Tim and Alvin said goodbye, calling the visitor Andy like they both knew him.

Lottie came in a few minutes later to change Tim's dressing, smiling.

"He can stay," Tim said. She slid the curtain around us while Alvin turned his TV on to a sports channel. Lottie expertly flipped Tim's sheet down to his pelvis and he pulled the gown off. He joked with her about "the free show." The change in his wakefulness seemed impossible. I wondered if he'd chosen to remain silent before, listening to me as I listened to him breathe, watching me through slitted eyelids. Without the shapeless gown, his weight loss was startling. Lottie peeled the surgical tape from the edges of the large bandages, apologized for the hair she took along the way, and lifted the pads off, laying them underside up, across Tim's legs.

"Anybody else been by?' I asked, trying to distract him. I remembered what a pain that was, as if every hair on my body were being yanked off, one by one.

"Just you, Christine. This young lady here," he said, and Lottie smiled. "She says a guy comes with Christine sometimes but stays in the lounge. Probably know who that is." He locked eyes with me, telling me I shouldn't speak my guess aloud. I was surprised he'd learned the Eee-ogg rule of not speaking names. "Oh and the EMT that knows you. The one that brang me in. Been by a couple times. Semper Fi and all that." Leonard. Surprising. Strangely, Lottie blushed.

Rusty lines of blood traced the wounds around an orderly row of surgical staples. They looked like motorcycle jacket zippers, installed across his skin. My zipper of surgical staples had looked nearly identical, though I'd only had the one. When you looked at them, metal against bruised flesh, an orderly row of dull silvery teeth with a few stray bars around your navel, you didn't believe your body would ever close enough to remove them.

Tim's biggest strip followed the same pattern mine had, sternum to pubic hair—that would be the splenectomy. There was no way to wear undershorts while the staples were in. Even the lowest Low Rise waistband still rubbed the bottom few staples. You were stuck with your butt hanging out the gap in the back if you got out of bed. When they changed the dressing, your only covering was the top sheet you'd been sleeping under, and you tried to keep it from slipping too far down. Every day, the nurses assured you they'd seen it all before, but it didn't change the sharp knife of your vulnerability, your inability to ensure your own privacy.

Tim's second staple strip was a large diagonal across the left side of his chest, from low sternum up to his shoulder muscle, looking like a zipper slash pocket for his heart. I assumed that just sealed an especially large gash.

"How many?" The incision length seemed almost double mine, just by the sheer gap between my height and his. At twenty-six, I was definitely done growing. Though I couldn't tell with him lying in bed, my full height was probably still no further up than his Adam's Apple.

"Doc said over two guns, so something like eighty? Right nursey?"

"I'm not technically an OR nurse, Mr. Sampson, and definitely not an OR *nursey*, but that sounds about right, not counting whatever's inside, and up here," Lottie said, gently touching his jaw. "Those look pretty good. They might not leave much of a scar. They usually try to be pretty careful with the face. You had one of the best, Mr. Sampson."

"Don't they all think they're one of the best?" he asked.

"It would be unprofessional of me to say. These look good, not much drainage. You're closing up, sir. We could probably put these pads back on but I'll get fresh, 'cause you're nice."

"Nah, these are fine," he said, looking at the blood-tracked cotton squares.

"Get new ones," I chided, and she smiled, a whole different person these days.

"My insurance company thanks you," he said, and turned to Lottie. "Go with the boss's orders." She left and I suspected I only had a few minutes before her return.

"Do you want me to bring you home? I mean, to my place? No bullshit here, I know it's been a long time, but—"

"I'll be fine. Christine'll pick me up, but if not, I might need a ride home." I reached into my wallet to give him a business card, but he reached a hand up to stop me. "I know how to get ahold of you, if I need to."

"Okay," I said, not sure if I felt better or worse. "Well, I better head out, before they do the official Go On Home announcement. Margaret hasn't been by to see you, probably."

"Hah! Too busy with BINGO. But you know, she'd have no cause, really."

"You're her *uncle*. The only link left to the dad she so fiercely guards."

"Don't get your shorts in a bunch, now," he said, somehow half goofing and half serious. "You know she's got her own heartache to tend to. I was teasing about BINGO." He shrugged.

"Like what? What could be so important?" He looked me straight in the eye, frowning, and then flicked his eyes in a variety of directions, something dawning on him.

"I heard you wrote the obits. Isn't it, though?" I honestly didn't know what he was talking about, but was beginning to feel that heaviness, the way my scar throbbed when I unconsciously clenched my torso muscles, bracing for a blow.

"We share. I do a couple days a week, and . . . people die every day. What did I miss?" That list held very few possible names. My mom tended to keep track of who was dying and who had new babies, but some slipped through the cracks.

"Her man, what was it they called him? Bull Hoof Stew? Something weird like that."

"Moose," I said, my belly seizing tighter. "Moose-Knuckle Stew? No. Can't be . . ."

"Six months, maybe? Heard he was taking inventory upstairs in that garage you worked at sometimes. They didn't know how long before anyone noticed him missing. Word is it was one of those widow-makers. If you don't get it that second, show's closed. But you can't know how true something is when you get your news through people talking."

He leaned back and reclined the bed a bit; I approached his head and adjusted his pillows. "Thanks," he said. "Tough to reach up and do that."

"I remember," I said, working until he touched my arm to indicate it was good enough. "Was really tough to adjust them, and do a bunch of other things I took for granted. Being alone really made me understand how my life had changed there."

"Apartment, you mean? I imagine it was. Funny how quiet can seem like an obnoxious noise when it tells you how alone you are. Anyway, I guess that explains why you weren't at the wake or the funeral. I stayed the whole time. Went to the graveyard. They let him be buried out on Skid Row." The Rez graveyard was loosely organized around clans. If a couple wanted to be buried next to each other, they had to go where the wife's clan was, like it was a different period in history, the man moving in with the woman's people. If you were one of the miscellaneous outliers, but had been a meaningful community member, you went to the strip of graves everyone jokingly called Skid Row.

"Stew's dead? Really dead dead?" Even as I said it, I wanted to pull the statement back. Until a few seconds ago, he was still alive in my head. It was like he'd just now died, and for everyone else we knew, his grave was probably already covered in grass.

"There another kind of dead I don't know about?" Tim said. One word he'd said lingered: *widow-maker*. It was a word he knew. *Widower-maker* also existed. "Anyway, people's lives are just plain messy. They do what they can, you understand?" I didn't. People remained an ongoing mystery to me, but I nodded. "See you tomorrow?"

"Probably," I said.

"Come here." He reached his right hand up to mine, and I closed mine around his. Once again, it wasn't a handshake. That same something else. That same something more. "Thank you. Thank you for coming. All this time, I wasn't sure you were really here, at first."

"Well, you never delivered on your promise of going to Lakeside Park," I said, fighting to blink back tears, myself, something that never happened to me.

"Promise," he said. "We'll go. You know, over the years, I've come to like that song. I bought a copy of the album even."

"You lie!" I hissed, a bit of Rez slang.

"I swear," he said, laughing a little, then proceeded to name every song on *Caress of Steel*, in order. If it was a lie, he'd rehearsed. "Anyway, that stuff they give you to dull this," he added, gesturing to his torso. "It fogs you up some. Last night, I swore the middle of the night nurse was crying and carrying on and some other fellow comes in and she yells at him, but—"

"That wasn't no hallucination," Alvin yelled over, "unless we're sharing one."

Tim laughed dutifully, then lowered his voice. "When I knew for sure it *was* you visiting, and that you were really here, I didn't want to say anything that would scare you off." He made sure we locked eyes. "So I would see you come in and listen to you being here, glad to know it."

"Didn't you think I'd come?"

"Hard to tell. Christine's pretty much all I got in the world, I mean, Hayley, too, but she lives so far away. For day-to-day life, I'm gonna be a Special Occasions Dad for her probably forever." He almost always noted that Hayley wasn't around because she'd moved away. Since almost no one left the Rez quite that permanently, the families of those few who did made sure everyone knew why they were absent. "That's it for visitors. So when you came, I don't know, it was like a safety net or something. More than . . ."

"If I'm such a safety net, how come you don't tell me what really happened?" I asked, and we both noticed Alvin's TV volume inching down, and I nodded. Eee-ogg lived everywhere, I guess.

"You come see me, when I get home. We'll have a talk. May not be the one you want, but we'll have one, just the same. We got catching up to do, if nothing else." Tim let go of my hand and rested it on his chest, exhausted, as Lottie came back in and finished up. I asked her if she had another minute, when she was done. She nodded and I leaned in and patted Tim's shoulders. It wasn't exactly an embrace, but it was the kind of exchange between two people needing to acknowledge the massive, jagged gap they were working against, a fear of falling back into it, if they weren't careful. Given how wiped out he still was, I was sure he'd be sleeping deeply by the time I hit the parking lot.

"So what's changed?" I asked Lottie, waiting for me in the visitor's lounge.

"I don't know what you're—"

"Don't lie. You're no good at it," I said. "You know what I'm talking about. You've been meaner than a roo(t)-squuht-naeh for years, and all of a sudden, you're Little Jeet-neh." I wondered if Dusty had finally told her we were related. Not that being related prevented meanness; Rolanda had no issues expressing her own venom all these years.

"When you first got here, I thought you were doing your Eee-ogg job," she said. "And I know how that turns out for people." Dusty apparently never did explain the relationship between my article, Dusty's prices, and Lottie's savings account. Probably she could have figured it out, but a lot of people learn not to ask questions if they fear the answer. "When you came back, and then again, I knew it was different. Why do you come for him? He's nothing to you but someone's dad. It's not like you're even related or anything."

"Well, that's not your business, and it's not true," I said. "I know a lot of people at home only hang out with family. That all their friends are family and the only time someone new comes into the picture is when there's some jigging going on somewhere." She laughed and turned red again, surprising me. When I was younger, Dusty and Lena were the most scandalous girls I knew. "But who I'm close with is my business. And Tim is one of those people."

"But no one I know ever sees you and him together. Anywhere!" she stressed. "I've asked around."

"And you say I'm chasing Eee-ogg? Okay Kettle. What we have is our business." I was not giving her the satisfaction of confirming even one detail. She could use some mystery.

"Okay," she said. "Sorry. But after you've been here? He's a different person. Better, more awake. And I'll tell you," she added, dropping her voice. "He ain't like that after Christine leaves. I mean, he's not agitated or anything. Just . . . not the same as after your visits."

"Nyah-wheh," I said. "I appreciate that. I know you didn't have to say." I left and did a few Rez Laps, thinking about what she'd said, and what he'd said. I knew what Tim and I were likely to talk about, when we met up at his house.

I wondered where Christine and Randy were spending their days and nights now. We'd each moved on. All the aspects of my old life had fallen off when I'd gotten involved in my new life: Technically, the Rez was ten minutes from my apartment, but by the time I'd finished *Cascade* duties, I was wiped, most days. Sometimes, all I had the energy for was to drift through a few videos on MTV before crashing. One nice thing about Rez life was that almost every month, there was some community function going on, and you could drop in and visit with any number of people from your life with the time you could manage. No one expected you to go to everything, but you were guaranteed to find a few people to visit with at any gathering. Trying to maintain an apartment and a job, and staying balanced between the Two Canoes, was getting so tough I didn't know how I'd keep it up.

So tough, I'd literally missed the funeral of someone I'd once had a very complicated friendship with. And I didn't even know what to say, or how to approach the love he'd left behind. I didn't think Margaret would ever stop blaming my mom for stealing Gihh-rhaggs away from her family, like he hadn't had a mind and heart of his own. Or blaming me for not busting Stew in his long-term affair with her half sister. I couldn't blame Margaret in either case.

I hoped they'd come to some peace before Stew stepped out, but I also couldn't file the idea that he might have had company taking inventory, when he departed from our world. Did people change their ways? Randy Night hanging in the hospital lounge left an unsettling vibe.

The sky was still light when I left and I headed to the graveyard. Stew was deep in Skid Row, the start of a new row where the woods dropped off across the rocky escarpment. His headstone proclaimed the lie of his life here: Stewart Broad Moose. His real last name, Napier, was nowhere on the stone. What would happen if his relatives from wherever he'd come from showed up, being told he was buried here? Could they find him, or would they wander our graveyard, see the stones with the names disappearing from one hundred and fifty years ago, and wonder why no Napiers appeared anywhere in this long meandering gathering place for the dead?

At home, for the first time, I heard the sound of being alone that Tim had described. I ate in silence, looked at future columns in progress, and went to bed. In the morning, I checked work messages. Some part of me hoped Randy would turn himself in, but it was only a small part. I recognized the number on the last message, and it stopped me dead. DogLips Night cleared his throat before he spoke, a terrible, snappy sound, like a fish makes when you pull it from the river and it lands on the concrete, gasping in its new, terminal, environment.

"Hey!" he yelled, "get your old man outa my summer cottage. I called you a week ago, but you don't call me back. It's eviction day." DogLips knew better than to think of calling my ma—she might just show up at his house with a baseball bat for implying she had responsibility for My Old Man. "Do it right, I might get Tiffany to let you buy her steak dinner." He laughed, still busting my nuts about my high school crush on his daughter, years-old jokes being a Rez Specialty. But this joke abruptly dissolved into hacks.

Normally, I wouldn't have considered this my problem, but Hillman's words, and in truth, Christine's observations from years ago about My Old Man, lingered in my head. I had to change my ways before I could expect anyone else to. As soon as I finished Obits and Blotter the next day, I headed home, to the reservation. I wasn't sure where I was supposed to go, so I passed Tim's place, the Summer Cottage, Hillman's, and landed at my ma's first.

CHAPTER TWENTY-FIVE

Ape Zero

I pulled into my ma's long driveway, crushed stone sunk back into mud. When the world felt too strange, or foreign or irritating, I went home. Tonight, she occupied the corner chair.

"So Tim Sampson's out of the ICU," I said, walking in. She held up the recent *Cascade* with my "Assault Victim Improves" story. The first story had been on the front page—blood and violence—but this was buried on Page Six. She thought journalism was my latest stupid decision. After I'd explained my initial internship, she said those were for kids who didn't need to worry about bills. Even after I became a full-time reporter, she'd encouraged me to get a job pumping at one of the Rez gas stations, because I could just write in between customers. She said she saw my name so infrequently, she assumed it couldn't be too demanding.

"I'm working at the *Cascade* full time, these days," I'd said. "Just because my name isn't always on there, doesn't mean I'm not working." What I did was ethereal to her, even if I offered proof of success, like making home repairs on her place. She'd subvert them. When I replaced crumbling dining room drywall with tongue and groove, she scotch-taped newspaper articles to the paneling. None I'd written, just Bigfoot sightings, a cat with two faces, stuff like that. If I gave her framed pictures, she'd stack them face down on the TV like books.

Whenever I mentioned these changes, she'd say I should have spent the money getting a trailer for our property, or improving my old room and moving back home. More and more, this house was changing from the home I'd known. My apartment wasn't quite home, but neither was this place any longer, and I suddenly had a sliver of understanding about My Old Man's life. When he used to loiter at our house, and I'd try to send him back to the Summer Cottage with other drifters, using every Rush album I had if the Bowie didn't work. I wondered if that hardwood floor and his group of fellow anchorless drifters offered him familiarity, as our house grew into something else.

"I'm doing what Hillman believes I should," I said, words like lazy flies. "For Tim."

"Glutton for punishment. I was teasing when I suggested it," she back-tracked, now that I'd started. "What makes you think it'll work any better this time?" she added, trailing her smoky laugh.

"Can't hurt. And I made my own decisions. I agreed to carry on, at least the knowledge."

"You already got that, according to you. All this time, what have you done?" She still thought that our lives remained on the same line. My brother and sister had settled into their own trailers near each other, their parallels closer than ever before. I understood she was critical that I had the knowledge and refused to use it, even though she'd made the same choice with tea leaves. Somehow, she felt I was the one disrupting our continued place in the community, that I'd somehow lost that lesson alone. "Why this?" my ma said. "*That* part of my life is gone. Just 'cause he was My Good Man's brother, that don't make him anything to me. Just a man that played cards here." To her, I couldn't possibly be tied to Tim on my own.

"I know him. I'm doing it for him. If he wants it. And I guess for me," I said, startling myself. I hated debts. You'd think the way I spent time with debts, they'd feel like family.

"Why you telling me? Only thing I'd do is try talk you out of it, since you don't think you're gonna keep following through. That what you want? An excuse to drop it?"

"No. I just thought you'd want to know."

"Well," she sighed, exasperated and shaking her head slowly. "You have no idea about the costs. None. What. So. Ever. Once people hear you're practicing, they won't come visit you when they feel good. It's like with the tea leaves. Notice how few visitors we ever had? Real visitors? They want a familiar face to tell them bad news, instead of a stranger. But then you become the person who told them bad news." She shook her head, apparently disgusted with herself. "I couldn't stand to look at their faces anymore." I'd hoped to convince her to do one more reading, maybe two.

"I don't intend to make a regular practice of this." I said. "Gonna be a one-time shot, and then back to my life." I wondered about the various crossroads where I'd almost turned onto a different path. If I hadn't run into Tim before I enlisted in the Marines? If I hadn't gone to Randy's New Year's Eve party? If Tim hadn't been in the Marines with someone who'd become an Admissions Counselor at a college a few miles from the Rez? If I'd never gone to college? That random series of crossroads lining up to send me this way seemed impossible. To even think of the possible paths that would have thrown me elsewhere made my head want to explode, like that guy in *Scanners*.

And yet, if Gihh-rhaggs hadn't fallen in love with my ma, and betrayed his last love for her, what would my present life be like? "I swear. It's just gonna be this once, and that's it."

"Once? Hah!" she exclaimed, ripping a cig from her pack in a frenzy. "You *can't* do this kind of thing, and expect not to attract attention. One *yes* opens the gates to all the others, and saying no ain't exactly one of your specialties. You'll have to learn to be like those apes you loved when you were a kid." *Planet of the Apes.* I'd blabbed about their constant historical shifts and subversions and convoluted minutiae so much that it'd seeped into my ma's toolbox of examples.

Lacking a better metaphor, she was preparing me to be like Aldo, the major force in their cosmology, according to *Escape from the Planet of the Apes.* Aldo was Ape Zero. He'd been enslaved, had heard the word "no" so many times that it became the First Ape Utterance, the zero-point-zero-one percent fluke, like my surgery mishap. He was "a mutant," the ape whose freaky vocal cords and brain came alive and spread awareness and revolt among the apes like a virus, sparking that resistance flame. But Ape History had a way of being rewritten on them, just like Indian History.

Audiences knew the *real* first talking ape had been Cornelius and Zira's own son, from the future. If I said "No," was I Caesar, talking offspring of time-traveling chimps? Or was I Aldo, the mutant gorilla, starting everything with his singular No?

Denying people wasn't the way my family operated. We'd felt a million slammed doors on our faces; "No" was a word we rarely used. My ma's first uttered "no" occurred only after a long buildup, but once spoken, it stood. I'd seen the faces of those she'd turned. I didn't ever want to be the person pushing the door closed, the recipient of those longing and desperate looks.

"A lot of the medicine's the same," she said, trying a different volley. "Aspirin, heart medicines, stuff for cough, infections, just go to Towne Pharmacy. People don't need Hillman's brand anymore." She knew what it was like to be noticed, even when she'd try to disappear.

"I know," I said. "It's Hillman's other kind I want to offer to Tim, not the kind you can get at Towne Pharmacy. I'm taking chances, but . . . you know what it's like to have someone appear, unexpected, and change your whole life." Normally, she'd have accused me of being melodramatic, but she knew better. I didn't know how Gihh-rhaggs entered her life, but he'd invited her to go to the track that night he died, and at the last minute, she'd decided to stay home. She knew intimately how one small decision could change the entire course of a life.

"I want to ask you . . ." I said, reaching for a teacup. She knew the rest of the sentence and left it hanging, then sighed and put her kettle on, steeping it for the single cup before me.

"You know what to do," she said. I ripped the bag, sprinkling the flakes in the cup. "You gotta pour your own." As it steeped, I asked her if Christine and Randy were still together. She gave me a: *what do you think? Of course!* look. I poured the tea, steeped, and then drank it, swirling each sip, rolling the bones of my future. I gave the cup one last dance, drained, and handed it over. She looked at it one way, then another, engrossed in a monochrome kaleidoscope. She opened her mouth, but remembered I knew the way her voice changed when she lied.

She went to her bedroom and retrieved her ancient coins. Several Liberty silver dollars, a few Mercury dimes, even an Indian Head Nickel, a real one. "You won't be needing this one," she said, sliding the Indian Head back into her apron. "Take these others. They belonged to My Good Man. He asked me to hang on to them. They're real silver."

"I'm not hunting for a werewolf, Ma."

"You asked me to look. I think this is what you need." Eventually I took them.

"What I really want to take is this," I said, lifting the ancient lighter from her table. "I promise, I'll take care of it and bring it back." Its weight told me it was full. She said nothing, looking at the reflected son in her window, lifting one of the few things she held on to.

"Well, you know where those coins go, if you don't need them," she said. "I'm not worried about the lighter. It finds its way home when it's supposed to. But . . . it's going to cost you. More than these'll pay for. If you think your choices'll stay buried, then you learned *nothing* living with me. I hope you're ready to be seen in ways you didn't expect." For all my preparation, I'd wanted her truth-telling voice to assure me things would be all right.

"Margaret still living in her mom's place?"

"She is now. Since Moose Knuckle's gone."

"How come you didn't let me know he died?"

"You're King of the Eee-Ogg. With all the city gadgets telling you everyone's bad news, figured you knew," she said. True enough—often when she'd let me know something, it had already come through. "Besides, he was no friend of yours. When you gonna learn? Never tell anyone anything that can't afford to go flying up like a bunch of smoke signals. Keep your skut-yeah shut if you know what's good for you." Stew had shit-talked me after we'd parted ways. There weren't a ton of big secrets, anyway. I'd learned even by then not to give too much of myself. "Rub someone the wrong way, they take every scrap of dirt on you they had and spread it like fertilizer, seeing what might grow."

"What makes you think I even have dirt worth spreading?" I said, laughing. The truth was, I'd had more dirt on Stew than he had on me. All I'd done was keep my mouth shut.

A few minutes later I pulled into Margaret's, and like so many, she had the door open before I got to the stoop. Two fresh cups of coffee sat on the kitchen table oil cloth. "Expecting company?"

"Nah, I always keep a clean cup in the other chair and the machine's always on. Instant." Stew preference. He'd convinced himself that instant was tastier than coffee grown strong warming on the machine's plate. "Kind of makes it seem like he's still here, too."

"Listen, I'm sorry," I said. "I didn't know about Stew. Tim just told me." Her face showed no reaction to my mentioning her hospitalized uncle. "Not sure how I missed it."

"Figured you were just still mad at him," she said. I wanted to ask her if she knew where Christine and Randy Night were, in the middle of the night last week. "He liked getting under people's skin. Was a game. Funeral was small, but nice. Almost everyone from the garage came to the wake. Bus drivers and mechanics in their 'dress Carhartts.'" She was letting me know how absent I'd been. "And since I'm sure you want to know, yes, my half sister was there. And yes, I've thought what you're thinking. What can I say? He had a type."

"I'm sorry, Margaret." I pictured Gihh-rhaggs, Margaret, and Liz, concluding they all resembled one another a bit. Since Stew was drawn to Margaret, Liz's attraction, at least visually, shouldn't have been at all surprising.

"Well, you know Stew. Wore out his welcome every place he lived." I never understood his charm, and I fell for it, anyway. Part of it was fear. He could stomp my kid ass if he wanted to and he seemed just wild card enough to think that was fine. He lived by his own rules.

"You know," she said, "if I understood how short our time was, I'd have loved him harder. Maybe made him take better care of his diet." The radio on the kitchen counter was playing Jazz in the Nighttime, which she'd always hated. "Brian? If you'd been there? Say you were working with him? Could you have brought him back with the know-how Hillman gave you?"

"No," I said. "It doesn't work that way. Does Hillman seem magic to you?" She refused to answer, which could mean either: *yes, he does*, or *I can wish, can't I?* "Margaret, they call those heart attacks 'widow makers' for a reason. He was probably gone before he even knew it. And, uh, we never did inventory together. He didn't want my help for that." I'd let her interpret that in whatever way she needed. "And you know what I've found? I see a lot of people who almost lose someone, and they're incredibly grateful . . . for about a month."

"That is not even true!" she steamed. "He was the love of my life!"

"That's not what I meant," I said. "But even after close calls, people go back to being annoyed at the little things. The extra work he caused you, overshooting the toilet and splashing the floor, wearing muddy boots in the kitchen, farting so your couch became a permanent stink-bomb. All the things that drove you crazy. We can't live with the intensity of love."

"Wouldn't be like that," she mumbled, but I think she heard what I was saying.

"I just wanted to say I was sorry, in person." Then I asked if I could use her phone.

"Same place as always." I dialed the number and went out onto her stoop, confirming with Visitor Information that Tim had been discharged. Before I could do anything for him, I wanted to see for myself if there was one lone squatter left. I'd told DogLips I'd be at the Summer Cottage at nine. That would give me a couple hours to do what I really wanted to do.

"Nyah-wheh, Margaret," I came in and finished, deciding I didn't need to know anything about Randy Night from her. Tim was either going to tell me himself or he wasn't. "For everything." No matter how things rolled, Snake Eyes or Box Cars, it was time for me to lift up those dice in hand, blow inside for luck, and take care of business.

CHAPTER TWENTY-SIX

True Confessions

I t's open," Tim yelled when I rang the bell. The sun was below the wooded horizon. I'd made passes earlier, but Christine's car had been there each time. I walked in and up into the main house from the entryway. "Living room," he yelled, and I followed the sound of his voice.

"Mind if I turn some lights on?" I asked, bumping into things. "Long time since I was here, don't remember exactly where everything is." I whacked my knee on the kitchen extension, something I should have remembered. I'd gotten turned around in the dark.

"Wall switch. Left of the fridge." I backtracked, discovering a small accordion gate.

"You got a dog? Moving to Dog Street?"

"Christine. One of those little yappers. I don't want it shitting on the carpet, so I make her keep it in there." Tim sat on his couch, feet up on a hassock, newspapers beside him.

"Figured it was you," he said. "Didn't know what you were driving these days."

"Still your truck."

"Your truck," he corrected, reaching slowly over and turning on a light.

"Why you keeping your door unlocked? Kind of dangerous." I'd locked the door.

"No dangers. This is my house. Be pretty ballsy for someone to come uninvited," he said. Absently his hand slid under his T-shirt, his fingers running down the incision edge.

"Not any ballsier than beating someone with a tow chain and calling it in to the cops. Whoever did that wasn't fucking around. You gotta be careful, Tim. Especially living alone."

"Nah. Don't you worry. Besides, it's not practical. If someone came, they'd be gone by the time I got down there to answer. Kicks my ass just to get up, but the doc says it's better if I'm not laying down. Move around, he says, like it's nothing. I do what I can." He struggled and winced and finally, sat straighter. "Don't want to go back in with pneumonia or blood clots. Too much to manage the up and down stairs, though. Here, come sit down." I sat at the couch's opposite end. He seemed settled-in, coffee table spread out with water, snacks, and napkins.

"Want anything?" I said. "I can cook, not much, but something. Or go get you anything. Could pick up pizza." I wondered if any place would ever be brave enough to do Rez delivery.

"Nah. Want something? Dig in the fridge. Christine went shopping. Lot of easy shit, lunch meat, frozen stuff. Help yourself." In his sudden weight loss, and our distance, I saw how much older he'd grown. He wasn't *really* old, in his fifties, but his hairline gave him a widow's peak now, and grooves had formed near his eyes. His shoulder span was the same, and he was probably the same height, but his mass had been shed like a winter coat.

"Have you weighed yourself since you've been home?" His T-shirt billowed out, and his sweat bottoms sat low, distanced from the incision, his pale belly peeking out above them. I assumed all his clothes fit badly now, including those new ones I'd brought him.

"They did. Dropped thirty-three pounds. Doc said probably the best thing for me. Awful hard way to lose that extra baggage." He smiled and then stopped, jaw sutures still going taut.

"Didn't know. It's been a while since I've seen you."

"Almost six years, by my count. A lot of things can change in that time." We both nodded, and he turned on a ball game with the sound off. "Damn," he said, shifting. "There's hours when it's worse, like when I been up for a while."

"Many people come to see you while you were in?" I asked again, now that he didn't have an eavesdropping roommate.

"You, Christine, a couple cops," he said. "About it. You wind up in the hospital from a beating, people don't want that luck rubbing off on them. They'll laugh if you say that, but still, they don't come. Some people, probably, I've spoken with for the last time. Even folks who used to take my money in dice. They think whoever did this, well, they might be next in line."

"Guilt by association?"

"I was thinking 'Fellow Traveler,' but that's before your time. Guess yours works."

Almost nobody had come to see me, either, which was maybe why I'd felt his absence so sharply. My ma, of course, Mona, Chester, Auntie Rolanda, Roland, a couple more distant cousins and their families, Hubie and Margaret, Hillman—he might have been the reason some people stayed away. But almost no one else I'd ever hung around with had made the effort. Most, I expected that distance from, but Tim should have been different.

"Christine been around today?" I asked, hoping she'd concluded her obligation.

"Come and gone. Told her I was fine. She didn't need to come back. Had a feeling you'd be stopping today. Didn't think you'd want to see her."

"I don't have any problem with her."

"Seemed like you took care not to run into her during visiting hours—"

"That was for her," I said, probably partly a lie. After that last exchange I'd had with Christine, in the driveway of this house, I was the king of awkward interactions.

"So, after all this time, here you are. If all it took was an ass beating to get you to visit, I coulda arranged that a while ago," he said, that funny, clipped laugh pinching his sutures.

"I don't recall you coming to see me when I was in the hospital," I replied, regretting it even as it came out.

"Well, that didn't take long to come out," he said, suddenly seeming more alert. "Not like the old days when it took you near five hours of rambling to get to what you really wanted to say, whenever you were serious."

"I'm sorry. That isn't what this is about." I had the direction of this conversation entirely planned out, but real people weren't quite as cooperative as their imaginary counterparts, and you could never predict where they might take you, with or without your cooperation.

"Nah, it's all right. It's true. I didn't come, but I *wanted* to, if that makes any difference. I was afraid. After you see your wife die, it takes a lot to get you back into a place where the chances of losing someone are high. I made it to the parking lot for you before turning around. Three times. Each one, could barely drive home, I had the shakes so bad. For real, never been back in one until I woke up in the ER last week, and, well, it's not like I made that decision.

"Anyway, I'm sorry. Thought about leaving a message at the paper, but . . . I was afraid I might catch you in. If you'd picked up, I wouldn't know what to say. I tried, I really did. Even bought you a card. I didn't have your address, and I didn't want to send it to your mom's place. It's in my top dresser drawer if you don't believe me. Keep it with that letter you wrote me."

"You still have that letter? Why?"

"Why not? It's mine. What do you care?"

"It's not that I mind. You know, you read letters and most, you toss out," I said, excusing myself and heading down the hall to the john. Secretly, I felt a kind of joy that he still had the old letter, but I didn't want him to see the ridiculous prideful smile I felt welling up inside me.

"Not me," he said, loud enough to still hear. I glanced at the magazines on the little stand. *The library*, people joked. When I opened the door, he spoke again. "Go down to my room. Top dresser drawer. Far corner, under the socks. Your card, might as well open it. But the letter's mine." I wasn't sure I wanted to see that letter again.

"Maybe later," I said, coming back into the living room, holding a magazine.

"Kept it, figuring you might come someday."

"Well, you know, we have different lives now . . ." I said, and even as

I did, I heard the lameness and guilt. "*True Confessions*? Not what I would have pegged for your reading taste."

"Vestal's. Look at the cover dates and the labels. Never had the heart to throw them out."

"I haven't come, because . . ." I started, "I didn't think you wanted me to. When you didn't come to the hospital, I figured I'd done something to you that I didn't know. I was . . ." I paused, trying to find the right word. Being a writer didn't mean you had access to all the words you wanted at all times. It meant taking the time to find them and recognizing them when you did. "I was respecting your absence."

The Rez only had five entry roads, and nowadays I almost always chose the one past his place. In the evenings, he usually had the TV on, and its blue shadows caressed the closed curtains like anemones on ocean TV shows.

"Why the hell did you think that?" he asked, vaguely irritated. "Suppose we do have different lives. So what! Lots different these days, but that don't mean you gotta disappear," he softened, a thread of pleading in his voice that seemed so much like that New Year's Eve a million years before. And then, even softer: "So what is it you're doing here, anyway? No bullshit. I'm super happy to see you, even happier that you came to see me in there. One of those shirts you brang me." He tugged on his baggy T-shirt, confirming I'd been wrong with the size. "I read your stories faithfully. Even shit I got no interest in, if your name's on it, I'm in. And yes, I've read what's been hidden in them just for me. I've saved all those ones. I wanted to respond, but I'm scared, I guess. It's tough allowing someone to see your most vulnerable side. Even someone you've shown it to before." He looked down at his lap, as if there were a cheat sheet hiding there, and after a pause, continued.

"But I hope you're not looking for a story now. There's none here. Told the cops, I don't remember anything. And since they say the reservation ain't technically in their jurisdiction, chances are good they won't be back. Maybe if I asked them, but that's it." He looked at me when he spoke, but at the end, he closed his eyes and leaned back on the pillow.

"And you just happened to be on Moon Road in the middle of the night.

Some police investigator might buy that, particularly one that doesn't want Rez red tape, but I don't guess that's true, either." He shrugged, not giving me much. "They have enough active cases they aren't gonna waste time on someone who refuses to identify his attacker." At that, he looked down, studying the coffee table. "Just don't go thinking that your story was convincing or anything. Anyone from the Rez paying any attention to you would know that's a lie."

"That's why my story's good enough. No one here pays me any mind. Just you."

"But that's not why I'm here," I said, again. "I mean it." I had to stop myself from getting sidetracked, and from inventing sidetracks. "You want to put those events away in a box? Fine, it's away as far as the news or my job goes. I want to help you, but you gotta be honest for me to do that."

"Help me what?" he jumped in. "Solve the mystery? I think you know enough what I'm saying to know there's none to be solved."

"I understand that, Tim. I got it. And I promise. What I'm about to ask you about, will stay only between you and me. Totally private. You understand?"

"No, son, I don't," he said immediately. "I don't know what you want. I don't even know what you're saying here. You're rambling like the old days. You seem to be hinting at something you're offering me, but I guess I'm dense. Like I said before, I was coming home from the Spithouse, knocking back a couple with buddies, and decided to take a ride around the reservation before turning in, like we used to." He reached over and took a long drink of water, then slowly set the cup back down. "Some nights are lonelier than others. That's the last thing, before waking up." I could hear the studied phrases. He'd rehearsed them to himself, the way I did when I knew every word I said was going to be scrutinized. But I knew he was lying. If I could have kept him talking for a while longer, he might've given in, but it was time I was direct, and explained why I needed to know the truth.

"Listen, even though you're white, you've figured out a way to live among us. And people have grown so used to you, folks even talk about things they wouldn't around other white folks." I could hear my own evasiveness, the ways I wasn't saying what I wanted to say.

"You mean like the Skidaddles?"

"Please tell me you don't really call them that." He'd been around enough that people discussed our unseen world in his presence, even the death singers. Did he know about Tallman, the Little People, shape changers? Did he believe what everyone else did about Hillman's work with me? Only one other white man I'd known had that invisibility. Tim's brother, of course.

"Just yanking your chain, son, keeping you on your toes. Ow. You gotta quit making me laugh." He reached up and touched his face.

"Here, let me see that."

"Eh! It's fine. You gotta be in good light to see it and it's hard for me to move around." He frowned when I stood, I guess thinking I would have respected his dismissal. He eventually shifted and made room on the couch, near the end table lamp. I tilted his head and he grimaced. The sutures were tight and small, and a tiny row of surgical butterfly bandages lined up across the wound. That scar would be visible, even after they pulled the thread.

"Have you been skipping shaving?"

"Not skipping. Doctor's orders. Leave it alone, let it heal. Gotta keep looking at it. If a hair starts growing into the scar, I'm supposed to see if I can yank it, or call them to take care of it. Otherwise, get snipped in another week? They said the thread might bust on its own."

"Did a plastic surgeon do this?"

"Hell, got me. Don't think those are on standby at that rinky-dink hospital. They said it shouldn't be too bad. They tried to be neat. Besides, who's looking at my sorry ass, these days?"

"Can I see the others?"

"I guess. Gotta shower anyway. Christine's been helping, but I give her a break. I can do the shower alone. She bought me one of those stools. Only tough part is getting a shirt off. Wanna give me a hand?" He lifted his right arm and sniffed. "Maybe you wanna wait until after I shower before you look." He struggled to sit up and raised his arms into the air, waiting for me to lift the shirt like a little kid would. I grabbed it from the bottom hem and carefully pulled it up away from his belly, stretching the neck hole to slide around his face.

The same butterfly bandages ran right up his midline, from below the sweatpants waistband to the bump of his sternum, and then again, diagonally across his left chest, replacing the surgical steel staples that had been there last week. Beneath them, the scar, thick and purple, became nearly black down at the bottom. He'd been shaved in surgery and his belly and chest were covered in a uniform layer of stubble as his body tried to put itself back together.

"They said these things'll wash off on their own, but that I shouldn't rush them." He looked at the line of butterflies. "Longer I kept them on, the better chances that the scar would be less, what? Less obvious? Probably a load of shit they tell you to buy time while you get used to the idea of your new body. Hurts like I got a belly and chest full of rotten teeth."

"That's what I want to talk to you about. No story in the paper. None of that. I promise. This is between you and me and no one else, ever. I hope whatever connection we had . . . and lost. Man! I hate to say that! But it's true. I'm here to try and rebuild my end. You understand?"

Neither of us was good at this kind of conversation and I'd gotten worse. I was rarely in situations where I needed to dull my anxieties about saying wrong things and I didn't really drink much anymore, so I had no effective strategies to loosen my tongue.

"I'm guessing you've heard about what happened when I left the hospital," I said.

"All that voodoo with Hillman?" he said, eyebrows raised. "That he fixed you up good as new with his secret tricks? Sure, who hasn't heard that around here?" He still absently rubbed the edges of the line dividing him into halves, a new Prime Meridian of his body I already knew.

"Yeah, all that." Like most stories around here, that one was fueled by a little bit of truth and a lot of speculation. "You didn't hear about that whole Tin Man scare back in the seventies, did you? Too new here for people to talk about it in front of you?"

"Son, as God-fearing a Christian woman as Vestal was, she woulda been terrified of that Tin Man!" he said, laughing and then sighing. "That Tallman story was bad enough. That's why we don't have a second floor here you, know." Funny, most older Rez houses had an upstairs, but almost any built from the midfifties on had a basement and a main floor alone. I suddenly wondered if the fear of Tallman had changed the whole Rez architecture demands. You never knew where and when stories would take hold.

"She didn't want giants peeking in at night. No matter how ridiculous I said it was, that no man two stories tall could hide in these woods, she just shut her ears. She wasn't stubborn about a lot, but that? Insisted it had to be true. Made me swear never to spend any time at night alone in the woods, and to never build an addition up. She was gone by that Tin Man year, but I heard about it the whole year, mostly from Christine and Hayley. One day, people just quit talking about it, like it never happened. I don't think Christine ever watched that *Wizard of Oz* again though. Always wondered what it was in the grove really causing all the fuss."

"Couldn't say. But anyway. The thing I want to talk to you about? It's kind of like that. If you told someone in the city that you'd seen a Tin Man, they'd laugh in your face. But you know we live in a different place. I want to try to give *you* something, something from here that would also get you laughed at out there. And there aren't any guarantees."

"There usually ain't, but what are we talking about here? What Hillman did for you?"

"You see, what everyone believes and the truth? Often two different things. You already know that," I said. I could still say something irrelevant and get my ass out of here.

"Sure, seen it happen often enough," he said, scratching gingerly around the bandages on his belly. I remembered the constant cross between pain and itch as your body did its job. "My brother's name bumped up in status after he crashed his car, like he'd been something special alive. People claiming he did all kinds of good things. Even folks who wouldn't give him a ride if he had his thumb out on Dog Street. Truth? They didn't give him a ride for a reason. He was a shiftless shit who drank too much and gambled his money away and couldn't keep his pecker in his pants unless someone threatened to shoot it off. Worst? He left two daughters to their lonely mothers when he got bored." He puffed out his lip a little, grimacing, but determined.

"You and your mom . . . your brother and sister, you'd have probably been left the next time some barfly rubbed up against him at the right crossroads of drunk and horny, hoping he had more than that surplus of charm and a skilled hand. You caught him at the end of the line. I loved him, he was my brother, but he wasn't the miracle man your mom remembers." I had to wonder what their relationship had been like for such an unflinching assessment of Gihh-rhaggs.

"We knew his faults," I defended. "We just accepted them. Which is one of the things I've learned. Hillman trained me, and he's willing to do more, but as my ma is so fond of pointing out, I still have this." I lifted my shirt, revealing my own thick line of purple welts, and then dropped it quickly. Almost no one saw me this way. When I inadvertently caught glimpses in the mirror, I felt like Dr. West had delivered a curse onto me. I *had* become a mutant.

Even now, years later, I still felt most like Ben Grimm from the Fantastic Four. The other three members could walk around, looking totally normal, pass for regular average people. But for all the strength Grimm had been given, he could never escape the fundamental way he'd been changed, and anyone who encountered him knew it too. The superhero duds Reed designed for him were a joke, confirming his outsider status. The whole outfit was just a pair of blue satin briefs that more or less said "why bother?" Ben was The Thing, twenty-four hours a day. It felt melodramatic to still have such ruminations years after the fact, but there was no denying what faced me in the mirror every day. I remembered that I used to think of Tim as a living Ben Grimm, because he was so massively bulky compared to anyone else I knew. Now here I was.

"Hah! We match," he said, wincing again in his smile.

"Well, not quite. I don't have that one across my chest like you and the Tin Man."

"Oil Can!" he said, squeaky, laughing through a grimace, and then coughed, quickly pressing a throw pillow against the sutures. A key hospital discharge instruction, if you must cough. "No offense, son, but it doesn't look like Hillman did too good a job, if that's what you're offering."

"Hillman told me I had to be totally honest with him in whatever he asked. If I couldn't, then what he did wouldn't stick. Or it wouldn't happen at all. Or only a little."

"Been my experience that full-bore honesty's hard to come by," he said, trying to whistle. "Bet it's worse if people think you might be sniffing around for something to go in the paper."

"I don't get told a lot of direct lies," I agreed. "Mostly silence or, you know, Rez answers."

"Nah. Folks don't want you thinking they're wasting a good lie on you," he said, growing distant. "They look at you and say nothing. Like *you* did, that first night we went for a ride." He'd assumed I was doing a Rez Stonewall that New Year's Eve. I guess if you were around us long enough, you got to identify the strategy. If someone asked you a nosey question, you just acted like no one had said anything, as if their voice stopped projecting. But that night, I'd been afraid I might say something to set him off, stuck in a minefield with no map whatsoever.

"Well, anyway," I said, Rez Stonewalling exactly as he'd claimed. "Hillman asked me if I'd accepted that the surgeon screwed up and that humans do. It's like beadwork. You know, faithful beadworkers put one wrong bead in their work because only the Creator can make things perfect." A couple beadwork picture frames hung on the wall, his wedding picture in one, and the other shared by Hayley and Christine's pictures. I couldn't see if they had intentional errors. Some beadworkers ditched that belief, saying tourists treated flawed pieces as "factory seconds."

"I said I accepted, but I didn't, really. Maybe if that surgeon admitted his screwup, instead of filing a State Health Department Report that I spontaneously started bleeding like a mutant, I'd consider that. But people don't spontaneously start bleeding by themselves, particularly when they have a scalpel inside their body."

"Seems to me you still haven't accepted it," Tim said, lifting his eyebrows. His expression, his expectation, must have been met a thousand times with Rez Stonewalling before he finally got it. "You know? Another way to see it? You're here. He messed up, but he had enough going on to put you back together. Now, I'm not saying what he did was right, being too greedy with his nest egg to admit he fucked you up." He shrugged, acknowledging where his sympathies lay. "But you wouldn't be talking to me if he hadn't gotten his shit together quick."

"Yeah, Hillman's medicine decided the same thing. That I hadn't accepted it. So, it took most of the pain, and left the scar the same way it looked when I was discharged. Worse, actually. It separated and grew bigger that first month. But . . ." I said. This would be where he'd listen and we'd move forward, or he'd raise those bushy eyebrows, defining his usual doubts.

"Hillman showed me how to make the medicine that takes away the scars, and the kind that'll take away the pain if it doesn't leave on its own. He said your body remembers when someone else's hands have been inside. The medicine allows your body to understand that those hands saved your ass, but you have to allow the medicine to come to those terms." Tim stared at me, eyebrows in place, his own version of the Rez Stonewall. But doubt still flashed in his eyes.

I'd doubt this story too—still could, really. If I were honest with myself, I'd admit that I hadn't fully committed to everything Hillman offered. It was nearly impossible to reconcile evidence-based journalism with Hillman's world. But my offer to Tim was one part of the last two stages to complete my education. I didn't want to be in the position of an incomplete education by my own shortsightedness. And I could help someone I loved. Even though I hadn't done a single thing with the medicines in the years since my surgery, people had come forward from time to time obliquely asking for help, asking me to finish what I'd started with Hillman.

I reminded each that Hillman was still around. Some sought him, but others' church ties made them too afraid to cross his threshold. They wound up in Cavalry Cemetery on the Torn Rock. I never understood why they thought I was a safer bet than Hillman, since he'd been my teacher, but people tell themselves all kinds of things to get through the day.

"Tim, I haven't done this before. Haven't even offered, which I guess is why I'm not explaining it too well. You're my first. Or, you'd be my first. I'll need you to do whatever I ask, or it won't work. Understand?" I could show him things at Hillman's that would edge him closer, but I wanted him to arrive on his own. I wanted him to know people run for EMERGENCY EXIT from one another's lives, only to discover themselves back at the IN door. I wanted him to remember that night on those long stretches of Niagara County roads, where he'd committed to being in my life, and I committed to being in his. I needed him to believe in me one more time.

"I don't. I'm sorry. I really don't know what you're saying. You want to try on me what didn't work on you?" He smiled despite the strain, clearly wanting to seem supportive. "Listen. I live out here, but I'm not like you. I'm not from here. I think you're asking me to go into uncharted territory with you. I trust you. I do." He sat tall, and though I remembered how it hurt to stretch my belly like that, he tried not to show discomfort as he gingerly did the same.

"But before we go down that path, I gotta know something. If you start doing this? Aren't you kind of . . . risking it taking over your life? All you worked for? Went to school for? All the sacrifice. . . ." I knew he'd stopped because he'd also made major sacrifices for me, so I could be where I was that moment. "I've seen a lot in this world, but like I said, I never saw the Tallman or the Tin Man."

"I was thinking maybe you could trust me. You know what the Marines say. Semper Fi."

"Yes, I do," he said, that phrase sinking deeper than a tattoo. I thought about Hillman, waiting for me all these years. Another reminder that I'd have made a shitty Marine.

"Truth is, I haven't been faithful to one thing," I said. I wasn't responsible for massive, life-derailing lies, but I'd slipped out of every connection where someone wanted to change me, to make me something they wanted, or where I thought they did. Before this decision, I'd never thought I'd change my ways. "My entire life. I always look for the EMERGENCY EXITS. That New Year's Eve? I looked for an escape the whole time. I was positive you were going to beat my ass."

"Crossed my mind," he said, the corners of his mouth turning downward as he looked at his lap, picking at nonexistent lint on his sweats. "But you know that already."

"But something happened that night," I said. "We've never talked about it. What was it?" He leaned back and closed his eyes, sprawling in the couch corner. He remained still so long, I thought maybe he'd begun to doze.

"My brother," he said, finally, not moving his head, keeping his closed eyes facing the ceiling. "He'd taught me to *always* lie when we were out here. He introduced me to Vestal. Hell, I don't even know how they *really* met, all these years later." His eyes opened to narrow slits as we arrived at the same conclusion, particularly that now, his face thinner and bordered with a newly growing beard, the resemblance to his brother was unmistakable. "No one to ask, now."

"You told me you met when she picked you up hitchhiking," I said.

"Don't forget much, do you?"

"Comes with the job, or maybe the job's easier because my memory's good."

"That was true. From a certain point of view. But my brother had already shown her a picture of me in my dress blues. When she saw me hitching, she knew who I was. But was seeing that picture once enough? Or was it like I thought? That she saw a connection."

"Was it enough? Seems like it. You stayed together."

"Maybe he worked her hard, so we'd be in this together. Living here was gonna be risky. A white guy getting together with an Indian woman? Asking for trouble. Two white guys?" He whistled, like a bomb dropping. "One time at a Bug Jemison party, we were the only white guys. All half in the bag, Bug asked us why we insisted on chasing Indian tail. He said 'haven't you white guys taken enough from us already?'" I'd witnessed similar moments. Indian guys would do this at mixed parties. So the white guys would finally know what it felt like to be watched."

"I imagine you two had made Emergency Exit plans for yourselves," I said.

"We knew lies to get through the day," he said, like he'd been reading my mind, as he seemed to from time to time. "Even as boys, we knew rainbow-colored sludge shouldn't drip down our bedroom walls? Everyone there knew Love Canal was doomed before the *Cascade* covered it." Those places had their own private histories. I'd never have full access to them, in the same way I'd never write for the *Cascade* with our secrets, myself.

"But we knew how to tell each other the truth, me and him, and almost no one else. Even Vestal, for everything she was to me, I kept some things from her. Just things that would have hurt her unnecessarily. Things that were no longer a part of my life."

"Anything I should know?" Had Tim Sampson had other intimates on the reservation before winding up with Vestal? I couldn't say I was ready for a Yes answer.

"Nah, not right now. You and me? We're good at the moment. Better than good. You reached out, and reconnected, when I most needed you. When I couldn't even speak the need. I'm just blown away that you're here, trying to do this for me. What more could I hope for?" His voice hitched. "Now go on, get out of here, before I wind up crying for the third time in my adult life. You already got one of those two times pinned on you. Just you and Vestal."

"All this time? Tim?" I said, standing. "It wasn't for lack of desire. I'm sorry it took such a screwed up, horrible thing to get me to finally act. I'm sorry we . . . I, me. Sorry *I* wasted so much time. Now that I'm here, I don't want to pressure you into a part of the reservation experience you've maybe not come across." Not entirely accurate. I wanted him to desire it on his own, but I might be willing to push. His wall clock said it was closing in on nine.

"I'll be back in a few days," I said. Those bandages should be off by then. "I promise. It's going to be a strange offer, and you probably won't believe part of it, and you're definitely not going to like a part of it. All I can ask is that you trust what I'm going to offer you. It's big for me, something I've never done. I want to do it, for both of us. But I want to give you time to think, even if I can't give you details right now. You decide what you want then, I'll respect it. But know I'm offering from my heart. And I promise, I won't let this kind of thing mess us up again. I mean this. Not when it's so easy to lose everything and not even notice. Semper Fi."

"Don't be mad if my answer's no. But even if it is, between you and me? Semper Fi."

CHAPTER TWENTY-SEVEN

Summer Cottage

Tim's words stayed with me, a preemptive rejection, as I made my way to the Summer Cottage. I should have known that, remembered we'd lived in the same place but weren't of the same place, but it still stung. More accurately, it ached, making my own belly throb like the summer I'd healed. I concentrated on pushing that low-level pounding deeper in my mind. I had things to do. The Summer Cottage windows glowed and smoke trickled up into the gradually darkening sky as I pulled in. My Old Man wasn't ambitious enough to build a fire, even if someone else had cut the wood. But Rez nights in May could still dip into the fifties or even forties.

DogLips had implied he'd meet me, but mine was the only vehicle. Finally, I noticed a note taped to the door: *Come On In. Remember Your Skin. And I Will Throw You a Bone.* A play on an old song. My Old Man was the right age for it, but it didn't seem like his work. As far as I knew, he had no sense of humor. The knob turned easily, recently oiled.

"Hello?" I said, feeling like an expendable character in a slasher movie. Faint music bounced off the empty rooms. I'd never been inside. The guys who wound up here tended to be in the late stages of their drifting careers. Either they found ways to fit back in, or they huddled here with other drifters, hoping to make it through winter. Many lived on some combination of aid and off-the-books farm work, being flush a few days a month and scrounging the rest. I didn't know if My Old Man cutting off a couple of his own toes when an I-beam landed on his steel-toes qualified him for permanent disability, or if he'd found some other way to survive.

The layout was of a different era. The front door opened on a center hallway lined with other doors, like the world's smallest hotel. I saw how it attracted its vagrant population. You could have a little temporary privacy, though the interior doors were long gone. The back door was open on an intact screen door, where I glimpsed the front fender of another car.

The only furniture was a beat-up lawn chair in one room, next to a plastic milk crate holding what looked like Christine's old boom box, the source of the music. The scarred floor looked like hardwood. In the fireplace was an absurd set of fake logs illuminating the room with a flickering orange light to simulate flame. Either battery-operated, or DogLips had already had the electricity turned back on. I heard the screen door open and slam shut, footsteps following.

"So, you showed, as promised," Randy Night said, stepping in.

"Where is he?" I said. "I don't want to waste any more time with you, or him, for that matter," Whatever he'd had over me was gone. I'd always wanted to believe Randy could change, be a better person. That belief shaped the pattern of my life around him for all those years. My suspicion made sure I'd never again desire that old place.

"So is it true?" he asked. "Can you do what some people say? You and Hillman?"

"I can't speak for Hillman." No matter what I said, the dueling warnings of my mother and Hillman stuck in my brain. He insisted I wouldn't be able to help people I wanted, if I weren't willing to help people I didn't want to. And my mom understood that word would get out. It was already out, and I hadn't done anything. "What am I doing here? I've honored your dad's request to get My Old Man. That's it."

I assumed Randy was asking on behalf of his father. The snappy phlegm in DogLips's voice projected an urgent need that average congestion remedies weren't going to touch. DogLips sounded like someone in serious need of a miracle, or aggressive treatment. If Hillman had medicine for something that life-threatening, he'd never passed that information on to me.

"I already took care of your problem," he said, motioning me to follow him. "I don't know where your old man is, but he ain't here, and he won't be back."

"I don't want your dad leaving me another message, making this my problem again."

"Your old man left when I told him *you* were coming. Got right up, stuffed his junk into a sleeping bag, and headed out. Maybe he moved in with your brother. I hear he's like you, living alone, except he's doing it out here. And your old man won't be back," he grinned, "because I'm moving in. Me and my woman. We're staying near Love Canal right now. Something she arranged, but I'd rather put off cancer until it's absolutely necessary." He finished and took a pull from a bottle I'd just noticed. It looked like top-shelf liquor, but I couldn't tell in the growing dark.

"I don't think you're supposed to drink that stuff quite like that," I said, as he poured what looked like several shots down his throat. "Unless you're trying to avoid cancer by speeding up the process in other ways." He offered the bottle my way and I shook my head.

"Suit yourself," he said, taking another hit. I turned to leave, having no idea what I could possibly offer him. "Wait! Come out back, got something to show you." He walked without checking, confident I'd follow. He'd been busy for a while, or someone had. As I came out, next to some muscle car I'd never seen before, a fire pit blazed steadily, the real source of smoke I'd seen, and maybe a yard away a makeshift structure. I'd never participated, but a sweat lodge—even a rickety-ass, improvised one—was relatively unmistakable if you knew what to look for.

"There's questions you wanna ask," he said, walking to a galvanized water bucket. The Cottage at least had a functioning pump. Maybe there was working plumbing inside, but it seemed unlikely. The pump looked ancient and rusted like ours, but I could smell the fresh cold metallic water in the bucket. He must have just pumped it before walking in. Taking a long pull from the ladle, he offered me some. I shook my head. "Better take it. Gotta stay hydrated. If you want your questions answered, it's gonna be in there, and you know the rules."

He set the bucket down near me and stoked the fire, poking at it and shifting its components. Rocks glowed orange in the center. "Don't worry, they're not from the dike. You ain't the only one learning ceremony. I'm just more charitable with my knowledge. Trying to help you here." He grinned, like a ridiculous James Bond villain. River rocks risked exploding if used in a sweat. Even with peripheral knowledge, I knew that. If you were aware of traditional practices basics, you could spot fakers, people who claimed the ghost of some long-dead Indian princess gramma with giant cheekbones, long straight black hair, who always had to hide their secret identity to live among settler whites, and when their dads were drunk, they'd cry and say *never forget you're an injun* and punch their own chests and blah blah blah, endlessly, over and over. Always the same. It was like a story blueprint existed for over-educated white people who suddenly discovered how Indian they were when it became trendy.

"Randy, you're definitely not supposed to be drinking in there," I said.

"Done. That was just lubricant," he said. "You know how this has to be done," he added, matter of fact, unlacing his boots and kicking them off. "And I'm kind of naturally shy," he said, laughing. Next came the socks and shirt, which he put on another lawn chair out here. His insides might have been rotted, but he was vain enough to maintain the six-pack I'd never have again. Irritated that he knew I wouldn't risk his potential death from heatstroke, I pulled my boots off.

"Good boy. Knew you couldn't resist," he said, tossing two towels from a duffle onto the chair, and then a pair of gym shorts. "Bring a pair for yourself?"

"I'll have to go with what I've got on," I said.

"Lucky you still wear them. I prefer free-ballin'." He dropped his jeans and put the shorts on bare-ass, and shoveled a couple glowing hot rocks into the lodge while I stood and watched. "Come on, you chicken. What kind of medicine man ain't willing to do a sweat right?" All it had taken to understand I'd literally become a different person was that first *holy shit!* look I got in the gym locker room, six months after the surgery.

"Well?" He was testing to see if he could still pressure me. This time, I acted of my own choices. You had to wear something in a sweat, for modesty. I slid my jeans down, stepping out and folding them onto the chair. The breeze raised goose bumps all over. I hoped he knew what he was doing, and that he didn't have malicious intent. Flame-heated rocks were nothing to mess with. Finally, I slowly unbuttoned my dress shirt and hung in on the chair.

"Jesus, you *do* still wear little kid undies! You and Fuck Face. If you're not gonna free-ball, at least move to man skivvies. Boxers, or skimpy ones," he said. I still wore plain white briefs. Even now, the colored ones Roland wore made me think those were for tougher guys than I'd ever be.

"Nice scar, there," Randy added. "You tell the chickies to follow your Unhappy Trail? If you can't get rid of that, how the hell you gonna help me?" He set the shovel back near the fire and stepped inside, never breaking eye contact until he closed the flap behind himself. "Don't just stand there freezing. Open the flap and come on in, remember your skin, and get what you come for. The thing that only me and you know you want." Enclosed, he started mumbling a version of giving thanks, one I'd never heard before, his voice a steady beat.

Seamlessly, he'd gotten the upper hand. When I crawled through, feeling the air warming and the cold, damp earth on my shins, I knew I was going to have to take off the muddy briefs before putting my jeans back on. He said, "I just wanted to make sure you weren't wired for sound."

Unbelievably, even here, Randy Night thought I'd come looking for a scoop, maybe forgetting he'd lured me with the story that I had to help move My Old Man. In the low light, I could see virtually nothing beyond those glowing rocks. "Well?" I said. "Why did you do it?" He ladled some water onto the rocks. They hissed a plume of hot steam like a volcano, covering us.

"*Why* did I do it, why *did* I do it, why did *I* do it, why did I *do* it," he repeated, changing emphasis each time. "Well, I did it 'cause of *you*," he said suddenly, quickly, grinning. His teeth were all I could see of him in the dark.

"Bullshit." I'd been played into this for nothing? For another Randy Night Cheap Trick?

"No bullshit. To be clear, I did it for my woman. But what I did was *because* of you. We were digging around in Fuck Face's stuff one night when he was out, probably trying to track down Little Eva for another beej.

We knew he wasn't spending his evenings with you anymore, whatever you two used to be up to." I thought people had more interesting lives than to be preoccupied with my comings and goings, but apparently not.

"If he's not home, that's some shit Meduse likes to do. Still likes to remind him that she could throw him out any time she wants. It'll never happen, as much as I'd like his ass gone so I could move in. She loves him too much to ever be a real cutthroat like me." He paused and took a ladle of water, then passed it to me. And this time, covered already in dripping sweat, I took it.

"But you know how it is when you go snooping in someone else's shit." He disappeared until the steam broke a clear spot between us. "Sometimes you dig up things better left alone, things you shouldn't find. And sometimes those things . . . turn . . . out . . . to be valuable," he said, poking me in the chest with each of those last words. He'd been waiting for me all this time, willing, delighted to be so forthcoming about his participation, just to get to this moment.

I saw them, going through Tim's things the way I'd gone through my mom's possessions when she wasn't around, the way I'd found her scrapbook of Gihh-rhaggs, wedding favors, her own wedding pictures, where she and my dad stood flanked by the men and women in their lives. I hadn't a clue what objects of interest Randy found among Tim's belongings, but I had an idea about one thing Christine discovered that she shouldn't have.

"*Dear Tim, Dear Mr. Sampson*," Randy said, mimicking my voice with nearly unbelievable accuracy, adding just a hint of exaggeration and plea. "*I call you this because I want to show you the respect I have for you.*" He smiled wide. "Could you get any cornier?" It was the letter I'd written when I was eighteen. The one Tim had just informed me he'd saved.

One handwritten page, not even on standard notebook paper, it was largely a thank you, for everything Tim had helped me do, everything he'd done, all the times he'd gone out of his way for me. The ways I'd felt less lonely when I was around him. I confessed that he'd been more of a father to me in one year's time than my own had in the previous seventeen. What he'd done was what I'd needed. The freedom he'd given me was intoxicating. Knowing someone had my back if I needed, for the first time in my life, had gotten me through seriously hard days. My ma by that time was so burnt out from her years of struggling that she was more relieved than anything when I found someplace else to spend time. I remembered it most because it was the first letter I ever closed with "love," and meant it.

That letter also, however, documented something that should have remained only spoken between two people. It was a sentence Randy repeated now. *"I'm sorry I couldn't take that money from you to go on a date with Christine,"* he said, giggling. "What the fuck? He wanted to pay you to take Meduse out? He try to tie porkchops around her neck so the dog would play with her, too? Did he offer a bonus if you brought back a used rubber as proof? How much?" He started singing that David Lee Roth song, "Just a Gigolo."

I shook my head. At least I'd been smart enough not to commit the dollar amount to paper. "I'll tell you what I'm getting," he said, abruptly ending his song. "That Duster's pretty sweet, but it's just the tip." He motioned to the muscle car a few yards away, definitely several clicks up in price from the Nova Tim had bought for Christine.

"Meduse is like that perfume. She brings home the bacon, fries it up in the pan, and never ever, ever lets me forget I'm her man." That last bit he also sang, mocking a commercial. "Life's pretty good. Sometimes she wants me to pretend to be rough and, a couple times, I forgot I was supposed to be pretending." He finished, weirdly chagrined. "Isn't that what you came to hear? The ugly truth? You just didn't count on the ugliest mug being the one you find in the mirror every day." He crawled out and carefully slid a couple new hot rocks into the hole. They hissed and shot off a few splashes of scalding water.

I sat in the warm dark, thinking about the truth bomb Randy had just set off. As the rocks cooled, the cold and wet seeped in through the ass of my briefs and I carefully crawled out. He was already dressed, sitting in the lawn chair, one towel over his head like a hood. My clothes and the second towel were neatly stacked in his lap. I grabbed the clothes and set them on the stoop and, turning away, got dressed.

"Seems like you don't have what might help my old man," he said. "You're such a Boy Scout, you would have said, if you did." I shook my head and he held up his hand, understanding. "Guess we're gonna make a trip to see Hillman after all. My dad didn't want to."

"You can't have the upper hand in everything," I said, knowing DogLips Night's greatest fear: that someone would roll dice better than him.

"Think you can help me?" he asked. I looked to see if this was more of the long con.

"With what? I didn't know you were sick," I said.

"Sure you did. You know what I'm sick with. I wanna be a better person." I didn't believe it for one second, but he had, in fact, given me what I'd come for.

"Get in my truck," I said. "Passenger's side. Should probably lock up here, first, if you're really trying to keep the Cottagers out." I poured the rest of the water onto the fire and a great plume of steam, ridiculously looking like an eagle's feather, unfurled from the remains. I pumped more water and drank deep. I didn't have a specific protocol for what I should do to help someone with this particular problem. Just the same, I'd accepted the responsibility to be inventive, to add to the long history of new remedies to old problems, as well as matching old remedies to new ones.

I started the truck and Randy came out of the Cottage. As he started to walk around the grill, I climbed out, and said, "No, slide in here, this way," as Tim had that New Year's Eve, all that time ago. Normally, this would have elicited some smart-ass remark, but tonight Randy did as he was told. I backed out and we headed to the place that started this all.

The crime tape was all gone after this amount of time. But he knew where we were supposed to go, and guided me to where I should pull over. I'd brought some kindling and small stove-lengths from the pile behind the Summer Cottage and instructed him to make a small fire ring with field stones, to retrieve the wood, and I'd start the fire.

"Seems drier over here," he said, near a rock pile some farmer had cleared.

"You know where. You're the only one. Don't lie to make it easier. Even if I don't know, I imagine my medicine does." He sighed and stepped further into the field. It was a surprisingly quiet night on Moon Road. The partiers were still spooked, abandoning this place for now.

Once we got the fire going, we knelt, facing each other, the flames sometimes feeling like they were scorching. I dropped some tobacco and other select medicines on top, and they crackled in ignition, sending out a more pungent smoke. "All right, like I told you on the way here. Begin your apology while I get the smoke right for you to breathe in."

"I'm sorry I had Meduse—"

"Christine," I said, and I reached out, with one hand, locking onto his neck, keeping him in place. With the other, I placed my shell of medicines on the ground, within reach.

"Christine, sorry I talked her into calling her old man down here, telling him her car was stuck. I'm sorry that when he pulled up, he was so easy to take care of. He pulled his tow chain from the trunk and handed it right over to me. I didn't even have to use the bat I bought just for the occasion. Soon's he saw I had gloves on, he knew he wasn't having a good night, and the crazy bastard handed it over, anyway. I'm sorry he broke down on this road, crying like a bitch." He caught me there, like he'd hit me with a stun gun. If he were telling the truth, that he'd made Tim cry that night, then Tim was still not telling me the exact truth. Maybe I just didn't want to admit there was always some way the truth was malleable. "Just like you used to." And then he started to laugh, pushing away, throwing me off balance. I had to roll from the flame.

Randy stopped at this point, mostly because of my boot connecting with his ribs. He grunted a little, rolling over, and laughing harder. I didn't connect hard enough to have any real effect, but it wasn't for lack of trying. He'd watched me, on guard like he was with everything else in his life, moving enough out of range to catch a sidelong impact.

"Squier, you still kick like a girl," he said, lying curled up, protecting his solar plexus. "No wonder they always picked you last for kickball. Didn't take long for me to break your medicine man bullshit." He stood up, assessing himself. "Meduse was real easy. When we found your little love note, she went on this crying jag, hurt little daddy's girl routine. Easy to remind her of all the shit she gets around here for being half a white girl."

"Did she forget you're the one who gave her the most?"

"No way, man. Girls are way fiercer on each other than you or me ever would be. Got their own secret acid. So from there? Easy jump. I said her pops maybe needed a tune-up for thinking no one would put up with her ass unless he paid for it. And with a scroungy little pig like you, no less." He tried to stretch, and grabbed his side, wincing at a twinge.

"He wasn't even paying for Top Shelf Stud. And me? Her hero boyfriend? She was happy that I was willing to wake his ass up. People are quick to dole out an ass-beating, if they don't have to pick up the tow chain themselves." He rubbed his side more and came away with a swipe of blood. Not much, little more than a harsh brush burn. "Damn, you ripped my favorite shirt." He took it off and looked at the moon through the tear. "You might still kick like a girl, but I didn't *even* think you had the balls, for real. You want some of this?" he asked, fanning the tobacco embers with his shirt, like he was making smoke signals.

"This is for you, not me."

"You're as much a medicine man as I am a Lodge Elder. Only thing? You're the only one who knows I have a lodge." Disappointment and fear swallowed his shadowy face. "You know, people used to come to my parties just to see what I'd do to you next, and have you *still* come back for more. Carson used to do the same with those others. Doobie and Gloomis. We figured since all of your moms scrub Lewiston toilets for a living, you three have got yourselves such a taste for shit, whenever it's being passed out, you go asking for seconds."

"I thought you just wanted to roll me for my pay," I said, letting him know that I was aware of our fucked-up past.

"Oh sure, that was a bonus, even if the fins I lifted smelled like shit and Lysol."

"Like you ever limited it to fins."

"Mostly I made money betting you'd be back. My other, um, guests, couldn't believe how pathetic you were."

"Those same guys who crash their cars into each other's now?" I thought of the people we'd gone to school with who'd drifted in and out of the Night parties over the years. "I'm *so* disappointed I'm not cruising around with them anymore."

"No loss to them. You never did cruise with them. Just you and Fuck Face. And for the record? Oh yeah, you didn't bring your little reporter's tape machine. You take one more swing at me? You're going down. I bet

‚hat scar up your middle is easy to wake up, and I'm just the guy to be your alarm clock.

"And one other thing," he said, after a pause. "I'm kind of sorry I didn't finish him off when I had the chance. Would have been worth the risk. I'd have a place to live where your sorry-ass dad hadn't shat on the floor. Scumbag ruined the Summer Cottage." He said this last as if my father had been the only regular squatter—as if DogLips hadn't scammed some poor bastard out of the deed rolling dice at his table.

"I used to envy how everyone came to you," I said. "The same way they were drawn to your dad. I even envied that you had a dad at home. I guess there's a risk in having a dad so close. You're just like him, hanging on to people as long as they're useful. You gonna run the Summer Cottage like a holding pen for guys on the skids, until they get up enough money to lose it at your dad's dice table?" That shadow crossed his face again, the flicker of hope and worry.

"Was Tim the last call for the Night train when you ran out of money?" I continued. "Maybe I should thank you. That shit you did made me think about choices I've made." I started to walk away. "Done here. You've lost the track of the medicine."

"Not by my accounting. I don't need forgiveness." His voice raised in increments with each word, each step I took. "I was just doing a job. Meduse made me promise he'd survive. *Her* choice, not mine. He deserved me to finish, and I would have. Not a hypocrite like you."

"Yeah, you were always so good at keeping your word."

"If there's hard time involved I can. Don't mind a few nights in Nancy Jay, but no state pen for me. Meduse said she'd turn me in if he didn't make it, even though I could snag her on being an accessory. Mutually . . . assured . . . destruction. Ain't that what the white people call it?" Awareness of the Cold War didn't seem his style. Maybe he *had* become a different person.

"So I left him just like she wanted. Sweet enough, watching him just crying, why, why, why, over and over. I had to promise her not to tell him the reason I was doing it, but I mean, he had to know. So I hopped back in that car he got her and peeled out," he said, squatting near the smoke again. "Picked her up at the Shop-and-Dine. I think she had second thoughts and maybe called the cops. I was supposed to honk four times as I drove up Clarksville Pass so she could jump in. Might'a had enough time to call."

"That medicine won't do anything for you now," I said as he kept drawing the smoke around himself. "You're not really acknowledging." I stood and headed to my truck.

"Wait," he called, and paused. "Can't you really do *anything*?" I wasn't sure how to answer what seemed like such a simple question. I didn't know what I was doing there.

"Not without you meeting me partway. You're not thankful for the chance to change. The medicine knows it. It makes its own decisions. You're stuck with whatever life this is." His eyes narrowed. Whatever hope he'd had was gone. His regular disposition fully took back over as I climbed in.

"Maybe. But I can change, if I want. If you're for real chasing that crackpot Hillman, you're gonna have to watch for houses falling from the sky for the rest of your life," he said, then sang the Wicked Witch of the West's theme music. He couldn't decide if he desperately wanted to believe I knew medicine, or if he should be afraid I'd snare him with *witch-craft*. That tension had played out across the Rez in its mangled history, Christian missionaries casting all our traditions as dark magic, until our ancestors didn't know which way was up. That centuries-long fear lurked even now in Randy Night's bruised heart. "One last thing?" he added. "Meduse still believes in Hell. Keeps trying to talk me into getting saved by Pastor Clyde. I tell her it's okay. If I go to Hell, I'll have company. At least I'm not fucking over my family to get paid for a shitty story in that rag, the *Cascade*. Your sins are deep, brother. So stop by when you get lonely next door, Squier, or maybe wave when you're writing a story about us." He'd twice called me that, pointedly, so I'd know it was *my* nickname people used when I wasn't around. He was hoping for me to ask, but Tim had already clued me in years ago.

"I'd like to write *this* story. I'd figured out a fair amount. But Tim says he doesn't—"

"Tim? You mean Mr. *Sampson*?" he said, dragging the name the way you'd taunt a high school substitute teacher, dipped in sarcasm as thick as tar.

"Tim. Just Tim. He's lying. For you," I said, starting the truck. "Says he can't remember a thing. Nothing I can do about that."

"Maybe your buddy's got something more to hide, himself. Be careful where you stick your nose," he replied, turning his attention to flames. "Ya might find a hairy root dangling in front of it!" he shouted as I backed out, leaving him on Moon Road.

Randy Night couldn't be cured of being who he was, and I couldn't fix what wasn't wrong with me. My ma had walked away, maybe because she could only bear witness. I had the chance Hillman offered, to carry on the DNA woven within him. He'd never said why he'd chosen me, other than something about a natural affinity when I was a little kid, my ability to hear my ma's true voice, my sensing one of his medicines calling to me. I'd have to find my own way and not look for his road signs, not try to recreate his path.

Hillman's light was on, and he opened the door when I stepped up.

"I guess you been busy tonight," he said, as I stepped to his table for a pinch of what he called "strong medicine," among the easiest to find. Most folks considered it a weed called a Heal-All. People used it to treat so many things in the past, but it had been largely dismissed by science now. Hillman said it was even in a Robert Frost poem. He had never struck me as a poetry kind of guy. While I dug around in his plants and grabbed some more tobacco, he didn't stir.

Hillman's place was big enough that I could move in someday. He hadn't let me forget his offer of it to me. "*When* I don't need it anymore," he always said, laughing. Even with all his personally harvested medicines, and his Western medicine library—the *Taber's*, the *Gray's Anatomy*, the *PDR*—the place had plenty of room for all of his world, and my stuff.

"I did what you wanted me to do," I said, joining him at his table. "I tried healing my enemy before trying to heal my friend, but it didn't seem to work on Randy. There's so many near misses in our lives, so many times we barely pass a test. And sometimes, we just don't."

"He's maybe not the kind to make tough life changes," Hillman said.

"Hard to say," I offered. "He went along with everything I asked, even when I told him to do the things my heart told me to do. My own first steps. Then . . . things drifted."

"So maybe *you* weren't willing to make the tough life changes, isn't it though?"

"If you're asking me to accept him for being a mean bastard, that he's part of the equation that way, then, no, I suppose I didn't. I wanted him to want to be . . . fixable?"

"It ain't perfect," he said. "We're humans. We miss signs. Our own longing pushes us to serve our own desires. Always the struggle. Every now and again, even I still make mistakes." Was I one of those mistakes? If I had a chance of helping Tim, I had to be truthful.

"I also kicked him. I let him get to me. That's when I knew it was over." Hillman sat shaking, and as I watched him, I realized I'd been here before, that I was again living a double-exposure photo. He shook like my ma when Gihh-rhaggs had died . . . except *he* was laughing, not crying.

"Maybe you did right," he said at last, allowing his laughter to gain volume. "If he's still able to do the things he likes, and he accepts that's his life, maybe you done what you set out for. Sometimes, a kick in the ass is the right medicine." He smiled.

"It was in the ribs."

"Ribs," he said, nodding, considering. "I'll keep that in mind." He paused and got serious. "Where your medicine failed was in the doubt. If you believed in your kick, or what it could do, it could'a had a running shot. Things get tricky between brothers."

"We're not brothers." I didn't like Hillman's speculation about DogLips and my mother.

"If blood is all it takes, then me and you, we're brothers, the amount of my blood you carry around," he said, escorting me to the door. "The Good and Bad Mind are always brothers, wrestling for control. That story of brother killing brother, that's the story of other people. Only way you'll know if this worked is over time. Night." And with that, I was on the porch again.

I thought of one more thing I should do. Though it was late, when I drove over, Hubie's car was among a few in the fire hall parking lot. He was shooting pool, alone. Eight Ball.

"That thing you told me," I started, grabbing the other cue. "About feeling that first solo breath when you've been giving someone mouth to mouth?"

"Stripes," he said, taking the balls with more on the table. "What about it?"

"It ever get old?"

"Never. Each breath, each life, is someone different you've helped. It's always for the other person." For failing Kindergarten, Hubie had excelled as an adult. "You gonna help FF?"

"You, of all people, should be nicer about bad nicknames," I said, annoyed.

"What's so bad about Forever Faithful?"

"What?"

"My mom told me that when he started hanging out here, after the service, he was always so proud of his tattoo. Gihh-rhaggs wanted to straighten his ass out about being a show-off, so he gave him that name before, well, you know." Gihh-rhaggs would have hated Latin.

"Funny, I always thought it meant something else. Anyway, you might want to take a swing by the far end Moon Road tonight, or maybe the Summer Cottage," I said.

"I need my bag?" he asked, standing immediately, letting the name issue go as only a person with a bad, Krazy-Glue-sticking nickname could.

"Is your car ever without it?" I asked. He laughed, shaking his head no. If Randy was at the Summer Cottage, Hubie could assess him. He'd probably ask, but neither of us would ever tell. It was that way with friends, or the people you're stuck with. I wasn't sure how different those two things really were. Before heading to the city, I took a last Rez Lap.

It was after midnight, but I assumed Tim was still up. I'd walk to the door and grab the handle, knowing it'd turn easily in my hand. You only got so many times to try out new lives. I hoped it would feel like home when I opened his door, pulled out my medicine bag, and began my new life. If I wasn't good enough, at least I would have tried, finally. I let history unfold before I dropped the truck into Drive, the first medicine Tim had given me, and pointed its nose in his direction.

CHAPTER TWENTY-EIGHT

Patient Visitor

A strange car sat in Tim's driveway and the living room lights were on. I grabbed my Maglite, the closest thing I had to a weapon. It was like a higher-tech, deadlier version of the sawed-off lacrosse stick I used to keep in my jacket sleeve. All things being equal, the Mag felt like better defense. The door was unlocked and I tripped, taking the stairs two at a time.

"Hey, son," Tim said, looking puzzled and a little embarrassed for me. "What are you doing here?" His shirt draped down the coffee table's far end. Lottie Darkwinter sat on the edge of the couch where he was lying, pressing gently near the incision edges as Tim winced. The butterflies were gone, and the scars were exposed wide.

"Saw your light on. Listen, you—" I started.

"I did, too," Lottie said, standing. "We were coming from my mom's." Leonard Stoneham reluctantly waved from the hassock, in the far corner. "Thought it couldn't hurt to check up, long as I was in the . . . um, why you got a Mag with you?"

"He fumbles in the dark," Tim said, granting me a wink only I could see.

"We were just leaving," Leonard said. "Pressure's good, Mr. Sampson. Lungs clear. More you move around, better off you are. Semper Fi." Tim repeated Leonard's affirmation and I walked them out. Lottie asked me to try convincing Tim to lock his door. I agreed and thanked them for caring enough to stop. Dusty had told her Tim was a night owl, just like she and Lena had always been themselves. I turned the lock and headed back to the living room.

In the low light and the ongoing growth, Tim's beard looked fuller, almost identical to the one Gihh-rhaggs had always worn. They'd only ever looked mildly alike, since Tim usually had a much fuller face and chose perpetual five o'clock shadow. But since his time in the hospital, their shared DNA had become almost impossible to deny. At that moment, there was absolutely no mistaking their connection.

"What? What's the matter?" he said, noticing the surprise on my face.

"Nothing," I said, sitting. "I've just spent the evening with Randy Night."

"You did, huh? Barhopping again?"

"If there's one thing I'm certain of, it's that Randy and I will never barhop again."

"Don't ever say never, son." I used to like him calling me that, but it had lost a bit of its glow in our long silence. I already had one father who'd vanished like a magician's assistant. The word felt like a reminder of the impossible gap between our two vessels. "This world's too funny a place for that." Tim seemed to have forgotten that he'd been a man of absolutes for years. "Find the answers you were looking for?"

"Some clarification?" I shrugged. "He called me Squier again, trying to prod. He has no idea you told me years ago." Could you be re-embarrassed by the same action, years later? Particularly if it was as accurate and still stung? "Can I ask, was Vestal, you know, your first?"

"Not really any of your business, son, but I'll tell you. I'd been a Marine for two tours. By the time Vestal offered that first ride, I'd . . . satisfied my curiosities, come to know what I wanted and what was too complicated a way to live. Just say that. Why such a nosey question?"

"Seems like I'm getting a little old. Almost everyone I know—"

"People change, grow, at their own speed. You'll know what to do and when it's right. I was stationed in a lot of places. Back then, the Marines was the only thing I was faithful to. Don't rush yourself for the sake of getting it over with. Do things the way you want."

"Thank you. Sorry for being nosey. I didn't really have anyone else." I couldn't think of another person I could have asked, since the extent of my father's "Facts of Life Talk" had been to warn me when I was eleven not to jack off so much, because he wasn't paying for an exam my weakened eyes would supposedly need. I knew I was in a smaller and smaller minority, and that the older I got, the more embarrassing it seemed. Sometimes I felt like going to a singles bar, seeking out a one-night stand, just to get things over with, so the threshold didn't loom so impossibly large in my mind. But that didn't feel right.

Most of my life, I'd watched people use each other, or get used by other people, and then have to go home and rebuild themselves. I'd probably done it to others inadvertently, even just thoughtlessly trying to talk to Margaret about her dad, or the messiness with Christine, but those moments continued to haunt me. The idea of stealing intimacy from someone was like a crime to me. I'd wanted for so long to pass through that last door to adulthood, I kept believing the right person had to wander into my life at some point. And there was that other thing, too.

"Understood," Tim said. We were quiet for a minute. He knew more was coming.

"There's something I have to tell you."

"Even before you tell me all about this big mystery you're planning to spring on me?"

"Unfortunately, yes, and you're not going to be happy. If I trace it back to its most secret origins, it's truly my fault, too. So I want to say I'm sorry ahead." He raised his eyebrows. "I know you don't want to talk about what happened down on Moon Road, but I maybe got some answers you don't currently have," I said. "That letter I wrote you? I don't think it's in your dresser anymore."

Tim leaned back, understanding immediately. "Fuckkkk," he dragged out, a long-breathed resignation. "Wanna check for me?" Tim's bedroom was neat, the opposite of the dirty-clothing piles in TV show bachelor bedrooms. His bed was made with care. The dresser's surface held a watch, an untouched bottle of Obsession, and a few framed photos: Vestal and him, one of Christine and Hayley, and the one my mom had, where he and Gihh-rhaggs stood together, smiling out of their youths into a future that didn't happen. The top drawer was neatly divided, folded socks on the right, stacked by color, white briefs in the middle, including the new ones I'd just purchased—cardboard still inside—and colored boxers on the left, dark to light, like the socks. They looked like clothes on store shelves, professionally creased.

At the bottom, the letter was there, still in the envelope I'd handed over. It stuck out from under a square pale-blue greeting card envelope. Below those, a large white paper-sized envelope covered the bottom. These three adhesive sleeves were the only mismatched things in this drawer. The size of that last one seemed troublingly familiar. "It's here," I yelled. The blue envelope's seal was intact, only marred by a fingerprint smudge and my name. He'd intended to hand deliver it.

"Okay," he yelled back. "Guess it don't much matter, now." I was halfway down the hall when he asked me to retrieve it. I hoped he wouldn't reread it in my presence. Pulling it from the envelope, he held it close to his face, still folded. A piece of colored paper fell out, and I could see it was the invitation I'd sent him to my last Moving Up Day celebration. He slid it back into the folded sheet. "Still smells like you," he said. It had never occurred to me he'd know my scent as clearly as I knew his. "I suppose there's more than two people who know what this says."

"At least two more."

"Go into the kitchen, the drawer just below where the keys are hanging. My billfold's in there." He folded the fragile sheet of paper one more time and slipped it into the wallet's dollar bill compartment, telling me I could toss the envelope. Across its top, childish letters spelled out his name, in what I'd believed was adult handwriting. It didn't look a thing like my penmanship now. I slid it in my back pocket. "Something else, too, right? Something else Night told you?"

I could ask him if he'd cried during his encounter with Randy, but it was less important than my real questions. I felt an obligation to do my best, because it was for Tim. But our relationship was complicated. Friendships felt like they should come packaged in bubble wrap and triple-thick cardboard, with the silk screen of a broken wineglass on every side. Let one person defy the other's expectations, and you could send two people shattered, fragments and slivers tumbling in different directions.

"Tim? I haven't even explained what I really want to talk to you about."

"I'd be kind of a moron if I didn't have a pretty good guess. I'm willing to listen, but well, that's about all I can promise right now."

"Yeah, I know. But before any of that? I need to know. How come . . . how come you never came to see me in the hospital? Really?" We needed to talk about bigger things, but we had to start here. "For this to work, if you agree to what I propose, we have to be right with each other first. You and I. We're not right, at the moment. Something's missing." It was blunt, but I needed to be in the Good Mind before I began. This conversation was one door I needed to open, thankful for the opportunity to invite him through it, no matter what new world we found ourselves in, together, on the other side.

Silent for a bit, Tim struggled to sit up as he thought, trying to read my mind.

If he looked into my heart, the way the medicine would, what he'd see was me in a hospital bed, years before, talking with family and waiting, hearing him in every footstep until it passed by my room, and then Visiting Hours would be over for that day, and the next and the next, and suddenly I was discharged and he'd never come, not even a card or phone call.

I could have reached out, of course. But the way he hadn't come when I needed him most, and his silence afterward, those things had kept me from knocking on his door. That silence was a mold, growing in the dark, an indelible stain that expanded around us. Neither acknowledged the impasse, each eventually avoiding places the other would be. And suddenly a year had gone by. Even bleach wouldn't get that shit out. And then, five more years.

"Look," I prompted, "I understand your resistance. In the hospital, people always look funny, scary, not themselves. When my family came into the ICU, I could tell how scared they were. Maybe it was the gastric tube, or the drains, or the catheter. The TVs that kept chasing my vital signs across their screens like sad video games, or the big circular bank of lights floating overhead." Even as I described them, I could smell the strange antiseptic ICU air.

"I understand," I continued, "that part of it's just the sight of someone you know, in a johnny and maybe socks, staring up at you. *That* can make you not want to stay and visit. I've been the Visitor." You admire flowers and cards, glance out the window to the parking lot, not wanting to see others trudging in or out, or you watch nurses smoking, shaking their heads, talking about a patient who isn't going to make it despite their efforts.

"But when I was the patient? I got discharged, and still . . . no card? No visit? No call? I've never considered myself an especially demanding person." He bowed his head so he didn't have to do much, to avoid making eye contact. "Something you learn at the bottom of the economic scale. No bargaining chips. Pockets so empty, you can't even bluff. But during my week and a half in the hospital, you couldn't come? Or call? I sort of get it. I've never gotten around to visiting some friends before they'd been discharged. Life gets congested sometimes. But I didn't consider you just a friend. It was like . . . like a close family member hadn't come."

"I know. I. . . ." he said, then just let out a long breath. He lifted his eyes to look at me, but no words seemed forthcoming. It was more a silent plea for me to stop.

"At first, I hoped I'd run into you by circumstance," I went on, shrugging, needing to fill the silence, myself. "Seemed inevitable on this tiny Rez. I even told myself that as I started taking different routes on and off the reservation." No matter where I'd been, I always passed by his house now. "I knew you believed enough in our place that you stayed on the Rez, even after Vestal died. It's not the most inviting place for outsiders. Shit, it's even tricky for people like me, straddling those borders publicly." He pursed his lips, took in deep breaths, and then let them back out slowly through his nostrils. Each time I thought he'd say something, he stopped.

"Really, this time. I gotta know," I added, after his minutes-long silence.

"Thought it was the fear of hospitals," Tim said, finally, staring down at his hands folded between his thighs. "The chemicals and death swimming in the air. You can smell it. I don't know if it's in the vents or what, but as soon as I step in, I smell it and I see my brother. He didn't die at the crash site, you know?" I hadn't. "They were still working on him when I made it to the hospital." This was news to me, so many years after the fact. "Common enough. Nobody wants to go there. Hospitals ain't fun for anyone. How folks go work in them every day, you got me. Say what you will. They're doing yeoman's work. Lottie and your old buddy—that was him, wasn't it? The Jarhead from the bar?" I nodded. They'd only seen each other for a few minutes that night at the Spithouse, yet Tim remembered Leonard Stoneham.

"But it wasn't that," he said, looking up at me. "Really. I was afraid of losing you. Seeing you that way. That's the last sight I have of my brother, seeing the ambulance folks, medics, pumping on his chest, trying to breathe life back into him, and that sight never fucking leaves me. Was being selfish. Scared. Sat in that parking lot every night you were in. Not three times. Every single night. But I couldn't bring myself to walk through those doors. Sometimes I even walked around the parking lot, stared into those sliding glass doors. And after you came home, well, I couldn't face you. You know how that is. When you can't be who you believe you are. When someone knows your weaknesses, you see in their faces all the ways you're a failure."

"I wouldn't have shown that."

"You'd try to hide it. You try to hide everything from most people, but you and me, we've got something else. Or we did. I'd see. Then, you know, the longer you don't see someone when you've screwed up, the harder it is to find the path back to their house. Been lucky. Could always keep up with what you were doing in the paper, and with the Yee-hog." I corrected his pronunciation unconsciously, and he nodded. "Your mom talks about you. Not to me, but word gets around. You did good on my investment, son. I knew you would."

"Fair enough," I said. "And nyah-wheh. I appreciate that you think so."

"But you know, I could ask you kind of the same question. I know *I* screwed up in not coming to see you, but how'd you just walk away, yourself? Gotta admit, we spent a lot of time together when you were in school and then wound up in college." He said that as if he'd had nothing to do with my enrolling, having received a scholarship. He said that as if he'd never given me a vehicle. He knew the answer, but since he'd asked, I felt like I had to respond. It was hard to imagine telling anyone the realities of the life my ma had demanded our silence on, for so long. No case workers, no teachers, no bosses, not even friends.

The only friend who'd ever spent the night at our house was, of course, Randy Night, in those periods we held each other's secrets. The ways he was sneaking beer sips around the dice table at nine years old, the porn mags he lifted from DogLips's stash, the shipwreck of our house.

"Okay," I said. "I'll tell you. Everything, if you want, but the short answer is: charity and debt. I understand when people want to help you out, but when you can't return the favor, well, that debt builds in you, like an organ gone bad, slowly poisoning you from the inside."

"What I did wasn't charity, son. I did it because I wanted to."

"So you know then. It's hard to see," I said, "to understand how people fit into your life until you have distance, some space to see the pieces and the ways they make up something larger, the ways people invest in you. I mean, I sort of asked you this before, but I don't think you answered. Or maybe I've forgotten what you said."

"I doubt that. You don't seem to forget anything," he laughed, and paused a little. "Least in my experience. You might not see what you think you're seeing, but it don't change the way you remember the moment." Reminding me of the way I'd been so easily fooled by his fake encounter with Little Eva, he was cautioning me to always acknowledge that the truth was always complicated and unexpected.

"I might have agreed with you about my memory at one time, but since the surgery, it seems like pieces flake off at the edges, like photographs that have survived a fire." The stories I'd been keeping to myself, I'd written down, and they solidified in the writing. The act, itself, felt like a medicine of sorts. I did it for myself, and who knows, maybe I'd suggest the act to others looking to understand their own lives. The stories, the memories, came in bursts, frozen in a way I could understand them. They were probably exactly the kind of story Gary was asking of me, but some things were meant for privacy.

"You snagged me that New Year's Eve because you wanted to find out why I was making Christine so miserable. How I could do such a thing, when it turned out I—"

"Now, wait!" He pushed. "That is *not* what I said, or," he softened, "what I meant if I did say that." He leaned forward, his massive veined hands dangling between his thighs.

"You leaning forward because of those incisions? Are they hurting you right now? I remember. It was a long haul back."

"Not pain, exactly. Vulnerable? One of the first things you learn in Boot. Always protect your midsection. Never expose your underbelly."

"You protecting it from me?"

"Instinct, son," he said, still hunching forward. "Bracing for your question."

"It's not going to be hard. I just want the truth."

"Oh, is that all?" he laughed. "No, not hard in the least."

"Something happened that New Year's Eve. I know it gave me a way to see my future, to understand that I wanted things out of life I hadn't seen, myself. I know after it was over, you were worried I'd tell people about . . . well, about your exposed underbelly, I guess. Your vulnerability. I promised I wouldn't."

"You'll forgive me for not believing a cocky eighteen-year-old could be trusted to keep his mouth shut with a story perfect for party jokes." I couldn't argue with him. A big guy like him, breaking down and crying, looking for comfort? That was just not the way things were done on the Rez. I'd held the power to make him the butt of mockery for the rest of his days.

"Seventeen. I was seventeen," I corrected. "Okay, I get that. But at some point, you must have known I was good on my word."

"Yeah, the whole month of January, I waited for some random person to come up, carrying on, fake crying, grabbing on to me, looking to be held, and everyone would explode in cackles. I knew it was gonna happen, and I kept holding my breath, waiting, and then one day big paper hearts covered the school windows and massive white teddy bears holding stuffed hearts filled the shelves down at the K-Marts, and I realized almost a month and a half had gone by."

"I promised. I've never told anyone. Even now. And even when people would ask me over and over why we started hanging out." In a place this small, anything out of the ordinary drew attention, and people weren't shy about being nosey. Eventually, something more interesting came along and people forgot about our evenings doing Rez Laps, but it had been a drag for a while. Particularly with Randy stoking fires as he loved to. "But what happened with you after that? I mean, I'm not that good a hugger. I don't think I told you. That night? That was the first time, to the best of my memory, that someone had given me one."

"No need to exaggerate, son. I get the point."

"That's not an exaggeration. I've thought about it a lot. Seventeen years is a long time to wait. That connection, whatever it was—"

"It was an embrace," he interrupted. "See? You're so afraid of it, you can't even say it."

"Okay, that *embrace* made me realize I shouldn't have had to wait that long, and let's face it, you weren't embracing *me*, exactly. You were hugging what? Your loss? Your desperation? I just happened to be the only body in proximity."

"No, that's not true, either." He leaned back, slowly, his hands pushing against his thighs. "But I don't have the words to explain it. I know what it means to have human contact taken away from you. The girls quit letting me hug them years before. We all became different people when Vestal left—I mean, this house must be so painful to Hayley, she's moved to a whole different state. I get that, but I gotta stay here, at least until she's responsible enough to work out living arrangements with Christine, do upkeep on their own. I don't want some third or fourth cousin showing up needing a place to stay, and suddenly there's ten people jammed in here and my girls don't know how to show them the door. I can be tough for them, until they can be tough enough to protect their own interests."

After all this time, he never quite understood how things worked here. He did, in that what he'd just described could well happen. I couldn't argue that. But he didn't understand that this was our way of life. That we lived as groups of people, extended families, not tiny units, like the little pointy-bottomed people you wedged into little plastic cars in the Game of Life.

"Anyway, every once in a long, long while in your life. Impossibly long. Someone comes alone with the same need as you, at the same moment. It's like we briefly have invisible whiskers, like cats, like we feel more things around us than usual. I needed human connection that night, not the joking kind, not the ball-busting kind, and not the giving someone an ass-whipping kind. I know those are usually the choices you get. In that moment, though, you were giving off the exact same need." I considered the possibility. It was likely true. I'd probably been giving off that signal for so long, and so steadily, I didn't even feel what I was sending out anymore, because no one's antennae had ever picked it up before. "I took a chance. And it turned out, maybe? That hunch had been right?"

I admitted to myself that he had been. I'd only recognized it as relief that first night, that I'd dodged the pounding I was sure I was getting. But, in fact, other electricity *had* lingered in the air. That same charge had made it easy to keep my promise. "So, then what? You just drove around until you saw me again, knowing I'd have to be walking the roads at some point?"

"Don't be a smart-ass, now," he answered sternly. "You asked for truth and I'm giving it to you in the words I have. Can't help if they don't fit in your little package of the way things ought to be. The first time I saw you walking, I knew what I was supposed to do. I accepted that you and Christine weren't ever gonna be you *and* Christine. And by then, she was already involved with that little shit ass." Hearing him use this extremely Rezzy derogatory term made me smile. It fit naturally in his mouth, like he'd been raised a fluent speaker in Rez vulgarity.

"Seeing you in my headlights, just a scrawny little guy in a black leather jacket and dark jeans, walking alone with the pace of someone who's got nowhere to go, willing to risk getting hit, I knew I had to pick you up. I did it because I'd been that same guy, myself." He stopped for a moment, resting. "When I enlisted, I knew I could see action. There were hints we'd get involved in the trouble brewing in a tiny country I'd never heard of, across the globe. I needed to be somewhere I wouldn't be alone. Almost went career, even. Right when they were dangling bonuses in front of me, if I signed up for a third, I met someone who made me see other possibilities."

"Vestal? Through your brother?"

"No, it was before all this," he said, shaking his head, dismissing something. "Don't matter now, but once it was over, I'd been out long enough that I figured I should come home. My brother was making noises about this girl on the Rez, perfect for me. You know the rest of that part.

I got back here, settled in, and he invited me out here, already paving the way."

"A white person inviting another white person into a preexisting place, without regarding the people already here? How refreshingly different," I said, laughing to myself.

"You want me to pretty it up? We didn't think about those kinds of things then." I shook my head and gave him the *please continue* hand gesture. "Well, you know, one thing led to another. Vestal missed a month, so we hurried up and arranged a wedding. My folks thought I was rushing into things, but—"

"But Church Lady Vestal was having sex before marriage and she'd be damned if she was going to let that out, even if she didn't necessarily love you," I said, probably with a little too much glee in my voice. This would have been some sweet Eee-ogg, but I'd keep it locked up.

"We loved each other," he said. "Not sure we were in love just then, when we exchanged vows, but people didn't think much about options back then. You got someone pregnant, you did the right thing or the wrong thing. That was it." He sat up even straighter, slowly reaching up and clasping his hands behind his head, grimacing. I remembered this exercise. You had to keep breaking up the tissue as it healed, stretching it so you didn't lose more flexibility.

"Being *in* love came later," he said, finally. "Not many people get everything in the order they think it's gonna come."

"Tim, I don't wanna sound like DogLips. Boy, if there's one thing I don't want, it's that," I said. "But your wife's been gone a long time. If you . . . what's the word. . . . *crave*. If you crave human contact so strong, you'd embrace a scroungy stranger like me, then you should be out there. Looking, sending out your signals. Don't you think? I'm sure there's people who want to, you know, share the love you want to share."

"Spoken like someone who's never been in a relationship," he said. And though he was smiling to confirm he was Rez-teasing, it still stung like rubbing alcohol on a deep cut. "I built this place. Put my whole life into it. I did it for the girls. I can't risk their losing it just 'cause my bed's more lonesome than I'd like." For all the times I kept acting like he was an outsider, he'd adopted our way of life more than I thought, maybe more than I was willing to, myself.

"I've made my choices about my life. To the degree I have a say. I thought Vestal and I would have a lot more years together, but isn't that always the way? I figured out a way to live most of my time with a mask on, so I'd fit into the Rez here. It's not a mask for you folks, far as I can tell. It's just a different way of life. It's my job to change, not yours to change for me."

It seemed like a logical statement, flat out, but time and again, we'd all encountered people who wanted to change us, make us more American, to fit in. The Boarding Schools, like the place my grandfather went, were the most obvious and worst, kids dying in them because they couldn't make the transformation. But we'd each encountered our own weaker version of that same idea infecting the American mind. My current infection was a City Room editor named Gary Hughes, and since I had no way to cure it, if I wanted to stay at the *Cascade*, I did what people do. I endured, and waited to grow some insulation or some antibodies.

"That night? The reason I reached out?" he said, his words clipped. He was trying to keep his lips from quivering, his voice from shaking.

"Tim, I'm still okay with you crying. Aren't we beyond that?" He nodded, and though he kept his composure, the occasional tear did slide down his face, dampening his beard.

"I felt like I could . . . No, felt like I *should* reach out, because I saw you were wearing the same mask. And after? I felt less alone. Just knowing someone else out here felt the same kinds of things I did, had the same kinds of needs, it was enough. I'd seen behind your mask, and I continued to, ever since. And the closer we got, the less alone I felt. It was a gift that made life tolerable again. I hope, if nothing else, I made you feel less alone, too."

"You did," I said, immediately. "More than tolerable, and when you were gone. Jesus. And now? I feel that way again, if I'm being honest. Less lonely. But one more thing?"

"Son, I've given you everything I have," he said, suddenly weary, his eyelids heavy. I remembered that post-surgery feeling. I'd feel decent, almost normal, and then it was like someone hit me over the head with a pillow that had a brick buried inside.

"I'll be quick, I promise." He nodded, but moved around, lifting his legs back up onto the couch and sliding into place, so I'd know he meant to sleep in the extremely near future. "If all that's true—and I'm not arguing, because I did feel the same way. But then why did you help me find a future that I, myself, didn't even know I wanted? If my being here helped you feel less lonely, why did you help me to leave?"

"Easy to answer, but you gotta hit the road right after. Barely keeping my eyes open." I agreed. "When you tried to enlist in the Corps, I knew that wasn't the place for you. It was the right thing for me. Made me more the person I wanted to be. I'm not gonna pretend to know your life experiences, and I know you keep almost everything locked up, but you've let me inside enough, I know you probably better than most people. That a safe assumption?"

"Yeah," I said, and thought. "Probably better than anyone. Even Hillman. He only knows one side. The group side. You know the side that's just me. Like you said, behind the mask."

"When I saw you walking alone on the side of the road, your future stretching out in my headlights to infinity," he said, "I remembered my own walks through Love Canal like that. Walking alone in the dark can be risky." He had a way with words he never shared with anyone else, that I knew of. I wondered what his life might have been like if the right person had received his signal at the right time. That mystery person, in that other place, the one it ultimately hadn't worked out with. What if they had heard his signal? "Everything I've done, I did it for you to find your path. Like I was supposed to help you become the person you want to be. The one you need to be." It was almost as if he'd seen this moment years ago, the way our lives would forever be entwined. "I know it sounds ridiculous to think I could see the future."

"I guess you're forgetting what my ma used to do," I said, and we smiled. "I'm going to come back in a few days," I added, deciding in that moment to give him some real time to consider, fairly, like I should have to begin with. "It's time for me to make good on someone else's investment now, and on yours. But it's going to require you to trust me and do what I ask, if it has any chance of success. I want to see if I can use what Hillman taught me, to help you. You'd be my first. I know I've said that before, but I want you to understand. If you're not interested, there's no point in pursuing it."

"Well, we've come this far together, haven't we?" He motioned for me to hand his shirt back to him, but instead, I went to his bedroom and grabbed him a clean one. That large envelope in his drawer was calling me, and I was almost tempted to peek. Instead, I did what was right.

"Hey, under the letter, in the bottom of your drawer?"

"Nosy little fucker still, I see," he laughed. "It's what you think it is. When Christine started going with her man, she finally took your picture out of her mirror."

"Did you dig it out of the trash?" I asked, not fully sure I wanted the answer. He paused long, which I took as a confirmation he didn't want to admit, no matter how much I deserved it.

"Well, no. She left it for me, on my dresser. We never said a word." He let out a shaky sigh. "I got a good envelope and put it where I kept the other things. I'm glad she didn't throw it out, and I'd like to think I'd have retrieved it if I noticed it there. Believe me?"

"Yeah, of course," I said. It seemed strange that he didn't offer to give it back. He knew Randy had stolen it from me and sold it to Christine. "Haven't seen that portrait in a long time. Not sure I'd even recognize the person in it."

"Well, I do. I knew him pretty well, and I'm glad I have it. I mean, I'm not gonna put it up on the dresser in a beaded frame or anything," he laughed, kind of awkwardly. "But it's also kind of a piece of our story." I nodded in agreement, as equally odd and true as it was. "I should also tell you. When it was clear you weren't gonna wear that jacket, I slowly put money back into Christine's savings. Took me a while. She's got an eagle eye. But I paid it off. I figured if I bought it, maybe you'd consider wearing it one day. A shame for it to sit in a closet."

"Why did you do that?"

"Was kind of my fault to begin with. I encouraged her to figure out the things you loved."

"Thank you. For telling me." I felt uncomfortable that it did make a difference. "We good for now?" I asked, helping him into the fresh shirt. I shut off the lamp and turned on my Mag. A bright tunnel of light streamed from its eye. "I'm gonna lock this door," I added, as I reached it.

"Wait!" he yelled. "Come and get this." Digging into his wallet, he pulled a house key from a hidden sleeve. I slid it into my own wallet, nodded, and stepped back out, shutting off the Mag. I tried the door, and it was secure. We were both growing comfortable in our own darkness, each on the opposite sides of a locked door. But now, finally, we both had the key.

CHAPTER TWENTY-NINE

Commencement

I called to check on Tim and returned a few evenings later, as promised, letting myself in. He greeted me from his same spot on the couch. "Those look suspiciously like the same clothes I left you in a few nights ago," I said, spreading out the contents of my bag on the coffee table.

"White T-shirts and sweats all look the same," he said. "I buy a bunch of the same ones at once. Who cares what they look like? Just me here." He laughed, seemingly in a good mood. "I promise. I showered this morning. Today's the day, right?" He leaned over the table. I was relieved that he agreed to participate the way anyone else from the Rez would. We didn't have a direct conversation. We just moved forward like this was our intent, the whole time.

"Today is indeed the day," I said, revealing my package. The materials came together—the small bundles of dried plants and a couple of quahog shells, their mother of pearl interiors shimmering. My personal bundle vibrated in my pocket, as it hadn't when I'd tried with Randy.

"So what you got there, anyway?" I considered how Tim communicated in the sidelong rhythms of Rez life, and I flashed on my grandfather, what he'd faced in boarding school. How had he survived coming from here, where life happened through natural cooperation, only to be thrown into a military style world, where every part of his day was controlled with the sole purpose of wiping out the person he'd been his entire life? All that, so I could be here, now.

"Your future." I mix dried flakes from one bundle with others, adding water from my two-spout vessel, and poured the last of my tobacco to give thanks for being there. "Remember what I told you? Whatever I ask you to do? No questions, no fighting, and most of all, no lying."

I brought the lighter near the tobacco shell.

"What are you doing with Lionel's lighter?"

"Lion L?"

"Lionel, you know, like the train set," he said. "My brother?" He added this when I didn't respond, slightly incredulous. I repeated the name, sure I'd never known it my whole life. I hadn't been allowed to attend Gihh-rhaggs's funeral, only hearing second and third hand about its tense line of grieving women and children, years later. His obit was absent from my mom's scrapbook. "Your mom give you that?"

"She let me borrow it. When Margaret gave it to her—"

"Margaret? No. I did. Since Lionel never married any of those women he had kids with, I got his stuff. I was his only legal next of kin. I put this lighter and a few other things into a bag for your mom and dropped 'em off at your house early that morning."

"That money, too?"

"What do you think?"

"Does my ma know this? She always told me it was one of his daughters who dropped the stuff off the next morning. I guess I assumed Margaret."

"Pretty sure she knew. I didn't knock. Just slid the envelope between the screen door and the wood one. Should have recognized my handwriting. I didn't have the heart to tell her in person he was gone. Like my brother, I'm just the cowardly sort, when it comes down to it."

"You're sure it's his? I always thought it had been my grandfather's."

"Nope, it's his. I ought to know. I bought it for him, at the PX when I was in."

"Well, anyway, it's mostly never left her sight," I said. "She did give me these, saying I might need them." The old coins chimed from my bag into his palm. Her dreams of an escape route gleamed there. She was convinced every coin was rare and would bring her a fortune if she'd turn them in, but it meant giving up something of Gihh-rhaggs.

"Where's the nickel?" Tim knew what they were with only a casual glance.

"She took it back. I don't know why."

"I do."

"She said it's because these were all silver."

"What's that got to do with anything?"

"You can use silver to offer thanks if you don't have tobacco." This was one of Hillman's first lessons. He said there was a purist mentality to some medicines, a necessity to do things the right way, but added there was also room for improvisation. "And this is the last of my tobacco at the moment," I said, sparking it full.

"Go back in my room again. Same drawer, beneath the undershorts. Some coins like this, inside a cigarette pack. Take those instead, if you need. These? Bring them back to your mom, but don't tell her. Put them where she keeps them. Bet you know where that is."

"I do," I said, retrieving a Winston Lights soft pack I suspected had been his brother's final one, from exactly where he'd said—next to the large envelope holding my school portrait. Along with the old coins, the Winston paper sleeve held a bar token like the one Gihh-rhaggs had given me, an oversized Indian Head nickel. I asked Tim about the token.

"We got 'em the night I left for Boot Camp. I was trying to get Lionel to come with me, thought the Marines might straighten his ass out, too. Glad he was smart enough not to agree. He was never good at rules. We carved our initials into these. Then I took his and he took mine. See? The LS on it? We said we'd have a drink with them when I made it home safe, but we never got around to it. We each kept a part of the other. Don't know what happened to his."

"Gave it to me. Was in my jacket left behind when you and I went riding. Last I saw it."

"Well, you can keep that one if you'd like. A replacement. Those other coins you brought and that there lighter? That's, I guess what *you'd* call, some strong medicine for your mom, if I understand anything of your medicine." Something about his observation itched my brain, made me stop for a minute. "Shared history, like the way I keep things going with Vestal."

"Must have been easy to whiz no-handed with a catheter on." We laughed.

"True, but I wouldn't care to repeat that experience," he said. "So what are you going to use these for, anyway? Is it what I think? I appreciate your effort here. I guess. But remember, I'm not from here. Your magic might not work on a white body." He paused, just briefly, then added, "And I gotta ask you again, are you sure about this? Are you planning to keep doing it?"

"Well, that's a conversation for later. Now, I gotta ask you to take your shirt off—"

"You and Lottie, all you Indians like seeing me without my shirt," he said. I laughed and nudged him. "Haven't sprung any leaks. Sealed up good, if ugly."

"Lean back and I'll tell you what I'm going to use these for." The scars were still huge, puffy and shiny. I hoped I could give him what Hillman hadn't been able to give me. "If I've done what I'm supposed to do, this'll work, but I don't know if it works immediately. This is the stuff Hillman mixed up to put on me. He told me if I'm ready, I'll know the circumstance that would cause me to act. You saved me from some hardships that you have no idea—"

"I have some idea," he said, but quietly, not planning to elaborate.

"Okay, that may be, but it's just *some* idea. Anyway, now that I have the opportunity to return the favor to you, at least a little, it softens the sting of charity."

"I didn't do much," he said, uncomfortable with nearly any responsibility for someone else's successes or failures. "Really, less than I could have. Like I said. It was for me, too."

"I take that back," I said. "I'm doing it because it's something I can offer you. Period." He considered, silently. "When I put this stuff on your scar, you have to forgive the person who did this to you, and you have to speak that person's name. That's the beginning. You prepared to do that?" This was not anything Hillman gave me. As with my encounter with Randy, I was making the medicine my own as we went. This felt like a variation on the Ganoñhéñ•nyoñ'. A spoken acknowledgment. This was part of the journey, the transition. The truth.

"I think so," he said, looking over my shoulder, the way Gihh-rhaggs taught me to lie. I hoped it wasn't a family tic. "But before you begin, why did you ask me the other day if Vestal was my first? You're nosey, but even for you, that was pushing things. It seems somehow tied up in this. Is it?"

I hadn't expected this question, but if I demanded he be truthful, I should be, too.

"Well, you know how I . . ." I said, setting things down and lifting the front of my shirt, enough to make a sliver of my own scar visible.

"Yeah, the matching scars, sure. You think if you get it to work on me, it might for you?"

"No, I don't think so. I don't think it works that way." I lowered my shirt again, resigned. "But one reason I haven't, one reason I'm still, you know."

"Yeah, I remember."

"I'm afraid of what will happen. If I find that person I want to finally cross the threshold with, and I begin undressing, if they freak out . . . I've been an outsider my whole life. In one way or another. I don't know if I can face that. So here I am. And I got to thinking about you. What if *you* finally decide you want to be with someone again? I don't want you to have this same roadblock. Christine told me a long time ago, she thought our hanging out was somehow stopping you from getting back into dating, or whatever you want to call it."

"What I do with my life is not her business," he said. "I appreciate what you want to do, and I'm willing to go along with it, if it will make you happy. But let's say, on the off off off chance I ever connect with someone again . . . ? No one's gonna expect a man my age to look like I just rolled off the new car lot. I'm expected to have some dings. So no matter what, don't you worry. But, I want to say, honestly. Don't deny yourself. When the right person comes along, if they're worth it: when you take off your shirt and lower your jeans, they'll accept what they see."

"Maybe I'll believe that when the time is right."

"How about this? We do this, and you see if Hillman will give you another try. The worst that can happen is he says no, or it doesn't work, right? Deal?"

"Okay, deal," I said, and I was sincere, but mostly I wanted him to see this through. "Okay, are you ready to begin, in earnest? Do you forgive the person?"

"I do. I forgive her," he said, and I believed him. "My daughter, Christine." As I spread the mixture thinly over his scar, a wave of goose bumps rose on his belly, the new stubble, a thousand tiny antennae. My fingers met, and I covered the entire scar. The mixture tingled beneath my hands, some chemical reaction.

"I forgive her. But I don't because she needs it. I deserved what I got, even worse, really, taking away her loveliness the way I did. But that night? The reason I couldn't beat you when I'd wanted to so bad. I saw what she saw in you. I don't know what it is, and that sounds like horse shit as I say it. I thought anything I could do that might get you together . . ." His breath hitched a bit, a diaphragm spasm. His breaths rose and fell as his words came.

"Offering you money was wrong. I'm sorry. But I was at a loss. It wasn't my intent, but she's half white and tough as it is to be white out here, I bet it's worse in-between." He and Randy knew this same secret about Christine's particular loneliness I'd been wholly unaware of—or had lost sight of. I'd never had to face life's jagged edges as that kind of in-between. "The deal she's got herself into now? Only someone who still doesn't know her own worth would put up with his antics."

"Someone more you need to forgive."

"That little shit ass? Nah, there's nothing to forgive. He just did what she couldn't bring herself to do. Something broke that kid—well, you guys ain't kids anymore. But whatever happened to him, it was a long time ago, and there ain't no fixing him now." He sounded suddenly like Hillman, maybe knowing Randy better than I did. "Together, my girl and him, they must make up some kind of complete thing. If I brang her home to get away from him, she'd be back there in a day. They're like two ghosts who just don't realize it yet."

"Might not work unless you let it go," I said. I'd released my bitterness toward Tim. I believed when he said he'd sat in the parking lot every night. This was the truth. The air between us was electric. I understood the secret origin of our rift, and now, it could begin closing.

"Already let it go. In the hospital. I knew she was coming every night, just to throw suspicion off her man. Didn't figure out she read the letter. Thought she respected my privacy the way I respected hers. But she had more reason for concern. That's the way it is in my family. Men screw up, and women are left to clean up after us. But maybe it means, not just women. Everyone we're involved with. That's who's left to clean up. You ought to know that, Son, since you joined the clean-up crew." I didn't have anything to add. "Stuff feels funny. Tingly. Your hands are warm." He smiled. "Feels good. Surprising. Like this connection is something I need."

"Leave this on, okay," I said, letting go of the poultice and taping a gauze pad in place. I repeated this ritual across his heart, its rhythm steadily tapping the palms of my hands. "At least overnight. I'll come back in the morning," I said, helping him back into his billowy T-shirt. I didn't want to be around to discover the scars were probably exactly as they had been: that it was extremely possible I'd failed him. But it was part of the deal. He did not mention that Randy had made him cry. Maybe another Randy lie? Surely not the first one. But what if it wasn't? Did that silence count as a lie in Hillman's shadow world? Would it, in my version of that shadow world?

I brought the last from the shell up to his face, but he reached to stop me.

"Leave that one. I'm keeping the beard. It'll hide that line altogether, once it's healed up. Makes me look kind of like Lionel, if he'd stuck around." As if he'd read my thoughts.

"No harm in trying to get rid of it."

"Sometimes a scar's a good thing. Reminds you where you been. If I need reminding about valuing other people, and the costs from such ideas, all I gotta do is shave. If you have this gift you think you've been given, there's better things to spend it on than my mug." He started to stare intently. "Come closer?" he asked, and I did. "Are these still Lionel's glasses?" He touched the right temple of my frame.

"Well, I've been wearing them since I was nine or so. I think the statute of limitations is up and they're mine." We both laughed, but he kept his bushy eyebrows raised.

"Yeah, they're the same frame. Different lenses of course."

"Why do you still wear them? Figured I was just buying you some time."

"Well, the better to see you with," I said, and rubbed my hands like a cartoon wolf.

"Goofball," he said, and shagged my hair. "But seriously, the lighter? The glasses?"

"We all become a part of each other. My way of hanging on, maybe? Plus, I still like them. They're the kind I wanted when I knew my vision was getting worse." I thought about that for a minute. "Maybe I wanted them because they remind me of him. Who knows?"

"Son, I'm gonna get rid of that letter. Not tonight, but soon. Just so you know."

"I know," I said, and walked toward the door, where Christine's dog gate reminded me that nothing stayed the same.

"But I want you to know that I can," he continued, and I walked back to look at him. "'Cause I've memorized it. It meant the wrong thing to Christine, and I shoulda known better about where to store precious things. I kept it 'cause it's a part of you. Your handwriting. Your smell. Our history. When I'd come home from the hospital parking lot? I'd read it over and over. Sometimes even out loud, so the house didn't feel so empty."

"Funny, my handwriting doesn't look like that anymore. Be back tomorrow," I said.

As I headed again for the door, he yelled, "Hey! Ain't you gonna take your card?" I thought for a minute before responding. "You still there?"

"It's a Get Well card, isn't it?" I said finally.

"Sure, of course. What else?"

"I hope not to need it soon. I'm going to head out. It's late and you should be in bed."

"Wait! I got one more thing to say. I mean, I understand what you risk now, whenever you let someone walk out a door. You don't know if they're ever coming again. All that time we spent together, you never did share so much. Your face eventually said you wanted to share, but your voice was fully hidden behind a solid wall."

"Wall's down now," I said, and felt that it was true, maybe for the first time in my life. "But even after years, scars can be tender, easily awakened. Might have to take it slow," I added. "I promise, I'll be back in the morning, and tell you everything I have, my whole life story, if you want to hear it. I can't guarantee it'll explain how I disappeared for the time I did, but maybe we can find a way through it to catch up with each other. You game?"

"I got plenty of time," he said, smiling, remembering to stop short of the big grin. "Are we good now? You and me? Tell me the truth, please."

"Well, your people and my people haven't done such a great job of being good with each other for five hundred years . . ." I said.

"Five hun? Oh, Columbus. I get it, funny," he laughed.

"Funny isn't exactly the word that comes into my mind," I said. "But yeah. We're gonna screw things up between us again periodically. Let's hope we have a lot of opportunities to do that, and to strike treaties with each other."

"I'm open if you are," he said. "What you doing with those coins?"

"Hillman told me that sometimes you can perform some medicine on people who need it, but who won't take it. You just have to be near them," I said. He silently looked doubtful.

Stopping at my ma's place, I slipped her coins back in her jewelry chest, where the nickel sat. That nickel meant something to both her and Tim, something to do with Gihh-rhaggs. One of Mona's kids was asleep in the downstairs bed, staying the night. Chester was in the living room as usual, snoozing on the couch. As I was about to leave, my ma stepped out of the shadowy living room. "I didn't think you'd need them," she said. "Did he give you the ones he had? My Good Man's brother?" I nodded. "That's good. Hope for him yet." Again, I had that vague feeling they shared a part of the past I'd never have access to, and I understood from both that I never would.

Next stop was the Summer Cottage. I took Tim's silver coins from my pocket. In the moonlight, I discovered two bar tokens in my hand, one

carved with *TS* and the other with *LS*. Randy must have slipped the missing token into my Levi's pocket at his lodge. I'd like to believe he had a
sliver of kindness in him, but I knew he also still wanted to believe I might
be able to help DogLips. Maybe both things could be true. I dropped the
tokens in my medicine bag, and slid a Liberty Dollar of Tim's into the
earth. The ground swallowed it like the greased slot of a pinball machine.
Even if he couldn't get in, My Old Man would probably flop his sleeping
bag here on the back stoop. Maybe this dollar would send him on his way,
to find a peace of his own. Who knows? One day, some kids digging in
this backyard for the joy of playing in the mud would find this Liberty Dollar and feel like they'd discovered hope.

I burned the strong medicine just above the vague mud dimple. This
plant, Hillman said, he used when things were nearly hopeless, the kind
he'd probably use for DogLips Night. The smoke rose, moving toward the
window. I took some in myself, held, and after a while, I let it trail from
me, drifting up toward the moon and starlight, dispersing into the night.

Heading home, I cruised by the remnants of Love Canal. Christine's
Nova hulked in a driveway, the place Tim had inherited from his parents.
Technically, he had another place to go to. He was choosing to stay in the
Rez house and Christine was living here, instead.

I slid one of Tim's coins into the struggling weeds there, on the edges
of Love Canal's brown fields, and I burned the last of what I'd gotten from
Hillman. I breathed it in, again, hoping Christine forgave me my blind-
ness, my ignorance, the letter I'd forever scorched into her memory. Hearts
misfired all the time. It was neither her fault nor mine. We were never going
to connect, but I could have been better at seeing the way things were with
her, better at knowing only one of her antennae picked up the signals Indians transmitted. If I loved clichés, I might have whispered Smoke Signals
right then, but my journalist brain was always partly on these days. As with
Randy, her future was entrenched with mine. Particularly now that Tim
and I had found each other again, after years of us each wandering lost in
the dark.

After a few hours of sleep, I got up, dressed, and before I left my
apartment, I pulled on the Rush jacket as the sun rose. Though I'd tried it
on recently, I was still relieved it fit. And for the first time, it felt

comfortable. It felt right. I grabbed two coffees to go from the Rez coffee shack and headed to Tim's. His door was unlocked and he sprawled on the couch, engulfed in the warm yellow rays the morning sun filled the room with.

"Nice jacket," he said as I entered the living room.

"A gift I didn't deserve." He nodded. "Did you sleep there?" I passed him a coffee.

"Full bladder woke me up a couple hours ago, and then I just stayed up."

"Wanna look at that scar? See if I'm a successful medicine man?" I knew that even if it did work, it wasn't going to be overnight. I was just in need of a miracle.

"*We* got time. No hurry on the healing process. Why don't you tell me what you got? What you promised me last night. I want to know you like never before. From the beginning."

"Well, I suppose it starts with my ma and Gihh-rhaggs . . . your brother," I began.

"Lionel," he said, smiling a little.

"Still sounds funny." I reached in my front Levi's pocket and revealed the twin tokens. "Look what I found in my pocket last night. Think they'll work in your pinball machine?"

"Well . . . I'll be. I suppose that reappearance means something new to you," he said. I nodded. Another chapter in the gangly, knotted string of wampum Randy and I had built over our lifetime. "Christine must have had people over at some point. The last time I went to play the pinball, it didn't work right. Haven't gotten around to seeing if it can be fixed."

"People," I said. "Did those people do any visible damage?"

"Not that I can see, but not all damage is visible, you know?"

"Yes, I know." I didn't ask if Gihh-rhaggs's zero high score was intact, or gone for good.

"Okay, so, you were gonna tell me about My Good Man." We both smiled.

"That was what she called him," I began, "but he never quite grasped the language the way you have. He got some things wrong that you've gotten right." I thought for a minute, hoping I'd remember this right. "*Plus ça Change, Plus c'est Le Même Chose.*"

"French? You pick that up in college?"

"No, it's from a Rush song."

"Oh, jeez, still with that band, huh? Hate to tell you, it's not original with them."

"Yeah," I said, laughing. "I know. But it's a saying, you know, how some ideas work only in their original language? I guess it means the more things change—"

"They stay the same way, or something like that. I know a little French. *Entre Nous.*"

"Yeah. *Entre Nous*," I repeated. Just between us. "We'll let it be just that. Gihh-rhaggs definitely put things in motion, set things to growing, but probably the seeds were planted, really, at my house before he arrived. You know, that house in any small town, the one everyone always decides is haunted?" I guessed that's where everything began, but maybe I was wrong.

"You know?" He tapped the gauze pad on his belly. "Whatever happens, or doesn't happen, under these covers? I promise to do my best to hold up my end of the bargain."

"What do you mean?"

"Well, I got to thinking overnight. That lighter, your glasses. I'm not my brother. Whatever he was to you, I can't be that same thing. Not fair to any of us."

"Yeah, I know," I said. "He was . . . my mom's good man. Nothing's going to change that. Maybe what that makes you . . . is mine. *My* Good Man." He smiled wide, even though it hurt him some to do so. "We'll figure it out."

"I can live with that, Son, if you can," he said, with a committed nod. I'd been planning to correct him the next time he used that name, but just now, it felt right again. The day stretched out before us, like a road we could follow, trying to find our way back home, *entre nous*.

"But first. Ganoñhéñ•nyoñ'. The words before all other words. For those we have the chance to share our time with, we give thanks."

Acknowledgments

As always, thank you first and foremost to Larry Plant, MGM forever—no other role imaginable. Thank you to E.R. Baxter III, Heid E. Erdrich (Turtle Mountain Chippewa), Louise Erdrich (Turtle Mountain Chippewa), and Cynthia Leitich Smith (Muscogee Creek), who offered encouragement when this book felt like being lost. Nyah-wheh to children's lit advocate, Debbie Reese (Nambe Pueblo), who coaxed me to write for young people after hearing a story I'd read. So began our friendship, moons and moons ago. That story is a chapter in this book.

A *huge* thank you to Nick Thomas and Arthur A. Levine, for ongoing faith in my work that defies easy categorization, and to the rest of the LQ team: Antonio Gonzalez Cerna, Irene Vázquez, Meghan McCullough, and Madelyn McZeal. Thank you to Jim McCarthy for his relentless dedication, wise counsel, and insight in escorting this project to its most supportive home.

Nyah-wheh, as always, to my family. Covid's isolation has made me keenly aware of how the beads in our wampum belts are ever tight and ever at risk. You expect aunties and uncles to be a part of your story, but in many Indian communities, those two terms extend beyond blood and marriage. The "supplemental" elders from my community offered guidance as they saw fit. Many were lacrosse parents, or beadwork parents, or corn-farmers, but others were men who gave you their car keys and taught you how to drive, claiming you were doing them a favor, or women who taught you a traditional craft and how you might make a few bucks quickly if you needed to, or who let you know their couch was vacant, no questions asked. Many people from my younger years are gone, but a few are still around. I appreciate their generosity.

Thanks to Jeffery Richardson, helping to keep things afloat when I was stuck in deadline mania and couldn't quite manage those duties and regular responsibilities.

Thank you to Canisius College, specifically the Joseph S. Lowery Estate for Funding Faculty Fellowship in Creative Writing. Thank you also to my colleagues, students, and community, always keeping me guessing about the boundaries of universal experience.

Grateful acknowledgement to the editors who published chapters as short stories, in different form: "My Good Man," in *Boston Review* (2005); "True Crime" (2006) and "Secret Identity" (2019), in *The Kenyon Review*; "Forbidden Fruit," in *Wasafiri* (2017); and "No Heart," in *Yellow Medicine Review* (2008). This work was also supported by The New York Foundation for the Arts (NYFA), The Seaside Institute, and The Constance Saltonstall Foundation.

Thanks to Rush—Geddy, Alex and Neil (Gih-heh)—holding the flame, igniting the dreams, helping to facilitate my growth as a reader, writer, painter, and thinker, all while annoying family and friends and changing my wardrobe forever.

The Obligatory Culture, Art, and Music Note

Because I come from two distinctly different cultures, Haudenosaunee and American, some mash-up of these two influences inform my life and work. These notes offer signposts to "Easter Eggs." If that's not your thing, feel free to close the book. There aren't any post-credit sequences where characters reveal themselves as Shape-shifters or discover brand new powers.

Living within two cultures is often messy. Haudenosaunee cultural ideas guide a group of six related indigenous nations. I'm an enrolled Onondaga Eel Clan member, born and raised at The Tuscarora Nation. Until I was 11 years old, the only white people I knew were the few who'd married into my family and those on American and Canadian radio and TV. My world view was shaped by the tension of living between these two poles.

Our culture is oral, and its important cultural documents are made of wampum: belts and strings of purple and white beads. Our first treaty with invading Europeans is called the Two Row: two rows of purple beads against a background of white beads. It represents two separate journeys in the water: ours and Europeans'. The space between the rows represented peace. If you've ever been in a water vessel, you know you'll eventually feel the wake other vessels leave.

As with wampum, the verbal and the visual are tied together in my life. I've included visual art in my books from the start, but I can never predict what will come first. Toronto-based band Rush was going to play a key role in this story, so I knew their album art, tour books, and stage set design would likely influence the themes in the paintings, but this one was a struggle.

One of the best parts of writing for young people is your job involves keeping in touch with your younger life. Rush entered my life when I was 11, through a cousin's copy of *All the World's a Stage*, Rush's first live album. If you were young in that era, attending concerts was something you did without parents, a rite of passage. Tickets were under ten dollars, and we often slept outside the ticket office the night before they went on sale, to get good tickets, and to party wildly through the night. Sometimes you got rides with guys you barely knew and you might not have a reliable ride home. It was a different era. From 1980 to 2015, when Rush officially stopped, I missed only one tour. In 1982, I was too broke to afford the ticket and a ride.

It seems ridiculous that a Canadian power trio influenced so many different paths in my life, but it's absolutely true. I am an English professor but I became a reader of literature because of Rush. I didn't know at 11 that *All the World's a Stage* was from Shakespeare, or that *A Farewell to Kings* was a sideways reference to Hemingway. Many works I was assigned in college, I'd read on my own in high school because they'd been used in Rush songs.

Beyond the music, Rush had a reputation for carefully executing their album art. The covers had a sly sensibility, full of visual puns, very similar to a Rez sense of humor. I was immediately in tune with the ways they took seemingly simple ideas and explored them for all they were worth. Every album cover was an art lesson for me in pushing the limits of any idea, courtesy of Rush's longtime graphic designer, Hugh Syme. The album cover for *Moving Pictures* features at least four wholly different visual representations of that phrase. It's probably not a coincidence that my formal commitment to painting occurred the same year I began studying the execution of Rush album covers—1980, the year I turned 15—and the first year I saw them live. Many of my first twenty paintings were visual representations of Rush songs.

When I got to the last stage of organizing this novel, I didn't feel Rush was as universally present as I wanted them to be, so I added some nuance. The novel is now divided into seven distinct parts, each named for a Rush song. I decided that each painting should reference iconic cover compo-nents as indigenous art forms, in addition to hinting at the relationships in each. I knew first that The Man in the Star from *2112* would be recast as a traditional corn-husk doll. That figure played a major role themati-cally and as a plot point, and I decided to put him up against the iconic symbol for "man" used in Haudenosaunee wampum belts. I planned to use a dice motif from *Roll the Bones*, set to sixes, to create a Two Row Wam-pum to border the top and bottom of each painting. A game of chance plays a key role in Haudenosaunee cosmology, and a dice game recurs through-out the book. Any visual pun was worth exploring.

I had one bind. For the cover of *Test for Echo*, Syme had used a cul-tural icon from First Nations communities that Neil Peart spotted travel-ing across Canada. *Test for Echo* was released in 1997, and this novel's events concluded in 1992. The reference didn't quite line up. The ancient indigenous form on the cover, the inuksuk, or more precisely, the inunnguaq, is a figure made of arranged stones, "in the likeness of a human," and has become recognized across Canada. It seemed prepos-terous that, as an indigenous artist, I'd ignore this chance to communi-cate with another indigenous art form, as well as North American pop culture. Once I'd allowed myself this chronological cheat, and found a way to re-imagine the inunnguaq for myself, the whole series opened up. The tension between the fragile and the sturdy, the corn-husk doll and the inunnguaq, the complex history of treaties, and the risks in games of chance, were all keys to complementing the novel's central relationships. There are other puns (I'm sure you've guessed), but this extra-long state-ment should be map enough if you want to hunt.

Surprise! Post Credit Sequence

The story of Brian Waterson and Hillman originally played out in a ter-rible horror novel I wrote as an undergraduate in 1987, that will never see publication. It allowed me to see I could write a novel-length work, but it's not good. The two books bear passing resemblances, but Brian's been lurking in the background of virtually every novel I've published. It was time he got his own origin story.

About the Author

Eric Gansworth, S ha-weñ na-sae², (Onondaga, Eel Clan) is a writer and visual artist, born and raised at Tuscarora Nation. He's been widely published and has had numerous solo and group exhibitions. Lowery Writer-in-Residence at Canisius College, he has also been an NEH Distinguished Visiting Professor at Colgate University. His work has received a Printz Honor Award, was Longlisted for the National Book Award and has received an American Indian Library Association Youth Literature Award, PEN Oakland Award, and American Book Award. Gansworth's work has also been supported by the Library of Congress, the New York Foundation for the Arts, the Arne Nixon Center, and the Saltonstall and Lannan Foundations.

SOME NOTES ON THIS BOOK'S PRODUCTION

The jacket and case was designed by Alex Merto. The art for the interiors was created by Eric Gansworth using Winsor & Newton Designers Gouache, Loew-Cornell brushes, and 140-lb. 100% cotton Arches Cold Pressed Watercolor Paper blocks. The text and display were set by Westchester Publishing Services, in Danbury, CT, in Adobe Text Pro, a Transitional serif type designed in 2010 by Robert Slimbach for the Adobe Originals program. The book was printed on 78 gsm Yunshidai Ivory uncoated woodfree FSC™-certified paper and bound in China.

Production supervised by Freesia Blizard
Book interiors designed by Lewelin Polanco
Editor: Nick Thomas
Editorial Assistant: Irene Vázquez

LEVINE QUERIDO